D0458796

HALF WILD

HALF WILD

SALLY GREEN

VIKING
An Imprint of Penguin Group (USA)

VIKING
Published by the Penguin Group
Penguin Group (USA) LLC
375 Hudson Street
New York, New York 10014

USA ★ Canada ★ UK ★ Ireland ★ Australia ★ New Zealand ★ India ★ South Africa ★ China
penguin.com

A Penguin Random House Company

First published in the United States of America by Viking, an imprint of Penguin Group (USA) LLC, 2015
Published simultaneously in the UK by Penguin Books Ltd

IBRARY OF CONGRESS CATALOGING-IN-PUBLICATION DATA
Green, Sally (Novelist)
Half wild / Sally Green.
pages cm.—(The half bad trilogy ; 2)
Summary: In a modern-day England where two warring factions of witches live amongst humans, seventeen-year-old Nathan has come into his own unique magical Gift, but he is on the run with the Hunters close behind, and they will stop at nothing until they have captured Nathan and destroyed his father.
ISBN 978-0-670-01713-3 (hardback)
[1. Witches—Fiction. 2. Fathers and sons—Fiction. 3. England—Fiction.] I. Title.
PZ7.G826323Hat 2015 [Fic]—dc23 2014044805

Printed in the U.S.A.

1 3 5 7 9 10 8 6 4 2

Designed by Nancy Brennan Set in Fournier MT

For Indy

BOOKS BY SALLY GREEN

Half Bad

Half Wild

CONTENTS

You'll feel my heavy spirit chill your chest,
And climb your throat on sobs

Wild with all Regrets, Wilfred Owen

HALF WILD

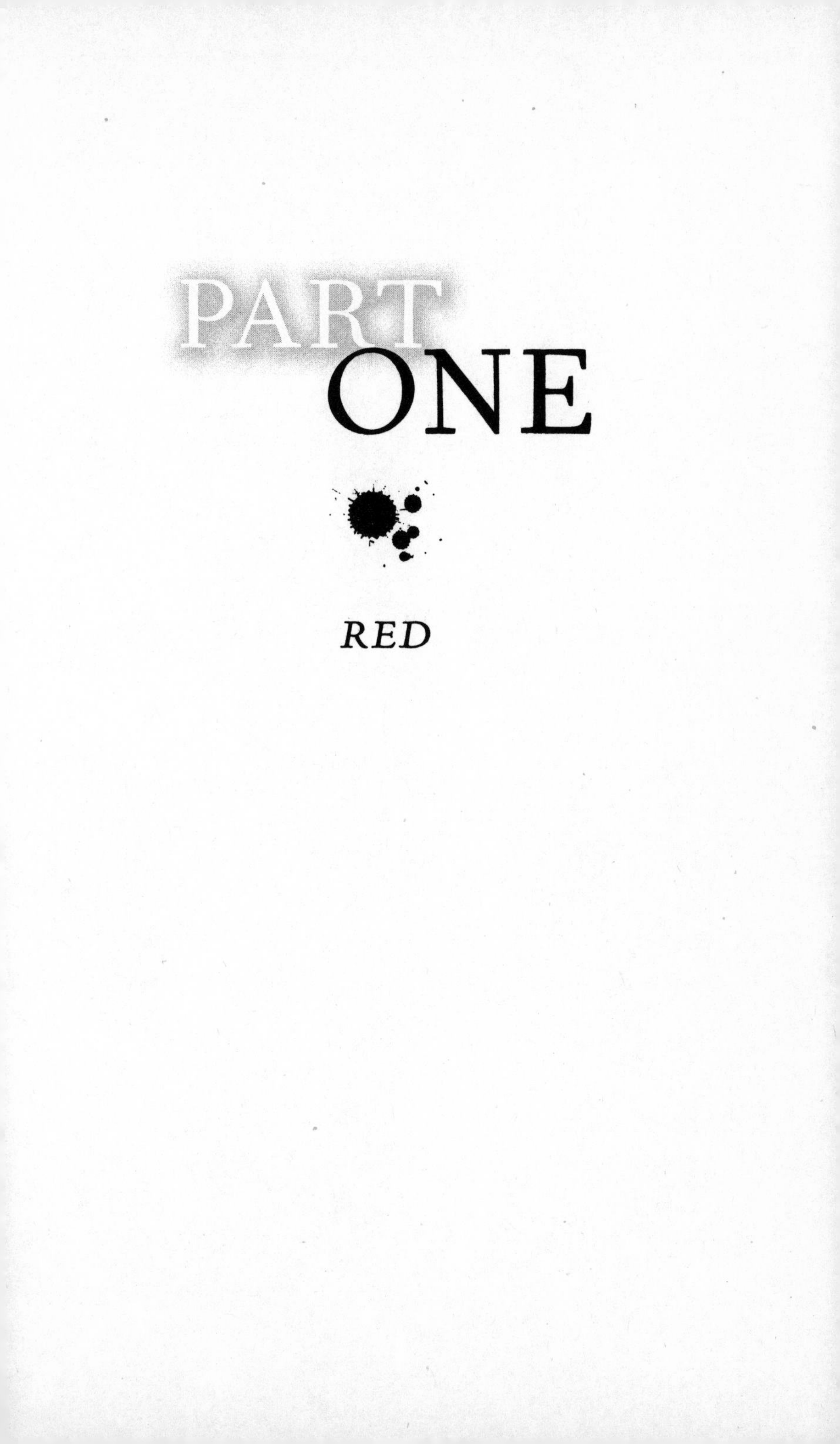

PART ONE

RED

A New Day

a crossbill calls

another bird replies, not a crossbill

the first bird takes over again

and again

the crossbill—

shit, it's morning

i've been asleep

it's morning, very early

shit, shit, shit

need to wake up need to wake up

can't believe i've been asl—

chchchchchchchchchchchchchchchchchch
chchchchchchchchchchchchchchchchchchch
chchchchchchchchchchchchchchchchchchch
chchchchchchchchchchchchchchchchchchch

SHIT!
the noise is here. HERE!

chchchchchchchchchchchchchchchchchchch
chchchchchchchchchchchchchchchchchchch
chchchchchchchchchchchchchchchchchchch
chchchchchchchchchchchchchchchchchchch
chchchchchchchchchchchchchchchchchchch
chchchchchchchchchchchchchchchchchchch
chchchchchchchchchchchchchchchchchchch

that level of noise means, oh shit, someone with a mobile is close. very close. i can't believe i've been asleep with hunters on my tail. and her. the fast one. she was close last night.

chchchchchchchchchchchchchchchchchchchch
chchchchchchchchchchchchchchchchchchchch

THINK! THINK!

chchchchchchchchchchchchchchchchchchchch
chchchchchchchchchchchchchchchchchchchch

it's a mobile phone, for sure it's a mobile phone. the noise is in my head, not in my ears, it's to the upper right side, inside, constant, like an electrical interference, pure hiss, mobile hiss, loud, three-or-four-meters-away loud.

chchchchchchchchchchchchchchchchchchchch
chchchchchchchchchchchchchchchchchchchch

ok, right, lots of people have mobiles. if it's a hunter, that hunter, and she could see me, i'd be dead by now.

i'm not dead.

she can't see me.

chchchchchchchchchchchchchchchchchchchch
chchchchchchchchchchchchchchchchchchchch

the noise isn't getting louder. she's not moving closer. but she's not moving away either.

am i hidden by something?

i'm lying on my side, face pressed into the ground. totally still. can't see anything but earth. got to move a little.

but not yet. think first.

stay calm and work it out.

chchchchchchchchchchchchchchchch
chchchchchchchchchchchchchchchchch
chchchchchchchchchchchchchchchchch
chchchchchchchchchchchchchchchchch

there's no breeze, no sun, just a faint light. it's early. the sun must be behind the mountain still. the ground is cool but dry, no dew. there's the smell of earth and pine and . . . there's another smell.

what is that smell?

and there's a taste.

a bad taste.

it tastes like . . . oh no—

don't think about it

don't think about it

don't think about it

don't think about it

think about something else

Think about where you are.

chchchchchchchchchchchchchchchchchch
chchchchchchchchchchchchchchchchchch
chchchchchchchchchchchchchchchchchch

You're lying on the ground, in the early morning, and the air is cool. You're cold. You're cold because . . . you're naked. You're naked and the top half of you is wet. Your chest, your arms . . . your face are wet.

And you move the fingers of your left hand, the tiniest of movements, and they're sticky. Sticking together. Like they're coated with drying, sugary juice. But it's not juice—don't think about it don't think about it don't think about it don't think about it

DON'T THINK ABOUT IT!
THINK ABOUT SOMETHING ELSE!

chchchchchchchchchchchchchchchchchch
chchchchchchchchchchchchchchchchchch
chchchchchchchchchchchchchchchchchch

THINK ABOUT STAYING ALIVE!

You've got to move. The Hunters are on your tail. That fast one was close. She was very close last night. What happened last night?

what happened?

NO! FORGET THAT.

chchchchchchchchchchchchchchchchchch

THINK ABOUT STAYING ALIVE.

WORK OUT WHAT TO DO.

You can look, move your head a fraction to see more. The ground by your face is covered with pine needles. Brown pine needles. But the brown isn't from the pine. It's the color of dried blood. Your left arm is extended. It's streaked in it. Crusted with dried brown. But your hand isn't streaked in it, it's thick with it.

Red.

chchchchchchchchchchchchchchchchchch

You can find a stream and wash. Wash it all off.

chchchchchchchchchchchchchchchchchch

You need to go. For your own safety you have to get out of here. You need to get moving. Get away.

chchchchchchchchchchchchchchchchchch

The mobile phone is close, not changing. It won't be coming closer.

But you have to look. You have to check.

Turn your head to the other side.

You can do it.

It looks a bit like a log. Please be a log please be a log please be a log please

It's not a log . . . It's black and red. Black boots. Black trousers. One bent leg, one straight. Black jacket. Her face is turned away.

She has short light-brown hair.

It's sopping with blood.

She's lying as still as a log.

Still wet.

Still oozing.

Not fast anymore.

The mobile phone is hers.

chchchchchchchchchchchchchchchchchch
chchchchchchchchchchchchchchchchchch
chchchchchchchchchchchchchchchchchch
chchchchchchchchchchchchchchchchchch

And as you raise your head you see the wound that is her throat, and it is jagged and bloody and deep and

red

Waiting

I'm back in Switzerland, high in a remote valley—not the one where Mercury's cottage is but close to there, half a day's hike away.

I've been here a few weeks now and I've gone back to Mercury's valley a couple of times. The first time I retraced my steps, looking for the stream where I lost the Fairborn, the magic knife I stole from the Hunters. That Rose stole. I found the stream easily enough, and it wasn't too hard to spot blood and some yellow stains on the ground. No Fairborn, though. I trailed up and down the stream, and all around that stained central spot: peering into bushes, looking under stones. It was getting ridiculous—I mean, looking under stones! I had to stop myself after two days' searching. I'd started questioning if I'd ever really had the Fairborn at all; if an animal could have run off with it; if it had magically disappeared. It was getting to me. I've not been back to look for it since.

I'm waiting here now, in this other valley, at the cave. That was what we agreed, me and Gabriel, so that's what I'm doing: waiting for Gabriel. He brought me here one day and hid his tin of letters in the cave—they're the love letters between his parents, his one possession. The tin is in my rucksack now. And I'm here. And I tell myself that at least we have a plan. Which is a good thing.

It's not much of a plan, though: "If things go wrong wait at the cave."

And things have gone wrong—big-time.

I didn't think we'd ever need the plan. I never thought things would go this wrong without me actually being dead. But I'm alive. I'm seventeen, a fully fledged, received-three-gifts witch. But I'm not sure who else is alive. Rose . . . Rose *is* dead . . . I'm certain of that; shot by Hunters. Annalise is in a death-like sleep, a prisoner of Mercury, and I know that she shouldn't be left in that state for long or the death-like will become just plain death. And Gabriel is missing, still, weeks after we stole the Fairborn—four weeks and four days. If he was alive he'd be here and if the Hunters have caught Gabriel they'll torture him and—

But that's one of the things I don't allow myself to think about. That's one of my rules while I wait: don't think about negative stuff; stick to the positive. The trouble is all there is for me to do is sit here, wait, and think. So every day I make myself go through all my positive thoughts and I tell myself each time that when I've been through them Gabriel will return. And I have to tell myself that's still possible. He could still make it. I just have to keep positive.

OK, so positive thoughts, one more time . . .

First off, noticing stuff around me. There's positive stuff everywhere and I notice the same positive stuff every positive bloody day.

The **trees**. Trees are positive things. Most are tall and fairly straight and thick, but a few are fallen and moss-covered. Most trees here have needles, not leaves, and the greens range from almost black to lime, depending on sunlight and age of needle. I know the trees here so well that I can close my eyes and see each one but I try not to close my eyes too much—it's easier to stay positive with your eyes open.

From trees, I move to the **sky**, which is positive too, usually bright blue during the day and light black at night. I like the sky that color. Sometimes there are **clouds** and from what I can see of them they are big and white, not often gray, not bringing rain. They mainly move to the east. There's no wind here: it never gets down to the forest floor.

What's next? Oh yes, **birds**. Birds are positive and greedy and noisy—always chattering or eating. Some eat seeds and some eat insects. There are crows flying high above the forest but they don't come in, not down to my level anyway. They're black. Sharp black. Like they've been cut out with scissors from a piece of black paper. I look out for an eagle but I've never seen one here, and I wonder about my father and if he really did disguise himself as one and follow me and that seems so long ago—

Stop!

Thinking about my father does not belong here. I have to be careful when I'm thinking about him. I have to be strict with myself. It's too easy to go negative otherwise.

So . . . back to the things around me. Where am I up

to? I've done trees, sky, clouds, birds. Oh yes, we have **silences** . . . plenty of them. Huge silences. The silences at night could fill the Pacific Ocean. Silences, I love. There's no buzzing here, no electrical interference. Nothing. My head is clear. I think I should be able to hear the river at the bottom of the valley but I can't; the trees blot out the sound.

So that's silences covered and then there are **movements**. Things that have moved so far: small deer, I've seen a few of them; they're quiet and brown and sort of delicate and a bit nervous. Rabbits too, which are gray-brown, silent. And there are voles, gray-brown, and marmots, which are gray and quiet. Then there are spiders, black and silent; flies, black, silent until they're close, then incredibly, hilariously noisy; one lost butterfly, cornflower blue, silent; falling pinecones, brown, not silent but making a gentle word as they land on the forest floor—"*thu*"; falling pine needles, brown, as noisy as snow.

So that's positive: butterflies and trees and stuff.

I notice me too. I'm in my old **boots**. Heavy soles, flexible cos they're so worn. The brown leather is scuffed and water gets in the right one through the ripped seam. My **jeans** are baggy, comfy, worn to threads, ripped at the left knee, frayed at the hems, blue once, gray now, stained by soil, some green streaks from climbing trees. **Belt**: thick black leather, brass buckle. It's a good belt. **T-shirt**: white once, gray now, a hole at the right side, little holes on the sleeve like some **fleas** have nibbled at it. I don't have fleas, I don't think. I'm not itchy. I'm a bit **dirty**. But I wash some days, always if I wake up with blood on me. My clothes don't have blood on them, which is something. I always wake up naked if I've—

Get back to thinking about clothes!

Where was I up to? T-shirt. And over my T-shirt is my **shirt**, which is warm and thick, wool—the plaid pattern still visible in green, black, and brown. There are three black buttons left on it. **Hole** on right side. **Rip** in left sleeve. I don't have **pants** or **socks**. I had socks once; don't know what happened to them. And I had **gloves**. My **scarf** is in my **rucksack**, I think. I haven't looked in there for ages. I should do that. That's something to do. I think my gloves are in there, maybe.

So now what?

More about me.

My **hands** are a mess. A real mess. They're tanned, lined, rough; the **scars** on my right wrist are hideous, like melted skin; my **nails** are black and bitten to nothing, and there are the **tattoos** as well. Three tattoos on my right little finger and the large tattoo on the back of my left hand. **B 0.5**. A Half Code tattoo. Just so everyone knows what I am: half Black Witch. And in case they miss these tattoos there's the one on my ankle and the one on my neck (my **personal favorite**).

But these are more than tattoos, more than brands: they're some form of magic too. If the Hunters get me, if Mr. Wallend gets me, they'll cut off my finger and put it in a witch's bottle and then I'll be in their power. They could use it to torture me or to kill me at any time by burning the bottle. That's what I think they'd do. The tattoos are their way of having control over me. They'd use it to try to force me to kill my father.

Except I won't ever kill my father. I couldn't, even if I wanted to, because my father is still the most powerful Black Witch I've ever heard of and I'm nothing compared to him. I mean, I can fight OK and I can run OK but that's not ever going to be enough against Marcus.

Shit! I'm thinking about him again.

I should go back to thinking about my body.

Sometimes my body does strange things. It changes. I need to think about that more. I need to try to work out how it changes, why it changes, and what the fuck it changes into.

I don't ever remember it but I know it happens because I wake up naked and a little less hungry. Though sometimes I'm sick, vomiting up the night's meal, then retching again and again. I don't know if it's cos my body can't take what I've eaten. I eat small animals mainly, though I don't remember catching them. But I know it's happening cos there're little bones in my vomit and rags of furry skin and blood. There was a tail once. A rat's tail, I think. I know I change into some kind of animal. It's the only explanation. I have the same Gift as my father. But I don't remember any of it: not transforming, not being an animal, not transforming back. Nothing until I wake up after it all. I always sleep so I guess I must be exhausted by it.

I got a small deer last night. Woke up next to its

half-eaten body. Haven't puked that up. I think my stomach's getting used to it. I've been hungry, dead hungry, but now I'm not. So I guess that goes to show you can get used to anything, even raw meat. Still, I could murder a proper meal. A burger, chips, stew, mash, roast beef, and Yorkshire pudding. Human stuff. A pie. Custard!

Careful!

Best not to think about what I can't have: that's the route downhill. Must be careful with my thoughts. Mustn't drift into the negative. And I've been good at staying positive today, so I can reward myself by thinking about other people, even **my father**, but I have to be extra careful with thoughts about him.

I met him. I met Marcus. He didn't kill me, which I never really thought he would, but given his reputation it could have gone either way.

I went through most of my childhood believing Marcus didn't care for me but it turns out he was thinking of me all the time, just as I was thinking of him. And he always planned to help me. He searched me out. Then he stopped time for me, which I'm guessing isn't a simple thing to do, even for him. He performed my Giving ceremony: let me drink his blood and gave me three gifts. And the gold ring he gave me, his ring, is on my finger, and I rotate it and hold it to my lips and feel its heaviness and taste the metal. The bullet my father took out of me, the magical Hunter bullet, is in my pocket. I sometimes feel that too, though I'm not sure I even like having it as it's a Hunter thing. And the third gift he gave me, my life, is still with me. I don't know if that really counts as I've never heard of any gift not being a physical thing before but he's Marcus and I guess he knows what he's doing.

I'm alive because of my father. I have my Gift because of my father, and that Gift is the same as his. Most witches struggle to find their Gift, maybe taking a year or more to work out what it is, but I didn't even have to look for mine. It found me. And I don't know if that's a good thing. Best to think of something else . . .

My family is a positive thing to think about. I don't often go negative when I'm doing family. I still miss Arran but nowhere near as bad as when I was Celia's prisoner. Those first weeks in my cage I missed my brother so much. But that was years ago . . . two years ago, I think. The Council took me just before my fifteenth birthday, just before Arran's Giving. Yes, it's over two years since then but I know he's OK and Deborah too. Ellen, my Half Blood friend, contacted Arran, showed him a picture of me, and I saw a video of him, heard his message to me. But I know that they're better off without me. I can never see them again but it's OK because they know that I'm alive, I've escaped, and I'm free. Being positive is what I do and that is a positive thing because the longer I'm away from them the better it is for the people I care about.

Sometimes I sit in the cave entrance, maybe lie down and sleep there for a bit, but I'm not sleeping too well and generally I feel more comfortable waiting up here in my tree where I have a good view. The mountainside is steep here; no one's going to come strolling by on a whim. But you never know. And Hunters are good at hunting. I try not to think about Hunters too much, although pretending they don't exist isn't sensible. So, anyway, I sit up in my tree and when it's dark, like now, I allow myself to remember the old days, before I was taken by the Council, before Celia, before they kept me in my cage.

My favorite memory is of me and Arran playing in the wood near Gran's house. I was hiding in a tree and when Arran finally spotted me he climbed up to join me, but I went further and further out on a thin limb. He begged me to stop so I moved back to sit with him, much like I am now, me leaning back on him, our legs astride the branch. And I'd give so much to sit with him like that again, to feel the warmth of his body supporting mine. To tell that he's smiling from the movement of his chest, to feel his breath, his arm round me.

But it's best not to think too much like that. Best not to think about what I can't have.

I remember Gran too, with her bees, her boots and chickens, and the muddy kitchen floor. The last time I saw Gran was when they took me away. I was in the Council building and was told that Celia was going to be my "guardian and teacher." That was the first time I saw Celia, the first time I heard her sound, her Gift that could stun me. It seems like a lifetime ago. Celia felled me with her noise and they carried me away and I had one last sight of Gran looking old and frightened, standing alone in the middle of the room where I had my Assessments. Now I look back, I think Gran knew she'd never see me again. Celia told me she died, and I know they drove Gran to kill herself like they did my mother.

I know now—

What's that?

Footsteps! At night!

My adrenaline kicks in.

Control yourself! Listen!

Light footsteps. Light enough to be a Hunter.

I turn my head slowly. See nothing. The cloud cover is heavy and no moonlight gets through to me here in the forest.

More footsteps. More adrenaline.

Shit! That's more than adrenaline—that's the animal in me.

Then I see her. A small deer. Nervous.

And the animal adrenaline is ready to burst out, the animal in me wanting to take over.

Calm! Calm! Breathe slowly. Count the breaths.

One in slow and out slow.

Two in slow—and hold—and out slow.

Three in slow—and I can feel it in my blood, setting it on fire—and out slow.

Four in slow and it's the animal in me, whatever it is that makes me change.

The deer moves away and is quickly lost in the gloom. But here I am, human, and the deer is not dead. I can control my Gift. Stop it anyway. And if I can stop it maybe I can allow it too.

I'm grinning. For the first time in weeks, I feel genuinely positive about something.

I've done well today, stuck to the lists, haven't strayed too far onto the negative. I can reward myself with some good thoughts, things I reserve for special occasions. My favorite ones are of Annalise. And this is what I remember . . .

Me and Annalise

•••.••

The two of us are sitting on the sandstone escarpment, our feet dangling over the edge. Annalise is fifteen; I'm still only fourteen. My leg is close to hers but not quite touching. It's late autumn. We've met here once a week for the last two months. Since we've been meeting we've only touched once, the second time we were here. I held her hand and kissed it. I still can't believe I did that. I was sort of carried away, I think. Now I think about it all the time, and I mean *all* the time, but I can't seem to do it again. Annalise and I talk and climb and run around but even when we're chasing each other I never catch her. I get close and then I can't do it. I never let her catch me either.

She's swinging her legs. Her gray school skirt is clean and pressed and neat. The skin on her legs is smooth and lightly tanned and the hairs on her legs above her knees are fine and blonde. And my leg is millimeters from hers but I know I can't make it go any closer. I force myself to turn my head to look at something else.

The cliff is steep and the drop is long but doable as the landing is on sandy soil. The tops of the trees are moving and rustling, almost talking to each other, gossiping, and leaves fall in little gangs. A cluster descends toward us and even before she moves I know Annalise will try to catch one. She stretches out her hand, her arm, and then her body over the edge of the cliff. She's going too far but she won't get hurt if she falls, although maybe I should grab her, hold her. But I don't move. She laughs and reaches out even further and catches the leaf, taking hold of my sleeve at the same time, and still I don't touch her. I pull my arm back so that she's safe but I don't touch her.

She's got the leaf. A small brown triangle from a birch tree. She holds it by the stem and twirls it in front of my face.

"Got it. No thanks to you! I nearly fell."

"I knew you'd be OK."

"Did you now?" She pats the leaf against my nose once, her fingers close to my lips. I move my head back away from her.

"It's for you. Here, take it."

I say, "It's just a leaf. There are plenty of them around."

"Hold your hand out. This is a special leaf. It's one I caught, at great personal risk, just for you."

I hold out my hand; I want the leaf.

She drops it into my palm.

"You never say thank you, do you?"

I don't know. I've never thought about it.

"And you never touch me."

I shrug. I can't tell her I think about every millimeter between us. I say, "I'll keep the leaf." And I push off from the cliff and drop to the ground below.

I'm at the bottom and I don't know what to do now. I was hoping she'd jump down with me. I look up at her and say, "Can we talk about something else?"

"If you come back up here and ask nicely."

I climb back up the cliff, fast as I can, showing off, but when I get near the top I stop. She's moved to the place where I normally climb over. She's blocking my way. There's a different route to the left that's harder and I go down a couple of holds and then back up and she's shuffled along to be sitting there now.

"Hi," she says, leaning forward and smiling at me.

The only way I can get up is by climbing over Annalise. "Excuse me," I say. "Can you let me pass?"

She shakes her head.

"If I say please?"

She shakes her head again and is smiling a huge smile. "For a badass Half Code, you really aren't very badass."

"Please, Annalise." My hold isn't good: my fingers are already cramping and my toehold is slipping. I won't be able to stay here for much longer.

"I can't understand how you were expelled from school. You seem such a timid boy." She says that in a teacher-ish voice.

"I'm not timid."

She leans toward me, grinning. "Prove it."

I have to either jump down or climb over her and I have to do one or the other pretty soon as my right leg is starting to shudder with the strain. I think I can get over her if I put my hand to the right of her leg but I'll have to somehow pull up over her lap and—

"I can't wait to tell my brothers what a frightened little thing you are," she teases. I look up at her face and, even though I know she's joking, just the thought of her speaking to her brothers about anything makes me mad. I see her smile disappear in an instant. I let go of the rock, turn in the air, and drop to the ground. She calls out, "Nathan! I'm sorry! I shouldn't have . . ." And she drops to the ground beside me, as graceful and light as ever. "I shouldn't have said that. It was stupid."

"If they ever find out we meet. If—"

"You know I won't tell them anything. It was a stupid joke."

I realize I'm overreacting and ruining the day, so I scuff around the sand with my boots and say, "I know." And I smile at her and want to get back to having fun. "Just don't tell anyone I'm really a wimp, will you? And I won't tell them what a badass you are."

"Me! Badass?" She's grinning again and her feet scuff the ground too. Then she makes a long line in the sand and says, "On a scale from badass here"— she sticks her heel in one end—"to nice, polite, and timid over here"—she walks to the other end of the line, puts her heel down, and looks at me—"where am I?"

I mutter to myself, "Annalise, Annalise, Annalise," and I move up and down the line. About three-quarters of the way to the timid end I stop and then shuffle a little nearer to the other end and then further and then further until I'm about a tenth of the way along the line from the badass end.

"Ha!" she says.

"You're far too bad for me."

She growls at me. "Well, most of my school friends would put me here." And she jumps to a spot near the timid end.

"All your school friends are fains," I say.

"But still capable of spotting a nice girl when they see one."

"And where would they put me?"

I move out of the way as Annalise shuffles along the line almost to where I'd been standing, close to the complete-badass end.

"And your brothers? Where would they put me?"

She hesitates but then walks past the badass end as far as the cliff. She says, "The fain kids at school were scared of you cos you beat people up. You had a bad reputation for being wild but they saw you in class most days, sitting quietly, so they knew that if they left you alone you'd leave them alone."

"But your brothers couldn't quite work that out. To leave me alone, I mean."

"No. But they were scared of you too."

"They beat me up! Left me unconscious."

"You beat them up first! But it's more than that." She hesitates and then says, "It's who you are. Or who your father is. It all comes down to Marcus. They're scared of him. Everyone's scared of him."

She's right, of course, but it's not as if he's going to appear any minute and back me up in a fight.

Then she asks me, "Are you scared of him?"

I'm not sure: he's my father. He's dangerous and murderous but he's still my father. And I want to meet him. I wouldn't want that if I was scared of him. I say, "I trust you more than anyone, Annalise, but if the Council ever hears me talk about him, or my feelings about him, or anything . . . I just can't talk about him. You know that."

"Sorry, I shouldn't have asked."

"I'll tell you who I am scared of, though: the Council. And your brothers. If . . ." But I don't go on. We know that if they find out we're meeting both of us are in big trouble.

Annalise says, "I know. I have the worst, most messed-up family ever."

"I think mine is slightly more messed up than yours."

"Not by much. At least you have Arran and Deborah. You've got nice people. I don't have any nice people. I mean Connor's OK if he isn't with Naill or—"

"*You're* the nice people," I say.

She smiles but it hits me then how sad and lonely she looks and how lucky I am to have Arran, Deborah, and Gran. And without even thinking I take her hand. I'm touching her! I'm surprised but it's happening and I don't want to overthink it. Our hands are similar sizes: mine's wider; her fingers are longer and thinner. Her skin is soft and skin-colored—not dirt-colored.

"How do you keep your hands so clean?" I turn her hand over slowly and inspect it thoroughly. "I'm all covered in red dust but you and your hands haven't even got a speck on them."

"I'm a girl. We're well known for being able to do amazing things, things that boys can only dream about." Her voice is shaky; her hand is a little shaky too.

I'm scared now but I'm not going to stop. I trace my finger round the outside of her hand as she holds it in the air. Over the thumb, down between the thumb and forefinger, then up the finger and down between the next finger and up and then down and then up and down and finally along her little finger and down to her wrist.

She says, "You always surprise me with how gentle you are. You're so far from the badass end of the line."

I want to say something back but can't think of anything that sounds right.

"You've gone quiet again," she says.

"What's so wrong with being quiet?"

"Nothing, I suppose. It suits you." She moves her finger to trace round my hand like I did hers. "But sometimes it makes me wonder what you're thinking." She continues moving her finger round my hand. "What *are* you thinking?"

I'm thinking I like her doing that. It feels nice. Is that

what I should say? I don't know. I say, "I . . . you're . . ."

She ducks her head down to look at me. "You're trying to hide your face," she complains. "Are you blushing?"

"No!"

She puts her finger on the end of my chin and turns my head toward her.

I feel a bit hot but I wouldn't say I was blushing.

She says, "You're so sweet."

Sweet!

I say, "I think I'm quite badass."

She giggles and gets up. "You're sweet and you're slow. You never catch me."

And she runs off and I run after her and that day, for the first time, I catch her.

Getting Darker

It must be past midnight. So that's another day gone. Another day of thinking positively. Another day of thinking about Annalise but not getting any closer to helping her. Another day of sitting in a tree, waiting for Gabriel, and him not showing up. I should try to sleep but I'm not tired. I'm rarely tired at night. Instead I seem to come alive a little more, though I know I get a bit darker too.

I could do some lists or go back to stuff Celia taught me: how to kill with a knife; how to kill with my hands. That's cheery. Or maybe facts. My family tree is a good one. Just recite the names over and over: Harrow, Titus, Gaunt, Darius, Leo, Castor, Maximilian, Massimo, Axel, Marcus, Nathan. Harrow, Titus, Gaunt, Darius . . .

Of course the list is a bit on the depressing side and I'm not supposed to do depressing but I can't be blamed if they were all killed by Hunters or tortured to death by the Council. Though Marcus isn't dead, or at least as far as I know he's still alive and well and living no one knows where. And he was with me, and saved my life, and performed my Giving ceremony, but he left, left me on my own, *again, like my whole life*.

"You did well enough on your own," he'd said. *Classic cop-out!*

Mustn't be negative. Got to stay *posi-bloody-tive.*

Shit, I'm in a black mood.

I need to try more memory tests. Yeah, I could recite all the Gifts my father stole, one for each human heart he has eaten. And that man, that killer, that PSYCHOPATH, sat opposite me and talked with me and gave me three gifts. And I can't hate him and I'm not even afraid of him. I'm . . . awestruck by him. That's positive, isn't it, to admire your father? Your father the psycho. Is he a psychopath? I don't know. I don't know what the definition is. Don't know how far down the path of eating people you have to go before you officially become a psycho.

I'm biting my nails again, only there's not much left to bite.

And here I am, sitting in a tree, biting my fingers—Nathan, son of Marcus, the kid who's supposed to kill his father, the kid who tried to prove he wouldn't hurt his father by returning the Fairborn to him but who cocked it up and lost the knife. And I know I wouldn't even last a second in a fight against Marcus, but everyone thinks I can kill him; everyone wants me to kill him. I managed to escape Wallend and those White Witches who want me to do it and I ran to Mercury and guess what? She wants me to kill him too.

Shit! I need to think of something more positive.

I need to think about Annalise again. I used to think about her when I was in the cage. I fantasized about her, imagined touching her and having sex and stuff like that. Not that I've actually had any sex or even much stuff like that. And the last time I held her hand was when I was sitting next to her on Mercury's roof, and then it all turned to shit and the wind was holding me back as Mercury lured Annalise onto the grass. I remember Annalise's body lying there, her chest heaving, desperate for air, and that last gasp that looked so slow and so painful before she was still, and I hate it. I hate that last gasp.

And, while I'm thinking about hate, I can make a good list on that subject. There's **my sister**, of course: darling Jessica. She has hated me from my birth with venom and I return the feeling in spades. There's her boyfriend, **Clay**, leader of the Hunters, brutal and arrogant. What's not to hate? And the other brute, **Kieran O'Brien**, Annalise's oldest brother, who used to be top of my hate list but is now just hovering at number three most days. Number two on my hate list is **Soul O'Brien**, Council member. He told me he wanted to be the one to give me three gifts, which is, frankly, freakier than keeping me in a cage. He might well be some kind of psycho too. And, talking of psychos, numero uno on my hate list is **Mr. Wallend**. The White Witch who worked on me as if I was a lab rat. The man who gave me my tattoos, which are the things I hate more than anything.

So that was positive!

Celia isn't on the list. I don't hate Celia anymore, which is a good thing, I guess. After all, to not hate someone who kept you locked up in a cage for nearly two years is positive. Surely. On the other hand maybe it shows that I'm totally screwed up by that whole experience. I don't know. But Celia's not on the list.

Mercury isn't either. Mercury doesn't inspire hate. It would be like hating the weather.

Mercury said she would free Annalise in exchange for my father's head or his heart. I won't deliver either. Somehow I have to find a way to get back to Mercury, find Annalise, break the spell she's under, and escape with her. Sounds difficult and dangerous but I have a plan, which is another positive thing. Except the plan is crap and stupid and won't ever work. And Mercury will kill me for sure.

Still, I shouldn't worry about that. After all, *everyone dies sometime*.

And at the moment I've got enough problems with the current plan. I've been here more than a month now and I'm struggling to imagine a positive scenario: a scenario where Gabriel can't get here not because he's dead or captured by Hunters but because he's lying in a luxury king-size bed, reading a book and eating croissants.

If he had been captured they'd have tortured him and he would have told them everything. Everything about me, him, the Fairborn, Annalise, and most definitely where they could find me, about our meeting place here at the cave. I'd have told them under Retribution and so would he. There's no shame in that. Retribution breaks everyone eventually and no one could hold out for a month. And yet the Hunters aren't here. But neither is Gabriel. So that means he's dead. Shot by Hunters that night when we took the Fairborn. Killed trying to save me. And here I am, sitting in a tree, trying to be positive.

Positive is pretty sick when you think about it.

Not Waiting

It's getting light by the time I reach Mercury's cottage. After my father gave me three gifts I fled from here, chased by Hunters. This is the third time I've been back since then. My chance to watch them for a change.

The first time I returned was two weeks ago, when I was absolutely sure that no Hunters were on my trail. I'd killed the fast one and lost the rest. I was fairly certain that they wouldn't expect me to return. After all, there would be no point in me coming back and it would be stupidly dangerous. Given that logic I was expecting there wouldn't be many Hunters at the cottage. Wrong! There were twelve. I think they were using it as a base from which to try to find Mercury. There was a magical cut in space that she used to travel to her real home. A cut like the one Gabriel and I used to get to the cottage from the apartment in Geneva. My father said that Hunters could detect cuts so I guess that by now either Mercury has destroyed the cut to her real home or the Hunters have found the way through and Mercury is dead too. And if Mercury is dead then I've no idea what will have happened to Annalise. But Mercury wouldn't be careless, or slow, or weak. I think she'll have destroyed the cut, covered her tracks well so this valley is a dead end for the Hunters as well as for me.

That first time I came back to the cottage Clay was here and in a foul mood, shouting a lot. Jessica was with him. She has a long scar from her forehead across her nose and cheek where I cut her—or rather where the Fairborn cut her. Clay didn't seem to mind that, though; he and Jessica still seemed to be an item. He put his arm round her and kissed the tip of her nose. At one point he came close to the forest edge, hands on hips, legs apart. He seemed to be staring straight at me. I was well hidden and he couldn't see me but it was as if he was waiting for me.

I came back to the cottage again a week ago. There were only six Hunters left and I expected Clay to be one of them: I thought he knew I'd come back but he wasn't here. Instead I had the pleasure of seeing Kieran. And there was a different atmosphere this time. The remaining Hunters were sunbathing, laughing, messing around. It was almost like a holiday camp, except these are Hunters and they're never on holiday. They definitely didn't look as if they expected the son-of-you-know-who to turn up.

I studied Kieran: he was stripped to the waist, his hair was sun-bleached, his face ruddy brown, and his body huge and heavy with muscle. He's almost as big as Clay. They'd set up an obstacle course of logs and climbing frames, ropes and a crawl net. Despite his size Kieran was always the fastest and he mocked the others for being slow. When it came to the sparring it was clear that the girls were beginners. Kieran's partner was good; Kieran, excellent. Still, I reckon I could take him in a straight fight but his Gift makes it much trickier as he can become invisible. One of the girls seemed to be able to set things on fire and another could send out bolts of lightning but they were both pretty weak Gifts. I couldn't work out what Kieran's partner or the other girls could do.

Hunters are mainly women but there are a few skilled male witches. They only recruit the strongest and fittest, partnering males together and females together. I've never heard of Hunters being anything other than British before now but two of the girls weren't. They spoke some English, but to each other and sometimes to Kieran's partner they spoke in what I think was French. As far as I know the White Witch Councils in Europe have never trained Hunters and never hunted Black Witches like they do in Britain. Gabriel told me that here in Europe the Whites and the Blacks each kept to their own areas and ignored each other, and Hunters were only used in extreme circumstances to track specific witches, my father being one of them. If they're recruiting local White Witches it seems to be a sign that Hunters are expanding their operations.

I watched them all day. I knew I shouldn't have. I knew I should have been at the cave waiting for Gabriel but I couldn't tear myself away. I watched Kieran shout at his partner and remembered the day he and his brothers caught me, cut me, tortured me. I'm more shocked now by what they did than I was at the time. I was fourteen, small, a kid. Kieran would have been twenty-one then, and he made his younger brothers join in, made Connor put the powder on my back, joked about it, joked at their weaknesses as much as mine. And he didn't just cut and scar me but branded me too: B on the left side of my back and W on the right. And that's what I am: a Half Code, half Black, half White, not belonging to either side.

And now I'm back a third time. I've approached the cottage from above, through the forest. The sun isn't over the mountain peaks to my left but the sky is light. I'm not sure why I'm here but I won't stay long. I just want to check on things one last time.

The cottage is built high on the steep valley wall, on the edge of the forest, with an open meadow of grass below. Most of the valley is covered in forest, though the high ridges and peaks are above the treeline and the gray rocks hold some snow in sheltered pockets even in summer. At the top of the valley there is permanent snow and the glacier, and from that runs the river. The river is far below the cottage and can't be seen from there but still it can be heard: its roaring is constant.

I pad down to the edge of the trees. There are no sounds except for the buzzing in my head that their mobile phones set off. The buzzing is faint, though. Not many phones. Not six. Two, I guess. Both in the cottage. So they must have pretty much given up on Mercury and they think I've gone and am not dumb enough to come back. But guess what? Here I am.

It's properly light now.

I really should go.

But I can't face sitting at the cave, waiting for Gabriel, when he has to be dead. Yet I want to see Gabriel and I promised him I'd wait, as he promised me, and I know he'd wait more than a month and—

The latch of the cottage door rattles and a Hunter steps out.

I recognize his bulk immediately.

Kieran walks round the cottage, stretches, and yawns, rolls his head on his thick neck as if he's about to start a boxing match. He goes to the woodpile, selects a large log, and places it end up on the sawn-off tree trunk that acts as a chopping block. He picks up the ax and steps into position. The wood doesn't stand a chance.

He's got his back to me. I slide my knife out of its sheath.

Kieran stops. He bends down to pick up the pieces of wood, loads his arms up, walks to the side of the cottage, and stacks the wood. A small bird flies past him, close. A wagtail. It lands by the cottage. Kieran watches it for a few seconds and then swings the ax onto his shoulder and selects another log to be chopped. He starts again.

The knife is still in my hand.

I can kill him now. In ten seconds he'll be dead. And I want him dead. I know that. But I've never killed anyone like this: when I could have walked away. And if I kill him

I'd have to flee the valley for sure. If Gabriel was trying to get back to the cave I'd be drawing more Hunters in. But I know Gabriel is dead; I just don't want to believe it. The Hunters will have killed him: Gabriel, one of the most special, most honest, most understanding of people. And here, alive and well and chopping wood, is one of the least special, most cruel of people. Kieran deserves to die. The planet would be a better place without him.

Kieran is swinging his ax back as I tread down toward him. I can kill him before he knows a thing. He's vulnerable: the ax is useless if I'm fast, my knife plunged straight into his neck.

I want him dead.

But, but, but . . .

I can't kill him like this. I want to kill him but not quickly, not like I'd have to do it. I want him to look at me as I kill him, to know it's me taking all he has, taking his life.

Or am I just thinking up excuses? Am I just unsure?

And the animal in me, the adrenaline, isn't here at all, as if it doesn't want any part of this.

The cottage door rattles again, then opens. Shit! I'm in plain sight of the Hunter, who steps out onto the grass. He's scratching the back of his head, still waking up, and looking down.

I retreat fast. Holding my breath as I run up the slope to the thicker growth of trees and stop under their cover to listen.

Wood is still being chopped.

The chopping stops and I hear faint voices: Kieran's partner and then Kieran but I can't make out what they're saying.

Quiet.

The chopping starts again.

I've got away with it.

I run.

You're Not Dead, Are You?

I'm going to leave the valley. Leave and never come back. I have to find Mercury and work out a new plan to help Annalise, a plan that doesn't involve Gabriel. But first I head back to the cave. I think I should leave something of mine just in case a miracle happens and Gabriel's alive and he does, one day, find his way there.

On the way back I stop and sit on the grass to work on a piece of wood that I'd found. I'm making a carving of a small bowie knife, like the one I'm using to carve. I'll leave the carving in the cave, in the nook at the back where Gabriel put his tin of letters, and then I'll go and never come back.

While I carve I remember Gabriel giving me the knife . . .

We've been at Mercury's cottage two days. I've only met her once, on the day we arrived, and since then she's left me to stew and worry that she won't help me with my Giving. So Gabriel and I fill our days with hiking and swimming. Today we leave Mercury's cottage just before dawn and set off hard and fast. Gabriel is leading the way and I'm following. Even with his fain body he's fast. His legs are long: one stride of his covers a third more than mine. We climb up a steep, rock-walled gully and I manage it OK. I'm copying how he does it and the holds he uses, and I'm improving but he's effortless.

At the top of a minor peak he stops and watches me. His eye has healed, though there's a scab through his left eyebrow and I think he'll have a small scar—a reminder of how I attacked him when we were at the apartment in Geneva. I could have blinded him.

He holds his hand out to me and I take it so he can pull me up the final step. There isn't much room on the rock and we stand close together.

The peaks in the far distance have snow on them. It's cool here but I'm hot.

"You're panting," Gabriel says.

"We're high. The air's thinner."

"This bit I'm breathing isn't so bad."

I nudge him with my shoulder.

"Don't start what you can't finish," he says, nudging me back.

There is a steep, long drop with sharp rocks behind me and a small drop to a grassy bank behind Gabriel. I push him but not hard and I'm holding his jacket so he doesn't fall.

He breaks my hold with a sharp lift of his forearm and shoves me back hard with the flat of his hand. I grab his other sleeve, cursing him and pulling myself upright. He's grinning like an idiot and there's more pushing and shoving, each push a little harder than the last, until I break his hold on me and with two hands jab him on the shoulders and he's falling backward, reaching for me, and he's not smiling and he looks worried. I grab him but I've leaned too far and I can't hold my balance and we fall together. I pull him to me and turn in the air so that I land on my back with him on top.

"Ow!"

I'm on the grassy bank but there are some flat, smooth rocks buried in it and they're hard in my back.

Gabriel rolls off me and laughs.

I swear at him. "I think I've broken a rib."

"Moan, moan, moan. You English complain all the time."

"I'm not complaining, I'm stating a fact. Just cos I can heal doesn't mean it doesn't hurt!"

"I didn't think you'd be so soft."

"Me? Soft?"

"Yep." He's kneeling beside me now and pokes me in the chest with his finger. "Soft!"

I've healed my rib and I grab his hand, twist and throw him to the ground so that I'm on top of him.

I poke his chest. "I'm not soft."

"You are but don't worry about it. It's one of the things I like about you."

I swear at him as I get up. I hold my hand out to him and he takes it and I pull him up.

We descend into the woods again, cross a stream, and ascend a steep, wooded mountainside, so steep that we have to use our hands to scramble up. Despite the slope the trees are tall, each with a hockey-stick curve at the base where it emerges from the ground. We arrive at a small area of scree below the wide, open mouth of a cave. The cave isn't deep, only four or five meters and the same in width, but it's dry and I could sleep in it, I think, without getting sick.

The smell is that forest smell: decay and life.

Gabriel says, "I thought, if anything happens . . . goes wrong, this is where we should meet."

"What are you expecting to go wrong?"

"I'm not sure but Hunters are after you; Mercury is dangerous and unpredictable." He hesitates, then adds: "You're a little dangerous and unpredictable too."

He's right, of course.

He takes a tin out of his small rucksack, saying, "I'll leave my things here." He's told me that the tin contains mementoes: love letters that his father sent to his mother, as well as the item Gabriel would have given to Mercury if she was to succeed in turning him from a fain back into a witch. I still don't know what that is. I won't ask. If he wants to tell me he will. He puts the tin in a corner of the cave and then fishes something else out of the rucksack.

He holds the package out to me.

"It's for you . . . I thought you'd like it."

I'm not sure what to do.

He says, "Take it. It's a present."

I can tell from Gabriel's voice, the way he hesitates, his hand not as steady as normal, that he wants me to like it. I want to like it, for him.

The package is long and flat. From the weight of it, it could be a book but I know it isn't—that would be too hard for me to like. It's wrapped in the bag from the shop, pale green with some writing on it, folded over at the top and crumpled from being in his rucksack. The paper of the bag is thick and waxy.

I squat down and gently open one end. Inside is tissue paper: white, thickly folded, new, not wrinkled. I carefully pull the package out and let the bag go. It seems to float to the ground. Everything seems special. The gift has a certain weight on my palm, a balance and a thickness.

"When was the last time you were given a present?" he asks, joking, nervous.

I don't know. A long time ago.

I place the package before me on the needle-thick ground, bright white on green and brown.

I unfold the tissue paper carefully.

As slow as I can.

As gentle as I can.

Still one fold to go.

"You'd better like it after all this."

I like it already. And I wait, enjoying the tissue on the ground, the almost-unwrapped present.

I lift back the tissue with my fingertips. The knife lies there, black on the white paper. The handle is covered in fine black leather. The blade is protected by a thick leather sheath. There's a clasp to attach it to my belt. The knife handle fits my hand well, not too big or too small. Not too heavy or too light. The blade slides out of its protective cover smoothly. It's a bowie knife, the blade dramatically curved. The poor light from the sky catches on the metal and reflects into the forest.

I look up at Gabriel. He's trying to smile.

"I like it."

I never apologized about his eye.

I've finished the carving of the knife. I would love Gabriel to see it but I know that will never happen. I stand and look back toward the cottage and I want to scream with frustration at the unfairness of it all. No one can ever be a friend to me like Gabriel was, and he's been taken from me, like they take everything, and I want to kill Kieran and all of them. But I know if I kill Kieran now the Hunters will be after me again and they might catch me, and then there'd be no one to help Annalise. For her sake, I have to be cautious.

I make my way back to the cave.

It's dark and I'm almost there, approaching it from along the hillside, when I see a flickering flame. A small campfire.

Could it be . . . ?

I stop. Then move ahead. Slowly. Silently. Staying hidden in the trees.

The fire is in the cave mouth. There's a small ring of stones with burning branches inside and a coffeepot standing on one of the stones.

But who made the fire? It can't be Gabriel, can it? Maybe hikers? Not Hunters, surely? They wouldn't have a fire or a coffeepot. There's no buzzing, no mobile phones. Not fains. Probably not Hunters either.

Could it be Gabriel?

He loves coffee.

A movement in the cave. A man's dark shape.

Gabriel?

But this silhouette looks shorter, stockier.

It can't be a Hunter, can it? There's no buzzing and there'd be two of them—or twenty . . .

Shit! Who is it?

The man comes out past the fire. He looks toward me. It's dark. I'm standing well back in the trees. I know he can't see me.

"Bloody hell, mate," he says. His accent is Australian.

I wonder if there are two of them and he's talking to a friend who's still in the cave.

But he walks slowly toward me . . . Hesitantly, but straight toward me.

I'm frozen, not breathing.

He comes a step closer. Then another. And stares at me.

He's four or five meters away, a silhouette against the glow from the fire. I can't see his face but I can tell that he isn't Gabriel.

"Bloody hell," he says again. "I thought you were dead."

He's definitely talking to me. He must be able to see in the dark. I don't move, just stare back.

Then, sounding more nervous, he asks, "You're not dead, are you?"

Nesbitt

My knife is already in my hand as I step toward the man, grabbing his jacket, using my momentum to push him to the ground and kneeling on his chest, the blade at his throat.

"OK, mate, OK," he says. He sounds more irritated than afraid.

"Shut up!" I snap.

The blade of my knife is pushing down on his neck but only the flat of it so it won't cut. I scan around to see if he's alone. I think he is but he could have a friend. I see nothing but the dark shapes of trees, the fire, and the coffeepot.

"Who are you? What are you doing here?" I demand.

"Don't suppose you'd believe me if I said I just like being in the great outdoors?"

"Don't suppose you'd mind me cutting your tongue out if you can't tell the truth?"

"Crikey, mate. Just having a little joke, a bit of banter."

I push the knife into his neck so blood dribbles out. "I can cut it out from here, I think."

"Nesbitt—the name's Nesbitt. And you're Nathan, aren't you?"

I can't decide if confirming this would make any difference but I don't think it'll help so I say, "What are you doing here, Nesbitt?"

"The boss sent me."

"Sent you to do what?"

"Run an errand."

"And the errand is . . . ?"

"A private matter."

"A private matter that you're willing to fail to carry out because you'll have your tongue cut out, your innards made outtards, your—"

He flips his body, jerks my arm away, and grabs me. He's bigger than me, much heavier, and strong too, but I break his hold and roll from him to my feet. He's on his feet too now: he's faster than he looks.

He says, "You're quick."

"You'd be quicker if you got into shape."

He frowns. "Not so bad for my age." He slaps his belly. "And you're not so bad for a dead kid."

I stand more upright, feigning relaxation. "Where did you hear I'd died?"

He grins. "I didn't hear you'd died. I *saw* you."

"You saw me? Dead? What? In a vision or something?"

"Vision! Nah. You don't remember, do you? Well, I guess you weren't in a fit state. You did see me, though, but . . . you called me Rose, which I—"

"What? You saw me when I was injured? You were in the forest too?"

"Yeah, oh yeah. I followed you from the train station. Got lucky that day. I was on my way to— Well, never mind that." He grins and winks. "But I spotted you and I spotted the Hunter. She hadn't seen you but she would have, and quickly too, if I hadn't distracted her and given you time to get away. Mind you, you left a trail a mile wide. A child could have followed that trail. I had my work cut out tidying up after you. But we lost the Hunter and I followed you through the forest.

"I stayed close behind you but when I had a nap you wandered off. I found you in a village shop. You were trying to read the newspaper, trying to work out what day it was. It was painful to watch, mate. It was two days before your birthday. You really don't remember any of that?"

I shake my head.

"Well, I got you back to the forest, still checking whether you were being followed, which I thought was a dead cert after the shop. To be honest, mate, I thought there wasn't much hope for you—I guess you had a Hunter bullet in you?"

I nod.

"Yep, well, I went to tidy up your trail—*again*—and when I got back it looked like you'd had a go at a bit of surgery on yourself, blood and yellow gunk everywhere, and . . . you looked pretty dead to me. Your skin was gray—gray and cold, mate—and your eyes were half open too, just blank, dead-looking."

"Do you have my knife? The knife I cut myself with?"

He looks around and up as if in thought. "No."

"But you took it from me."

"No, I took a knife from beside a body, which I thought was a dead body, on account of it looking very dead and with eyes half open and dead-looking."

"I want the knife back."

"I'm sure you do. But I don't have it anymore. Sorry, mate."

"Does your boss have it?"

He shrugs and smiles.

Rose died getting that knife and Gabriel's probably dead because of it, and Nesbitt just shrugs and smirks. So I kick at him, high on the chest. He's strong but I've surprised him and all my weight is on his chest now and I'm pushing the point of the knife into his throat. A new trickle of blood runs down his neck. "Does your boss have it?"

"Yes."

"Who is your boss?"

"Take the knife away and I'll tell you."

I push the knife further in. "Tell me." Blood is running freely now. He's healing but not fast enough.

"You make a convincing argument, kid. Me boss is Victoria van Dal."

I get the feeling he wanted to tell me anyway, to impress me.

"Victoria van Dal?" I've never heard of her. I guess she's a Black Witch if her friend was helping me escape from Hunters. I take the knife from Nesbitt's neck and wipe it clean on his jacket. I say, "I've heard her name. She's a White Witch, isn't she?"

"A White? Van? Kid, come on. Crikey, you've got the wrong woman there. She's a Black Witch. Black through and through. Great admirer of your father. And greatly admired by all Black Witches herself."

"So let's get back to the original question. Why did she send you here?"

He hesitates.

"I can still cut your tongue out."

"I'm not sure you're a cutting-tongues-out kinda guy."

"I admit I haven't done it before but I am an open-to-new-experiences kinda guy, a willing-to-have-a-go kinda guy, a what-the-heck-it's-only-Nesbitt's-tongue kinda guy."

And, although I'm sort of joking, I see Nesbitt's face lose its jokiness.

"I've come to pick something up. Some letters."

I stand up and he starts to rise but I push him back down with my foot.

He says, "I'm guessing that you've got them." Then he holds his arms out wide and says, "Which is OK. Which is fine. All I'll ask is that you give them to me so that I can give them to Van."

"And, supposing I did have these letters, why would I give them to you?"

"Well, Van'll be horrible if you don't. Horrible to me, mate. Which I'm sure is a concern to you even though you're hiding it well." He relaxes back on the ground and looks up at me. "She'll be horrible to me and she'll be horrible to your friend too."

"What friend?" I push harder with my foot.

"Well, I'm assuming he's your friend," he says. "The good-looking bloke with the hair. French. Has a girl's name."

I stare but see nothing. I feel sick with fear and excitement and daren't believe it.

"Gabri*el*," he says, emphasizing the "elle."

"He's alive?"

Nesbitt grins and nods. "You gonna let me up so I can tell you?"

And I feel like all this has been a bit of fun for Nesbitt. It's his idea of a game.

Kieran and Partner

We sit by his fire and Nesbitt makes a fresh pot of coffee and lays out his food for me: bread, cheese, tomatoes, crisps, an apple, and chocolate. I stare at it and lick my lips. I could eat it all in half a minute but I'm not sure I can trust him so I don't touch any of it.

"You look half starved, mate. Tuck in."

I don't answer and don't move.

He takes the baguette, rips the end off, and bites into it, chews, swallows, and hands the rest of the loaf to me, saying, "It's not that fresh but it's the best I've got."

I eat the food as slowly as I can. Nesbitt drinks his coffee and watches me.

I ask him, "Why do you keep staring at me?"

"You're sort of famous, kid. You know: son of Marcus; half White and half Black . . . and, to be frank, you've got freaky eyes."

I swear at him about the son-of-Marcus thing and swear at him about being a Half Code and then swear at him about my eyes.

"Hey, don't take it bad! You asked, I answered. But shit, mate, your eyes look real nasty when you do that."

Do what? All I did was look at him. I swear at him again.

"Can't believe no one's told you that before."

I remember Annalise saying she liked my eyes, found them fascinating, but I don't think I'm looking at Nesbitt the same way I looked at her.

In the firelight I can see that his eyes are unusual too, an aquamarine blue and green that swirls around as if in a current. Ellen has eyes like his. She's a Half Blood—half fain and half witch—and I guess Nesbitt is as well.

I ask him, "You're half something too. Half Blood?"

"Proud to be half Black."

"Not proud to be half fain?"

He shrugs. "I am what I am."

"And proud to work for Victoria van Dal?"

"Well, I call Van 'my boss' as a bit of a private joke. We're more like partners."

"Yeah? What's she like?"

"She's special: talented and beautiful. Beautiful hair, beautiful eyes, beautiful skin. She's generally beautiful all over. Not that I've seen her all over, if you know what I mean, kid. Strictly business, our relationship. And she keeps herself well covered up. It's like she's from a different time. You know, when people dressed up and took pride in their appearance."

I look down at myself and hold my arms out.

"No, I don't suppose you do know what I mean," says Nesbitt.

"I know she's a thief."

"A thief?"

"She sent you to steal Gabriel's letters and she has my knife."

"Well, as I said, stealing off a dead body isn't technically stealing."

"What is it?"

Nesbitt looks like he gives this serious thought, then shrugs and says, "Tidying up the countryside in your case, kid." He grins. "Like picking up litter."

"But taking the letters is stealing; they don't belong to you."

"Well, for a start, I haven't taken them cos they ain't here. Though I'm guessin' you have 'em."

I blank him.

He continues. "And anyway it wouldn't be stealing cos Gabriel told Van where they were. Said she could have them."

"Uh-huh. And why would Gabriel do that?"

"He wants to thank Van for her help." Nesbitt looks all innocent at me, begging me to ask what Van did. And I have to comply.

"What help?"

"Gabriel was in a bad way when we found him. He'd been shot. Hunter bullets, two of them. You know how bad they can be. They weren't serious wounds, and the bullets had passed through, but even so the magic did its stuff. He was out of it for a week. Van nursed him. She's good with potions, very good, the best. She saved him. Much like I saved you and—"

"You left me to die slowly from my wound."

"I hid your trail."

I shake my head at him. "So you wouldn't be caught."

"Kid! Mate! How can you say that?"

I roll my eyes. "Where did you find Gabriel?"

"He was staggering down a backstreet in Geneva. Coppers everywhere. Hunters everywhere else. What a mess! Van drove through it all like a demon, scooped Gabriel up, and off we scarpered into the night."

"And Gabriel is OK now?"

"Fit as a fiddle."

"So why didn't he come for the letters himself?"

"Ah. Well, there's a bit of a trust issue, isn't there? We don't want him running off without handing over the goods."

"I'm sure Gabriel could be trusted to show his gratitude if, as you say, Van saved his life."

Nesbitt smiles at me again and shrugs. "Yeah, true, kid. Peace and lurve and all that. But it's in the nature of Black Witches to not always act as they should. Particularly the good-looking French ones, I've found."

"So, where's Gabriel now?"

"With Van, near Geneva. Not far. A few hours by car."

"You can take me then—because, as it happens, I do have the letters. *I'll* give them to Gabriel and he can do what he wants with them." I give Nesbitt one of my best stares.

Nesbitt shudders, then laughs. "Sounds like a plan. Leave now or tomorrow?"

I think about it. I haven't slept properly for ages; it would be good to rest before we go. But I don't want to sleep near Nesbitt. I still don't trust him. And I don't trust the animal inside me either.

"Tomorrow," I say. "I've got something to do. I'll be back in the morning." Though all I've got to do is rest and think.

As I'm about to leave I ask him, "Do you have a Gift, Nesbitt?" He's a Half Blood but I think he has one.

"I can see in the dark. Real well."

"Useful."

"And you?" he asks. "You were trying to get back to Mercury for your birthday. I'm guessing you had your Giving. But have you found your Gift yet?"

"I was brought up to think it rude to ask a witch about their Gift."

"So how come you asked me? You forgetting your good manners, kid?"

I swear at him, telling him where to go to.

"Whites have strange ideas of what's polite, that's for sure. And you're a lot like them. Half White, brought up by them . . ."

Nesbitt is just pushing buttons, trying to find one that gets me going. Everything he says is some kind of niggle or angle or joke.

"So?" he asks. "Have you found your Gift?"

I don't answer. I'm too tired. I just turn and walk away.

I know I'm nothing like any White Witch I've ever met, neither the good ones nor the bad. And Nesbitt is not like anyone I've ever met before.

The night's cool. It's late July and, although the days are hot, we're high in the mountains and there are pockets of snow in the gullies on the north-facing valley wall. As I trek away from Nesbitt I try to work out how much of what he said is true.

It sounds like Gabriel was shot by Hunters as he tried to lure them away from me. He saved my life and risked his own in the process. And Van and Nesbitt rescued him but I don't understand why. Surely they didn't go to all that trouble just for some letters. It sounds like Van and Nesbitt came to Geneva at the same time as the Hunters. Could they have come for me? Could they be working with the Hunters in some way? Gabriel did tell me that Hunters use Half Bloods as informants. For all I know, Victoria van Dal doesn't exist and Nesbitt has been sent by Hunters. But that doesn't feel right. Why wouldn't they just come themselves?

And, if Victoria van Dal *does* exist, what does she really want? Me? The tin of letters? Gabriel told me that in the letters is something special—a recipe for a potion or instructions for a spell is what I'd always assumed. Whatever it is, Gabriel was going to give it to Mercury if she succeeded in helping him turn from a fain back into a witch. But Mercury never seemed in any rush to do that.

If this thing was so amazing, wouldn't she have been more keen to get her hands on it?

Then there's the biggest question of them all: is Gabriel really alive? He must have told Van about the cave but who knows what's happened to him since?

There's no way for me to know the truth of any of this. All my life I've been told how untrustworthy Black Witches are but so far they seem just about as trustworthy as anyone else. All I can do is go with Nesbitt and hope he'll take me to Gabriel. I don't have any other options.

On the positive side (and positivity is my middle name) Nesbitt says Van has the Fairborn. We went through so much to get that knife, to steal it from Clay, and I want it back. If I do ever get the chance to return it to my father I will.

I find a sheltered spot on a steep hillside and curl up between the roots of a fir tree. I take a deep breath, exhale slowly. I need to sleep, I need to rest. Tomorrow I'll see Gabriel.

I jump awake. It's still dark. I've no idea how long I've slept. A few hours, maybe. I listen out for any noise, scan for any movement in the dark shadows of the trees.

Nothing.

I lie back down and close my eyes but I'm wide awake. I don't want to sleep anymore. I want to go to Gabriel.

I'm fully dressed and I always sleep with my arm through one loop of my rucksack so all I have to do is stand

and I'm ready to go. I set off, eager to see Nesbitt, eager to get going.

The forest is silent and still. Nothing moving except me. But something is different. I stop and listen.

Silence.

The sky is lightening now, pale blue, not much more than white. I stop by a tiny spring. I know the water tastes good: I've been here many times before. There's moss on the jagged stones, the water seeps and dribbles rather than flows, and the life it brings is lime-green, plump moss. I hold my hand against the rock and let it fill with water.

That's when I hear it.

chchchchchchchchchchchchchchchchchchchchchchchch

It's not buzzing. I don't know why I think of it as buzzing—that doesn't describe it at all. It's static. The only way to put it into words is to say it's the sound of electricity. The sound of a mobile phone.

Nesbitt didn't have a mobile with him earlier.

Fains do, and so do Hunters.

Has Nesbitt betrayed me already?

I let the water fall, wipe my hand on my jeans, and draw my knife. The cave is across and down the slope from me, a few hundred meters away, and I move toward it. The hiss is faint but getting slightly stronger. I can feel the animal adrenaline rise a little but I breathe slowly, in and out, calm myself, concentrate on what's happening.

chchchchchchchchchchchchchchchchchch
chchchchchchchchchchchchchchchchchchchch
chchchchchchchchchchchchchchchchchchchch
chchchchchchchchchchchchchchchchchchchch
chchchchchchchchchchchchchch
chchchchchchchchchchchchchch

I'm twenty meters from the cave, level with it, my knife in my hand.

CHCHCHCHCHCHCHCH
CHCHCHCHCHCHCHCH

There's movement below me, a black figure partly hidden by the forest. Then there's a grunt. I tread softly but quickly down. The black figure moves away from me and is lost in the trees. Only Hunters can be that fast and quiet—no fain could do it. And I follow. We're racing downhill, fast and silent, and I gain on the figure and see it's not one but two men in black. And I'm jumping down a small cliff and sliding down the slope on my backside and I'm up again and below them now but they're further along and I see one black figure leap downhill onto the first. And I run to them and slow. The two black figures are fighting on a small area of flatter ground.

It's not two Hunters. It's Nesbitt. The Hunter was chasing him but now Nesbitt has got his arm round the Hunter's neck. The Hunter's face is quickly turning purple. Nesbitt looks up as I step toward him but he doesn't change his grip on the Hunter.

"Kid, you gave me a scare. For a minute I thought you were the other one. I'd love to ask this fella a few questions."

The Hunter Nesbitt is holding I recognize as Kieran's partner.

"He won't tell you anything and we've got bigger problems," I say. "The other one's invisible. And fast," I remember to add.

"Great."

Nesbitt keeps hold of the Hunter and his body jerks and struggles but seems to know it's already lost. It gives up. Hangs there. It twitches once again and then is still. Nesbitt lowers the body to the ground.

"I know the other Hunter," I say. "He wants me." And I know I want him too, and I think I can take him but I'm not sure, if he's invisible. I wonder if the animal in me will come to help.

I look up the slope. We've come a long way.

I say, "Your best chance is to run. I'll deal with the other one."

"Sure?"

I keep scanning the mountainside above me but it's all still and quiet. "Keep out of the way for a few hours is my advice."

"This one hasn't got a gun. Just a knife," Nesbitt says. "They weren't prepared."

"Are you staying or going?"

Nesbitt grins at me, says, "Good luck, kid," then bounds off down the slope. He quickly disappears but I imagine he'll be back to see which of us, if either, survives.

I turn the other way, going as silently as I can but hard and fast too, back to the cave, listening all the time. I crouch down on the bare rock above the cave and put my knife on the ground in front of me. I'm clearly visible to Kieran but he has to come to me. The forest is as still as ever. The sun is up now, shards of light angling down through the trees. One of the shards to my left blinks off and back on, as if an invisible body has passed through it, and the animal adrenaline races into my bloodstream and I want the animal to take over. A small cascade of rocks clatters and I turn to the sound. Another shard of light blinks off and on and the animal adrenaline is surging and I lick my lips and rise up from my haunches.

CHCHCHCHCHCHCHCHCHCHCHCHCHCH

The adrenaline floods into my system.

CHCHCHCHCHCH
CHCHCHCHCHCH
CHCHCHCHCHCH

CHCHCHCH
CHCHCHCH
CHCHCH
CHCHCH
CHCHCH
CHCHCH
CHCH
CHCH

One Last Look

"Nathan? That you?" Nesbitt calls as he comes up the slope.

He stops.

I don't move. Neither does Kieran.

"Oh shit." Nesbitt turns, bends, and coughs. He coughs again and watery sick slides to the ground. He straightens, takes a breath, and turns to me, keeping his eyes on me, my face, and not on Kieran's body, which is lying in the mouth of the cave.

"You OK?" Nesbitt asks.

I don't feel like answering and I just stay still, sitting on the ground. I don't remember what happened once I transformed. All I know is that I woke up near Kieran's body, his knife embedded in my left thigh. I pulled it out and healed. I found my clothes, which were in a small pile in the exact spot where I'd waited for Kieran, as if I'd shrunk to nothing and the clothes had dropped off me when I turned into . . . whatever animal I turn into. My father's ring was by the pile too. I sit and twirl it round my finger now. All the time I'm trying to remember something, anything, but it's all black.

"How long is it since you left?" I ask.

"I dunno. I guess about two hours."

The fight must have started about twenty minutes after

I left Nesbitt and would have been over in a few minutes at most. I woke and went to the stream to wash and have been waiting here for around an hour. So it seems I only slept for ten minutes or so—not long at all. But I can't remember anything between standing above the cave and waking up with Kieran's knife in my thigh and his blood in my mouth. I had to lie in the stream to get all the blood off. It covered my face and neck and chest.

Now Nesbitt is swigging out of a hip flask and looking at me, then down at Kieran. When our eyes meet he says, "Well, kid, I guess your Gift is like your dad's, huh?"

I don't answer.

Nesbitt puts his hand over his mouth, moves closer to Kieran, and peers at him. "Did you break his neck first or did that happen when you ripped his throat out?"

"Shut up."

"And his stomach is sort of all over the ground here, so I'm guessing you have big claws and jaws and—"

"Shut up."

"Just thought it might help to, you know . . . talk about it."

"You thought wrong."

"Drink?" He holds the flask out to me. "Might take the taste away."

I swear at him.

"Being practical about things, killing them both was the only sensible solution."

"I said shut up. We need to leave."

"Yes, and soon. But we don't need to panic."

"I'm not panicking." Though I'm itching to get going.

"Those two couldn't have told anyone what they were up to, otherwise the hillside would be swarming with Hunters by now."

"And what makes you think the hillside isn't swarming with Hunters?"

He grins. "Cos we're still alive. And I admit, mate, that I did get quite a way before I decided to come back." He takes another swig from his flask. "I don't think there's anyone but us and two dead bodies for miles. And they didn't bring guns. Hunters usually carry a full bloody armory. These are the guys from the cottage, aren't they? Gabriel told us about that place and I checked it out three days ago from a safe distance, a considerable safe distance. In fact, from the other side of the valley, with binoculars. Have you been at the cottage recently?"

"Two nights ago."

"They'll have found your tracks. You know, when I met you the first time I thought you left a trail cos you were ill, not cos you don't know how to keep hidden."

I swear at him again. I wasn't that careful but that's because I was planning on leaving. Or did I do it on purpose? Did I hope Kieran would find the trail? I'm not sure I really know.

Nesbitt continues. "I reckon they were out for a stroll; they never thought you'd be daft enough to go back to the cottage. They were wandering around, picking berries or something, when they saw your tracks—certainly not mine cos I never leave any and I wasn't stupid enough to go close to the cottage—and they followed the trail here. They should have gone back for their guns but they didn't want to risk losing you. We got lucky but they'll be missed soon. We need to get going. We'll have to leave them where they are. Not so nice if they're found by fains but I think the Hunters'll clean it all up before then."

"Let's get out of here." I lift my rucksack onto my shoulder.

Kieran's body is lying at my feet. His right eye isn't quite shut; the left side is pulp and tiny flies are caught in the blood. Nesbitt goes through Kieran's clothes, taking a knife, torch, money, but tossing the phone aside. He puts the booty into his rucksack before slinging it onto his back and walking away.

I set off but can't help looking back one last time. More flies have collected on Kieran's face so that from a distance he looks like he's wearing a black eyepatch. His neck is mostly gone, the white of his spine visible below his head, but his upper chest is intact. I didn't eat his heart, that's for sure, but his stomach is open, his guts hanging out in a red and purple morass. And I wonder what sort of animal does that to a human being.

PART TWO

GIFTS

Van Dal

We hike fast. Nesbitt must be in his early thirties. He's fit and clearly a good fighter but I have to slow down for him and stop when he wants to rest. I could run all day, all night, and all the next day, even though I've hardly slept. I can almost sleep while I run.

Nesbitt won't say where we're going but when we leave the mountains and the forest we walk along a path between fields, toward a town lying below us. I can see a railway line and ask him if we're going by train. He says, "Public transport? For us? No, mate, we need to find a car."

"*A* car or *your* car?"

He doesn't answer but gives a little skip of delight as he spots a gleaming gray saloon. He says to me, "I love the new Audi. And these keys"—he holds a key fob, dangling it in front of me, grinning as he walks backward—"these electric sensor ones, are so much easier than the old style."

He walks up close to the driver's door and presses the fob. The door unlocks. We get in and Nesbitt rubs his hands. "Leather seats, air con, cruise control. Gorgeous."

"But you don't own it."

Nesbitt laughs. "Ownership is theft, mate. Ain't that what those fains say?"

"Not that I've heard." I pick up the fob. I don't know much about cars but I can see it's for a BMW, not an Audi.

"Van put her magic on it and it opens the car you're nearest to." Nesbitt pulls out and screeches off at a frightening pace. I put my seat belt on tight. "We'll be at the house in a couple of hours. It's a humdinger of a place."

"Van's house?"

"Not exactly. There are many empty houses and it's a waste not to use them. We maximize underutilized resources, like these cars that are left standing around."

"I guess you never ask if you can maximize."

Nesbitt grins. "You guess right, mate. Though, if Van did ask, people would agree. She has a potion for that. She's got a potion for most things."

Nesbitt is right. It is a humdinger of a house—a modern, sprawling, kingpin-of-the-drug-world sort of humdinger of a house. There's a three-meter-high wall round it with a solid metal gate that looks like it could withstand a rocket attack and is operated electronically, presumably by the person watching through the cameras that are fixed on the gateposts. Van clearly found a way round the security system. I don't see how potions could circumvent electronics, though I guess it's the same way she can get cars to unlock.

We've left the Audi and walked the last couple of miles to the house. "They'll find it. Missing a bit of petrol but no harm done," says Nesbitt.

"Are you really bothered about that?" I ask.

“Well, some of these cars have trackers on them. Use ’em and lose ’em is my advice.”

At the gate we stand beneath the cameras, waiting. Nesbitt has pressed the buzzer and now speaks into the microphone.

“Hey! It’s me. This is Nathan. You know how I thought he was dead? Well, turns out”—Nesbitt shrugs—“he’s not.”

I glare at him.

“He’s a good kid really.” Nesbitt looks up at the camera and in a loud, slow stage whisper says, “He has the letters.”

There’s no reply, not even the buzz of an entry system.

The sun is fierce and the tarmac under our feet is like a furnace. The metal gate seems to throb with the heat but then it starts to move, silently sliding to the side, and we walk up the long, straight drive. I look back and the gate is already closing. On the ground along the inside of the wall and the bottom of the gate is a thick roll of razor wire. The house is as much a prison as it is a fortress. Ahead, half hidden in the tall pine trees, is a low building made of glass and stone.

A man comes out of the house and watches us approach. He’s dressed immaculately in a pale blue suit. The palest of blues, almost white. His trousers are wide and he’s wearing a waistcoat of pale blue too. As we get closer I see his shirt is white and his tie is pale pink, with a matching pink handkerchief in his jacket pocket. He turns his back on us as we get nearer and goes back inside. The man is tall, taller than me, and slender. His hair reminds me of Soul O'Brien's, that white-blond, super-slick look, cut with precision to the nape of his neck. It only now occurs to me that I've assumed there'll only be Van and Gabriel here but it seems there's at least one other person.

"Who's that? Who else is here?" I ask Nesbitt.

He glances at me and starts to dance around in front of me, flapping his arms, singing, "Ain't nobody here but us chickens . . ." He clucks and flaps and sings and laughs all the way to the house.

We go into the house through the wide, cool entrance hall and into a living room that has a wall of windows overlooking a long, wide lawn down to Lake Geneva. The room is huge, big enough for a party, a ball I suppose, though it's full of sofas and low tables set out in three groups.

The man has his back to me. He picks up a silver lighter from a low table and turns to light his cigarette so that I can see his profile. His skin is clear, pale, and looks incredibly healthy, and as he inhales and swallows the smoke I realize that this isn't a man. This is Van.

She turns to look at us both and I'm amazed at how beautiful she is. She looks like a boy and yet a girl as well, maybe twenty years old.

"So?" She says this to Nesbitt. Her voice doesn't match her looks but it does match her cigarette habit. She sounds like she smokes sixty a day.

"So. Hi there, Van. Good to see ya, good to be back. This is Nathan."

Van inhales deeply on her cigarette and then slowly breathes out a fine trail of smoke. She comes closer to me and says, "Delighted. Genuinely delighted." Her eyes are pale blue, as pale as her suit. I've only seen the eyes of two Black Witches before now: Mercury and my father. Both were different and totally unlike White Witches who, to me, have silver shards that twist and tumble in their eyes. But Van's eyes have jewels of sapphire that turn, grow, and diminish, and then when they touch each other give off sparks that seem to turn into more sapphires. They're the most beautiful eyes I've ever seen.

"You have Gabriel's letters?" she asks me. I notice that the smoke trailing out of her mouth isn't gray but extremely pale pink, like her tie. The smoke almost seems alive as it curls slowly up Van's cheek, then turns and mingles with the air in front of her eyes, and the deep blue of them deepens further.

I'm vaguely aware that I reply but I'm not sure what I say.

Van's eyes remain locked on mine and sparkle even more as she says, "Nesbitt, you were supposed to get them." And she turns her gaze on him.

I take a step back but it's hard. I have to force myself to look away from Van.

Nesbitt says, "I was supposed to bring them to you, which I've done. I could've taken them off Nathan if I'd had to but it would have involved violence and it seemed best to avoid that. He's a decent fighter, this kid, in an unconventional sort of way—brings out the animal in him. Anyway, he's here, he's got the letters, and he's keen on seeing his mate Gabby."

"So . . ." she says. She has come closer to me again, closer than before, close enough for me to feel her breath on my face. I expect it to smell of cigarette smoke but it's strawberries.

"So . . ." I say.

The strawberry smell is faint and I inhale deeper, to get more of it. This woman is the most amazing I've ever met. I inhale more and say, "My friend Gabriel . . . Nesbitt told me that you saved his life. Thank you. I'd like to see him."

"I'm sure you would," Van replies. "And I'm sure he'd like to see you. And we'd all like to see the letters."

The letters are in the tin that Gabriel has always kept them in and I've not opened it, except the one time when I first found it in Mercury's apartment. But now I have an urge to take the tin out of my rucksack. As I bend down to reach inside I breathe different air, air that doesn't smell of strawberries. I stand up again, holding the rucksack, not the letters.

Van smiles at me and I feel my knees buckle a fraction. Annalise is beautiful but there's something mesmerizing about Van. She's literally stunning. But I've got to keep her at a distance.

"I need fresh air," I say, and walk to the windows and draw the door to the side. "Let's talk out here."

The air outside is clean. Though it's intensely hot.

Van follows and gestures to a shaded seating area on the

patio. I walk to a low sofa but I don't sit until I see where she goes and then I move opposite her.

She calls to Nesbitt. "Ask Gabriel to join us, and bring lemonade and tea for four." She gestures to the seat, saying, "Please, do sit. I'm sure Gabriel won't be long."

We sit in silence for a few minutes, Van smoking her cigarette, then I say, "Nesbitt told me that Gabriel had been shot but that he's recovered. Is that true?"

"He was shot twice and Hunter bullets are nasty things but, yes, Gabriel is over that." She knocks the ash off her cigarette and takes another long drag before adding, "He hasn't quite recovered *himself,* though. He cares for you very much, Nathan, and I'm afraid that Nesbitt, my idiot assistant—"

"Business partner," Nesbitt corrects as he walks out onto the patio with a pitcher of lemonade that he places between us. He mutters, "Gabby was in the kitchen so I've broken the news that you're here."

Van continues. "Nesbitt, my idiot assistant, told us you were dead. As I say, Gabriel cares for you very much. He—"

I see a movement to my right and, as I turn, Gabriel steps onto the patio and stares at me. I can see he can't believe I'm here. He looks frail and thin and he says something very quietly.

I stand and I'm not sure what to say. Words won't cover any of it. I want to tell him I owe him my life but he knows that.

I step toward him and he strides to me and holds me tight and I hug him back. He says something under his breath, the same as before, I think, but it's in French and I don't know what it means.

He holds his head back to look into my eyes. He's not smiling and his face is drawn and gray. His eyes are the same fain brown but the whites are veined with red.

I'm not sure what to say and it comes out all garbled. "I waited at the cave. I made it out of Geneva because of you. I kept hoping you'd be alive. I'd be dead if it wasn't for you."

He would normally make some sarcastic comment but now he leans into me again and says something else in French.

We stay together. I hold him, feeling how thin he is, how his ribs are sticking out. I won't let go, though, not before he does.

He says, "I thought you were dead." And I realize that's what he said in French. "Nesbitt said he saw your body."

"Nesbitt is a fool," Van chips in.

Nesbitt walks out with a tray crammed with tea things and says, "I heard that. If you'd actually seen his body . . ." And he places the tray down and sets out the china teapot, milk jug, cups, saucers, and sugar, muttering as he does so about me being gray and cold with my eyes half open.

When Nesbitt's finished he sits down and picks up the teapot. "So, I'll be mother, shall I?"

* * *

We spend the next half hour catching up on what has happened. Van begins with "Do tell us what happened after Gabriel left you, Nathan."

I shrug. I'm not sure about saying anything, not sure how much she already knows.

"Let me start you off. You, or rather Rose, stole a knife from a house in Geneva. Not any old knife but the Fairborn. Not any old house but the Hunter base, and not from just any old Hunter but Clay, their leader. Rose certainly was a talented witch. However, it was not the best of plans and she paid with her life. And you were shot too." Van draws on her cigarette and breathes out a long stream of smoke toward me. I smell the strawberries faintly. "Do tell us what happened next, Nathan."

I look at Gabriel and he nods.

"I was shot and wounded and couldn't run. Gabriel saved me by drawing the Hunters away." I try to turn the subject back to her and ask, "And you saved Gabriel but what were you doing in Geneva that night? I thought all Black Witches had fled. The city was full of Hunters."

"Let's complete your story first," she says, smoke curling out of her mouth with each word. "You were wounded but you had the Fairborn. You escaped Geneva through the forest—"

Gabriel interrupts. "But why were you in the forest? Why didn't you go back to Mercury's cottage through the cut at the apartment?"

"The poison from the bullet made me ill. I got lost. It took me a long time to find the apartment and when I got there it was swarming with Hunters. So I set off on foot—I thought I'd have plenty of time to get back to Mercury before my birthday. I stole some food, clothes, and money. I felt better at first with the food but I became weaker and weaker until I collapsed. I cut the poison out of me and then I passed out. I wasn't dead—obviously—but I wasn't far off. That's when Nesbitt saw me. I woke later and set off again for Mercury."

Van inhales deeply. "Of course the question on everyone's mind is, "Did you make it?""

"I made it. But Mercury didn't perform the Giving ceremony."

"Ah. Because you didn't have the Fairborn?"

"Because she was busy fighting Hunters."

They all wait, looking at me.

I say, "My father gave me three gifts."

Van blinks. "That must have been very special."

"Yes."

I notice Van glance at my hand and my ring. I ask her, "Do you know him? Marcus?"

"I met him briefly a couple of times, years ago. He doesn't come to Black Witch gatherings anymore. Hasn't for a long time."

"Do you know where he lives?"

She shakes her head. "No one knows that."

We're all silent for a second or two, then Van says, "And

your Gift is like your father's, I'm assuming, from Nesbitt's little jibe. That is a rare Gift."

I try to remain blank. I don't want to think about the animal now. I haven't felt him at all since I killed Kieran this morning.

"And then what happened?" Gabriel asks.

"My father left. The valley was swarming with Hunters. Mercury was furious with me. She told me she had Annalise and would only release her in exchange for my father's head or heart. Then the Hunters were on us and I ran. Eventually, after about a week, I lost them. I went back to the cave and waited for you."

"You waited a long time."

I shake my head, but I can't tell him I was about to give up.

Van says, "Yes, it's fortunate for us all that Nathan is so patient."

Gabriel's mouth twitches. "I've always thought that—Nathan: such a patient person."

"And that brings us all rather wonderfully up to date," says Van. "Nesbitt found you at the cave when he went to collect the letters. Ah! Talking of the letters, please may I have them now?"

I say to Gabriel, "What do you want me to do with them?"

"I promised I would give them to Van."

"And you want to keep that promise?"

"She saved my life."

I look at Van. Her face is serenely victorious.

I say, rather pompously, "Of course, Gabriel, they're yours and I must give them to you, just as Van should return the Fairborn to me, as it is mine."

Van smiles, still serene. "Yours? You stole it from Clay. In fact, Rose stole it."

"And it was stolen by Hunters from Massimo, my great-grandfather. It belongs to my family."

She sips her tea and then says to Nesbitt, "Do you think we should give him the Fairborn? After all, you retrieved it."

Nesbitt bares his teeth like a bad dog and shakes his head once.

"I have to agree with Nesbitt. You were rather careless with it the first time. If Nesbitt could take it from you . . . well, a child could. It needs to be kept in a safe place. It's a dangerous and powerful object. For the moment, I think I'll look after it."

"It's mine!"

"Actually, my darling boy"—Van looks at me and her eyes sparkle in a dramatically blue haze—"I agree with you. However—and I mean this in the kindest way possible—I don't think you should have it. Not yet. It's an unpleasant thing, full of evil magic. I can assure you I will keep it safe." She reaches for the teapot. "More tea?"

No one answers. As she pours she says, "Nathan, the letters are Gabriel's. Do return them to him, please."

I look at Gabriel and he nods.

The Amulet

Gabriel opens the tin, flicks through the letters, and takes one out from the middle of the pile. It has a smudge of soot on it from when I first went through them months ago, when I found the tin hidden in the chimney in the apartment in Geneva.

Gabriel puts this letter on the table between himself and Van, saying, "The amulet. It's yours. Thank you. I'd be dead without you." He opens the folds of the letter and we all lean forward to look.

Van says, "Thank you, Gabriel. It really is beautiful."

I move closer still. I'm not sure *beautiful* is how I'd describe it. It's a fragment of parchment, yellowed, with faded black-ink markings on it—writing, but not like any I've seen before. This is laid out in a series of circles. Only there are no full circles, just semicircles, because the parchment is ripped in half.

"What did your mother tell you about this?" Van asks.

"Not much. She thought it might have some value because of its age. She told me her grandmother found it in an old house in Berlin. By 'found' she meant her grandmother stole it. But that's all she knew."

"Did she know where the other half was?"

"No, this is all we ever had."

"And Mercury never saw it? You never told her what it was?"

Gabriel shrugs. "I didn't tell her it was ripped in half. I thought she wouldn't be interested if she knew that. I told her I had an amulet that my mother had given me, that it was old and valuable. She didn't ask any more about it, I supposed because there are quite a few like it."

"There are quite a few amulets, that's certainly true, and most are poor magic. I think it was lucky for me that you didn't describe it. In fact, I suspect it was lucky for you too. I think Mercury would know what this is and she'd have killed you for just this half." Van folds the amulet back into the paper with great care and slides it into her jacket pocket.

"Why?" Gabriel asks. "What's so special about it?"

Van turns to Nesbitt. "I think we need champagne, don't you? I'm sure there'll be a wonderful selection in the cellar." She smiles at Gabriel. "Or would you boys prefer to stick to tea?"

Later Gabriel and I are alone together in his bedroom. We've both drunk champagne. I don't understand why I was drinking and what I was supposed to be celebrating and I didn't really like it. I've never had champagne before, never drunk any alcohol before. Gabriel and Van talked about it as they would discuss a good book.

As we walked to Gabriel's room the corridor seemed to be tilting. When I pointed this out Gabriel called me a "lightweight" and then went on ahead. He turned back to watch me make my way toward him. It was good to see him smile; almost as if he was back to his old self. And now we're alone, sitting together on his bed, and finally I can ask him for his story.

"After I left you I ran. That was it, nothing more complicated. I ran and the Hunters followed. I shouted, urged you to hurry as if you were with me. It fooled them enough to think we were together. I was lucky. The best protection I had was other people—fains, I mean. I stayed where it was busy, and there was lots of confusion, lots of people, things Hunters hate: fains, fain police, noise, panic, and lots of shooting. I hoped they'd think I was a fain but at the same time I had to keep them after me. I was shot, twice, as I was running. Neither were serious wounds but the poison from the Hunter bullets weakened me and, as I can't heal, I knew I wouldn't last long. All I could think was that I should keep running. I remember seeing a car drive up to me, which must have been Van. Then I remember nothing until I woke up here in this room days later. I'd been ill but I think after that, after I'd recovered, Van drugged me and I told her everything. Everything about me, about my family, the letters, and the amulet . . . and about you. I'm sorry, Nathan. I know it's private. I—"

"It's OK. I don't care about that. I'm just glad you're alive. That's what's important. I thought you were dead. I didn't want to believe it but it was the only logical explanation; I knew you'd be at the cave if you could be."

"I'd be dead if it wasn't for Van."

"But why was she there in Geneva? Why risk her life for this amulet—half an amulet?"

"I don't know. She told me that she'd recently learned that I might have half of it. It wasn't hard to find out that I was in Geneva and working with Mercury. At first she was afraid that Mercury would get it but after Nesbitt said that you'd died she became much more concerned that it would fall into the Hunters' hands."

"Why? What does it do?"

"It doesn't do anything. It's only half an amulet. But amulets, whole amulets, heal and protect. She's gone to a lot of trouble to get this and I think she intends to get the other half, and maybe together they'll work again."

"And you really know nothing else about it?"

"No. It was just one of those things my mother had. I value the letters more." We're sitting together on the bed and now he shuffles back and leans against the wall. "Van can keep it. I'm not interested in any of that."

"Any of that?"

"Things. Stuff. Amulets, knives, whatever."

"I never thought you were."

He leans his head back, keeping his gaze on me. "It's good to see you, Nathan. I'm glad you're alive. Very glad." He looks tired: his skin is gray and there are dark circles beneath his eyes. He says, "Who'd have thought we'd be here? Alive. Sitting in a beautiful house. Drunk on champagne."

But his comment about "things" and "stuff" is making

me wonder if it was wrong for me to want the Fairborn. I thought that if I had it I could show my father that I won't kill him. Maybe I don't need the Fairborn to do that.

"What are you thinking?"

"About *stuff*. The Fairborn. My father."

"What's he like?"

"My father? I don't know. I really don't know him. He's a lot smarter than I expected; cleaner, I mean. He wore a suit. By looking at him you couldn't tell that he's killed hundreds of people."

"I asked what he was like, not what he wore."

"So what do you want me to say? He's amazing? Powerful? Well, he is. Only more than I thought was possible. He did this thing that sort of stopped time—snowflakes were hanging in the air, waiting to fall, but we carried on talking as if it was all normal. I still had the Hunter bullet in me. He cut it out. Then he gave me three gifts: a ring, the bullet from my body, and my life." I hold the ring out to show Gabriel. "Then he cut his palm and I drank his blood. I think all along, all my life, he was planning to give me three gifts. He was waiting for me to return to Mercury's; he knew I'd head back there. And he did all that, stopped time for me, saved my life by giving me three gifts, and then . . . then he left! He left me again! Left me to Mercury and a valley full of Hunters."

Gabriel doesn't say anything.

"I always thought that if we met I'd explain to him, *show* him, that I would never kill him. And I tried to do that but it was as if he wasn't listening. He could have killed me but he saved my life. It was the most amazing and wonderful thing and then . . . it wasn't."

"He's your father but he also believes the vision—that you will kill him."

"He said, 'I'm not a great believer in visions. But I'm a cautious man,' or some crap like that. Basically he doesn't trust me. He didn't believe that I'd lost the Fairborn. So it seems stuff *does* matter, Gabriel, because I couldn't give it to him and so he left me again. The stupid thing is that I hate him for that. Not for killing people, not for eating their hearts, but because he left me when I was a child and then he left me again."

"You don't hate him. You're angry at him." Gabriel laughs a little. "Which at least means you're not giving him special preference as you're angry at most people most of the time."

I swear at him and then say, "I'm glad you're alive, Gabriel. Someone else for me to be angry at." My head's swimming still and I slump down. "I need to sleep. So do you."

I don't actually sleep but I stay with him for as long as I can, which isn't long as it's almost dark and I can't stand being indoors at night. I have to go outside.

I check out the grounds. They're large, wooded, sloping down to the lake, enclosed on all sides by that high wall and razor wire. But the lake cannot be walled and there's a narrow beach of rocks, a small wooden jetty, no boats. The mountains opposite are silhouettes now. The moon appears as the clouds disperse in a warm breeze. It's perfect for a swim.

The water is cool. Calm. The moon's reflection seems to fill the water. I swim out a long way and float on my back, looking at the sky.

Then I feel something brush against my leg and instantly my animal adrenaline is released and races throughout my body. But not so much, not so much, because I tell myself to calm down and take slow breaths, and I tell myself it was just a fish or something floating in the water. And I keep taking slow breaths and the adrenaline has gone, disappeared as if it was never there.

The moon is still bright on the lake's surface and I wonder if I can make the adrenaline come back. I think about possible dangers in the water, monsters lying in the depths, hiding in the dark, swimming up to me—a long, thick eel that could swallow me whole. I submerge myself, breathing out, feeling the cold, noticing how dark it is and imagining the eel coming to me . . .

Nothing happens. Of course no eel appears but my animal adrenaline doesn't either. I swim back to the surface and look around, almost hoping for a monster to show up, but it doesn't and after a minute I kick slowly to land.

Gabriel is sitting on the grass near the shore, watching me. I dress and go to sit by him.

He says, "I'll sleep out here with you."

I collect some wood, make a fire, and sit by it, feeding it twigs and branches until they run out, and then I collect more. I wonder if Gabriel's going to ask why I'm not sleeping but he doesn't speak. He falls asleep just before dawn. And I feel then that I can finally close my eyes. I've never turned into an animal during the day unless I've been threatened by Hunters, and I don't think it'll happen. But at night . . . who knows?

We both wake a few hours later and already Gabriel looks better. He has more color, and smiles when he sees me.

I need to talk to him about Annalise but want to put it off some more.

"Did you sleep?" he asks.

"The same as you. Enough."

"Good." He stands and stretches. "We need breakfast. Coffee and croissants and rolls and eggs . . . I'm in the mood for eggs."

Gabriel and I spend the day eating. Both of us are underweight—or at least we are at the start of the day. In the afternoon we swim and lie in the sun to dry off. It's another day of pure blue skies and throbbing, intense heat.

Gabriel says, "We've talked a lot but not about that subject we disagree on."

"I don't want to disagree with you, especially when we've only just met up again." But I know we have to talk about Annalise. I need to rescue her, which sounds ridiculous and heroic and stupid, but I have to do it. I can't leave her a prisoner of Mercury. I say, "I have to help her."

"No. You don't."

"I do, Gabriel. Annalise is in trouble because of me. She's in a coma or whatever it is because of me."

"It's not a coma and you owe her nothing."

"I want to help her, Gabriel. I need to free her. Annalise is my friend. I like her . . . a lot. I understand that you don't trust her but I know she won't betray me, hasn't betrayed me."

Now he looks at me. "How did the Hunters know about Mercury's apartment in Geneva?"

"What?"

"You heard me. How did they get there? You said the apartment was swarming with them. I didn't lead them there. I didn't go anywhere near there. So how did they know about it?"

"Marcus told me that Hunters have a way of finding cuts. They must have detected it somehow."

Gabriel sits up. "No, Nathan. I don't think that's how it works. I don't think they can detect them from long distances. If they could do that they would've found the other cut to Mercury's real home."

"We don't know that they haven't. And anyway Mercury had time to destroy the cut. They won't have been able to find it."

"You build up excuses and come up with explanations but the obvious explanation you won't admit to is that Annalise told the Hunters about the apartment."

"You said yourself that I shouldn't leave the apartment but I did. Someone, I don't know who, an informer, a Half

Blood, could have seen me when I followed you. They could have alerted the Hunters and so they were there when I got back."

Gabriel is silent but lies back down.

I say, "You have to agree that's a possibility."

He doesn't look at me, which I take as an admission that I'm right.

I say, "Gabriel, I trust her. She tried to help us. She told me how Hunters protect their base, what spells they use."

"She has to build up your trust to convince you of her devotion. Nathan, spies don't go around with big banners that say, 'I'm a spy.' The whole point is that they behave like they're on your side."

I remember Annalise sitting next to me on the roof of Mercury's cottage, her whole body shaking with fear and I know she didn't betray me.

"I have to try to help her, Gabriel. It's what you would do for me and it's what I must do for her."

He says nothing.

"I like her a lot, Gabriel. You know that."

Gabriel puts his arms over his face. He still says nothing but I can see his chest is heaving.

"I've got a serious favor to ask you," I say.

I wait.

So does Gabriel.

"Will you help me find Mercury?" Because we both know that, wherever Mercury is, she's got Annalise with her. "I need your help, Gabriel."

He doesn't reply. Doesn't uncover his face.

There's nothing more I can do, so I go down to the lakeshore.

A while later he joins me and we both look out over the calm water, the mountains beyond, and the sky, clear and blue above that.

Gabriel says, "Van told me that you were dead. Nesbitt described your body, your wound. He had the Fairborn and I knew you wouldn't have let him take it if you were alive. I knew you were dead. There was no doubt in my mind." He glances at me but looks away again across the lake. "I wept. I wept a lot, Nathan. And I had this idea that I'd go and find your body and hold it to mine and not let it go, ever. I would stay with you, starve, but at least I'd die holding you. That's all I thought was left to me."

"Gabriel . . ." But I don't know what to say. I don't want him to starve or die. "You're my friend, Gabriel. My best, my only friend. But . . ."

He turns to me. "I'll stay with you always; go where you go always. I don't want to be anywhere else. I couldn't stand to be anywhere else. If you go to Mercury then I'll go too. If you want me to help free Annalise then I will."

I turn to face him and see how angry he looks. I say, "Thank you." I think it's the first time I've thanked Gabriel for anything but I know that he doesn't want my thanks; he doesn't want any of it.

A Proposition

"I have a proposition." Van started the elaborate evening meal with this comment, though we have yet to hear what the proposition is and the meal is nearly over.

Van is sitting at the head of the table, I'm to her left, and Gabriel is sitting opposite me. He and I have been together all day, eating, swimming, sunbathing, and occasionally arguing. Gabriel says that we're on holiday and that this is what fain holidays are like. We don't argue about Annalise; she isn't mentioned again. We do argue about who runs faster (me, by a mile, and yet Gabriel seems to think he wins every race because of some handicap system that applies to fain bodies), swims further underwater (me by fifty meters but yet again the handicap system reveals my failings), climbs faster (there's a climbing wall in the garden—as in most drug-baron homes, I expect—and this one Gabriel wins before the handicap system comes in; after the handicap is applied I'm relegated to slug speed). We eat a lot and discuss food a lot: whether croissants are better dipped in coffee or hot chocolate, bread with peanut butter or chocolate spread, chips with mayo or ketchup, that sort of thing. I realize how much I've missed him. He's good to be on holiday with but now the games are over.

The dinner is formal, with a lot of crystal and cutlery and candles, though I'm dressed in my old clothes. Van is immaculate in a cream-colored suit and Gabriel is wearing new clothes he found in the house. He and Van make a beautiful pair. Nesbitt is a lot less beautiful and has on the same black clothes he's always in. He's both chef and waiter and I have to admit he's pretty good. In fact, now I think about it, he's pretty handy at most things: cooking, serving tea, hiding a trail, strangling Hunters. As far as assistants go, Van has the best.

We've had soup, then lamb, but no dessert. "I think we're all sweet enough" is Van's comment. I snort a laugh.

She turns to me, saying, "I'm serious. Nesbitt told me that you threatened to cut his tongue out but you resisted. I suspect your father wouldn't have held back." Van watches Nesbitt walk away with a pile of plates. "Anyway, I'm glad you didn't do it." She hesitates and glances at the doorway through which Nesbitt has just exited. "Nesbitt and I are old friends and, much as my life would be infinitely more peaceful should Nesbitt be mute, he's a lot more useful with a tongue in his head."

I'm trying to work out their relationship. Van says she and Nesbitt are old friends and she looks like she's only a few years older than me, but she acts as if she's older than Nesbitt. They appear to be like a master and servant who've been together for decades.

I say, "Nesbitt told me you're an expert at potions."

"He's very generous. And certainly I prefer potions.

For example, I would never use anything as crude as a knife to cut a tongue out. Potions are extremely adaptable and more precise than even the sharpest blade. A certain potion dropped on your tongue and you would eat it—your own tongue, I mean."

"I've never heard of that. My gran's Gift was potions too. She had a strong Gift."

"I take it you're referring to your grandmother on the White side of your family?" Van doesn't wait for me to reply before going on. "Most White Witches know little about the power of Black potions. Potions have infinite uses and strengths. They are, in my humble opinion, the most powerful of weapons."

"And you've used that weapon? Made someone eat their own tongue?"

Van gives the faintest shrug. "I have few enemies; most I have dealt with."

Nesbitt has returned to clear more plates and bowls and as he piles them up he says, "Tell 'em about the potion for those who don't repay you." He grins at me and Gabriel. "I earn my keep, boys. You should think about earning yours."

"I'm not sure that those details are for the dinner table," Van says. "Though it is very effective."

"I think Gabriel has repaid you for your help," I say to Van.

"Yes. All in all I like to think we have done well by each other. Gabriel is alive and well, and I have half the amulet as he promised. Gabriel has been gracious and helpful: the perfect patient and the perfect guest. And you, Nathan, have your own charms."

"Yeah?" I can't believe Van finds anything about me charming. I look at Gabriel, who is grinning, no doubt at the comment about my charms, but I tell Van, "We'll be leaving tomorrow."

"That is, of course, entirely up to you."

"It is."

"May I inquire as to your plans?"

"You can inquire all you like."

"I assume that you're intending to find Mercury and help your friend Annalise escape. A worthy quest for a young man who is blinded by love." She smiles at me and then turns her smile on Gabriel.

"I'm not blinded by love."

"No. Of course not," Van says. "And even so the quest is a worthy one."

Nesbitt brings coffee and places the pot centrally on the table between us all. Van continues. "It feels rather unfair that I know your plans and you don't know mine. And I'm nothing if not fair." She waves at Nesbitt to indicate he can pour the coffee. "I too am on a quest of sorts."

"To find the other half of the amulet?" I ask.

Van shakes her head slightly. "That is something I hope to do at some stage, yes, but it isn't my first priority."

"And what is?"

"Since you left the world of White Witches, Nathan, a

lot has happened. The old Council Leader, Gloria Dale, has been ousted. Soul O'Brien used your escape from the Council building to bring about her downfall. No prisoner has ever escaped before and you are the son of Marcus. Your escape was both unprecedented and unforgivable."

"But I was a prisoner of Soul." Or at least I think I was.

"It doesn't matter who took you there or why. The Council guards failed to guard you and the magic protecting the building failed to retain you. The building, the guards, the magic are all the responsibility of the Council Leader. Gloria took the blame and Soul made sure she took it all."

"I always wondered if my escape was made easy. It certainly wasn't made difficult."

"My sources say that Soul allowed your escape. Though it did not go entirely as he planned. You were supposed to have had your finger chopped off and made into a witch's bottle before that happened. They were going to force you to kill your father and then murder you. But I see you still have all your fingers." She waves her cigarette at my hand. "Nonetheless, your escape has still worked to Soul's advantage. He brought down Gloria and took control of the Council himself."

"So now there's a man in charge of the Council and another leading the Hunters? That must be a first. I can't see it going down well with White Witches."

"Well, no. Most females, of course, have stronger Gifts than men. You and Gabriel are unusual in that regard."

Nesbitt coughs to bring attention to himself but Van ignores him. "Anyway, men actually don't hold both those two key positions. Clay also fared badly due to your actions. Many White Witches have died protecting the Fairborn, and yet it was stolen on Clay's watch without him even getting a bruise. There was a call for him to go too . . . and he went."

"So who's in charge of the Hunters now?" But somehow I have a feeling I already know.

"There was one person who did get rather more than a bruise the night you stole the Fairborn. She's a little young and somewhat inexperienced but intelligent and highly gifted. And also horribly disfigured, so they say. Your half-sister Jessica."

I remember the Fairborn in my hand, its power and its desire to cut, and how it sliced down her face. I say, "She was Clay's lover. I guess that relationship is over now since it's served its purpose. She'll be loving the job more than she loved Clay."

"Jessica is loyal to Soul and is already extending the Hunters' range across Europe. Soul is bringing the White Witch Councils of Europe under his influence. He's winning them round to his point of view. He wants them all to report to him and for them to drive out the Black Witches from here as they have been from Britain." Van shakes her head. "I'm a Black Witch and have no love for Whites but in Europe we have a long tradition of live and let live. They stick to their traditional areas and we stick to ours. There's a harmony."

Van pulls her slim silver case out of her jacket and takes another cigarette, saying, "Soul has no interest in harmony. All he wants is more and more power." She lights the cigarette, inhales deeply, and blows the plume of green smoke high above us. "He plans on killing all Black Witches in Europe. And he will kill anyone, Black or White, who stands in his way. He is no true witch."

"And your quest is to stop him?"

"Yes. To restore harmony and balance we have to prevent Soul from taking over all the Councils of Europe and we have to stop the Hunters who work for him."

"Who's *we*?"

"An alliance of all witches."

"*All* witches? You mean Whites as well as Blacks?"

"Yes, all witches who want to retain the traditional values."

"Traditional values of hating each other?"

"Traditional values of mutual distance, respect, and tolerance. We all respect the individual, whether White or Black. And we're looking for new recruits."

"Me? I'm neither Black nor White."

"You're both." She looks over at Nesbitt. "Half Bloods have joined too."

"So, let me get this right: you're banding together with a bunch of White Witches to battle the Hunters who are expanding into Europe. And you want me to join and fight alongside White Witches?"

"Yes."

"Ha! You talk about balance? Well, I hate White Witches and they hate me. That's the sort of balance I'm used to."

"You don't hate all White Witches. Your half-brother Arran and half-sister Deborah—"

"Are they joining?"

"I believe so."

I'm not sure how I feel about that but I imagine it's true. They would both believe in the cause.

I say, "I can't see either of them being much use in a fight."

"An army isn't just made up of soldiers." Van drags on her cigarette. "We all bring different attributes to the cause. Yours is undoubtedly your ability to fight. Others, like Arran, can heal the wounded. Others, like Deborah, provide information."

I study her. "How many recruits are there?"

"A few. Some White Witches have fled England already. Those that find Soul too extreme and have said so. They've lost everything and want to fight back. Some Black Witches have also joined: those who see the future will be bleak if they do nothing. The numbers are small but growing."

"You don't need me then."

"Few of our recruits can fight."

"Ah."

"And you, Nathan, need us. Even if you are able to wake Annalise and escape from Mercury, do you really think your troubles will be over? They'll hunt you to the ends of the earth. And, while you may be able to run, your precious Annalise will, I'm afraid, not last two minutes."

"We'll hide."

"They'll hunt."

And I know she's right, of course. There'll be no end to it.

I look at Gabriel. He says, "I'll go with you, whatever you choose to do."

I shake my head. "It's not my fight."

Van smiles. "It's your fight more than anyone else's."

I get up and walk round the table. I really don't like this. I've no desire to fight against Hunters or risk my life for some cause. And I certainly can't see myself fighting alongside even one White Witch. All I want to do is find Annalise and go and live a quiet life by a river, undisturbed, forever.

I walk out of the dining room, wander into the lounge, and sit on the sofa, looking out over the lake to the mountains beyond.

Nightsmoke

It seems that I'm not going to be left alone even here. I've been sitting on my own in the lounge for only a minute before Van follows me into the room, Gabriel comes to sit on a chair near me, and Nesbitt stands leaning against the door frame.

Van says, "Soul is a danger to us all. The Alliance's cause is—"

I interrupt her. "I'm not interested in causes. I just want to get Annalise back."

"And how do you plan to do that? Mercury is formidable; her Gift is exceptional." Van paces the floor in front of me. "Let me guess. Annalise is in a death-sleep from which only Mercury can wake her. You hope that if Gabriel uses his Gift to transform into Mercury he can break the spell."

I have to admit, but only to myself, that that is my plan and it does sound a bit lame.

"There's more than one problem with your plan."

"I didn't say that was my plan."

"You have a better one?"

If I did I wouldn't tell her that either.

Van continues talking and pacing. "First problem: Gabriel is still unable to access his Gift. Second problem:

you don't know where Annalise is. Third problem: even if you find Annalise, and Gabriel can transform himself into Mercury, you still have to work out how to undo the spell. Fourth problem: even if you find a solution to problems one through three, Mercury will try to kill you if she finds out what you're up to—and I think she'll have a good chance of succeeding."

"I admit there are a few hurdles."

"Indeed." Van sits on the edge of the coffee table in front of me. "Though I might be willing to help you over those hurdles."

"If I join the Alliance?"

"Yes."

"How?"

"How can I help you? Well, let's start with your first problem: Gabriel." She smiles at him. "No offense, darling."

He shrugs.

Van continues. "I can help Gabriel recover his Gift."

"There are others who can help me do that," says Gabriel.

"Well, there's Mercury, of course, and a few others, but each one will demand much in return."

Gabriel says, "And aren't you doing that?"

Van smiles. "I think you'll find I'm a lot easier to deal with than most. And I'm here and I can help straightaway. I understand you aren't in any rush to rescue Annalise, Gabriel, but you've been a fain now for many months. You've been unable to access your Gift almost as long as you were able to use it. You need to get back to your true self soon."

He looks at me. "It's not the end of the world, not having a Gift. There are worse things."

"I will help Gabriel recover his Gift so he'll be able to transform into Mercury, but even then he may not be able to wake Annalise. It all depends on Mercury's spell. However, I have another option if that fails."

"Which is?"

"I'll make Mercury do it."

"Ha! How?"

"It's no harder than getting her to eat her own tongue. There are potions that will allow it. I can make her want to wake Annalise."

"And you'll just get her to drink your potion, will you? 'Here, Mercury, do have a sip of this.' "

"Not all potions need to be drunk."

I wonder if that means she'll use her smoke or something like that. But, whatever she does, I have to admit it sounds like she has more chance than I do of getting Mercury to wake Annalise.

"And a potion will help Gabriel find his Gift?"

"Yes." Van looks at me, leans back, and says, "And I can help you too, Nathan, if you wish. Controlling a Gift is always hard. The more powerful the Gift, the harder it is to control."

"I'm learning."

"Good. You'll need to have full control of it to fight with the Alliance and take on the Hunters."

"I still haven't agreed to join."

"But you will because my help is the only way you'll be able to rescue Annalise. And even together it won't be easy. We won't be able to waltz in there and waltz out again. It will take planning and care—but it is possible."

"If I do join I want the Fairborn back."

"Agreed."

I expected her to complain about that, and now there's nothing more for me to argue about without going round in circles. It's getting dark and I really want to be outside. I stand, saying, "I'll sleep on it."

"Yes, it's getting dark. Unpleasant in here at dusk. But I have a simple remedy. Nesbitt," she calls, "bring the night-smoke."

Nesbitt goes to the far end of the room and fetches a bowl of milky liquid. He strikes a match above the surface of the potion and a green smoky flame slides across the creamy surface of the liquid, moving as if it was alive.

"If you inhale the fumes you'll be able to stay indoors. It clears your head wonderfully."

She leans over and breathes deeply.

I approach the flame. It smells of milk, grass, and forest. My headache is already receding. But I say, "I prefer sleeping outside."

"I'm sure. I'm a Black Witch too, Nathan. Don't forget that. I suffer as you do indoors at night, and Nesbitt does also, to a lesser degree. But we've learned to use the nightsmoke and I suggest you do too."

Gabriel and I follow Nesbitt to the bedroom. I open the window and sit by it but Nesbitt says, "No cheating, mate, it's for your own personal development." He sets the bowl of nightsmoke down on the windowsill and closes the window. "Just breathe this as you would fresh air."

After he leaves I sniff cautiously at the green smoke.

"Nathan," Gabriel says, "you haven't spoken to me about your Gift."

I inhale a little more smoke. I know Gabriel's probably the only person apart from my father who has any chance of understanding but I don't want to think about it now. I've got enough on my mind.

"I take it from that gushing response that you don't want to talk about it?"

I lie on my stomach on the bed with my head near the bowl and nod at it, saying, "Did you ever use this stuff?"

"No. When I had a Black Witch body I preferred to sleep outside or nap inside during the day and stay out at night." He comes over and sniffs the vapor deeply. "It doesn't do anything for me in this body. I can hardly smell anything."

"What do you think about what Van said? Will this Alliance really work? Could they ever take on the Council and the Hunters?"

"I'm not sure. There are some Black Witches with incredible powers but working together isn't their strong point. In fact working together is almost impossible. Van is unusually tolerant, so she might be able to work with Whites, but I'm not sure others will."

I pass my hand through the green smoke and waft it up to my face. It's a clean smell. In fact, it's more than a smell: it's a clean feeling in my nose and throat and head. It's the feeling of being outside in a meadow. I'm not sure about the smoke, though—it's a potion after all, a drug.

I open the window and sit on the ledge.

"I'll sleep outside."

Gabriel puts a towel over the basin. The flame goes out with a faint sigh. He says, "At the moment I'm not sure we need to worry about joining the Alliance. Mercury is more dangerous. She's no fool, Nathan. She's lethal."

"If we plan carefully we have a chance. If it's too risky we don't do it."

"However much you plan it can still go wrong. Read any history book."

"You know I can't read."

There's nothing more to say so I climb out of the window and walk toward the lake. I need to swim, to see if I can get in touch with my Gift and maybe sleep a little. I don't need to think about Van's proposal much. I know there's no other option really. This is my only chance to help Gabriel recover his Gift and to save Annalise. I have to make it work.

Rain

It's later that night. I'm swimming. Everything around me seems gray. It's overcast and muggy. The moon is totally hidden. The far mountains are a dark outline against the dark sky. The lake water looks black. Inky.

I float on my back, looking at the sky. I think it must rain soon. The wind seems to be picking up a little and at that moment several things happen. I hit a patch of colder water, a crow calls one sharp cry, and a wave slaps the side of my face and the water goes in my eyes and up my nose. I close my eyes. Instead of seeing blackness, I see the forest above the cave and I know Kieran is with me. I can't see him—he's invisible—but I can smell him, feel him, and I can taste his blood. My leg is on fire, a knife stuck in it. I rip my jaws at Kieran and he appears, and my eyes are filled with black inky liquid; the blood from his throat is up my nostrils. Kieran makes one last cry, like the cry of a crow, and then he's still. The vision lasts a few seconds but it's clear to me. It's not a dream: it's a memory.

Later I'm sitting by a fire I've made near the lakeshore, still not properly warm. It starts to rain but I stay there, trying to remember more about being an animal. I see through the animal's eyes, feel his pain, smell and taste the blood, hear Kieran's scream . . . it's like I'm experiencing the animal's body, feeling what he does, but I'm not inside his mind. I'm not making decisions. I'm a passenger.

The light shower turns to a downpour and I'm soaked and shivering. The fire is out and I head toward the house to shelter under the eaves. I'm nearly there when I see a figure dart out of the house and onto the patio. He places five large, wide bowls on the table, then runs back round the side of the house and inside, out of the rain. I'm not sure what Nesbitt is up to but I follow him and look in the bowls as I pass. They're just empty bowls, though they're all unusual: they're made out of stone and have thick, uneven sides.

Round the side of the house I see Nesbitt has gone into the kitchen. A green glow is coming from nightsmoke he has lit by the window. I quietly open the back door and step inside the small cloakroom. There's another door that opens onto the kitchen. It's not quite shut but Nesbitt won't know I'm here if I'm still. Then I hear voices and realize that Van is there too.

"I've put the bowls out."

"Good. We should have enough from tonight. I'll see you at breakfast."

"I've been thinking," Nesbitt says.

"Oh dear, must you?"

"About the kid."

"Hmmm?"

"I think you should tell him."

"Tell him what?"

"Who you're working with—"

"Who *we're* working with," Van corrects.

"He'll find out eventually and . . . well, I don't think he'll like it."

"He doesn't have to like it. I don't expect him to like it. I don't care if he likes it. The point is he will do it. He'll join because he doesn't have any other option. So there really is no point in muddying the waters."

"Yeah, but . . ."

"But what?" Van sounds impatient now. "You really are getting more and more like an old woman, Nesbitt."

"He's a Half Code. And . . . you don't know what it's like, Van, but I do. Or at least I know what it's like being a Half Blood. He doesn't know where he belongs and at the moment he doesn't belong anywhere, not with the White Witches and not with the Blacks. He could belong with the Alliance, but to belong to them he'll have to trust them—trust you—and, well, that's going to be a problem."

"Yes, you're quite right, Nesbitt. How surprisingly thoughtful of you. May I ask what you are doing to build a bond of trust and friendship between yourself and Nathan?"

Nesbitt snorts. "He doesn't know it but he's my friend already."

Van laughs, which I've never heard before; it's pleasant and genuine and amused. Her voice is softer now. "Nesbitt, all I can do is reassure you that it's a problem I'm aware of and will deal with but I've got other problems stacked up in front of me. First we have to rescue the girl and I'm not entirely sure how we're going to do that."

Nesbitt barks a short laugh. "Yeah, well, ain't that the truth of it."

Van opens the door and says something I can't hear and the door closes.

Who could the rebel be that I'd take offense to? Just about any White Witch would be the obvious answer.

The rain is easing and soon stops. I look down and there's a puddle around my feet. Nesbitt will guess that I've been here but there's nothing I can do about that. I head off back to the lake, walking through the trees to the side of the lawn. I find a huge, spreading cypress tree where the ground is still dry under its canopy. I stop there and then move to hide further behind the trunk.

There are two boats on the lake. They have small lights at their sterns and both are traveling at the same slow speed. There are four people in the boat nearest and two in the one further off, and they're all looking to the shore, toward me; they all have binoculars.

Hunters!

And there's something about the stance of the most distant Hunter that tells me who it is. She's tall and slim and straight.

Jessica.

I race back to the house and into the kitchen. The bowl

of nightsmoke by the window is like a beacon. I pick up a cloth and smother it. Nesbitt begins to object and I tell him, "Hunters! On the lake. Six of them at least."

Nesbitt is already leaving the room. "Get Gabby and come to Van's room. There's stuff to take. We leave in five minutes."

"If they've seen the nightsmoke we won't have five minutes," I reply, running after him.

"Then hope they haven't seen it."

Less than a minute later Gabriel and I are in Van's room. She's carefully packing vials into an already full carpetbag. She says, "Nesbitt went into Geneva yesterday to buy some provisions. I think he must have been spotted."

She opens the drawer by her bed and takes out the Fairborn. She drops it into a large leather bag, which she then picks up. As she strides to the door she points to a pile of leather-bound books and the carpetbag. "Bring those."

We all head to the garage at a fast pace, meeting Nesbitt on the way, a large bag slung over his shoulder.

A minute later Nesbitt, Van, and I are in the back of a black limousine. Gabriel is wearing a chauffeur's cap and is driving. And we're out of the sunken garage, climbing into the pre-dawn light, along the drive, and out through the electric gates. It's probably only five minutes since I saw the Hunters but it feels like twenty.

The road looks normal but Hunters aren't likely to be driving up and down in tanks.

Gabriel pulls out and turns right, away from Geneva. Half a minute later a van drives past in the opposite direction and Gabriel calls to us. "Hunters in that. Three in the front, who knows how many in the back."

No one replies and we all scan each vehicle that we go past. Half an hour later we've left the lakeshore road and are heading north and we've not seen any more Hunters.

"Where are we going, by the way?" Gabriel asks.

Van says, "North is fine for the moment but soon we'll need to turn east. I know the perfect place. It's an old castle but nicely secluded and remarkably well maintained. It should be free at this time of year."

Slovakia

We arrive at the place just as it's getting dark. We've been driving all day, apart from when we stopped to change the limousine for a less conspicuous car. The castle looks more like a large country house with turrets. Set in a thick forest at the end of a long drive, it definitely is secluded.

Van and Nesbitt go inside. Nesbitt says he'll have some food ready in ten minutes. I'm hungry but I've spent all day in the car and I don't want to be inside now when I'll have to use the nightsmoke. I tell Gabriel that I'm going to sleep in the forest. When he says he'll come with me, I shake my head.

"No. I'm better off alone, Gabriel. You stay in the castle."

"But—"

"Please, Gabriel. I'm too tired to argue. I need to be alone."

I go into the trees and find a sheltered place. I'm almost dizzy with tiredness but this place is good. It's old and quiet and I know Gabriel won't come when I've asked him not to. I close my eyes and welcome sleep.

I wake to a faint noise. Footsteps. Not human but small and hesitant. A deer.

My animal adrenaline rises quickly but I breathe slowly in

and out—really, really slowly—and hold my breath, and hold it and hold it and say to myself, "Calm, calm." I don't want to stop the animal taking over; I'm noticing the increasing adrenaline as it's released into me and I'm letting it build slowly. I hold my breath and then breathe out. The slower the transformation the better, I think. I don't want to shock my body. I want to get used to it and more than anything I want to remember what happens when I've transformed. I breathe in slowly and I tell myself to stay aware. I hold my breath in and then let it out in a long, steady stream and allow the adrenaline to flood through me.

i see the deer. the animal i'm in follows after her. he's totally silent, keeping low, only moving when he's sure he won't be spotted. the deer stops. her ears twitch. she raises her head and looks around. she's beautiful. i don't want to kill the deer but the animal i'm in is bunching his hind legs, ready to charge forward. i say to him, "no, don't kill her." i'm calm, talking to him quietly, trying to tame him. the deer tenses. she's sensed something and she bends, ready to jump away, as he leaps at her and i'm shouting at him, "no, no"—

I wake up. It's still dark. I know by the taste in my mouth that the deer was dinner. My hands and face are covered in blood and, raising my head, I see its remains near me. I remember some of what happened. I remember hearing the deer when I was me, in my human body, and I remember the animal adrenaline rising, and I must have transformed but I don't remember that. No, I don't remember any of that. I do remember that I tried to stop him attacking her. I was shouting at him from inside his body but the animal I'm in didn't listen. He killed her anyway.

I feel the deer's body: she's still warm.

I find a calm pool in the river to wash in and then I lie down near it. I can't sleep now. I'm not tired but I'm confused. The animal didn't pay any attention to me. He is me but isn't me. He killed the deer even though I didn't want him to. He does what he likes.

When it's light I go to the castle to look for Van. I'm frustrated by my Gift; I'm frustrated by everything. We're not getting closer to helping Annalise, and Gabriel needs to get back to his witch form. I stomp from kitchen to dining room, music room to ballroom to gunroom, eventually coming across Nesbitt, who says, "Van's in the study. She'd like a word."

I head the way Nesbitt has come, pushing open a heavy oak door, and am greeted by, "You look like you could do with one of these." Van lights a cigarette and offers me one but I shake my head.

The study is wood-paneled. There's a large desk made of chrome and black glass, covered with rows of plates. I go over to take a closer look. On each small plate is a heap of different-colored material. The piles are mostly fine grains, herbs perhaps, but some are coarser than others and some look like large seeds.

I reach out to touch one of the piles. "Please don't," Van says and I withdraw my hand. She's sitting on a chair at the side of the room and is dressed in a pinstriped man's suit today. "I've been working on the potion for Gabriel, finding the correct combination of ingredients."

"You've got it?"

"Yes, now that the final two ingredients are here."

"Which are . . . ?"

"The rain that fell when we were in Geneva is one. Nesbitt collected some of it: fallen at night, at full moon."

"That really makes a difference?"

She looks at me as if I'm mad. "Everything makes a difference, Nathan."

I remember my gran said that plants' properties were different depending on the cycle of the moon when they were picked, so I guess rainwater could be different too. And why not anything else? My healing abilities change with the moon.

"And what's the other ingredient?" I ask.

"Oh, I think you know that," Van says, and stubs out her cigarette.

And the way she says it and looks at me gives me the feeling that something of me is the ingredient. "My blood?" I guess.

Van smiles up at me. "Oh no, dear boy—it's much darker than that. We need to use your soul."

Magical Mumbo-Jumbo

I'm sitting behind the desk in Van's study, watching her smoke another of her cigarettes.

"Gabriel can't find his way back to himself because his Gift is so strong—exceptionally strong. He has become such a good fain that he can't recover that element of himself that is the Black Witch."

"I guess that sounds plausible," I reply.

"Gosh, thanks, Nathan." She comes over to lean on the desk close to me. "But that Black Witch element of him is still inside. He needs to find it and he needs a strong witch to guide him to it."

"But why me? I'm not a Black Witch; I'm a Half Code."

"White, Black, half and half—it doesn't matter. He needs a witch he trusts. And he trusts you completely. He also believes you're a great witch."

I shake my head. "No, he doesn't."

"Have you any idea what he really thinks of you?" She drags on her cigarette. "He sees you as the ultimate witch."

"What?"

"The rejoining of Black and White in one person. As the original witches were, with the strengths of both sides."

"Oh! But . . ." But I really don't know what to say to that.

Just then there's a knock on the door and Nesbitt comes in, carrying a tray. "Grub's up!" he says. "Just brought you some tea and toast, Van."

"Thank you, Nesbitt. Could you ask Gabriel to join us as well, please?"

"Now?"

"That's the general idea," Van says.

And Nesbitt disappears, saying, "I'm not actually a servant, you know. I'm a partner in this relationship and I think we both know who the most hardworking one is . . ." But his whinging fades as he walks down the corridor.

"I'd be lost without him."

I'm not sure how to say that they seem totally incompatible so instead I go with, "He's very handy."

"Yes, he is. I trained him in most things. And, to be fair, he's a good learner. We've been together for twenty-five years."

"Twenty-five?" Van looks no more than twenty to me but she always acts much older, more experienced. "How old are you, Van?"

"A rather rude question if you don't mind me saying. But one of the many uses of potions is the option to keep a more youthful appearance."

Gabriel comes into the room and closes the door, virtually pushing it in Nesbitt's face. His complaints can be heard through the heavy wood.

"Gabriel, thank you for coming so quickly. I was just telling Nathan that we are nearly ready to help you get back to your true self."

"OK," Gabriel says cautiously, and sits down opposite me.

"So what do we do?" I ask.

"You both drink the potion I make. You'll be bound together and enter a trance, and together you'll find the essence that is the old Gabriel. Think of it as a cord. You find it and then make your way back along it to the here and now."

I look at Gabriel and shake my head slightly. He meets my eyes and, as if he knows what I'm thinking, says, "It's magic. None of it makes sense—yet it all makes sense."

I roll my eyes and turn to Van. "And what if we don't find the essence or we follow the cord the wrong way?"

"Then you stay in the trance."

"What? Forever?"

"Until you die of starvation."

"Not a nice way to go," I say.

"I always thought I'd be more the shot-down-in-a-hail-of-bullets type." Gabriel smiles at me. "But I tried that and it wasn't so great either."

"So how long should it take?" I ask.

Van lights another cigarette and blows out the smoke. "As long as it takes."

"You mean you don't know."

She doesn't reply.

"And how likely is it that we don't find it?" I ask.

"I've really no idea. It's entirely down to you two."

"I don't like it but I'll do it."

"I'm so glad you're enthusiastic, Nathan. That always helps." Van rests her hand lightly on my leg and pats it. "Fortunately this location is an advantage. Trees and a river and ancient hills are so much more you." And she looks into my eyes and the blue of hers sparkles. "Unfortunately we still have one small problem."

"What's that?" I ask.

"It will be too dangerous to perform under anything more than a new moon."

"What? But that's two weeks away." I'm standing now.

"Yes." Van blows another slow, steady plume of smoke into the air.

"But Annalise . . . She could die. Hunters may find Mercury and kill them both or capture them."

"I think we can have some confidence in Mercury's abilities to hide from the Hunters. After all, she's been doing it for decades."

"But Annalise will be getting weaker. We can't just wait here for two weeks."

"Yes, we can, and that's exactly what we're going to do, Nathan. You're right—Annalise will be getting weaker but we still have time. She can survive in that condition for many months."

"It's easy for you to say when you're walking around alive and well and free."

I go toward the desk. I want to swipe all her piles of herbs onto the floor. But Gabriel must see where I'm heading and he blocks my way. I swear at him and storm out of the room, slamming the door behind me. I feel childish for doing that but then I see Nesbitt standing in the corridor, smirking at me. I'm not sure if he's been eavesdropping but I push him aside and kick and hit everything I can on my way out of the house.

Telling Gabriel

I find a way to fill two weeks. I know I need to get back to my peak fitness, and there's nothing much else for me to do, so I start training. I get fitter cos of the training but also because of my Gift. Since I got it my body has felt stronger, more alive. I train with Nesbitt and Gabriel during the day and I train at night too. I can keep going all night easy enough if I have a couple of naps during the day.

Most mornings, first thing, I go for a run with Gabriel and Nesbitt but I always end up running on my own after a couple of miles. We meet up at dawn and they groan a bit and make a few comments about the weather and their aching muscles and we do some stretching. And I think today might be all right with them but every day turns out pretty much the same, with Nesbitt winding me up. He takes the piss out of me for everything—mainly for being impatient but also for being silent or miserable, or he takes the piss out of my boots or my hair, my face, my eyes. There's always a comment about my eyes. Sometimes I really do think he wants me to hit him.

Mostly I think if I stay with them he'll get bored with teasing me but then I feel myself getting mad and so, one way or another, I leave them behind and run on my own, and it's better like that. I don't know why I even bother with them first thing but every day I hope that somehow it'll be good to be together. It never is.

After my run I have breakfast. I make porridge. Nesbitt makes fancy stuff—eggs florentine yesterday—for Van and Gabriel. He does all that and waits on Van while I eat in the kitchen. Gabriel always stays with me. Nesbitt sometimes has porridge with us; that's when he's sort of OK. He doesn't talk too much then, and I just eat.

After that I have a morning nap, lying in the sun if there is any. Next I do more training, then I go hiking, usually on my own, sometimes with Gabriel. Then it's lunch followed by another nap. Late afternoon or early evening I do some fighting practice with Nesbitt. He's good but I beat him every time. I always comment on how old and slow and fat he is, and he always smiles and laughs and takes everything I say as a compliment. Gabriel sometimes watches us but he doesn't join in the fighting or the banter. Mostly he practices his shooting; he's good with a gun and also with a bow and crossbow. Like Van, he manages to make everything he does seem easy and elegant. I try the guns too but I hate them.

In the evening I shower in the castle and we have dinner, with Nesbitt acting as chef and waiter. When it gets dark I move to the forest. And then the day is over and there's one less until I see Annalise.

I've been sleeping in the forest. I like it here. The forest is a good place; when I'm alone in it I feel relaxed. I only transformed that first time. Every night I wait to see if it'll happen again. I want to learn about it, learn how to control it, and I do think this remote, ancient place is perfect for that.

I skipped food for a day to see if that would work but it didn't. I think it might be because no animal, no potential prey, crossed my path. Tonight I'm trying something different. I've not eaten all day and I'm going hunting, but I don't want to kill anything. I want to transform, hunt but not kill, and persuade the animal me to come back here. I've brought some meat from the kitchen and I lay it out on the ground.

As soon as it's dark I set off through the forest. I know there are some foxes in the area so I'm heading to their den. I work my way slowly and silently through the trees until I can see the tangle of branches that surrounds the entrance. I crouch down on my haunches and wait.

I have to wait most of the night but as soon as a small fox sticks her nose out of the den my animal adrenaline kicks in. I breathe slowly and steadily, waiting. I want to control it, see if I can at least hold it off until I'm ready. I don't want to kill the fox. I want to transform and find a way to stop myself killing her, even if all I do is make the animal me go back to the meat that I've left behind. I have to learn how to control him. Stop him from killing.

I breathe slow and watch; the adrenaline is in me but it's not overpowering. I tell myself, "We follow her. That's all. We follow her and let her live."

The fox hasn't sensed me and is trotting away. I stop the controlled breathing and concentrate on the smell of the fox.

i'm in the animal body. the den is in front of me. there's a strong smell of fox, much stronger now. the fox is moving away fast. he, the animal i'm in, goes after her. i tell him, "no, let her go," but he keeps following the fox. i say, "no, stop," and again "no!" i try to turn the animal round but he keeps on going after the fox. i have no control over him. he's gaining on the fox. "no!" i shout, angry at him now. "no!" but he's gaining quickly. his strides are huge compared to the fox's. the fox stops, turns, and i shout, "no! don't kill her. there's better meat nearby. no!" and try to hold the animal body still, try to stiffen his muscles, but i have no muscles and it doesn't work. he is racing to the fox and is on her and i'm shouting, "no! stop!" but tasting blood . . .

I wake up. I still taste blood. The body of the fox is by my head. A mess of fur and guts and bone. I want to pick it up and hurl it away. I hate the animal me. Hate him. He can't be me. I didn't want to kill the fox. I told him not to kill it. He didn't need to kill it. I shout and swear with frustration at the fox's stiffening body but I'm really shouting at the animal in me. I hope he can hear me. I hope he knows I hate him. I don't want this Gift. I hate everything about it.

By dawn I've calmed down. I'm not sure what to do about my Gift. If I can't control it I could kill anyone. I'm not sure if I should ask Van about it. She's knowledgeable about many aspects of witchcraft, so perhaps she can help me, but I don't want to rely on her. I want to work it out myself. And I haven't even told Gabriel yet.

At dawn I wash quickly in the river and go to meet up with Gabriel and Nesbitt for our run. They're standing together, talking, and Gabriel smiles as I approach.

He says, "You're looking even more messed up than usual," and he reaches over to my hair, saying, "What's that?"

I back away from him, tearing at my hair, finding bits of stuff, dried blood and other bits . . . tiny bits. And all I can hear is Nesbitt sniggering as he says, "Last night's leftovers?" I turn back to him and before I know it my knife is in my hand and I'm striding toward Nesbitt, who's pulling his blade out too.

Gabriel moves between us. "Nathan. Calm down."

I push my hand against Gabriel's chest but I can't speak. I know I shouldn't do anything but if Nesbitt says one more word I really will stick the knife in his fat guts.

Gabriel stays there, barring my way, and Nesbitt stands behind him, grinning.

"Nesbitt, go back to the castle. I need to talk to Nathan."

And Nesbitt, still grinning, salutes Gabriel behind his back, then turns and dances away.

Gabriel touches my arm. "Nathan. He's just winding you up."

"And that means I shouldn't kill him?"

He doesn't reply at first. Then he shakes his head. "Please don't. He's the best cook for miles. And I don't want to end up doing the washing-up. Get your own back by complaining his soup is too salty. That'll hurt him more than a knife in the guts."

"He drives me mad with all his stupid comments." I take a breath and say, "I overheard him talking to Van when we were in Geneva. He said that I didn't know it but I was already his friend." I shake my head. "I just don't get him."

"I think all this is Nesbitt's way of showing he likes you. He's half Black Witch, Nathan. Don't treat him like a fain."

"I don't!"

"You don't show him any respect."

I look over to Nesbitt's figure in the distance. He's not dancing now but is walking slowly to the castle. "I'm not sure I feel much respect for him."

"I think you do. He's a good fighter. A good tracker. He's just bad at jokes."

I feel stupid holding my knife now and I put it away.

Gabriel reaches out and feels my hair, pulling at bits in it. "Tell me about this stuff."

I try to speak but I don't know what to say. The forest

behind me is quiet. The wind is moving over the trees and they seem to be hushing each other. I want to find the right word to begin but can't.

"Is it to do with your Gift?" he asks. "Can you tell me?"

I manage to mumble, "I have the same Gift as my father, the turning-into-animals thing. I'm trying to learn how to control it but . . . I can't."

"Is that why you want to be alone at night?"

"Yes. I'm dangerous. You shouldn't be near me. No one should."

I look into Gabriel's eyes but don't focus on them so that I can manage to say, "I caught a fox last night. I thought I might be able to stop him but I couldn't."

"Him?"

"The animal me. I tried to tell him not to kill the fox but he doesn't listen to me. He wanted to kill it. To eat it. And he did. I experience it all, see it, hear it, smell it. Taste it. But I can't control it." I glance at the ground, then back at the trees behind me. I'm not sure I can say all this but I force myself to go on. "His first kill, my first kill, wasn't a fox."

"What was it?" Gabriel asks quietly.

"A Hunter." I've remembered more of it since it happened and now I can't un-remember it. "I woke up with her blood on my hands . . . in my mouth. Over my face. My hands were dripping with it. I didn't remember it at first but now I do. I ripped the Hunter's stomach open with my claws and her guts were half hanging out and I buried my head in her stomach. I remember that clearly—red everywhere and the taste of it and pushing my face inside her to bite into her and rip her apart.

"I mean, I killed that other Hunter in Geneva. I broke her neck. I thought that was bad enough. But this one—I had my head, my snout, inside her."

"That was the animal. The other you."

"The animal's still me. Another part of me." I take a breath before I say, "She was still screaming, Gabriel. I had my face buried in her and she was still screaming."

I look away and then back to Gabriel. "I thought having my Gift would be great and in a way it is. I feel stronger physically but inside, right inside, in that place where you got lost or whatever, I'm . . . it's like there's someone, some-*thing* else living in me. And he comes out and takes over. But I know he's still me, another part of me, a completely wild, uncaring me." I pause, take a breath, and I tell him, "I killed Kieran too."

"Kieran? Annalise's brother?"

I nod. "I'd seen him at Mercury's cottage and I thought about killing him—I mean, fighting him and stabbing him—but I didn't do it. I walked away. But then he and his partner trailed me. Nesbitt killed his partner and I, the animal me, killed Kieran."

And I'm beginning to remember more of it now. "Kieran screamed too. Once. I ripped his throat out. I can remember the taste of him and how slick he felt in my mouth. I licked his blood."

My eyes fill with tears and I feel stupid and like I'm a

hypocrite for crying cos I wanted Kieran dead. I disgust myself by crying. I turn away from Gabriel and try to straighten up, wipe my wet cheeks with my sleeve. When I turn back Gabriel's eyes are on me still.

"It was bad. Nesbitt was sick when he saw Kieran's body. If Nesbitt was sick . . ."

"None of this means you're bad, Nathan."

"It doesn't mean I'm good!"

"You killed him like an animal would. I know that might not be a comfort to you now but the animal acts on instinct. An animal isn't evil, isn't good or bad."

Then he says, "Can I ask you something?" He hesitates and says, "Did you eat the Hunter's heart? Or Kieran's heart? Did you take their Gifts?"

I shake my head. "The animal kills them, rips them apart. But he's not interested in Gifts. He just wants to kill."

"I think he wants to survive. He's not evil, Nathan."

Gabriel is close to me and he reaches forward and brushes away more of my tears with his fingertips. His touch is gentle.

It's good to feel him.

And Gabriel leans closer and closer and, very slowly and gently, he kisses me, on the lips, with infinite tenderness, so that our skin is barely touching. I pull away a little but he stays close to me. "Don't hate yourself. Don't hate any bit of yourself."

Gabriel pulls me to him and holds me and I feel his warm breath through my hair.

I'm not sure what to do about Gabriel holding me and kissing me. I don't know what I feel about it. He does it to show me how he feels. But he must know I don't feel the same way. I can't change that. But I do love him. He's my friend, my best friend, and I love him loads and loads. And I keep on crying and he keeps on holding me.

We stay like that a long time. The trees stay the same too and I still look at them and only them. When I've finally stopped crying Gabriel releases me. We sit down on the grass and I lie back and cover my face with my arm.

"You OK?" he asks.

"I'm the son of Marcus, the most feared of Black Witches. I'm a Hunter-eating animal. And I'm a complete crybaby. Course I'm OK."

"Accept your Gift, Nathan. Don't fight it."

"I'm not fighting it. I can't fight it. It takes over."

"Then welcome it and learn from it. Don't judge it. It must be very confusing for the poor animal. You want it because it's like your father's Gift, but you don't want it for the same reason. You like the power. You hate the power. I feel sorry for the poor beast inside."

"Say that when you're faced with the beast outside."

"All you do is tell me the bad stuff, the things you hate. Tell me the good bits."

"There are no good bits."

"Liar! I'm a witch, Nathan. I know what it's like to have a Gift."

I close my eyes and remember. I know I have to be honest

with Gabriel, so I say, "It feels good. It feels good when the stuff, the animal adrenaline, whatever it is, surges through me. I'm afraid of it but still it feels amazing and powerful. And . . . all my senses are super alert, super aware. And I'm sort of watching him, the other me, and he's . . . absorbed. That's what it is to be him: to be totally absorbed in what he does, not thinking but being purely physical."

I look over to Gabriel. "Do you think that's what it is to be an animal?"

"I don't know. That's why you have this Gift, though, Nathan. Not because you're an animal, not because you've no morals, but because you need to feel it. That's how you are, how you exist best—by feeling things."

"Oh."

"You're a true witch, Nathan. Don't fight the animal. Experience him. That's what he's for." He pauses and then says, "Can I ask—what animal do you become?"

I don't even know that. I remember the fox's eyes staring into mine last night and I tell him, "A hungry one."

Using My Soul

It's the day of the new moon. Van says that when we're ready Gabriel and I must drink the potion she provides before cutting the palms of our hands, which she will then bind together. We will stay like that until we find our way out of the labyrinth of Gabriel's mind. There's a catch, of course. "You both have to prepare your bodies. Gabriel, you must exercise gently and eat well. Nathan, you must spend the night before the ritual inside."

"What?" I say. "Why?"

"It will heighten your senses and make the trance you enter all the more real. That's why we waited until the new moon, so you could stay inside for the full night."

"I don't see why a shorter time with the fuller moon wouldn't work then?" I say.

"The full moon will drive you mad, and Gabriel needs you conscious and reasonably sane. The new moon will be unpleasant, extremely unpleasant, but you'll survive and be stronger at the end of it." She opens her cigarette case and picks one out. "Of course I could be completely wrong; there's always a first time. However, I believe that this is right for you. It's an instinct. It's my Gift, Nathan, and I trust it."

I'm not sure about the whole idea but I have no other option. The last time I was inside overnight I was sixteen. I hadn't received my Gift and it was bad. I don't often think about it, and whenever I have, I've not been able to work it out. As much as part of my brain was saying, "This is stupid, you're just inside, you're fine," my whole body was in agony and soon all I could think about were the noises and the fear and my screaming to get out.

I spend the day in the forest on my own, resting. The animal inside me seems to be resting too. I've not felt him stir since I spoke with Gabriel. I lie on the ground and watch the sky turn from pale blue in the morning to deep blue at midday and then briefly in the evening to violet before going gray. I'm hungry and thirsty; my stomach grumbles, which feels ridiculous given what I've got to go through. I'm sure I can do it. I want to, for Gabriel, to show him that I know he's making a sacrifice for me and I'll do what I can for him. It's only one night inside.

It's getting dark as I walk up to the main door of the castle. Van opens it immediately. She must have seen me coming across the lawn. I wonder if she'll say anything but she doesn't; she just leads the way through the entrance hall, down the corridor, wooden floors dark and echoing, to a door at the end. I follow her through the door and that's when I stop.

There are stone steps down.

"The cellar," Van says.

I wonder about the animal in me but he doesn't stir. Van

leads the way down into an empty room with a stone floor and brick walls and one faint light in the ceiling. It's more cell than cellar.

"Nesbitt will be at the top of the stairs. The door will be locked but if it's too hard for you he'll let you out. He'll check on you every hour."

I don't say anything. Already the room feels oppressive. I sit on the cold floor and watch Van climb the steps. Then the door shuts and I hear a key turn in the lock.

I know the animal isn't going to appear. It's too harsh here. He's hiding. I've only been inside for a minute, two at most, and I feel sick and dizzy but that's not so bad and this is for Gabriel. And for Annalise. I get up and walk to the far wall and back, and I do it again, but already that isn't good. The room feels like it's tipping up so I sit back down, and the walls are falling in on me. But I know they're not. They are not! They're walls and they're upright. I'm OK. I'm feeling sick. And I have a stinking headache. It isn't pleasant but I'm OK. I sit still and concentrate on my breathing and not being sick.

I hear the door open above me. An hour has gone by already.

"You OK?" Nesbitt shouts.

"Yeah. Fine," I shout back, making my voice sound stronger than I feel.

The door shuts.

I sit there another minute or two and tell myself I'm fine, I'm fine, and then I retch and I'm sick on the floor and my stomach is in a knot and all the muscles in my body cramp up. I feel the walls coming down on me but I know, absolutely know, they can't be. Walls don't do that. They don't. I'm hot and sweat blossoms out of me and I retch again and again and my stomach is agony and nothing more comes out when I retch but my stomach keeps doing it and I'm curled up in a tight ball.

Then Nesbitt is standing over me. Another hour must have gone by. And I look for him again but he's gone.

I'm shivering now, my body cold. And I'm retching again. There's not much to come up but my stomach seems to be determined to turn itself inside out. I'm still lying curled up at the bottom of the steps. And that's where I stay. I can't move. Can't stand. I can't even crawl. But I can cope with it. I can do it.

That's when the scraping noise starts. It's quiet at first but builds up until it fills my head and then suddenly stops. Silence. And I wait, listening for it; I know it'll start again. While it's quiet I tell myself it's not real: I'm in a cellar; there's nothing here to make a noise. *It's not real*. But then my head is filled with a scraping sound like nails down a blackboard and I wedge my head against the steps and shout. Shouting helps. And cursing. If I shout loud enough I can drown out the scraping noise. Then it goes silent again. And I can breathe and I wait for the scraping and it starts again . . .

Nesbitt is here. He's patting my shoulder and I look up

at him and then he's not there and I'm not sure if he ever was. The scraping has stopped. It's quiet and all I can see is the floor, which is changing from gray stone to red. Dark red. And everywhere I look I see red. Red all around me so that I feel it's choking me. And I'm screaming at the red and choking and clawing at my throat to breathe.

Then I feel hands round me. Holding my arms down. And Gabriel's voice, quiet in my ear, telling me, "It's nearly over. Nearly over."

And my cramps are easing and the banging and scraping have gone. And my stomach retches one last time and the red veil lifts and I see the stone floor and Gabriel's shoulder. And I want to cry with relief, with joy at the freedom, at being able to see again. I say, "It's dawn."

Gabriel moves off me and helps me to sit up.

"If that's the gradual, less intense method . . ." And I'm going to make a joke but I can't because I do feel different. I feel intensely aware of everything. Every movement of my body. The dampness of the air. The floor, the grains of loose dirt on my fingertips. And *colors,* even in this poor light—the grays of the room and the black and brown of Gabriel's hair. I look into his eyes and see that they're fain as they've always been but I see something else too. "I can see something in your eyes. I've never noticed it before. Hardly there. Twists of gold but far back and distant. Things witches have."

Gabriel smiles. "Let's go outside."

He helps me up and as soon as I step outside I heal and the intensity is beyond anything I've felt before. The air feels and tastes so incredible that I'm almost drunk on breathing. I sit on the grass and the animal in me flares up and fills me with adrenaline again but nothing more, just the joy of being free.

Van and Nesbitt approach. Van puts a tray on the ground between Gabriel and me. On it is a long strip of wide, fine leather; a bowl containing the potion; two small cups made of stone; and one other thing—a wooden stake, about thirty centimeters long, which tapers at both ends to sharp points and widens to be as thick as a pencil in the middle.

I don't know what the stake is for. Van hasn't mentioned this. I thought we were going to cut our palms and hold the cuts together but I see no knife and I have a bad feeling that this is where the stake comes in.

Van picks up the potion and dribbles it into the two stone cups. She holds them out to us. "Drink."

We watch each other and together lift the cups and drink. It tastes disgusting and gritty, like drinking mud.

I move my arm to put the cup down and already the tray looks wrong, like it's too far away and my hand can't reach it. Nesbitt takes the cup from me.

Van has lifted the wooden spike. She's holding it lightly between us. "Nathan, hold the palm of your right hand against the spike. Gabriel, your left hand. Focus on the stake." And I do as she asks and that helps: it's the only thing that isn't moving in and out of focus. Then Van says, "Push your hands together."

And I smile because it seems like a weirdly good idea and I push and see the wooden spike come through the back of my hand. I wait for pain but all I feel is warmth and elation at seeing the blood drip off the pointed end. My hand feels hot in its center and then Gabriel's hand grasps mine, our fingers overlapping, blood running down our wrists.

Van binds our two hands together with the leather strip. She says, "Don't heal. I will twist the stake and rethread it at dusk and dawn until Gabriel is back with us."

I feel like I'm floating out of my body. I watch Gabriel and I lower our arms so that our staked hands rest between us on the ground. The tray has gone.

I have an urge to touch the stake, so I stretch my left hand out to it. My fingertips touch the end that appears out of Gabriel's hand. I wrap my fingers round it and as I do I feel my body sinking and in an instant I'm panicking. Mud rises up from the ground, bubbling around me, and there is no ground and all I see is mud and all I feel is Gabriel's hand in my right hand.

The First Stake

I wake, drowsy, fuggy, my body aching. I blink my eyes open. It's daytime, light and sunny, and the sky above me is a perfect deep blue. I look around and recognize the roof terrace of the apartment in Geneva. Gabriel is with me, holding my hand just like he did when we were about to go through the cut to meet Mercury. Gabriel is on his haunches and he's looking away, his hair hanging forward, sunglasses on. His left hand is clasping my right.

And somehow I know I have to find the cut, that this is the way out. The way to find Gabriel's real self. I'm crouched in the corner of the terrace, my back to the sloping tiled roof. The cut is above the drainpipe. I've seen Gabriel use it, been with him when he slid his hand through it. Now I've got to find it and keep hold of him and see where the cut takes us.

I'm confident I can do it. I know where the cut is. I raise my left hand and slide it into the space above the drainpipe.

Nothing happens.

But perhaps I missed. A little higher, I think. Still nothing happens. So it must be to the left a tad. No! Then to the right. No, again. Then lower. Maybe I'm doing it too fast, being too impatient.

I say to Gabriel, "Where's the cut?"

He doesn't reply and I turn to him, annoyed. He knows where it is—he should help me.

But as I turn to him I see what he's looking at. There's someone standing on the ridge of the roof. A woman. Tall, slim, dressed in black, a Hunter. And as I look at her more Hunters appear and stand watching us. And my left hand is now frantically searching for the cut. And I say to Gabriel, "Where is it? Where is it?"

And I can feel his hand gripping my hand but he says nothing and I'm shouting at him to tell me where it is. And all the time I'm trying to find the cut and the Hunters are coming toward us.

There must be twenty of them now; more are climbing through the window onto the terrace. And still I'm desperately searching and I'm shouting at Gabriel to help me. "Where is it? Where?"

But he doesn't answer. The Hunters are all around us. Standing over us. They each hold a truncheon, like the one Clay used on me the first time he met me. He beat me unconscious with it. A Hunter raises hers and swipes it through the air onto Gabriel's shoulder, and I feel the blow reverberate up my arm. Another Hunter swings her truncheon hard into the side of Gabriel's face. Blood and teeth spray out but again all I feel is a shock wave up my arm. Yet another Hunter steps forward and I try to move to protect Gabriel—but I'm stuck in place, and all I can do is watch as they form a black wall round Gabriel and take it in turns to step forward and attack him. No one has hit me. Nothing has hurt me. And I know I should find the cut; if I could find it we could still escape. But my left hand won't even move now—I'm paralyzed.

Then Soul climbs out of the window onto the terrace. He smiles at me. He says, "I've always liked you, Nathan. Thank you for bringing this Black Witch to me."

And he moves to the side and I see that Mr. Wallend is with him. He has a pair of shiny chrome clippers in his hand. He says, "It really won't hurt at all."

He snaps shut the clippers and I laugh because it really doesn't hurt. My little finger is cut off and resting in the palm of his hand. He puts it into a bottle, stops the top with a fat cork, and holds it up and smiles at me. The bottle fills with green smoke. And I too seem to be surrounded by a green mist.

I'm choking in it. I can't breathe and I have to gasp for air and I hear Mr. Wallend say, "Shoot the Black Witch. Shoot him and you'll be able to breathe again."

And I feel a gun in my left hand and I'm choking and in the mist all I see is a gray outline of Gabriel and I know I'll die. I can't breathe. I need to breathe. I know I've only got seconds.

Wallend says, "Shoot him. Shoot him."

"No!"

And Wallend takes the gun from me and points it at Gabriel's head, pulls the trigger, and the green smoke engulfs me.

* * *

My eyes open and Gabriel is gripping my hand and staring at me and I know he has had the same vision as me. I shake my head at him. "It's not real."

But, before Gabriel replies, the pain in my hand takes over. Van is turning the stake. My hand before was warm and numb but now it is hot and throbbing. I realize it's dusk. A whole day has gone by but it seemed like minutes.

Van says, "More potion. Then I rethread the stake."

She holds another small cup out to us. Gabriel's eyes are on mine. I want to tell him that I will make sure we live. I won't let us die. I want the drink now. I want to feel dizzy and out of it so I swallow it down in one gulp and shudder at the bitter taste and then let the cup drop from my hand. Gabriel has drunk his too.

"I'll find the way next time," I tell him.

He nods.

Van says, "Now I'll draw this out and put a new stake in."

And I'm surprised by how drawing the stake out is not painful at all but feels good, a relief. My hand is hot and sore. Van holds up a newly prepared stake and puts the sharp point against the wound in my hand. She pushes it through and the pain is excruciatingly intense and I gasp and—

The Second Stake

We're climbing up steep, bare rocks. Gabriel is above me and he helps me onto a narrow ledge, pulling me up until I stand next to him so that our arms are touching. I look around. We're in the mountains: Switzerland, judging by the green slopes below and the snow-capped peaks in the distance.

"They're coming." Gabriel points down into the valley at the numerous black specks, like ants crawling around below, but crawling in our direction.

"We need to go," I say, and turn to head up the mountain.

"How far is it?" Gabriel asks.

"Just over this peak," I say. "Not far." And somehow I know I'm right. If we get over the peak we'll be safe. We'll find the way back on the other side.

I set off and for once I'm faster at climbing than Gabriel. He's falling behind. But it's an easy route and I know he'll catch up. I'm nearly at the top when a gray mist descends. There are narrow paths, each looking the same, each about thirty centimeters wide, like a spider's web through the rocks. I follow one and it leads to a cliff edge and then I follow another and reach a different cliff edge. I run back but I've no idea which way I came up or which way is down.

"Gabriel!" I call. "Gabriel!"

"Here!" a voice replies but I know it isn't him.

I run in panic and see a figure in the mist and then stop and retrace my steps as I know it's another Hunter. I run in a different direction and call again for him and someone replies but again I know it's not Gabriel.

I stop and calm myself. I know I can work it out. I follow a path as far as it goes, scramble over a long, flat boulder, jump down, and reach two large standing stones, squeezing between them. The mist clears for a few seconds and I see the valley below. A new green valley without any Hunters in it. The path is steep but easy to run down. I shout for Gabriel.

He doesn't answer.

"I've found the way!" I shout. "I've found it!"

I wait and wait.

"Gabriel?"

Nothing happens. The mist sits there as thick and gray as before.

I know I must go back for him. I tell myself that I'll remember this path, over the flat boulder and between the two standing stones. I creep back, keeping low, hoping that if Hunters are here I'll be able to steal between them without being seen. Black shapes move and disappear and I dodge back. I take a different path and hear a grunt and I know it's Gabriel. I know they've got him and are hurting him. I move forward and hear another grunt to my right and I follow it. Further to my right I see one black shape standing over another and I know it's Kieran. He has a gun in his hand and looks up at me as I approach. I say to myself that Kieran is dead and he can't hurt me and he can't hurt Gabriel.

Gabriel is lying on the ground at his feet.

Kieran kicks him hard and Gabriel groans and rolls onto his front. His eyes open, fix on me, and he says, "Nathan."

Kieran presses the barrel of his gun to the back of Gabriel's skull.

I can do nothing but plead and plead and plead. I say, "Please, no. Please." And in my head I'm saying that Kieran is dead, it isn't real, Kieran is dead.

Kieran says, "But you killed me. So now I get my revenge." And he pulls the trigger and—

The Third Stake

•⁘•

Van is pulling the old stake out. Gabriel is sitting close to me, his head down. He's covered in sweat. I am too.

I say, "I found the way but we have to stay together."

He mumbles, "Yes, together."

Van gives us each another dose of the potion. She helps Gabriel hold his cup as he drinks. It's getting light now but I'm not sure what day it is or how long we've been here.

Van pushes the stake through the wound left by the previous one and everything now is sore and hot and aching, and I grab the stake when it appears out of Gabriel's hand.

"We stay together," I say but I feel my voice is faint and I'm falling forward.

I wake up lying on the ground in a forest. The trees are not so old but tall and thin. Silver birch.

"France," Gabriel says. "Verdon." And his voice sounds happy.

"Your favorite place," I say.

Neither of us moves. I just want to be here in this special place and watch the trees.

"Take me to Wales," he says. "Your favorite place."

I'm about to say it's too dangerous when I realize that I

can do it. I want to show him the place I love. I want to go back there. I stand and Gabriel stands with me, my hand holding his. The hillside slopes down in front of us and I ask, "What's that way?"

"The gorge," Gabriel replies.

I don't know how to get to Wales and I look around and wonder if there are any Hunters hiding in the trees.

"Have you seen any Hunters?" I ask.

"No," he replies.

"Do you know the way to Wales?"

"No. You show me."

But I don't know which way to go: the gorge is too steep to climb down and the rest is just woodland and scrub.

I stand there. Wales is north but hundreds of miles away. We could go that way, though. There are no Hunters; there's nothing to stop us. I've just got to choose the direction and lead the way. And still I stand there. I have the strangest feeling. A feeling I never thought I'd have. For a few seconds, I want my cage back, so I don't have to make any decisions. But I've escaped from the cage. And as soon as I remember that, as soon as I realize I'm free to go where I want, I feel the animal adrenaline in me and I know what to do.

I run.

I'm holding on tight to Gabriel's hand and running fast, through the forest and down the slope. We're going faster and faster and the only thing ahead of me is the gorge. And I push harder and faster, gripping Gabriel's fingers, and as I get nearer I see how wide and deep the gorge is. I hear him in my head, the other me, the animal me, and I want to laugh as he roars at me, not in fear or terror but as if to say, "Yes!" All I can do is run faster and faster and leap off the edge and reach forward. Somehow I find a cut in the air and I'm sucked through it, still holding on to Gabriel and hearing the animal in me roaring. And we are swirled through the black tunnel of the cut, quickly spinning into the light, which hits us as hard as the ground.

We're on a mountainside and the smell of it, the air, the dampness, the light—everything says that I'm back in Wales. The hillside is grass-covered with some bare stones and to our right a small stream tinkers its way down. Gabriel is still holding my hand and I look at it and see that he is bound to me with the leather strap and the stake is there too.

We go to the stream and drink. The water is pure and clear and cold. I'm home. The animal in me knows it too. And I think I know what to do.

I take hold of the stake and drive it into the earth by my side. Nothing happens. The animal in me howls a complaint. The earth is the right way but I've not done it properly yet. I hold Gabriel's hand tight and look in his eyes and pull him to me. Our clasped hands are between us, the stake is between us, over each of our hearts. And I tell him, "This is the way back." Then I push Gabriel away from me and fall forward and feel the stake enter my chest—my heart—at the same time as it enters the earth and the animal's heart too. The earth and my blood and spirit mingle. And the earth holds me and something is returning up the wooden stake into my wound and between it all is Gabriel's hand, still held in mine.

I open my eyes and see Gabriel looking at me. His eyes are those of a Black Witch. Dark brown with gold and chocolate flecks twisting and fading and exploding.

PART THREE

ON THE ROAD

Do Obama

Gabriel, the new Gabriel, showers first. We've gone back to his room. I've healed my hand and now have a round wound on both the back of my hand and my palm to add to the other scars. I healed it in a few seconds. Gabriel's hand healed too. I watched. It took him about twenty minutes but it would take a fain weeks. He was grinning the whole time. I think from the buzz of healing and also the buzz of being himself.

He's a bit unsteady on his feet but insists that washing is more important than food. I'm spaced out with lack of food and sleep but more than wanting food or a shower I want to be with Gabriel. He's so pleased, so confident. So Gabriel.

Van enters the bedroom. "You did well, Nathan. And you'll be pleased to hear that I want to move on quickly. I need to get to an Alliance meeting in Barcelona by tomorrow. We leave after breakfast."

The door to the ensuite opens slightly and Gabriel stands there, a section of him revealed, bare-chested with a towel round his waist, damp hair, big grin, and eyes that are coffee-bean brown with gold twists moving leisurely around the irises.

"I get the feeling this discussion isn't just about what's for breakfast," he says.

"Nathan will tell you," Van replies. "We're leaving soon but first food and a small celebration—it's not often that the potion works." And she walks out of the room.

"I think that's her idea of a joke," I say, turning back to Gabriel.

"Yep," he agrees and opens the door fully. "So, what do you think?"

"Of the new you?"

He nods. "The original version." He holds his arms out and does a slow turn so I can see him from all angles.

"You're . . . remarkably like the fain version. Except that your grin is so wide it's going to break your face open."

He just grins even more.

"But your eyes are different, really different. And there's something else. Turn again." I watch him closely and I try to analyze it but there's nothing I can actually point to. "I guess it's the way that Black Witches move but I can't say exactly what it is." He's hardly moving anyway but something about the way he holds himself is different. "You look more comfortable in your skin, more relaxed." I shrug. "But I'm not sure it's that; you always look comfortable."

He turns back to me and controls his grin. "Thank you. From you, that's a great compliment."

"I'm not paying compliments. I'm just trying to describe you."

"And what I'm trying to say is that"—he hesitates and even, I think, blushes a little—"you're very comfortable in your body."

"Me?" For someone who's normally so right about people, he couldn't be more wrong.

"I thought I understood you before but now I realize more than ever how strong a witch you are," he says. "Your real Gift is your connection to the physical world and when we went to Wales—"

"We didn't actually go to Wales. We were in a trance."

"We went to Wales. You and your animal and me, we were there. I'm not sure how to describe it but you became part of the earth and the earth became part of you."

I just shake my head quickly and I'm about to say, "We didn't go to Wales," but I don't. I'm not sure what happened. I don't know where we went. But something significant did happen and the animal in me came too.

"So?" Nesbitt says to Gabriel as he piles bacon into a toasted sandwich and holds it up to take a bite. "Can you do Obama?"

Gabriel sighs dramatically. "This is the problem with my Gift. Everyone thinks I'm some sort of performing monkey. 'Do Obama.' 'Do Marilyn Monroe.' 'I'd love to see Princess Diana,' 'Hitler,' 'Kanye West'—whoever he is." He's complaining but grinning all the while.

We're sitting at the ridiculously long dining table. Nesbitt has cooked and laid out a buffet for twenty. Scrambled eggs, bacon, sausages, mushrooms, tomatoes, some kind of fish, porridge, boiled eggs, bagels, honey, hams and cheeses. Meters of food. Van is having toast and coffee.

Then something occurs to me. "But they're fains. You didn't become them, did you?"

"Yep."

"But you didn't get stuck as them?"

"No. I only got stuck as me being a fain."

Van says, "When Gabriel was being Obama he was just taking on the outward appearance. Inside he was still Gabriel. He was trying out what it was like to look like a fain. But when he made the more radical decision to actually try to *be* a fain—inside—then he got stuck. He did it far too successfully."

"I'm too talented for my own good."

"Yes, Gabriel, you have a wonderful ability; however, please no transformations just at the moment. Let's savor having you back with us as yourself."

Nesbitt starts to clear the table. He's on the other side of it from me when he says, "I'm still waiting to see Nathan turn. Not sure what he becomes: wolf or wild dog."

"You want to spend the night with me and find out?"

"No thanks, mate," he replies. "I want to cook breakfast, not be it."

"You know, Nesbitt, I really don't think I'd eat you. I can't imagine you'd taste that good. Too fatty for me."

"Don't worry about me, kid. The second you start to turn, I'm getting my gun out and shooting you."

I stare at him but before I can think of anything to say, he adds, "Don't look so alarmed, mate, my aim's spot on. I'd just wing you. You heal quick—no harm done."

And from his voice I know he's serious. I mumble to Gabriel, "See? People ask you to show your Gift by turning into Obama; me, they shoot and say, 'No harm done.'"

I'm trying to keep light and happy for Gabriel. I need to ignore Nesbitt but when I reach for more bread I see my hand and all the scars on it and the black tattoo and I want to scream at Nesbitt that it hurt, that every scar I have hurt, and my body is covered in scars that have healed quickly but they all hurt, and I can't say about any of them, "No harm done."

I stand up, push my chair back, and walk out of the room, saying, "I thought we were leaving."

Barcelona

We're back in the car and roaring up the drive with a spray of gravel. Nesbitt is driving. Gabriel and I sit in the back.

I say to Van, "You said you were going to a meeting of the Alliance but we still have to find Annalise. That's the top priority."

"We're doing both. We need to find Mercury's home. And Mercury only trusted a few people with that information. Pilot is one of those people."

"So we're going to see Pilot?" I ask.

"We will when we know where she is," Van replies. "But she's being almost as elusive as Mercury at the moment. She fled from Geneva when Clay and the Hunters arrived, apparently heading to Spain, but I don't know where in Spain and it's a big place."

"So, what do we do?"

"We go to Isch, a supplier. She'll be able to help."

"Supplier of what?"

"All the things that a Black Witch might desire. Ingredients, information, assistance."

"And this Alliance meeting you mentioned, that's also in Barcelona?"

Van drags on her cigarette. "As luck would have it."

But the way her face is serious and drawn doesn't make me feel lucky at all.

We drive straight through to Barcelona, only stopping to change cars once and using the nightsmoke to make it bearable after dark. We park up on a busy Barcelona shopping street the next morning. Nesbitt looks like shit with stubble and I tell him so. He just says, "And you're looking beaut too." We're all crumpled and tired except for Van, of course, who seems as fresh as when we set off, as fresh as she always does. Gabriel looks good whether he's crumpled or not.

Nesbitt nips out of the car to get two pizzas for me and Gabriel. We've got to wait in the car while the grown-ups go and talk business.

Van eyes the pizza boxes with disgust when Nesbitt returns. "Fortunately, Isch is very hospitable. I'm sure we'll be well catered to there. She travels for most of the year but always spends a few weeks in the summer in Barcelona."

It's August now and I can only hope that Isch does know where Pilot is cos I'm sure we're running out of time to help Annalise. It's been two months since my birthday, two months since Annalise was put in her sleep. I've no idea if this is all in vain and Annalise is already dead anyway. But, as ever, it's best not to think about that too much.

"Keep him out of sight, Gabriel," Van says.

"I am here. You can speak to me."

"Yes, of course." Van turns her eyes on me. "Please,

don't get out of the car. Don't do anything until we're back."

Nesbitt says, "Don't want a stray Hunter seeing you."

"You're the expert at being seen," I reply.

Nesbitt opens his mouth but for once no words come out. He looks genuinely sorry, though.

"How long will you be?" Gabriel asks Van. "When should we start to worry?"

Van smiles. "You really don't need to worry about us. We'll be a couple of hours, maybe more. Mustn't rush; manners at all times."

It's mid-morning and the car is hot in the August sun. I sprawl across the seats, open a box, and start to eat a slice of pizza. But Gabriel says, "I'm going to follow them. Stay here." And he's out of the car and walking up the road.

I catch him up in a few seconds and tell him, "I'm coming with you."

"OK, but keep well back. I'll follow them. You follow me."

I drop back as Gabriel turns into an alley but I keep him in my sights. He moves fast up another alley, which is darker and a lot quieter. I follow Gabriel down a couple more alleys, still keeping my distance, and then he goes right and when I reach the corner he's gone.

Shit!

This alley is even narrower. The houses are all four stories high. I move slowly forward. All the doors are shut and I can see nothing through the grubby windows. I reach a dead end and turn to work my way back when Gabriel appears out of a door on the left. He beckons me forward.

"They're in there. Some sort of meeting. I think this is Isch's house but I heard them mention the Alliance. Do you want to try to listen in?"

I nod.

He turns back to the door of the house, which is shut again.

Then he pulls a hairpin out of his jacket pocket. It has an unusual black skull on the end of it but I've seen it before. It's one of the pins that unlocks doors.

"Did you steal that from Mercury?" I ask.

Gabriel shakes his head. "Rose gave it to me."

He puts the pin in the lock and pushes the door slowly open. I follow him inside. This seems to be the entrance to a large apartment. There are cooking smells coming from the room ahead. I follow Gabriel up the wide stone stairs and through a door on the landing into a dining room. At the far end are French doors that lead onto a narrow balcony that stretches the width of the apartment. The doors from the dining room lead onto the balcony but so do the doors from the next room. These other doors are open. I move so that I'm against the wall and out of sight from the room but close enough to hear the people inside talking.

Van is speaking. Talking about a Black Witch. She seems to be assessing whether this person will join the Alliance. Nesbitt gives his opinion, which isn't very positive.

A woman's voice joins in. Van replies to her. Calls her Isch.

And then I hear another voice. A voice I recognize straightaway. I'd know it anywhere and I feel like I can't breathe. My impulse is to run. I look at Gabriel and he sees that something is wrong and grabs at me as I take a step toward the doors and he pushes me back against the wall. And I manage to hold myself back. I calm myself, taking deep breaths.

Gabriel mouths, *What's wrong?*

I whisper, "It's OK. I'm OK."

And he stares at me, questioning me with his look.

"I'm OK," I insist, holding his gaze. And I think I am. "I know who's in there. Why they didn't want me here."

He looks at me intently still. "Who?"

It's strange but I can't say her name. I shake my head, and feel like the choker is on me again and I can't breathe. And all the times she hit me and slapped me and shackled me and deafened me with her Gift, all that floods into me. I push Gabriel away as I pull out my knife and step into the open doorway, and I say, "My teacher and guardian."

My Teacher and Guardian

Celia stands. She's dressed the same, in her army gear, black boots, green canvas trousers, green shirt. Her hair is the same short, spiky crop, so thin I can see her scalp. Her face is as pale and ugly as ever.

"Nathan. It's good to see you." She says it as if I'm some old friend she hasn't seen for a few weeks.

I shake my head. "No. It's not."

I step forward, my knife out. Nesbitt stands then and I see he's pointing a gun at me. Gabriel steps forward too and his gun is pointing at Nesbitt.

"What's going on?" I ask. "Why is she here?"

Van stands up and motions to Celia to sit down. "Celia is working with the Alliance. She's one of the White Witch rebels helping us bring down Soul, the White Council, and the Hunters."

I shake my head. "No."

Van says, "Nesbitt, please put that gun away. I'm sure Nathan isn't going to harm any of us."

Nesbitt spins the gun on his finger. "I wouldn't kill you, kid, you know that." And he puts the gun back in his jacket.

"Gabriel, please, you too," Van says.

But Gabriel keeps the gun on Nesbitt. "Not until Nathan says."

"Point it at the White Hunter, Gabriel," I say, and he swings his arm to point the gun at Celia.

Van sighs. "Nathan, this is exactly why I didn't want you here, not until I'd met Celia, and not until I'd had a chance to talk to you, to explain how the Alliance will work and who is joining."

"And you expect me to join! With her!"

"Yes, I do." Van sits down and gets out her cigarette case. "Who did you think would be involved, Nathan? Who? Just the nice White Witches? We need fighters, people who know how Hunters work, and I can assure you there is no one better than Celia." Van lights her cigarette, inhales deeply, then sends a plume of red smoke in my direction. I don't think she's trying to calm me with it but just show how annoyed she is.

"I wasn't going to tell you about Celia until after Annalise was rescued but perhaps it's better this way. If you can't work with Celia then you can go and live under a stone somewhere for all I care. If you want my help in rescuing Annalise then you will be part of the Alliance afterward and that means working with Celia."

She knows I don't really have any option. But she must also know that I could still leave after she upholds her part of the bargain. I guess she's assuming I'll feel honor-bound to help the Alliance once they've helped me. Well, we'll see about that.

Van drags on her cigarette again and says, "Nathan, please tell Gabriel to put the gun down."

I hesitate and then I make a show of putting my knife away. I say, "Gabriel, please . . . give me your gun."

He holds it out to me without hesitation and I take it and walk over to Celia and push the barrel against her forehead. I want to know what it feels like to be able to do it, to have power over her for once.

Celia looks up at me and holds my gaze. Her eyes are pale blue with a few small specks of silver. I make a shooting sound and she doesn't even blink. I keep the gun there, feeling what it's like.

I say to her, "You haven't used your Gift." She could bring me to my knees with it.

"I won't use it on you, Nathan. We're on the same side now."

"Are we?" I don't take my eyes off Celia's but I ask Van, "How do you know she isn't a spy?"

"She *is* a spy, Nathan. For us. Celia has been useful in providing us with information about Soul, the Council, and the Hunters."

"I'm in Spain on official Council business, Nathan," Celia says. "They've brought me out of retirement. I'm meant to be tracking down a list of the most-wanted Black Witches. You'll be pleased to know that your name is at the top, along with your father's."

"I'm a Half Code."

"Since your escape from the Council building you've

been designated as Black. I don't know how much Van has told you but your escape led to many changes. Soul took over the Council and his friend Wallend got free rein to do what he likes. Which is why I'm helping the Alliance. I'm no lover of certain Black Witches, Nathan, you know that, but I'm no lover of criminals or monsters either, and Soul is the former and Wallend the latter."

"You didn't seem to mind Soul or Wallend before. You didn't seem to mind keeping me in a cage under Soul's orders."

"As I say things have changed since your escape."

"Yes. Now I'm the one with the gun at your head."

She looks at me, still calm, still the same controlled Celia. "I understand that you're angry with me, Nathan. But I am not your enemy. I never was."

I swear at her. And again.

"Soul is your enemy. He's the enemy of all true witches, as is Wallend. They're corrupt. They're not true witches. Soul is a danger to all of us, Black and White. I've spent my life protecting White Witches from the dangers of Blacks but now they are less of a threat to the White community than Soul is." She blinks. "I honestly believe that, Nathan."

"I have a gun to your head. I'm a danger to you."

"Well, there is that. But if you don't pull the trigger I intend to work with the Alliance to bring Soul and his cronies down. It isn't possible to do that with White Witches alone. They're either in Soul's pocket or too weak. If anyone complains about him they're punished."

My thoughts go to Arran and Deborah but I can't ask about them. I don't want to hear about them from Celia.

Van says, "Please put the gun down, Nathan."

"No."

"I can show you the atrocities that Celia has uncovered." Van holds some papers out to me. "Photographs of White Witches being tried and executed for objecting to Soul's regime, memos about each one. Details of who, when, and where. Death warrants signed by Soul." She flicks through more paper. "Black Witches in France being slaughtered. Lists of names."

"I'm not interested."

"You should be." The other woman speaks now. This must be Isch. She has papers in her hands too. "Some Black Witches think I have no feelings, no concern for others, but these things"—she holds a piece of paper out to me—"are a concern to all witches."

I take the paper. It's a photograph of three people: mother, father, daughter. The father is hanging by his neck from a beam. I guess this is their house. The mother and daughter are on their knees. The mother, her face bruised, is crying. The daughter's face is strange. Blood runs from one empty eye socket. A knife is being pushed into the other one.

"Your sister, Deborah, went to great lengths to get us this information. She's working for us. She believes as we do—"

"Shut up." I need to think and I can't when they talk about Deborah. But I can believe that she's one of the

White rebels; she can't stand any injustice. I focus on Celia, though. I say, "They've killed Black Witches for years in Britain and Celia joined in. They persecuted White Witches who helped Black Witches. And she joined in."

"Most Black Witches fled Britain, Nathan," says Van, "though I know many were killed. But this is different. Soul is slaughtering them—us. It's already on a much bigger scale and getting worse."

Celia says, "And Soul is not just a danger to Black Witches. Nathan, your father killed my sister but already Soul has done worse. He's killed my old partner, a retired Hunter, and my niece is on death row. Their only crime was objecting to Soul's regime. Soul is supposed to protect White Witches. He is betraying us."

I know Celia isn't lying. That's one thing about her. She may have kept things from me when I was her prisoner but she didn't lie. I drop my arm, turn and walk out of the room and onto the balcony where I can breathe.

Isch

Gabriel is with me, sitting on the floor of the balcony. I don't talk, don't want to talk. I've still got the gun in my hand but I've had enough of guns so I hold it out to Gabriel and he takes it.

After a few more minutes I say, "I think Celia might know something about Arran. He was always being watched by Hunters. Can you go and ask her about him and Deborah?"

"Yes, if you want. But can't you ask her?"

I shake my head. I'm fighting back tears, though I don't know why—lots of memories of Celia and me. I say to Gabriel, "I was just a kid. She chained me up in a cage, beat me . . ." And I think of all the times she hit me and used her Gift against me. "I tried to kill myself because of her, Gabriel. I was just a kid."

An hour later Celia has gone and I'm sitting inside with the others. Celia told Gabriel that Arran is working in London, training to be a doctor. He will join the rebels—that's where his sympathies lie—but he's in danger and is always being watched. Everyone knows he hates the Council. Deborah is working for the Council, in the archives. It's a junior position but she has access to all the old records and she's managing to get ahold of recent ones too. She has an unusual Gift for that apparently. She's risking her life every day to send information to Celia, but Celia hopes Deborah will soon flee as she's always under suspicion.

I'm finding it hard to concentrate on anything. Celia wasn't on my hate list, and I don't think that I do hate her, but I'm angry. Gabriel, it seems, was right about that—I'm angry at most people, most of the time, and I'm angrier now than I was when I was a prisoner because now I can look back and see the injustice and brutality and I can do nothing about it.

And as much as I'm shocked at my feelings about Celia, I'm also surprised at my feelings for Gabriel. He trusted me. He drew his gun to protect me and then gave it to me without question, without hesitation, when he must have wondered if I'd go too far. He can't have known what I'd do because I certainly didn't.

I look over at Gabriel. He's sitting on a low cushion, as I am. His hair is tucked behind his ears. He is handsome and brave and gentle and intelligent and funny: the most perfect friend. I've had few friends: Annalise, Ellen, and Gabriel. And I know he's the one who knows me best, believes in me most. Even Arran didn't trust me like Gabriel does. And when Gabriel kissed me, he did it so I didn't feel bad. He did it to show me I'm not a monster. He must have known he was risking me pushing him away. And it would be so much easier if I didn't care for Annalise like I do. If I felt for

Gabriel what I feel for her. He says he can't bear to be away from me and I'm like that with her. I can't imagine living happily unless I'm with her. That's the only place I want to be: at her side.

Gabriel turns to me, meets my gaze, and then his expression changes. "What?" he asks.

I shake my head and I mouth, *Nothing*. Then I force myself to turn from him and pay attention to what's going on around me.

We're sitting on large cushions that form a circle in the room. The floor is covered with rugs, Persian I guess, not one rug but many; they must be two or three deep and they're soft and silky. The room is dim but rich—all reds and golds.

I'm sitting opposite Isch, a large woman dressed in layers of color—purple, gold, red—from her turban to her silk slippers. She has plump hands that flit around as she talks. Her nails are long and painted gold and her fingers are almost hidden under numerous jewel-encrusted rings. We've been introduced and offered tea. Now two young girls enter the room, carrying large, round wooden trays. The tea is poured in small glasses. There is what looks like Turkish delight on a plate, nuts and fat black grapes.

Isch watches the girls leave and when the door is closed she asks Van, "What do you think of them?"

"The girls? Who knows? Until an apprentice works with you, it's impossible to say how things will turn out."

"Perhaps I should ask what you think, Nesbitt?"

He swigs his tea in one gulp, then says, "I'm sure you'll get good prices for them."

"I'm not so certain. Troubled times bring shortages of certain commodities. Demand for herbs and flowers for protective potions is sky-high already but that doesn't mean it's the time to take on a new apprentice. Prices for them are plummeting."

I've been sitting quietly up till now but I can't resist saying, "You sell the girls?"

Isch turns to me. Her eyes are brown, like Gabriel's, but smaller, lost in the plump beige skin of her face. Her nose is small too but her lips are full and painted a bright red. She says, "Of course the girls are sold. Boys too but few want boys."

"Sold like slaves?"

"Not at all like slaves. They're valued apprentices. Think of their prices as transfer fees. They're more like professional footballers than slaves."

"Do they get paid those sorts of salaries? Football salaries?"

Isch laughs. "They get the best training for free. They get the thrill of learning from another top player if they're good enough. It's how I learned. And Van."

"And what if they're not good enough?"

"Some owners put up with poor results; most don't. Hence the market in new apprentices."

"I was told Mercury ate little boys—would those be her failed apprentices?"

"I'm not sure she eats them but she does find uses for them—ingredients mostly, bottled for later use."

"And my father? Does he have apprentices?"

Isch hesitates. "He's never bought from me. But perhaps you'll soon be looking for an apprentice? And then I will ensure you get the best."

"No," I say. "I don't want a slave."

She picks up her glass of tea, sips it, and says, "Well, if you should ever change your mind."

"Are you intending to sell any of those girls to Mercury?" asks Van.

"Mercury doesn't deal with me directly at the moment. I hear the Hunters were close on her tail in Switzerland and since then she's cut herself off from everyone except Pilot. She's being extremely careful. I've already sent a girl to Pilot for Mercury. A nasty little thing but very bright and fast to learn. Mercury will be looking for the best to replace Rose, now that she's gone."

"She's not gone. She was shot. Killed by Hunters," I say.

"Alas," Isch replies but her mouth is a wide, bright red smirk. "Still, as ever, disasters bring many business opportunities."

"Well, I hope you make a tidy profit," I say.

"Could you tell us where Pilot is?" Van asks. "We too intend to do some business with Mercury."

Isch regards Van and then says, "In the Pyrenees, a small hamlet beyond Etxalar. The last house at the top of the road."

"Thank you." Van picks up a Turkish delight, which is a pale rose color, the same as her suit.

We're in the car twenty minutes later.

Van slides on her seat belt and says, "Let's go."

Nesbitt is typing into the satnav as the car screeches away from the curb.

"You trust Isch?" I ask. "She wouldn't just send us into a trap? She seems motivated by money."

"She's a fine Black Witch. She wouldn't sell us out."

"She sells girls into slavery."

"The girls are free to go if they wish."

"They're not free if they have nowhere else to go, if they have no one to help them, to look after them."

"You want to go back, buy them, and care for them?"

I don't reply.

Van turns and looks at me enquiringly.

"I don't think I'm the answer to their problems."

Van smiles. "No, indeed."

Pilot

It's well past midnight when we arrive in the tiny mountain village. The journey here took nearly six hours but we haven't stopped. We left the car in a different city, I've no idea which one, and Nesbitt traded it in for a new 4x4, but we've left that at the bottom of the hill with Van, as even that's conspicuous here. There are few cars in this area and all of them are old and battered. Gabriel, Nesbitt, and I are now walking through the village and up the hill. Pilot's house is the furthest and there is a faint yellow glow from a light in a downstairs window.

Van thinks her presence will be a problem. She and Pilot have had disagreements in the past, though she's not mentioned that until now. But anyway this negotiation is down to Gabriel, as he knows Pilot and she trusts him.

I'm going ahead and doubling back to the others as they're so slow.

"You're like a puppy off the lead," says Nesbitt. It's dark but he'll be able to see the finger I raise to him. "Take it slow, keep an eye out. Can't be too careful these days," he mutters.

We arrive at the small house. Nesbitt knocks gently on the door and we wait.

And wait.

And wait.

A shadow passes across the light inside. There are no sounds.

"Gabriel?" A quiet voice but not from the door—from behind us.

We turn as one and there's a woman standing in the path, an incredibly tall woman with black hair almost down to her knees.

Gabriel takes charge, spreading his arms wide and saying, "Pilot, it's good to see you."

She doesn't smile but she leans toward him and they exchange two kisses on the cheeks, which seems promising. Gabriel speaks in French, introducing us, I think. And that's when I sense that Nesbitt and I aren't going to get any kisses, ever. She can barely hold back a snarl from me and looks like she wants to spit at Nesbitt. Then she flounces off; only *flounces* doesn't do justice to her stature. We follow her slowly round behind the house, Gabriel ahead, while I say to Nesbitt, "She looks like she can't stand to have us near her."

"Don't take it personal. She's just a snob. Some of them are like that. Van's unusually open-minded, and young Gabriel is too, of course. Isch is just interested in business. You'd be surprised how liberal a lot of Black Witches are but some . . . some are snobs like Pilot. She can't stand mongs."

"Mongs?"

"Mongrels. Half Bloods. She only likes pure Blacks."

"I bet being half White is worse in her eyes than being half fain."

Nesbitt nudges my shoulder. "Don't worry, mate, I don't mind you." And he puts his arm round me. "Us mongs should stick together. All for one and one for all."

I push him away and he laughs.

Behind the house there's a patio area screened by vines with a lit firepit in the center. It looks like Pilot wasn't asleep. Or maybe she sleeps here. We sit on large, dusty cushions that surround the fire—or rather Pilot and Gabriel do. Nesbitt and I are relegated to the outer circle on threadbare rugs.

Pilot calls inside and a girl appears. She's thin and her hair is a straggly, mousy mess, almost alive with head lice. She scowls when she sees us and seems to barely listen to Pilot's instructions before going back inside.

Nesbitt leans toward me. "She's been told to bring us some water. But I wouldn't touch it, mate; she's bound to have spat in it."

A few minutes later the girl appears with olives and a carafe of wine. She spends the next few minutes going in and out of the house, bringing bread, olive oil, tomatoes, peppers, all for Gabriel and Pilot. Nesbitt was right: we just get water, and the glasses are filthy.

Gabriel talks to Pilot. I think he's explaining what's happened; I think I hear my name once or twice but he's talking in French so he could be saying anything.

The talk goes on and on.

The house is old and ugly. There's a low, plastered wall round the patio that was once painted white but is now gray. A structure of wooden trellis rises from the wall and connects to the house and over this is a thick growth of vines.

Gabriel and Pilot are sitting cross-legged. Pilot puts a log on the fire, Gabriel keeps his eyes on her, and they talk.

Nesbitt is splayed across his rug, half asleep. He says to me, "Sounds like this is going to take some time." I lie down too, trying to remember when I last slept.

I wake. The sun is jabbing at my face through a gap in the trellis.

Nesbitt is lying on his back, his arm over his face, but I see his eyes are open and I think he's listening to the conversation that's still going on between Pilot and Gabriel. Nesbitt yawns.

I sit up. A cricket lands on the rug beside me. It chirps and then jumps away as I reach for it. I realize now that the noise of the crickets is all around, and it sort of swells and dims, almost pulsing with the heat. It's a sound similar to mobile phones but it's in my ears not in my head.

I stand, stretch, and yawn, and then I walk to the edge of the patio to look through the trellis and up to the dry hills that surround us.

Gabriel and Pilot have gone quiet.

I can hear crickets. Lots of crickets. But also, maybe,

sometimes in a lull I catch a **chchchch** in my head. It's so faint that it might not even be there. I move to the corner to listen rather than look.

Nesbitt is standing beside me now. "What?"

"I'm not sure. Can you see anything?"

Nesbitt looks through the trellis. He shakes his head. 'I see better at night."

And I think I catch it again, so brief and quiet that it's almost drowned out by the crickets—but it was in my head, I'm sure.

"There's someone out there with a mobile phone," I say. "Maybe a fain."

"Just one?" Nesbitt asks.

"I dunno," I say.

"Let's take a look."

I turn to Gabriel. "Wait here? We'll scout around."

He nods. Pilot looks not too worried.

I circle wide to the left, Nesbitt to the right. The crickets jump ahead of me and fill my ears with noise. When Pilot's house is a distant square I turn uphill, slow now, keeping well to the left of the house. The hill seems to go on and on. I veer left a little more and come to a dry valley, three meters deep, steep-sided. I send a rock clattering down it. I curse inwardly as I stop and hold still. I'm surprised to be rewarded for my sloppiness as in return I hear . . .

chchchchchchchchchchchchchchchchchchchchchchchchch

I can't tell where the mobile is but it has to be uphill and I think I can hear it when its owner moves, like he or she did when the stone fell. I guess that if the owner of the mobile is a Hunter she's lying on the ground on the edge of the valley, watching Pilot's house. She'll be well hidden and the noise from her mobile blocked so that I hear the phone only when she rises up to look.

I move fast now, downhill, then stop. Listen again.

Just crickets here.

I move slowly and carefully down into the little valley, each footstep chosen so that no stones are dislodged, and at the bottom I stop and listen again.

Just crickets.

Then up the other side, slow and careful. Keeping low, I run quickly over to a stand of olive trees and through them, looking to my right. No movement. I stop, look left—nothing—and turn round to survey the whole area. I can make out a few houses that form the edge of the village way down the hillside but Pilot's house is out of sight.

I turn back to face uphill, close my eyes, and listen.

chchchchchchchchchchchchchchchch

I think I know where the Hunter is and I'm sure it's a Hunter now. There's no reason for anyone else to be up here, hiding. For a second, I consider trying to unleash the animal in me but I stand the best chance as a human. Celia has trained me for combat and it's time I used the skills she taught me.

I move as fast as I can back to the right, toward the dry valley. Then I see her. A black figure laid out on the ground, in plain view from here but hidden from Pilot's house. She's looking through binoculars. It seems like she hasn't realized that Nesbitt and I are scouting around.

But where is her partner? And are there two Hunters or more? Very possibly more.

And how did they find Pilot? Did Isch betray us, or Celia, or did someone spot us in Barcelona and follow us here, or have they been watching Pilot for days or weeks? And is Van safe or is she already a prisoner?

It will be hard to get to the Hunter quietly. She's in a good spot, not easy to attack from behind, but that's what I have to do. I know I can beat her in a fight but the problem is getting close to her before she raises an alarm. I really don't want her turning round and shooting me.

I set off, keeping my eyes on the black figure . . . it's like a child's game. I'm in plain sight if she turns round—let's face it, I'm *dead* if she turns round—but her job is to watch the house and if I'm silent she won't turn. So, slowly down the valley side, hardly breathing, keeping my eyes on the ground now to find my next foothold and—she shifts on her stomach, readjusts her binoculars—the loose, sandy ground slides away under my left foot but quietly. I take one more step to the floor of the valley. Now I keep my eyes on the Hunter, two meters above me. My knife is ready in my left hand.

I take two swift, large strides forward, grab her ankle with my right hand, and yank her down. She's good—she yelps and twists and kicks me but already I have the knife in her throat. The blood spurts over my hand. The glints in her eyes go out. I'm surprised how quick that happened.

My ribs hurt. I think she broke one with her kick. I heal, get the buzz, and I'm still holding her body, still holding the knife in her throat. I pull it out, my hand shaking a little as I wipe the knife clean on the Hunter's shirt. She has a radio and earpiece. I take them, my hand shaking again as I touch the Hunter's skin. I try the earpiece but I can't bear it hissing in my head. That's why I could sense them from so far away—not just their mobiles but the radios too.

I get her binoculars and move up to where she'd been watching from. The binoculars are great. I can see Pilot's house and the patio and the vines; I can see part of Gabriel's head but not Pilot's. The binoculars do their job but the vines do theirs as well. The Hunters don't know that Nesbitt and I left there, if they even knew we arrived.

I scan the hillside for the Hunter's partner and for Nesbitt. Way over the other side of the hill I can make out a black figure, a Hunter, then further up again I see another dark figure. Nesbitt? No! Another Hunter. Then further again another figure. Another Hunter. Shit! And I've no idea where Nesbitt is.

The alarm would have been raised if he'd been caught, though, so . . .

Then I spot him. He's doing what I've just done, approaching the Hunter across from me from behind. Which is fine but I have a feeling that Nesbitt doesn't know about the other two further up the slope and I think they will be able to see him. Shit!

I slide down into the valley to the body of the Hunter and grab her gun. I'd rather not use it but if I have to I will. Then I run uphill, keeping to the dry valley bottom, being as careful as I can to keep the sounds down but speed is more important.

I go three hundred meters; I reckon that's enough. Then I'm up to the side of the valley on my stomach and scanning through the binoculars. Nesbitt is way below and across from me, kneeling over the Hunter, who looks pretty dead. But the Hunter furthest from me is shuffling back and must be able to see Nesbitt. The Hunter nearest me is still but not relaxed, looking back to where my dead Hunter is. They know we're here now. They've seen Nesbitt and radioed each other and are now wondering why Hunter number one isn't responding.

I have to get to the Hunter nearest to me quickly and hope Nesbitt can deal with the other one.

My Hunter is a hundred meters below me and to my left. I reckon silence isn't an issue anymore, so I get as near as I can as quick as I can as quiet as I can. I point my gun at the

Hunter but I know I'm not a good enough shot unless I'm close up. I'm almost on her when she hears me and turns. I shoot and get her leg. She rolls away and shoots, and I'm amazed that she's missed me. I shoot again, emptying the gun as I run at her, and then my knife is in her stomach and I'm pulling it up, out, and stabbing it into her neck. The sparkles in her eyes last and last, silver and brown. I glance at my hand, her blood covering it. When I look back at her eyes there are no sparkles and I turn quickly away.

The side of my head stings. Blood is pouring out. Her bullet didn't miss but grazed my skull. I heal again as I put the binoculars back up to my eyes.

Nesbitt is by his dead Hunter, picking up her gun, then turning to look toward me.

I scan uphill and see the last Hunter. She looks from me to Nesbitt and gets her mobile out. She's contacting base. The place will be swarming with Hunters in no time if she does.

I'm off toward her. Shouting at Nesbitt, *"Shoot her!"*

Nesbitt shoots. Lots. I thought he'd be better than he is.

The Hunter's squatted down and is on the phone and then shooting back at Nesbitt and I'm almost on her. But she's made the call now. I'm running fast toward her. She turns and shoots at me but misses badly. She's spooked. Nesbitt shoots at her but the Hunter is off, running down the slope toward Pilot's house. She's fast but I think I can reach her before she gets there. I'm lurching down the slope but the slope is helping the Hunter too and she reaches the patio and she's shooting everything. Everything. It's like some Hollywood movie gone mad.

I reach her but she's pulling at the vines and falling backward toward me to the ground. Backward, black shiny hair in a ponytail moving toward me, her hand still gripping the vines, though I know from her body that she's already dead.

She lands on the ground. Her face is blank. There's a bullet hole, small, deep and perfectly round, in her forehead.

And Gabriel is kneeling there, his gun pointing at me. His arm straight. His face blank too.

"It's me," I shout, holding out my arms just in case.

Nesbitt skids to a halt beside me, saying, "And me." Then he says, "Shit!"

Pilot is lying on the floor, slumped sideways. The little girl is kneeling beside her, holding her hand. There are two red stains on Pilot's body, one on her shoulder and one on her stomach.

Gabriel leans over Pilot, feeling for a pulse. "She's still alive."

I tell him, "There were four Hunters watching the house. They've phoned in, contacted base or whatever they do. We have to go."

"There might be more at the car. They may have got Van."

Nesbitt says, "I'll check. If I'm not back with the car in two minutes you'll know there's trouble." And he's gone.

Gabriel crouches down to the level of the girl and speaks to her slowly and quietly in French. She doesn't say anything and is still holding Pilot's hand. Gabriel asks her something. She nods. He takes Pilot's hand from her and she runs inside the house.

I go to the side of the house and climb onto a low wall from where I can see down the road, and I hear the engine before I see our 4x4 reversing at high speed toward us. Van and Nesbitt are inside.

I go back to Gabriel. "Nesbitt's here." There's a screech of car tires at the other side of the house to confirm it.

Gabriel picks up Pilot and she screams.

Gabriel says, "I told the girl to get whatever she needs. We're going in one minute."

And he carries Pilot round the side of the house.

Ten seconds later the girl appears, wearing clumpy boots and carrying a small, pale pink rucksack that looks like it's going to burst open. I go to her and grab her hand. But she snatches it away and runs round the corner of the house to the car.

On the Road

We're in the 4x4, hurtling along a track, probably away fast enough but no one dares say it yet. The way Nesbitt has been driving we're more likely to be killed in a car crash than by Hunters' bullets.

Gabriel and I are sitting in the back of the car. Pilot is laid out across us, her bare feet on my lap. Surprisingly they smell of peppermint. But the main smell in the car is fear. The air is heavy with it. We've been driving for three hours and hardly spoken: every minute further away feels like we really have escaped. I can see the side of Van's face and her jaw is more relaxed now but even she was scared. Van has given Pilot a potion to take the pain away and thankfully she's been asleep since she took it. Up to then her screams were getting to me, getting to us all, I think.

I turn to Gabriel. He's holding a cloth over Pilot's stomach. The cloth is all blood now. Pilot looks like she won't survive another minute but she looked like that half an hour ago. Two Hunter bullets are still in her. Van took one look at the wounds and said she couldn't remove the bullet in Pilot's stomach and, the way she said it, I knew that was it. There was nothing we could do. It would just be a matter of time before Pilot would die.

The girl is kneeling in the footwell by Gabriel's legs, smoothing back Pilot's hair and whispering to her.

Gabriel asks me, "You OK?"

I don't know. I say yes and turn away to stare out the window.

"Well, I'm not," Nesbitt says. "I'm desperate for a piss."

The car comes to a sliding stop. We're in low hills, farmland. Who knows where. Nesbitt switches the engine off and gets out. The rest of us sit in silence, letting the dust settle.

Nesbitt stands by the car and pees. "Boy, do I need this."

Van asks Gabriel, "How's Pilot's pulse?"

"Faint. Slow."

"She has strong healing powers but the poison from the bullets will eventually overpower everything."

Nesbitt leans back into the car and says, "So, Gabby? Did Pilot tell you anything before she got shot? You were talking long enough."

"Yes, but I learned little. At first she said that she didn't know where Mercury's home was but I was sure she did. I flattered her as much as I could, telling her that she was unique in knowing Mercury so well, but of course I imagined few people had ever actually been invited to her house. Still she wouldn't say anything. I said it was strange that, above everyone, Mercury trusted Rose, a White Witch by birth, as the one person to be granted access to her home. That did it. Pilot couldn't resist saying that she'd been invited too and had gone to Mercury's home several times. It was she who 'introduced' Rose to Mercury years ago. She took Rose there herself.

"But she said that she was honor-bound as a true Black Witch and friend of Mercury to reveal nothing about it. Mercury wanted her home to be secret."

Van says, "So are you telling us that she didn't reveal where it is?"

"That's pretty much it."

"All that for nothing!" Nesbitt kicks the side of the car.

Gabriel goes on. "I said that perhaps Mercury had abandoned her home now, with the Hunters close on her tail. That perhaps they'd found its location. Pilot laughed at that and said it would never be found. She said that she was planning on taking the girl there as a replacement for Rose." Gabriel glances down at the girl sitting by his feet.

Van says, "I don't suppose she would have told the girl where Mercury lives?"

"Pilot insisted that only she knew and that she would never tell anyone. She also said that she was safe in that village. That there had been no Hunters anywhere near it. I think they must have arrived around the same time as us. Which makes me think that either Isch told the Hunters where we were going or they followed us from Barcelona."

"They didn't follow us or I'd be dead too," Van says. "They would have seen the 4x4. And Isch would not have told them voluntarily or quickly. Perhaps one of her girls?" She looks at Nesbitt. He nods.

"So Isch is dead or captured by Hunters. If captured she'll tell them about your meeting with Celia and that I was there," I say.

"I think that's a fair assumption."

Nesbitt curses and walks round the car and kicks it again.

The girl shifts now and Gabriel says something to her in French. She answers in French.

"Pers?" Van smiles at the little girl. "Her name is Pers?"

"Yes," Gabriel replies.

There's more talk. Van joins in, speaking French too, and then, to top it off, Nesbitt reappears at the driver's door and joins in.

The girl speaks again and looks at me and I'd like to say something to her but even in English I can't think of the right words, about Pilot and how I'm sorry and I don't know what will happen to her now and life's pretty shit all round but maybe Van will look after you although really she's not a great surrogate mother and Nesbitt would make an interesting father figure but anyway it's better than being a slave to Mercury.

And then I see her eyes aren't looking for anything from me. And she starts shouting. I don't know French but I'm guessing she's cursing. Her face is close to mine and I'm shrinking right back against the car door and she spits in my face. Gabriel has his arms round her, holding her away from me, saying things in her ear, but I don't think it's helping much as she kicks me and Gabriel has to wrap one of his legs over hers to keep her still. I open the door and fall out. I get up, wiping the spit off my face, looking at the tangled coil of arms and legs and hair.

"What was that about?"

"She don't like mongs much to start with but she seems to blame you for the Hunter attack."

Van has got out of the jeep and walked round to join us. She takes out a cigarette and Nesbitt lights it. Then Van holds the case out toward Gabriel. Pers shouts something and kicks again, and I realize Van was offering the cigarette to her. Van turns to Nesbitt, saying, "Highly spirited." And she drags on the cigarette, swallowing the smoke. She says to Gabriel, "Find out what you can about her."

Gabriel talks to Pers and she speaks to him in a more polite voice. Van listens and translates for me. "Her parents are dead, her father years ago, her mother recently, by Hunters; she escaped. Isch took her in and told her she'd grow up to be a great witch. Pilot was going to take her to Mercury. She's ten, so she says."

Van comments, "I'm not sure Mercury would have been that impressed: she's a nasty little thing. But she might prove useful. If Mercury is looking for an apprentice Pers might be our way in."

"We have to find Mercury first."

"Yes, that is becoming a tiresome problem." Van draws

heavily on her cigarette again. "Gabriel, you have asked Pers if she knows where Mercury's home is, haven't you?"

"Yes. She says she doesn't know. I believe her."

Van drops the cigarette to the ground and looks at it. "Yes, I do too. Which means the only way to find out is to get Pilot to tell us."

"A potion?" I ask.

"Yes, but it's not that simple. A truth potion would be best but they take time to make and need to be adapted to the person, and they work so much better if the person is weak-willed and healthy. Here we have a skinny, dying patient with a strong will. Much trickier."

"So?"

"The other option is a potion to access her memory of the place, go where she went, see what she saw."

"A vision of it?"

"Yes. I can make a potion with something from Pilot and something that belonged to Mercury." She looks not very hopefully at Gabriel. "I don't suppose you have anything?"

"I have a hairpin, which I got off Rose. Mercury made them and gave them to her."

Gabriel shows it to Van, who shakes her head. "It's magical. If I use that it will interfere with the potion's magic."

"There's no other option. We have to try the truth potion," I say.

"There isn't enough time," Van insists. "She'll sleep for

a couple of hours with the drug I've given her. I'll talk to her when she wakes. Maybe her situation will help change her mind. But for now we're all tired. We'll rest until then."

"We staying here?" Nesbitt says, looking around at the vast nothingness.

"Yes," Van replies. "This will be Pilot's final resting place."

The Map

It's getting dark and I wander off into a field and lie on the bare earth and close my eyes. My brain is mush.

I think of Annalise as I fall asleep. I'm walking with her by a river, through a meadow, blue sky overhead. We lie on the ground together and the birds call to each other. The breeze ruffles my shirt, the sun warm on my face. I roll onto my side. Annalise is looking up at the sky; her skin is glowing, flushed with the sun, and she's talking, moving her lips, but I'm not paying attention, I'm just thinking how I like looking at her. I blow in her ear, expecting her to smile, but she doesn't; she keeps on talking. So I lean over her and kiss her but she doesn't kiss me back and so I move to be over her, to look into her eyes. Her eyes are the same blue as ever but they're not focused on me: they're focused on nothing and the silver glints are still. Frozen. And I seem to fly up and be unable to touch her. She's lying on the ground, her lips moving, but she's not talking at all; she's gasping for air, taking her last breaths. I fly further from her and see she's on the ground by the cottage and Mercury is standing over her and the gale is holding me back and I'm shouting at Mercury. And I wake and sit up.

Gabriel is with me. "What happened? You were shouting."

"I'm OK. I'm OK. I have something of Mercury's."

Van is grinning. "It's perfect."

"Yes?"

"Yes." She's holding the piece of paper that Mercury gave me. The piece of paper she drew a map on so I could find the house that Clay was using as a base.

The folded piece of paper has been in my pocket for months: flattened, soaked and worn, so that it's rounded at the edges and there's a hole in the middle. But it is from Mercury—it used to belong to her. Even better, it has Mercury's handwriting on it, which is still visible, and, most importantly according to Van, Mercury gave it to me—it's not a thing stolen but a gift.

It's the perfect item for the potion.

"Of course this means that you must receive the vision from Pilot."

"OK."

"That means you make the potion and you drink the potion. The potion is like a river cutting through the land of the mind, carrying memories from Pilot to you."

"OK," I say, a little more cautiously now.

"You must make the cut that it flows down and be what it flows into."

"I cut her?"

"We need her blood for the potion. Lots. You must bleed her to death."

"What?"

"She's dying anyway, Nathan."

I used to think that I would never kill anyone. I remember, as a kid, hearing stories about Hunters killing Black Witches and stories about my father killing Hunters, and I thought I'd never do that. But so far, at the grand old age of seventeen, I've killed five people. And now I'm going to have to kill another. But Pilot isn't trying to kill me. She's dying anyway but I'll be the one who kills her. Another death on my hands.

And I'm shocked at how little I think about those people I've killed. I thought murderers would be haunted by memories of their victims but I hardly give them a thought. I want to think of them now, sort of as a mark of respect, and possibly to convince myself that I'm not totally lacking in feeling. There was the first, the Hunter in Geneva whose neck I broke. I do remember her well. Then the Hunter in the forest, the fast one, the one I killed when I was an animal. Then there's Kieran, who I don't want to give any respect to. And then came the two in Spain. The first one was in the dry valley. I stabbed her in the neck. The second one was under an olive tree. The ground was strewn with olives. I remember them well: green olives, fat, ripe, some split open, staining the ground. I can't remember the Hunter very well. I remember the ground beneath her better than her.

I've killed five people.

Soon to be six.

If I can go through with it.

Pilot is lying on the ground. Her head is on a pillow made of a rug from the car. Pers is sitting beside her, holding her hand. Van has spent the last hour surrounded by vials and jars from her carpetbag. She's been mixing and grinding ingredients, preparing them for me, and now she says she's ready. She speaks to Pilot. Gabriel says, "She's telling her we don't have to do this. All Pilot has to do is tell us the location. She's saying she can help with the pain."

"And what's Pilot saying?" But I think I can guess.

"Basically, no."

Van then speaks to Pers, I guess telling her what's going to happen. I expect Pers to spit at Van, to fight and complain, but she just holds Pilot's hand and whispers to her.

Van says to me, "Pers is a sharp little vixen. Don't be fooled by her cute exterior, Nathan."

Pers doesn't strike me as cute in any way. I know she already hates me, and I know that she'll hate me more for doing this to Pilot. There's always room for more hate.

Van has told me what to do. I must cut down Pilot's arm vertically, into the vein. Pilot must see and know what I'm doing. I must collect her blood and add it to the potion that Van has made up using the map. I must take as much blood as I can. Pilot will die. Pilot has to die. It's best if I drink the potion as she dies.

Van says, "Pilot has many memories in her head; she

must really understand what you need to know and how badly you need it. When you cut her think about Mercury, think about Pilot's blood, and think about taking Pilot's memories of Mercury's home."

Pilot is wearing a dress with wide sleeves and Gabriel has pulled one up to reveal the pale skin on the inside of her long, thin arm. The blue vein seems to lie boldly but deeply within it.

I have the knife in my hand, put the point to Pilot's skin, and then take it away. I'm not ready. I've got to get my head together. Got to think the correct thoughts.

"It's the only way to find Mercury, Nathan," says Van. "The only way to help Annalise. But you must be sure. The potion won't work if you're not sure. Remember, Pilot will be gone anyway in a few hours. There is nothing we can do to save her; she's dying."

Gabriel says, "But you are going to kill her. You are taking the last few hours she has from her. You have to be sure."

Van looks at him. "Gabriel, what would you do if Nathan was held by Mercury? If you had to cut Pilot to find him and try to rescue him?"

Gabriel doesn't reply. He stares at Van and then turns away.

She says, quietly and slowly, "I think you'd skin her alive."

He turns back to look at me and I see the gold glints tumble slowly in his eyes as he says, "Ten times over."

"But you don't think I should do this. Why? Because I don't care enough about Annalise?"

He shakes his head. "I know you do, Nathan. You don't need to prove it."

"I'm not proving anything. I'm trying to find a way to help Annalise."

"And this is the only way," says Van.

I think of Mercury and finding her home and push the knife's point into Pilot's arm and draw the blade down. Pilot doesn't flinch but she grunts and says something, a curse, I think, and, even though I told myself not to look at her face, I do. Her eyes are black; as black as mine. She says some more things, more curses. I can smell her breath, which is rancid. It's good that I can concentrate on Pilot's face. I know I have to believe in what I'm doing. Pilot stops cursing and her eyelids flutter but don't close. She stares at me until the end and then beyond, but the flashes of gray in her eyes, which were weak even before I cut, finally disappear, and her blood flows more slowly and then stops.

"Quick," orders Van. "Before she dies."

I add some of the blood to the stone bowl that Van passes me: the pulp of the map and Van's other ingredients lie in the bottom. "Add more," Van says. "Stir it in."

I think there'll be Hunter poison in it too but Van has said that I can counter that. She says I can counter everything.

"Find Mercury, Nathan. Find Mercury and save Annalise. Remember, that is what you have to do."

I put the bowl to my lips and sip the potion. It tastes of stone, strangely dry, almost peppery, and gives a hot feeling inside my throat and stomach.

"Think of Mercury," Van reminds me. And I swallow all the potion while remembering Mercury standing over Annalise. When I've finished I drop the bowl.

Pers is looking at me, her eyes black and full of hate, and suddenly I'm furious with her for judging me for what I am and what I have to do. I have to get away before I hit her so I stand up but my legs collapse and I'm surprised to find that Nesbitt catches me and lowers me to the ground.

My body's weak but my mind's on fire. I want to find Pilot's memories but I don't know where to search for them.

I close my eyes.

I see Pers. She's kneeling above me. I'm lying on the patio in Spain. I've just been shot. Then Pers is gone and I'm walking through a grove of olive trees and stopping to pick up something: a stone, a sharp stone. Then I'm on a beach and picking up a pebble and the sun is hot on my face. Then I'm by a river and I'm placing the stones in a small dam. Damming it up.

This is Pilot's way of resisting me accessing her memories. Van had told me Pilot might do this, fill her mind with false thoughts, not memories at all. I concentrate on Mercury, her hair, her gray dress, the cold chill she could summon in a second. I see her. And then I'm standing by a large blue lake. It's cold and the pale blue mackerel sky is reflected on the water. I pick up a stone, the biggest I can find. I'm going to carry it to the end of the lake to dam up the river. As I walk along, carrying the stone, I glance up and see that in the lake is an island and it's the strangest of things. A white island. And I realize that it's not an island at all but an iceberg floating in the lake. I'm still carrying the heavy rock along the shore but I want to look at the iceberg, to feel the cold and the breeze, to think of Mercury and her chill breath. But I keep looking down, looking at the stones at my feet and walking to the river, then dropping the rock in the water, damming it up.

The vision is near Mercury's home. Van is sure of that. But it's not much help. I've gone over it many times now but I'm not finding anything new. All I get are the same things over and over. Me in Pilot's head, lifting rocks and putting them in a dam.

I ask for advice and Van says, "She's dead. And they aren't real memories. Find the real ones."

"Thanks. Very helpful," I reply.

And I try again and come up with the same stuff.

It's late, dark. I'm pacing around outside, in the garden. We've moved on from where Pilot died, where I killed her. We've got another car and another house to stay in. I think we're in France but I'm not sure. The others are inside. Nesbitt at least provides a good meal for us all but he's complaining about how long it's taking to locate Mercury. He's nervous about information Isch will have disclosed to the

Hunters if she's been caught. Celia is in danger, may be revealed as a spy, but Van says that there's nothing that can be done except trust that Celia can look after herself.

We've been here a full day now. Waiting for me to find where we should go next. The back door opens and Gabriel comes out.

"Tired?" he asks.

"Tired—yes. Angry—yes. Pissed off—ninety-nine percent of the time. Fun to be around—never."

Gabriel smiles. "Who wants fun when you can have interesting?"

We sit down on some blankets under one of the trees. We slept here last night. "Any brilliant ideas?" I ask.

"On how to find the memories?"

"Yes."

"Keep going over them. Find the way through."

I rest my head back against the tree and say, "It's so boring. The same thing over and over."

"Boring but necessary." He looks at me. "If you want to find Annalise do it again."

I look at him. I realize he's right. He'd do it all a thousand times for me.

I go over each memory: the olive grove, the beach, and the lake. But I think the lake is the real memory. That's what appeared when I began thinking of Mercury. I go back to that and I see it again. The lake, the sky reflected in it, and I feel a cold breeze which seems real—that's a feeling I've not had in the other memories. I concentrate on the breeze. I shiver and look to my right. I'm in Pilot's head. I've heard something. There's a hill, tree-covered and brown. There are pockets of snow. There's a road by the lake and I walk along it. In the lake is the iceberg, its reflection mirrored perfectly in the water. I turn back to the hill and see Mercury beckoning me and I walk toward her, to her home.

The Shape of a Word

I spend the night going over and over the memory. Looking for more clues. I see Mercury's home clearer every time. It's not a castle, country house, cottage, or eyrie—it's much more difficult to find than that. It's a bunker. Completely underground, completely out of sight, inside the hill.

The next morning I try to describe the place, the lake, and the hill. Gabriel says, "Can you draw it?"

That I can do. Everyone watches as I draw the lake with the iceberg floating in it. The land around is undulating; there are no trees or shrubs, just yellowed grass and bare ground; patches of snow lie in wide hollows. As I draw I realize that there's a sign by the road that runs along the lake.

"Can you see the place name?" Van asks.

I don't know what the sign says. I close my eyes and describe what I see. "It begins with a V and is a sort of medium-length word."

"Well, that's a big help," says Nesbitt. "It's somewhere cold and begins with a V? Sure rules out a heck of a lot of places—"

"Yes, it does, thank you, Nesbitt," Van interrupts. "We need maps. Can you read maps, Nathan?"

"Yes. There's something else as well. I know the shape of the word."

"The shape?" Nesbitt laughs. "Well, why didn't you say that before? The *shape* of the word . . . that makes all the difference."

"Nesbitt, if you can't contribute positively do you mind awfully not contributing at all?" Van turns back to me. "The shape?"

I shrug. I draw it in the air with my finger.

"Good. And how long is this word? Do you know the number of letters?"

"Or what the letters are?" Nesbitt chimes in again. "I mean, that might be a question worth asking."

"The sign was by the road, a long way off." But I know it wasn't *that* far off and it's just that I can't read the sign and, every time I try to remember it or focus on it, it goes to a jumble of black on white.

Gabriel gives me a book, saying, "Which word is it most like?"

Nesbitt flaps his arms and shakes his head. "I can't believe this."

I put the book down and stare at him. Van and Gabriel stare too.

"What?!"

"Why don't you bring the atlas, Nesbitt," says Van. "Then prepare lunch and go for a long walk."

While he's gone I look through the book and try to find

a word that reminds me of the place name that I saw. I don't find any.

Gabriel brings scissors and cuts up some letters. He rearranges them until I say stop.

"That's sort of what it's like. What does it say?"

"Volteahn. It doesn't mean anything. And"—he's leafing through the atlas index—"it isn't listed as a place."

"Is there anything similar?" Van asks.

Gabriel studies the index.

I get up and go to the kitchen. Nesbitt is slicing a loaf with a bread knife. He glances up when I enter.

"Hey, mate."

I guess I don't look too happy because he says, "You know I didn't mean anything."

"I can't read, OK?" I walk up to him. The knife is pointed at my chest. It's a bread knife but it could still kill me.

I walk further so the point of the knife is hard against my skin.

I push. The point begins to go in but then Nesbitt pulls the knife away. There's blood on the tip.

"OK?" I insist.

"Yes, sure, Nathan. I was just kidding around." His voice is the same, and his stupid grin, but now I'm close to him I see that his eyes have lost their movement: the flow of blue and green is frozen. He's afraid.

And I'm so surprised that I stop. I never realized he was scared of me.

"Nathan, what's happening?" Gabriel asks as he comes into the kitchen. He hesitates, then says, "We think we've found it. The place."

"Seems I don't need to be able to read," I say to Nesbitt. "And," I add, "your soup is too salty." I turn and walk away.

Nesbitt says, "Too salty? Too salty? I . . . but . . ."

As I walk out of the kitchen I notice Pers. She's sitting in the corner on the bench. She must have been there all along. I recognize that look in her eyes again and she bares her teeth to hiss at me as I leave.

Gabriel points to the name of the village on the atlas. "Is that it? Veltarlin. Is that the name you saw?"

"I can't be sure. It looks the same. The lake seems right but I'd need a more detailed map to be certain."

Nesbitt joins us at the table. "You got it?"

I say, "Yes. It has to be the place: it's cold and begins with a V."

"Righto." Nesbitt grins at me.

"Now what?" asks Gabriel.

Van stands up, stretches back in a stiff arch, and then paces round the room. She takes her cigarette case out but plays with it rather than opening it. "We'll head there. We can get more detailed maps on the way to ensure you're correct. Assuming it is, Nesbitt will form the advance party."

"An advance party of one?" he asks.

"Don't pretend that you're anything other than flattered."

"With the aim of . . . ?"

"Scouting it out with extreme care. Watching. Observing. Locating the entrance or entrances. Looking to see if anyone goes in or out. Assessing what spells Mercury might be using as protection. Most importantly, making sure that you're not seen. And then returning to base."

"And where's base?"

Van comes back to the atlas and places the tip of her finger, her perfect fingernail, on a place a few centimeters from Mercury's hill and her bunker.

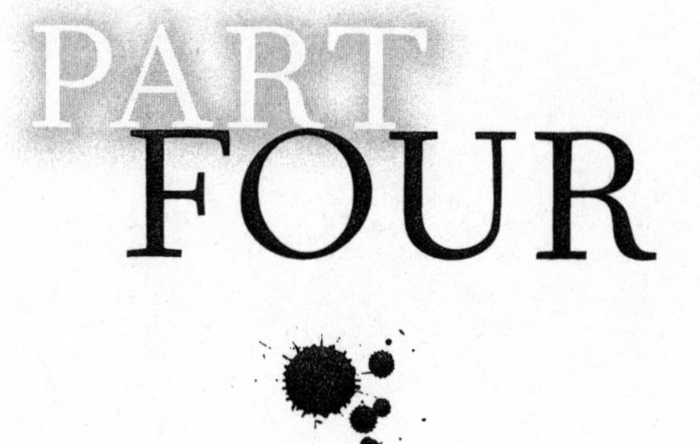

PART FOUR

THE BUNKER DIARIES

Being Positive Again

We're at the base, another vacant home, several miles from Mercury's bunker. We've checked the place on a detailed map and I'm certain now that it's right. We've been here for seventy-two hours and Nesbitt has been gone for seventy-one and a half. Van has spent all the time making a persuading potion that she can use on Mercury to make her wake Annalise. She's mixing and sampling, and glaring at us if we make a noise. Pers is still full of hate and evil stares but I give as good as I get. Gabriel and I keep to ourselves, hanging out in his bedroom or the kitchen.

I slept outside the first two nights. We're north, far north, and it's cold. The first night I wondered if I'd transform but nothing happened. The second night I sat cross-legged on the ground and watched the sun set and went over what I could remember of when I'd been in animal form, when *he* had taken over, and I thought of what it was like to be inside the other me and to see things in a different way. Nothing. But then I went back to the vision I'd had when I was helping Gabriel. I remembered being in Wales, the stake through my heart, connecting me to the earth and to him, the animal me. And then it happened; I felt the animal adrenaline slowly build in me, and I did welcome it and I transformed.

I remember most of being the animal, not all. I didn't hunt anything. It was as if he was showing me around, helping me work out what it's like, helping me get used to it, but I was always the passenger; he was in the driver's seat. I was just in his body, though I don't know what the body was. Judging by the paw prints, I think I was a wolf or large dog.

I feel like I've gained some control over when I can transform. I'm sure I can stop it now and I can make it happen too.

So tonight I'm staying inside, as me, partly cos I'm hoping Nesbitt will be back and partly because I don't want to transform again so soon. I'm lying on one of the two beds in Gabriel's room and I'm feeling positive.

Positive Thought Number 1

I am alive. I have my Gift and I'm beginning to be able to control it. This is a big deal. *I am alive. I have my Gift and I'm beginning to be able to control it.*

That is super positive.

Positive Thought Number 2

I like Annalise. I've been thinking about her quite a bit and I like her. A lot. She likes me too. I think.

Positive Thought Number 3

Annalise is probably not in pain or suffering at the moment. She's in a death-like sleep and it's dangerous but the death-like bit of it is probably not obvious to her.

Positive Thought Number 4

We know where Mercury's bunker is now. If Annalise is in there I really believe we'll find a way to get her out safely. We have a good chance of beating Mercury. Four against one are pretty good odds. She's on home turf but we have the element of surprise. She's very powerful. We're quite powerful. We've a good chance. Of course she could just freeze us all instantly in some ice storm or blow us away—literally—or, I don't know, send giant hailstones down to beat us to death.

Positive Thought Number 5

There are four of us against Mercury, which means that I haven't killed Nesbitt yet. And I don't think I will kill him now. He doesn't get to me like he used to.

Positive Thought Number 6

If we live through this I'll be with Annalise. I know all our troubles won't be over and there's the whole Alliance thing, and living a quiet life is still a long way off, but I will be with her. I really want to kiss her for real, and do other things I've thought of doing with her for years and never even had the chance and—

"You OK?"

It's Gabriel. He's here with me as always.

"Yeah. Just thinking about stuff . . . you know. Positive stuff."

"Oh, right. You're thinking about her. Annalise."

"A bit. I think we have a decent chance of making this work. Of saving her. And of living through it."

He doesn't reply.

"Don't you think?"

"Mercury will try to kill us and I think she'll try very hard. She's good at it."

I'm trying to keep things positive, so I say, "And I think the Alliance has a chance too. I mean, this could be a huge change. In a year's time the whole witch world could be different."

Gabriel gets up and I turn to look at him. He leans against the wall, staring out the window. The sky is dark, overcast. The room is glowing faintly green from Van's nightsmoke.

He turns to look at me, then back out the window. His movements are stiff, jerky, as if he was going to say something but changed his mind.

"Are you angry?" I ask.

He doesn't answer straightaway but then says, "A bit. Possibly a lot."

"With me?"

"Who else."

"Why?"

"I don't want to die, Nathan. I don't want to die saving a girl I despise. A girl I don't trust. A girl who I think has betrayed you and will betray you again. And being selfish for a while"—he turns to look at me—"I don't think you're even vaguely interested in what I want, are you?"

I try to think of things to say, how much I like him, how I appreciate him, how I know he's helped me. Crap words but maybe better than nothing. I start to say, "Gabriel, you're my friend. You're special. I couldn't—"

He interrupts me, loud now. "Do you know how special I am? Do you even care? You're so caught up in your own dramas that you don't see anything around you."

"Gabriel—"

"The first person I killed," he interrupts again, "I shot in the head. Point-blank range. She was kneeling at my feet; I'd tied her hands, her ankles. She was crying. Begging. Begging me to let her live. I shot her in the head, standing facing her, barrel of the gun to her forehead. She was looking up at me. I lowered the gun, pointed, pushed the gun against her skin, and pulled the trigger. To make sure, I shot her again through the side of the head, as her body lay on the ground. To make really sure, I pushed her body onto its back and shot her again in the heart."

"You're trying to shock me." I get up and go to him but I'm thrown for a second by how he looks.

He looks harrowed.

"Who was it?" I ask.

"A girl. Someone who betrayed my sister to White Witches. Her name was Caitlin. She was a Half Blood my sister trusted, whom I trusted. And you might say at this point, 'Oh, so Gabriel makes mistakes; he trusted someone who betrayed him—he's not perfect at judging people.' And you know what I say to that? I say, 'You're right. Of course you're right.' People are hard to read and you know what's really tricky about them? They change, Nathan. They change. My sister trusted Caitlin and she was right to because Caitlin was good and kind and nice and she was trying to help. She was on our side, at the start. But you know what? They made her betray us. They do that; they turn people."

"That doesn't mean it's happened with Annalise."

"No, it doesn't. And I may be wrong, Nathan. She may not have betrayed you. But, when I see Annalise, something about her reminds me of Caitlin."

"Gabriel—"

"To be fair, I realize Caitlin didn't have much choice, but she did have *a* choice. She was half White Witch and if she didn't do what they wanted then they'd have made her life hell. But because of her they caught my sister. My sister loved a White Witch. Caitlin carried messages between them. But then my sister went to see him, went onto White

Witch territory. She was always impulsive, full of life and excitement. They caught her. She was seventeen. The boy was too. He was imprisoned for a month and released. My sister was hanged. I don't know what they did to her before they killed her. What do you think they'd do, Nathan?"

I don't reply. I know he doesn't want an answer.

"I still hate Caitlin. For weeks after I shot her, I wished I could do it again, so I could do it slower, cause her more pain and fear, make her suffer like my sister suffered."

I go to him. Hold him. It's the first time I've done this—gone to him.

I think he might break, might cry. But he pushes me away and stares at my face. "I think of my sister a lot, how much she suffered, what they would have done to her. I love you more than my sister, Nathan. I never thought that would be possible but it's true. And I think you're right. I think we do have a chance of beating Mercury, and I even think the Alliance has a chance. But more than that I think you'll be killed, Nathan, and I think you will die a bad death, a painful, long, slow death. And I'm helpless to stop it because you can't see that Annalise is wrong for you. You refuse to see it. So all I can promise is that I'll try to help you and if I fail, if you die, I'll cause whoever did it more pain than I gave Caitlin."

He walks out.

So that was positive.

We Make Our Plan

"No. No. No." Nesbitt is back and not being positive. "Look, I told you. There'll be a protection spell."

It's the next morning and we're sitting round the kitchen table, forming our plan. We're trying to work out how to get into the bunker without Mercury knowing.

"What about digging our way in?" Gabriel asks.

"Of course." Nesbitt slams the palm of his hand into his forehead. "All we need is some mining equipment, explosives, lifting gear, a few diggers. Shouldn't take more than a couple of weeks."

We know he's right. And I know that the only way in is the way I've thought all along.

"I have to go to the door and knock."

They all look at me, except Gabriel, who acknowledges I'm right by keeping his head down.

"She won't kill me. Not straightaway anyway. She'll want to know if I've got Marcus's head or heart."

"How long do you think it'll be before she works out the answer?" Nesbitt says.

"About ten seconds," Gabriel replies, looking up at me.

"Yes," I say. "But she'll want to listen to what I have to offer. Last time I saw her she had just heard that Rose was dead, Marcus had given me three gifts and Hunters were invading her valley. She was furious and afraid. She'll be neither of those when I walk in this time."

"You hope," Nesbitt says.

"So," I continue, "I'll say I want her to release Annalise. What will she accept instead of Marcus's death?"

Gabriel comments, "Yours probably."

"There's the risk of that but I'm betting that Mercury will want to cause me as much pain as possible. She'll want to show me Annalise, revel in her victory. I think she'll invite me in. I think she'll talk to me."

They all stare at me.

"And then what?" Gabriel says. "Now you've done that so successfully."

"And then . . . And then you guys will have sneaked in behind me and will overpower Mercury, give her the persuading potion, find out how to wake Annalise, and we'll make our escape."

Nesbitt laughs. Gabriel rolls his eyes.

Van says, "It might work."

We all look at her in surprise.

"Getting us all in is the trick. Mercury knows that Pilot was going to bring her a new apprentice," Van says, looking at Pers, who is scowling in the corner. "Perhaps there's a way of using her."

"I could take Pers to Mercury. She'd trust me," Gabriel says. "I can watch Mercury to see what spell protects the entrance."

Silence. Van smokes her cigarette.

I say, "I don't think Gabriel should come." If Mercury sees us together she'll be more suspicious. "How about . . . I arrive with Pers. I've rescued her from Pilot's attackers. 'Don't know what to do with her, thought she'd be happy with you, Mercury. Oh, and by the way, how's Annalise?' Mercury takes me to Annalise and Pers has time to work out the entrance spell."

"She's French. She doesn't understand a word of English. And she doesn't want to help you anyway," Gabriel says.

"Tell her I'm bound to get killed and she'll have the chance to watch. That should motivate her."

"No," Van says. "You and Pers are needed to get in but someone else will have to learn about the access spell. This idea is good, though. With a few small changes it might work . . ."

Mercury's Bunker

The next morning we're ready. It's early. There's a clear, pale blue sky. It's going to be a lovely day.

Nesbitt says, "I've checked all around. This is the only entrance. Mercury must have a cut inside because I just don't see how she can get the groceries in from this spot. The big question is . . . is she home?"

"Only one way to find out," I say.

The entrance to the bunker is a narrow tunnel in the hillside. It gives no indication of how far it stretches as within a meter it's black. The wooded hillside overlooks the lake. There are no footpaths, dog-walkers, or people. This isn't England; this is Norway. Remote Norway.

Gabriel and I walk up to the entrance: the first wave of our infiltration. Gabriel has transformed to look like Pers and is wearing her clothes. He looks just like her, walks like her, talks like her, and scowls like her. I'm fairly sure that he's going to spit at me at some point, for authenticity.

Our plan is for me and Gabriel to get into the bunker first. I'll tell Mercury that I'm bringing Pers from Pilot and while I'm here I need to see Annalise, to be convinced she's still alive. Mercury takes me to Annalise, and Gabriel slips away to let the others in. Nesbitt and Gabriel together surprise and overpower Mercury and give her a sleeping potion that Van has concocted. We think the two of them will have the strength to do this if they can get close enough without her suspecting. While Mercury is unconscious the persuading potion can be administered by Van.

There are numerous ways that the plan could go wrong and, if Mercury even smells a trick, we're all in trouble, in which case we've agreed that we forget the plan to save Annalise and concentrate on saving ourselves. As Nesbitt said, "We can't help her if we're all dead."

We go into the tunnel entrance. The air is still and even colder than outside. I switch on my torch as we walk slowly and cautiously forward. The walls are uneven, solid rock, as is the floor, and it feels like we're being hemmed in: the walls narrow until we can no longer walk comfortably side by side.

Ahead there is a door, or rather two doors. There's a gate of metal bars and directly behind that a solid-looking wooden door with black metal studs embedded in it.

I pull on the gate but it's padlocked. The torchlight seems to have dimmed and the silence has deepened around us.

I reach through the bars of the gate and knock hard on the wooden door with the flat of my hand, and then my fist, but it doesn't make much noise. I bang again, harder, using the base of my torch. Even that sound seems to get swallowed up by the tunnel and I'm not sure if Mercury will be able to hear us. But maybe she can sense we're here. Who knows what magic she will have protecting her home?

I bang again and shout, "Mercury! You've got visitors."

We wait.

I'm about to bang again when I think I hear something and Gabriel leans forward as if he's heard it too. It's the sound of a bolt being pulled across rusty metal. It screeches and complains and then goes quiet. Another bolt and more scraping of metal and then . . . silence. The wooden door swings open slowly and, as it does, I smell something unusual, something spicy. I glance at Gabriel and he nods quickly to confirm that he's smelled it too and that it's something to do with how the door opens. It doesn't require a key or a password but something that smells spicy!

The door opens onto blackness. But I know Mercury is there because the temperature drops dramatically.

I raise my torch and there she stands. The same horrendous figure I remember: tall and gray, like a warped and rusted iron stake, her hair a bundle of wire wool piled on her head, her black eyes flashing with sheet lightning.

She sends a blast of freezing air in my direction. I get icicles in my hair and nostrils. I have to close my eyes and turn away from her. My back goes numb with cold, the wind so strong that I'm bent over and holding onto the tunnel walls for support, trying to protect Gabriel with my body.

Then, as quickly as it began, the wind stops. I straighten up and turn to face her.

"Mercury!" I say by way of hello and now regret that I haven't planned what else I need to say.

"Nathan. This is a surprise. And I see you have a new friend."

"She's not a friend. This is Pers. Pilot was going to bring her to you to be your apprentice, I believe, but . . . Pilot's dead."

Mercury says nothing but her eyes flash brilliantly.

"Hunters killed her. I was there. I escaped with Pers."

"And why have you come here? You wanted to drag Hunters after you to my home—again?"

"No. They've not followed me. That was a week ago."

"A week. A year. They'll be following you all the same."

"I've lost them."

Mercury curls her lip. "And how did you find me?"

"That doesn't matter." I know if I tell her Pilot told me she won't believe it. "The point is I'm here."

"And why are you here? I said to kill Marcus and bring me his heart. I don't see that anywhere."

"I wanted to talk to you about that. We didn't have much time to discuss your offer, what with the Hunters shooting at us."

"It's non-negotiable."

"You're a businesswoman, Mercury. Everything is negotiable."

"That is not."

"You originally wanted me to kill Marcus in return for

giving me three gifts, but before I set off to steal the Fairborn we agreed I would work for you for a year instead."

Mercury sneers at me. "And is that what you're offering me now?"

"No. In return for Annalise, I'm offering you Pers."

Mercury studies Gabriel and eventually says, "She was due to come to me anyway. I'll take her." Mercury opens the padlock with one of her hairpins, grabs Gabriel by the shoulder, drags him through the doorway, and pulls the gate shut. "But you and your father are different matters."

"But—" I grab hold of the gate.

"No negotiations. Come back when you have Marcus's head or heart."

This is just about the worst possible—and yet totally anticipated—reply.

"I need to see Annalise," I say, clinging on to the gate.

"No, you don't," Mercury replies.

"I do. How do I know she's alive? I don't even know where she is. For all I know, you left her to the Hunters. I'll do what you ask, Mercury. If I can, I'll do it. But I have to know that Annalise is alive. I have to see her first."

Mercury hesitates. She hasn't closed the padlock yet. She's thinking about it. That's something.

"I'm risking my life to come here, Mercury. You can kill me easily. All I ask is that you let me see Annalise."

"Last time we discussed this you said you'd never kill your father."

"That was before he left me to the Hunters. I nearly died—many times they nearly caught me—but I managed to get away, no thanks to him. I'd waited all my life for him to come for me. I thought he'd take me with him. I thought I'd learn from him, be with him, but no; he'd rather leave me for the Hunters to catch and torture to death."

"He's a cruel man. I'm glad you're realizing that, Nathan."

I bow my head and cling to the bars, saying, "I'll do anything for Annalise, Mercury. And I'll risk my life to help her but I need to see her first. Please . . ."

I daren't look up. All I can do is hope that Mercury's hatred blinds her to the fact that I will never kill Marcus, could never kill him. But I have to make her believe that for Annalise I'd try.

I drop to my knees. "Please, Mercury."

The barred gate swings silently open. I hesitate and look up.

"I will boil you alive if you try any tricks," Mercury says, and she steps back and into darkness.

I get to my feet and go in. Mercury closes the gate and then shuts the wooden door and slides two large bolts into place. Then she takes a pinch of some grains from a small stone bowl that's carved into the tunnel wall and sprinkles them over the bolts. The spicy smell fills the air again. I think the grains must fix the bolts in place.

The tunnel continues pretty much the same inside but there are a few oil lamps hanging along the walls, flickering a yellow light. Mercury keeps Gabriel in an iron grip and steers him along the tunnel as it curves to the right and I follow. She sweeps through a curtain of heavy material and I follow her into a large room, a grand hall, with roughly cut stone walls lined all round with tapestries. The curtain we came through is also a tapestry. There are no doors and I suspect that each tapestry conceals a different tunnel.

Mercury stops in the center of the hall and releases Gabriel. She says, "Stay there," and Gabriel does a wonderful confused look.

I say to Mercury, "Pers doesn't speak English. Just French."

Mercury mutters something to Gabriel and he gives a Pers-like scowl. She walks round Gabriel, looking at him from all sides.

"So, Pilot is dead. That is a great loss to us all. And Gabriel? I take it he's dead too?"

"I arranged to meet him at a place in the forest. He never turned up. Then Hunters arrived." From that description, it should be clear what must have happened: Gabriel was caught and tortured to reveal the location of the meeting place.

"I'm sorry," Mercury says.

"Really?" I scowl now. "I find that hard to believe."

"Gabriel was an honorable Black Witch." She pauses and runs her fingers through Gabriel's hair, then lifts a strand and lets it drop. I think Gabriel has even got Pers's head lice.

I know I need to keep things moving. I say, "Where's Annalise?"

"You risk much for Annalise, Nathan. Are you sure she's worth it?"

"Yes. I'm sure."

Mercury comes to stare into my eyes. "True love. It's a powerful force."

"If I have to choose between Annalise and my father then I will. But I need to see her. Show me that she's alive and I'll do what you want."

Mercury leans closer to me and strokes my cheek again. Her finger is cold and dry as bone. She says, "You always smelled so good, Nathan."

"I can't say the same for you," I snarl. "Show me Annalise."

"I love it when you fight back, Nathan. It's quite delicious. Come, before I change my mind."

She turns and walks past Gabriel, saying something in French as she passes, and Gabriel scowls and sits on the floor. I follow Mercury to the far end of the hall, to a tapestry of a hunting scene, a man on a horse with a dog running beside him and a deer with arrows in it. Behind the tapestry is a tunnel identical to the one leading from the entrance. Mercury is already striding down it.

It's looking good for our plan. Gabriel should be on his way back to the entrance as I follow Mercury down the tunnel, which is more like a corridor. There are wooden doors on both sides and Mercury is already at the furthest one. She goes through it and I slow. I've been so anxious about dealing with Mercury that I'm unprepared for seeing Annalise.

I step through the doorway, expecting a cell but finding I'm in a bedroom. There's a chair, a table, a tall chest of drawers, and a wardrobe all in a rich dark wood. An oil lantern hangs low from the center of the room, giving light and scent, and below it is a bed and on the bed is Annalise.

I feel my heart racing in panic: Annalise is pale; her eyes are closed. She's laid out on her back, which somehow makes her look more dead than asleep.

I touch her hand with mine. It's cold. Her face is thin. I lean over and listen for her breathing but can't hear anything. I feel for a pulse in her neck and find none.

"This isn't right," I say. "She's not asleep."

"No, Nathan. She's not asleep. She's in a death-like sleep. No breathing, no pulse to speak of; her body—and her mind—is shut down to the lowest of levels. But there is still life in her."

"How long can she survive like this?"

Mercury doesn't reply but goes to Annalise and smooths her hair on the pillow.

"Mercury! How long?"

"A month more. Then it will probably be too late."

"You have to wake her. Now!"

"I don't see Marcus's heart."

"Wake her and I'll get it. If she dies I never will."

Mercury smooths Annalise's hair again.

"Please, Mercury."

"Nathan, begging doesn't suit you."

I curse her. "Wake her now! Wake her or you get nothing."

And I'm convinced she's going to laugh in my face but she says, "I've always liked you, Nathan." She turns to look at Annalise. "And I admit she is looking frail. White Witches have no strength. A Black Witch could survive three times as long."

"Mercury, you gain nothing by letting her die. You're not giving me enough time to get to Marcus. It's impossible."

Mercury comes to me and looks into my eyes. "So you will kill him? Your own father?"

I look back at her and say it like I mean it. "Yes. I'll find a way."

"It will be difficult."

"I'll find a way. But only if you wake Annalise. Now."

"She'll remain my prisoner until you fulfill your half of the bargain."

"Yes, yes. I agree."

"She will be my slave. I warn you, Nathan, I have little patience with slaves or prisoners. I'll treat her badly. The sooner you destroy Marcus, the less Annalise will suffer."

"Yes, I understand."

"Very well."

She turns and kisses Annalise on the lips and, as she

does, Annalise's lips are parted and words on hot breath flow out of Mercury's mouth and into Annalise. Mercury straightens and smooths her hand down Annalise's arm, brushes the backs of her fingers down her cheek, saying, "I have begun the process. The spark of life is reignited but it will be hours, maybe a day, before the next stage can take place and she wakes."

I go to Annalise and take her hand.

"What's the next stage?" I ask Mercury, turning to look at her, but she's walking toward the door, leaving already. I've no idea if Gabriel's had enough time to let the others in. I need to delay Mercury but I don't know how without raising her suspicions. "Is there anything I should do? Will she need water or—"

Mercury half turns, saying, "I told you—"

She's interrupted by a call. It sounds like Pers but Gabriel wouldn't be calling. I don't understand the words but I have a bad feeling.

Mercury looks irritated rather than angry and leaves the room. I go to the doorway, planning on following her. Mercury pulls the tapestry aside and stands there, her back to me. I can see through into the great hall and I can hear Pers again. Now she runs up to Mercury. It's the real Pers, dressed differently from Gabriel. She sees me too and shouts and points. I've no idea what she's saying but I can guess.

Mercury doesn't even reply but turns to me and I duck back into the bedroom as a bolt of lightning flashes past. I risk another quick glance into the corridor and see the tapestry falling back into place. Mercury has gone into the great hall. The noise of thunder fills the bunker and the walls of the corridor shake like they might collapse.

I run to the tapestry but before I get there I hear a gunshot, and then an explosion, and another and another, so that the vibrations of each one add to the next until the whole bunker seems to be shaking. There is now a howling gale that I have to battle against to push aside the tapestry and look into the great hall, where I see Van facing Mercury.

Nesbitt is at the far end of the hall, his gun pointed at the body of Pers, who is splayed on the floor, a neat bullet hole in her forehead. For a second, I'm in shock but it isn't Gabriel; it's the real Pers—the one wearing different clothes.

Nesbitt turns to point the gun at Mercury but the strength of the wind increases and he can't hold the gun steady. He can hardly hold himself upright.

I spot Gabriel, no longer in disguise. He's kneeling in the corner of the room, a gun in his hand, but he can't hold it steady either. He shoots and misses.

Mercury raises her arms and swirls them over her head and the wind strengthens to a furious pace, picking up all loose items—cushions, papers, a small table—so they circle the room in a tornado. Even the heavy wooden chairs slide around in a strange circular dance and the wind forces me backward into the shelter of the corridor.

Mercury stands in the middle of the tornado, howling in fury. A flash of lightning jumps out, strengthens and grows.

Van screams and only then does the lightning fade. Nesbitt fires his gun but he cannot hurt Mercury. She'll kill us all.

The tapestry over the end of the corridor whips in my face and I step back. I want the animal to take over. I want to be him, even if it's for one last time. And I let the animal adrenaline flood through me and I welcome it.

I'm inside him. Inside the animal. But this time it's different: now we both want the same thing.

We

•••••

the tapestry whips in our face. we snap up and pull it down. we're strong and huge and even on all fours our head is high off the ground.

there's the howl of the wind, which sounds like a woman but the words don't make sense anymore. they're just noise, screeching sounds, furious sounds.

the woman in gray has her back to us. her dress is flying wildly, ripping apart in places. her hair is vertical, in a whirlwind of its own. lightning flashes out of the storm around her. she spreads her arms and her hands throw lightning across the room. the wind drops a little. the other woman is on the floor, crawling away. the older man is near her. he's angry and frightened, for himself and the woman on the floor, but he has a gun. he steps forward and shoots but the gun's empty, and he's shouting and running at the lightning woman but she throws her arm back and a surge of wind picks the man up and flings him hard against the wall. lightning woman doesn't turn to look at what she has done, she only looks at the other woman, who is crawling away, and lightning strikes the floor near the crawling woman. the flash is dazzling and the thunder echoes in the room.

we catch a movement to our far right. a young man is in

the entrance to another corridor. blood is running down the side of his face.

we swing back to the lightning woman. she's the only threat. she'll kill us if we don't kill her. we move forward. we smell her now, a metallic smell of anger.

the woman on the floor is still alive. she is exhausted but she is saying words.

the wind drops more. the lightning woman's hair falls around her neck. she's speaking again and then another lightning flash hits the ground. the woman on the floor screams a short, sharp scream and drops limp. smoke rises from her clothes. her hair is burning.

we move forward to the lightning woman. her body stiffens. she's sensed something. we get ready, tensing our rear legs. lightning woman turns. she sees us. she's surprised but she doesn't step back. she raises her arm to send wind or lightning but we're on her already. and she's on the floor beneath us, in our grasp. she's thin and brittle but hard, lost in our hug.

lightning strikes around us, around the room, dazzling. loud. louder. brighter. crashing close but not striking us. the storm is wild, howling, fiercely cold. we are in the eye of it. but we keep hold, crushing the woman to our chest. her ribs crack. crack, crack, crack. we push our claws into her side and rip them in and up, splitting bone, tearing through her. hot blood running out. we claw again. through the tough skin and down, crashing through ribs and guts to her hip bone.

the wind has gone.

still and quiet now.

there is no fear. it has faded with the last flash of lightning and thunder.

a small flame licks up the side of a tapestry. smoke and steam hang in the air.

the lightning woman is still.

we loosen our grip on her body and let it drop hard on the floor. we smell her from shoulder to guts, all open and red.

her blood tastes good.

we take her in our jaws, lifting her slightly as we bite. the redness of it and the smell of it are good.

Pink

•·•·•·•

i'm in a bathroom.

i'm shaking.

but i'm me.

i run the bath, washing the blood off my arm.

i remember every second of being the animal. i remember it all.

i lie in the bath, slide under, and submerge. when i surface again the water has turned pink.

i think i'm going to throw up and i get out and stand by the toilet but i'm not sick.

i've stopped shaking.

Kissing

“Can I talk to you?”

Gabriel stands in the bathroom doorway. I’ve got my back to him, though I can see him in the mirror. He steps further into the room. He is incredibly, perfectly beautiful and worried and human, and I look at myself, at my reflection. I look the same as ever but I’m not.

I tell Gabriel, “I can remember all of it.” I even remember transforming back. Once Mercury was dead I stayed with her, almost feeling her life dissipate into the silence around me. Nesbitt staggered to Van and knelt over her, checking her pulse, talking to her, telling her to heal. She was burned, smoldering and blackened. Nesbitt spoke quietly to her. He smelled of sorrow. Gabriel came out of the corridor. He no longer held a gun. He walked toward me, arms out, palms facing me. Not quite meeting my gaze, looking at the floor and glancing up, and he sat on the wet rug near me. I lay down by him and rested, and the animal adrenaline left me and in a second I had transformed back. I returned to this me. Nathan.

Gabriel says, “That’s good, that you remember.”

“Yeah, maybe. I don’t know.” I turn to face him. “It’s different when I’m the animal. I’m not the same.” I say it so quietly that I don't know if he can even hear me.

"Don't be afraid of your Gift, Nathan."

"I'm not afraid of it, not anymore. But once I'm transformed, when I'm the animal, everything is different. I'm sort of watching him but also part of him, feeling all the things he feels. And it feels amazing, Gabriel, to be completely, absolutely him—to be completely, absolutely wild. I don't want to be an animal, Gabriel, but, when I am, it's the best feeling. The best, wildest, most intensely beautiful feeling. I always thought a person's Gift reflected something about that person and all I can think is that my Gift reflects my desires, and my desires are to be totally wild, totally free. Without any control."

"You enjoyed it?"

"Is that wrong?"

"There's no right or wrong here, Nathan."

I don't know if I can say it but I want to tell him, so I do. "It feels good."

He comes closer to me and says, "I love it when you're honest with me. You're more in touch with the real you than anyone I've ever met."

And I know he's going to kiss me again and I put my hand out against his chest to stop him.

But then I look at him, at his face, his eyes, and the gold in them tumbling around, and I don't know why I'm fighting this too. I'm curious about him. And just touching his chest is something. It's nice. It feels good. I'm not sure what I want to do and I know I'll stop if it doesn't feel good.

I slide my hand up to his shoulder and behind his neck. I'm leaning my head the slightest amount, bending forward, and he doesn't move. He's so still. My hand is round his neck, in his hair. I'm not looking in his eyes but at his lips and as quietly as I can I say, "Gabriel."

I'm so close to him our lips are almost touching, and then I move closer so our lips *are* touching as I say his name again. It's like a kiss but it's not really a kiss. And it's nice and I want more. I move my lips without saying his name, still barely touching, then closer, caressing his lips with mine. And he kisses me. I don't care anymore about anything. I want to feel more and I'm desperate and kissing Gabriel on the mouth harder and harder and pulling his body to me as hard as I can, my arms round him, our mouths open, tongues licking each other, our teeth clashing, and then I'm pushing him away. Pushing him hard against the wall. And then I back away from him and walk out of the bathroom.

I'm supposed to be with Annalise. I don't understand any of what's happening to me.

The Locked Drawer

It seems like a lifetime since Mercury kissed Annalise to wake her. I've been sitting here with Annalise for three or four hours and I'm glad she's still asleep. I can sit on the chair by her bed, my head rested back and my eyes half open, and look at her, at her pure beauty, and if I think about that I don't have to think about other stuff.

There's a knock on the door and before I say anything Van walks in. I can see that she's healed well and fast but one side of her face is scarred.

"Nesbitt said you were here. Any change?" she asks.

"Nothing. Mercury said she'd done the first stage of the process; she said it'd be hours before the next. But I've no idea what that is. I don't know if I have to do something or what."

Van sits on a chair on the other side of the bed. She's wearing a new clean suit and looks as perfect as ever. Even her hair isn't looking too bad, though I can see some of it has been burned off around her right ear.

She lights a cigarette and says, "Let's wait and see. I would assume the next stage is when Annalise starts to wake."

I close my eyes and doze. I think of Gabriel. I wanted to

kiss him, wanted to know what it was like, and it was nice, good. I liked it. But I'd rather kiss Annalise. And Gabriel is my friend, though I've probably messed that up, but I hope not because Gabriel of all people should understand. Though I'm not sure what there is to understand.

I open my eyes and sit up. Without really thinking about it, I say to Van, "Do you think I have to do something?"

"To wake Annalise?"

"Yes."

Van tilts her head to the left and she sits up a little. "Do something like . . . ?"

"I don't know. The old stories say the prince wakes the sleeping princess with a kiss. Mercury kissed her but maybe I need to as well."

"I can't believe you haven't tried it," Van says. "Though two kisses doesn't feel much like Mercury's sort of thing." She looks at Annalise. "But it has to be said that nothing much is happening now."

I get up and go to Annalise and gently lower myself down and kiss her lips. They're cold. I try again, harder. I feel her cheek: it's cold. I feel for a pulse in her neck: nothing.

I sit back down and stare at Annalise. "I'm sure this isn't right."

Van drags on her cigarette and says, "Do you notice anything about that chest of drawers beside you?"

I turn and look. It's a tall oak chest of eight drawers. The furniture in the room—the wardrobe, bed, chest, and chairs—is all the same wood.

"I've been looking at it for the last hour and now it's beginning to annoy me. Why does every keyhole in the chest of drawers, indeed in this entire room, have a key in it, except that top drawer?"

I look round. She's right: all the drawers have locks but each one has a tiny key in it. The door to the room also has a lock and key, as does the wardrobe. I try the top drawer but it won't budge. All the other drawers open and each one is empty.

Van stubs her cigarette out on the arm of the chair and gets up, saying, "I think you're right: you do have to do something to wake Annalise but it's not a kiss that she needs; it's something else. And that drawer is where I'd put the something else." Van tries to open the lock with the key from the drawer below. It doesn't work. "We need the right key."

"Mercury didn't use keys," I say, and I walk quickly out of the room. I know Gabriel has one of Mercury's hairpins but I'm not sure I can face him at the moment. I'd rather face a corpse.

It's still smoky in the great hall. I look to where I dropped Mercury's body. It's not there but there are two tapestries rolled up, lying next to each other at the side of the room. The bigger one must contain Mercury's body, the smaller one, Pers.

I drag the longer bundle to a space in the middle of the room and unravel it. Even this is unpleasant. She's stiff and unrolls with a jerk onto her front and then onto her back, until Mercury is lying there, eyes open, staring at me. Her eyes are still black but with no stars shining or lightning flashing in them. I carefully feel through her hair and pull out all the pins. Seventeen of them! Some with red skull ends, some black, white, green, and some made of glass. I can't remember which ones are for which tasks, though Rose did tell me that some open doors, some open locks, and some kill.

I put the pins carefully into my pocket. All I have to do now is roll Mercury back up. I flop the end of the tapestry over her and move round to slide my hands underneath her, and, as I do so, I see something slip from Mercury's blood-stained dress. It's a silver chain and locket with a complex clasp that slots inside itself. The locket is held within an intricately designed nest of woven silver and gold. It won't open. I pick one of the hairpins with a red end and push it against the locket.

I'm not sure what to expect—some special potion or valuable jewel—but inside the locket is a tiny painted portrait of a young girl who looks like Mercury. But it isn't her. Mercury isn't vain enough to wear her own picture. It must be her twin sister, Mercy, my great-grandmother. Marcus killed her and now I've killed the other sister. Black Witches are renowned for killing members of their own family and it seems in that respect I'm turning out Black.

I close the locket and replace it in the folds of Mercury's dress.

I roll her body back up and drag her to the side of the room.

In the bedroom with Van I show her the hairpins. "The red skull ones open locks." I put the point of one into the keyhole and there's a satisfying, quiet click. The drawer slides smoothly open and inside is a tiny purple bottle.

Van takes it and pulls out the worn cork. She sniffs at the bottle and jerks her head back, eyes watering. She says, "This is the potion to wake Annalise. I'd suggest just one drop."

"On her lips?"

"That's romantic but not very effective. In her mouth, I'd say."

I take the bottle and, while Van holds Annalise's mouth open, I tip the bottle up. A glutinous blue blob of liquid grows at the bottle's lip and I'm just beginning to think that it's too much and not right as the drop falls into Annalise's mouth.

I keep my hand on her neck, feeling for a pulse. A minute passes and there's nothing. I still keep hold of her and another minute passes, and then I think I feel something—the faintest of pulses.

"She's waking," I say.

Van checks Annalise's neck. "Yes, but her heart's weak. I'll see what I can come up with for that." And she leaves the room.

Annalise Not Breathing

This isn't good. This isn't good. Annalise's heartbeat is far too fast. It's getting stronger all the time but it's not normal, not regular. My hand is on her neck, feeling her pulse, which is racing faster and faster—and then I feel no pulse, nothing. It's stopped. This is the second time it has stopped. Last time it started again on its own after ten seconds. I count the seconds:

Five

And six

And seven

And eight

Come on come on

And ten

And eleven

Oh shit oh shit

And a beat, faint, faint like before, and another, and another, each a little stronger. This is the pattern. Oh shit! If it's a pattern it's going to happen again and again.

I still have my hand on her neck. Van hasn't come back and I'm not sure—

Her eyes flutter open.

"Annalise? Can you hear me?"

She's looking at me but not seeing me.

And her heart's going faster and faster again, and harder and stronger, but far too fast now.

And it stops, again.

"Annalise. Annalise."

And four

And five

And six

And seven

And eight

And nine

Please, please breathe

Please

Please . . .

Her eyes close.

Oh no, oh no.

But then I feel it again, faint but there, her pulse.

It's building again but not so fast. Am I just trying to convince myself? Annalise doesn't open her eyes.

"Annalise. It's Nathan. I'm here. You're waking up. I'm here. Take your time. Breathe slow. Slow."

Her pulse seems to be steadying, fast but not racing as frighteningly as before, and she feels warmer too. I hold her hand and it's so thin, so bony, it scares me.

"Annalise. I'm here. You're waking. I'm with you."

Her eyelids flutter again and they open. She looks ahead but still isn't focusing on me. Her eyes look wrong; they look dead. There are no silver glints in them. And now I feel her heart begin to accelerate again, going faster and faster. Oh no. Her eyes are still open and her heart is racing so fast and so hard I think it's going to burst out of her chest and then—

"No. No. Annalise. No."

I check but I know her heart has stopped again.

I can't count anymore. Can't face it. Oh shit. Oh shit. Do I do heart massage or something? I need her on a hard surface for that. I slide my arms under her, lift her, and she's so light, far too light. I lay her down on the floor gently and I'm not sure what to do.

I put my hands on her chest and push and push. There's a song I think you're supposed to do this to; I vaguely remember Arran telling me. It's fast. That's all I remember. I push on her chest, massage her heart, get it beating again. But really I don't know what to do. I don't know if I'm doing it right but all I can do now is keep going. I have to keep going.

"Nathan. What's happening?"

It's Van. She's kneeling beside me.

"Her heart keeps stopping. Her eyes opened but they looked dead and her heart's stopped again."

"You're doing the right thing."

"I think I've broken her ribs. I don't know how hard to do this."

"You're doing fine. Ribs can heal."

Van feels Annalise's neck, her forehead, her cheek.

She passes me a cigarette. "One breath every minute

into her mouth until the cigarette's gone. It'll strengthen her heart, though it might weaken yours."

I inhale on the cigarette and as I breathe the smoke into Annalise's mouth I feel myself go light-headed. I inhale again and feel OK but as I breathe out my head swims as if I'm giving Annalise all my strength. My lips are close to hers. I look into her eyes but nothing has changed. I take another puff of the cigarette and as I breathe out into Annalise's mouth my lips brush hers. Her eyes don't change. I do it again, another breath out, and my lips are clumsy on hers and I look at her eyes and they're glinting.

"Nathan?"

"Yes, I'm here." I feel Van touch my shoulder and murmur, "I'll leave you now."

Annalise says, "Is this real?"

"Yes. We're both real."

"Good." It's a breath as much as a word.

"Yes, very good. You've been asleep, under a spell."

"I'm cold."

"I'll try to warm you. You've been asleep for a long time."

Her eyes are focused on me; the blue is intense and the silver glints move slowly, and she says, "I'm so cold." But her hand moves, searching for mine, and I hold it. I pull a blanket down to cover her and lie close to keep her warm and I talk to her. Just repeating the same things: I'm here, she's going to be OK, she's been asleep, take it slow.

She's slept for months but seems exhausted by it. Her body is too thin; her bones are sticking out and her face is drawn now that she's woken. She looks more frail and ill than when she was asleep.

We lie together and I hold her close to keep her warm.

She asks, "Were you smoking?"

"Yes. We shared a cigarette. Not tobacco, something else."

She doesn't reply. I think she's gone to sleep again but then she says, "Nathan?"

"Yes?"

"Thank you."

And she sleeps.

Getting Stronger

Annalise is asleep in my arms. We've been together like this for hours and it's good. It's what I've battled for and waited for. It's not perfect, though. Annalise is frighteningly thin and weak.

There's a knock on the door. I don't want to move as I don't want to wake Annalise. Her face is snuggled against my chest, her forehead warm now. I'm hot. Sweaty.

The door opens and an icy wind comes toward me. It's not Mercury.

"How is she?" Gabriel's voice is almost civil. He's standing in the doorway to the bedroom. He looks pissed off.

"Sleeping. She's weak. Really weak. I think she needs food. And liquids, I suppose." I try to sound matter-of-fact, like I'm discussing a medical problem, not the girl in my arms.

Silence. A long silence.

Then he leaves, saying, "I'll get Nesbitt on to it."

I want to say thanks but he'd hate that and anyway he's gone.

Annalise sleeps on.

A short while later Nesbitt appears with a bowl of something. "Soup. With a little pick-me-up of Van's in it." He puts it down. "Gabriel's in a foul mood for some reason. Can't understand him myself; after all, we've rescued the girl."

I ask, "What time is it?"

"No idea. Why?"

"I'm sure it must be after dark but I don't feel bad."

"Oh that. Yes, it's night. Van says Mercury must have had a spell for the bunker. To make it habitable. Very impressive apparently. Van doesn't know how to do it."

I remember now. Mercury had a similar spell for the cottage in Switzerland.

After Nesbitt has gone I wake Annalise as gently as I can. She opens her eyes and says, "I feel dizzy. And a bit strange."

"You've been under the spell for months." I don't say *wasting away* but that's what appears to have been happening.

"Months?"

"Two months."

"Wow, that's a long sleep." She sits up a little and looks around. "Where are we?"

"Mercury's home in Norway."

"And where's Mercury?"

"She's dead."

Annalise thinks about this for a few seconds and then says, "So we're safe?"

"As safe here as anywhere, I think." I lift the soup bowl up. "You need to eat this."

"How did you find me? What happened to Mercury?

Tell me everything that's happened while I've been asleep."

"I will if you eat."

"Deal. I'm hungry."

I feed her soup. I talk while she takes tiny sips, and eventually the bowl is empty and I've told her everything, even about my Gift, even about killing Hunters, and even about killing Pilot. She asks a few questions, not many. Mainly she's quiet, taking it all in. She asks about the Alliance and says it sounds a good thing. And she asks about my Gift and I try to explain but it's hard and I end up just saying that I transform. She insists that killing Hunters to protect myself is understandable but she doesn't comment on Pilot except to say, "I would have died if it wasn't for you."

So I've told her everything. Only of course I haven't.

I haven't told her that one of the Hunters I killed was her brother and that I killed him by ripping his throat out. I haven't mentioned that I tasted his blood. I haven't mentioned anything about the blood, in fact. I haven't told her that when I'm an animal I have a tendency to eat things, like deer and foxes and rats.

And I haven't told her that I like being an animal.

And I definitely haven't told her that a few hours ago I was kissing Gabriel.

But I know this is not the time for that. Annalise nearly died. She's still not well and I just want to savor the good things about us being together.

Annalise looks at me and asks, "What's wrong?"

I shake my head. "Nothing. I'm just worried about you. Your heart kept stopping."

"Well, I'm feeling a bit stronger. I want to see if I can walk around."

I get up first and Annalise swings her legs out of bed and stands and wobbles. "Whoa! Dizzy again." I grab her and she clings to me. "But OK with you here."

She leans on me and I hold her. She's as fragile as glass. I'm careful not to squeeze too hard as I remember her ribs. "Do they hurt?" I ask.

She shakes her head. "A little sore." But she winces when I touch her ribcage. "But I'm alive. I'm awake." She smiles at me. "And my healing is working. I can feel it."

She puts her hand up to my cheek. "You saved me, Nathan. You searched for me and risked everything for me. You're my prince. Coming to my rescue."

"I'm no prince."

She leans her face up to me and kisses me on the lips. "Whatever you are, thank you." Then she stands back and stares at me. "You look tired."

"Rescuing people from evil witches is exhausting, I've discovered."

"*You* need to rest now." She turns. "Oh, look. A bed! That's handy." And she pulls me to it, saying, "Come back here with me."

And I let her guide me to the bed and she lies down and I crawl onto it and I lie next to her. She smells so good. Even after all this time asleep, she smells clean and of her.

She says, "You *are* my prince, my hero. No one else in the world would have done what you've done. Not even my family. In fact especially not my family. But you, the one person everyone told me was evil . . . you risked your life to help me."

She holds me. And I close my eyes. And lying there is good and warm and smells nice and I say to myself that in the morning I'll tell her about Kieran.

She kisses me on my lips nervously, and a bit clumsily for Annalise. I kiss her back, pulling her body against me, and then she's crying. And I know she's crying with relief, at being alive, and I wipe her tears away. And she looks at me, her eyes sparkling. Her cheek is soft under my fingertips and under my lips and I kiss her face and neck and down her throat. And she kisses me too, in the same way, over my face. And we're clinging together, my head against her chest, listening to her heart beating faster now, and I tell myself that she's alive because of me and her heart beats because of me and that has to be good, that has to be good.

Digging

I wake up in bed, close to Annalise, so close that I can feel her warmth. I'm not used to sleeping with someone and it feels strange but nice too. She still smells of her but not so clean now, and I want to kiss her. I open my eyes. She's smiling at me. She looks less pale.

"How are you feeling?" I ask.

"Better. A lot better. And you?"

"I'm good. But hungry, though!"

"As luck would have it Nesbitt just brought us some breakfast. I think he was using it as an excuse to meet me and to find out what we're doing, but anyway it's food and I'm starving too."

"I thought I heard someone." Normally I'd wake up instantly at the sound of someone's voice but for once I've been in a deep sleep.

We eat the porridge—there's enough for ten—and there's jam, honey, and raisins. Annalise eats a large bowlful and lies back, saying she feels good but stinky.

"You're not stinky."

"I need a shower, though." She gets up and walks to the door, saying, "I feel so much stronger. No dizziness."

I think that's a hint that Annalise can get to the bathroom safely alone. I lie on the bed and while I'm waiting for her to come back I fall asleep again.

I wake up as the door clicks open. I'm feeling revived, and pleased that I woke at the slightest sound, though I'm less pleased when I see it's Nesbitt entering the room, not Annalise.

"Had a good sleep, mate?" I'm sure he doesn't expect a reply. He picks up the porridge stuff, saying, "Time's marching on. You've got to get up."

"I'll wait for Annalise."

"She's with Van. You've been asleep for hours, mate. Annalise and Van are checking out the bunker—it's a rabbit warren. And I've been getting the range going and tidying up the mess in the hall. And Gabriel"—he grins—"Gabriel has got the job of gravedigger and you're going to be his assistant."

Gabriel and I are digging on the hillside. It's slow work. The ground is hard, dry and full of large stones and roots. We have to use a pick and an ax to break the earth before we can make any impression with the spades. It takes hours and is done in silence after I realize Gabriel isn't going to reply to anything I say, which is about five minutes into the job.

We finish late in the day as it begins to rain. The sky has darkened and a freezing wind has risen. The rain quickly turns to hail. I'm in the bottom of the bigger grave and I toss my spade out and ask Gabriel to help pull me up. I'm not sure if he's making me wait or just leaving me but after a minute more of sleet I know I'm on my own. I clamber out, slipping in the mud and getting covered in it. Gabriel is sheltering under a tree, watching me. I want to say something about him and me, and about me and Annalise, but as usual I've no idea how to begin, so instead I say, "I get the feeling you'd like me to be in there permanently." I indicate the grave with a nod of my head.

He doesn't even reply to that but asks me, "Are you going to join the Alliance?"

"I said I would, and—"

"Black Witches aren't renowned for keeping their promises."

"I'm not a Black Witch, Gabriel. I'm half White. And I want to do what's right. I think—"

"And what do you think's right about joining them?"

"Soul is evil. He should be stopped . . . I told Annalise about the Alliance and she thinks their cause is right. She wants to join."

Gabriel scowls. "I bet she does. Except, of course, that stopping Soul will involve killing, lots of it. Being whiter than white, being on the side of good is fine and noble and I'm sure Annalise will love that. Until she sees it up close and personal."

"I don't think either of us are under any illusions . . ."

Gabriel turns his head away from me and we're silent for a few moments. I've never seen him in a mood like this and I can tell it's pointless trying to explain things. I pick up my spade to go back to the bunker.

He stands in my way and says, "Talking of up close and personal . . . have you told her about you? Have you told her about your Gift?"

"Yes . . . mostly."

"Mostly?"

I shrug.

"And you've told her about Kieran?"

I shake my head.

"But you're planning on telling her?"

"Yes. Just not yet."

"I never had you down as a coward—so that shows how much I know about people."

"I'm trying to do my best with her, Gabriel. I'm rubbish at talking about stuff and I know I need to tell her but it's hard. And we *are* talking; we're talking about lots of things. You know me, and know my Black side so well, but Annalise sees the other side of me. And I admit I'm scared that she may never understand me or accept me like you do. I'm terrified of that. But that doesn't mean she doesn't know the other side of me, the good side. She's always been able to see that. I want to be with her. I want to be good."

He looks at me. His face is dotted with raindrops but I think there are tears too.

"I love her. I always have. You know that."

"And me?"

And I know he means how I feel about him and me kissing him.

"You're my friend, Gabriel."

"Do you kiss all your friends like that?" But he asks it without the harshness of his other questions. It's a real question.

"Just you."

We're silent. I want to say something but as ever words fail me completely and I daren't reach out to him. I know that would be wrong.

Gabriel says, "You know if we join the Alliance we'll be lucky to end up in one of those." He nods at the grave. "If we get caught we'll be cut up into little bits, and I'm not sure what they do with the bits." He jabs his spade at the ground and says, "I hope I do end up in a grave. My sister hasn't got one—a grave, I mean."

I nod. "All the time they kept me in the cage, I knew they could kill me at any time, and if they caught my father then they'd kill me for sure. I thought they'd bury me by the cage. But I never thought I'd have a grave or mourners or anything. And now if I'm caught and tortured and . . . well, if it happens that way, if I die that way, then that's what will happen. I don't want it to and I'll do what I can to make it not happen but, let's face it, my life isn't ever going to be peace and harmony. I can run wherever I want but they'll come after me, Gabriel. Whether I join the Alliance or not. You know that.

"I have a dream of a quiet life by a river but I can't have it, at least not while Soul and Wallend are alive and there are Hunters in the world. I'll always be looking over my shoulder and the Hunters'll catch me sooner or later. I have to fight for the Alliance and hope that when it's over I'll have the life I want. A life without persecution, outside a cage. I'd like to have one day free like that. To think that nobody was after me. Nobody was hunting me. A day to enjoy. But first I have to fight."

"It'll be bad, Nathan. The fighting."

"Mercury once told me that I was made for killing. I'm sure she didn't envisage I'd kill her. But I'm beginning to think she's right. That is what I'm made for. That's why I'm here."

Gabriel shakes his head. "No one's made for killing. And you aren't."

"And you? What will you do?"

"If you fight then I fight too."

"If you don't believe in it, Gabriel, don't do it."

"I can't not be with you, Nathan. I wanted to leave you in that grave and walk away and I couldn't. I can't walk ten paces away from you without it hurting me. I treasure every second with you. Every second. More than you know." He looks down and then back up into my eyes. "I'll be your friend forever. I'll help you with each breath I take and I'll stay with you. I love you, Nathan. From the day I met you, I loved you and I love you more each day."

I don't know what to say.

"But that doesn't mean I think you're right about things. The Alliance won't be interested in you apart from how many people you can kill. And I think you'll kill lots. And as for the girl you say you love, who doesn't know the first thing about you because you're too afraid to tell her the truth—well, I think you're right to be afraid because she will not understand you; she cannot. And the more you kill and the more she sees that half of you . . ." He shrugs. "I think she'll end up dreading you."

And I think he's finished but then he says, "As for me I'll always love you. Even when I'm buried deep in one of those." He nods at the grave. "I'll still love you. Forever."

Gabriel goes into the bunker and I stand in the rain, letting it wash some of the mud from my clothes.

The Fairborn Is Mine

We've all found our way to the kitchen for food and warmth. Gabriel is speaking to me normally again and Annalise is beside me, though they haven't actually spoken to each other yet. Annalise first met Gabriel in Geneva and sensed then that he didn't like her. I've told her about his feelings for me, and she was surprised but said, "I thought he hated me because I was a White Witch. At least that explains things a little more." I haven't told her that he doesn't trust her, that he thinks she'll betray me.

There's a range in the kitchen, which is like the one in Celia's house in Scotland, and I'm sitting in front of it, my boots propped up against it to dry. Steam is coming off my damp clothes. The kitchen is a surprise. There's no fridge, no freezer, and definitely no microwave but there is a good store of food in the pantry. There are tins, pots, and jars. Three hams, strings of onions and garlic, a sack of potatoes, and shelves of round cheeses. And Nesbitt has found the wine store.

"We'll bury Mercury and Pers tomorrow morning. First thing," Van says.

"And after that? What are you going to do?" Gabriel asks her.

Van looks at me and says, "There's a meeting with the White rebel leaders in Basle in four days' time. I'll be going to that. I'd like you to come with me, Nathan, if you are joining us."

"I said I'd join you and I will. And you also said that you'd return the Fairborn to me."

"I did, didn't I? And I rather expected you'd want it as soon as possible." She takes her cigarette case out of her jacket and says, "Nesbitt, please give the Fairborn to Nathan."

Nesbitt takes the knife from a leather bag that is at Van's feet. He holds it in his hand, looking at it. I know he's not going to just hand it over; that would be too easy for Nesbitt. He looks at me and smiles but he's holding it out to Gabriel. "You want it, Gabby?"

Gabriel shakes his head.

"Go on. Take it. Take the knife and stab me."

Gabriel smiles now. "That's a tempting offer." He reaches over and then hesitates and looks at me, suddenly cautious. "You've used it?"

I nod. "Twice." Once on myself and once on Jessica, and both times the knife felt like it had a life of its own. A soul of its own. And it was bent on cutting open everything.

Nesbitt, grinning, is still holding out the knife.

I say, "Please take that smile off his face, Gabriel. You'd be doing us all a favor."

Gabriel reaches for the Fairborn. His left hand is on the sheath and his right on the handle. He pulls. It looks odd, almost comic: Gabriel pulling and then tugging. The knife seems to be stuck in the sheath.

"Won't come out, will it?" Nesbitt says.

Gabriel looks at me. "No."

Nesbitt takes it and makes a show of trying too.

Van says, "It's made for you, Nathan. For your family. It recognizes its owner and will only cut for you, your father, his father, and so on. It's an extremely powerful object. The magic to do that—to recognize you, to last for a hundred years or more—is exceptional."

Nesbitt tosses the knife over to me. "So not much use to anyone but you."

I catch the Fairborn, stand, move round the table, and slide the blade out of its sheath in a second, putting the tip under Nesbitt's chin. "It really wants to cut you, Nesbitt," I say. Only I'm not just saying it: the knife does want to cut; it feels alive in my hand. There's a darkness to it, a murderous quality. The Fairborn wants blood.

There's something too serious about the Fairborn to torment Nesbitt with it. I look at the knife. The handle is black, as is the blade, which is a strange, almost coarse metal with no shine to it, although it is razor-sharp. It's heavy. I slide it into the sheath of worn black leather and the Fairborn reluctantly goes back. Then I slide it out and it almost rushes into my hand, and I force it in again and I'm getting the feel of it now. I let it slide out once more and then force it in hard.

Scars

It's a bit like one of my old fantasies, only miles better, warmer and much sweatier than I ever thought it would be. I can't move because I don't want to wake Annalise. She's curled up against me now but in the night we were tangled up, all legs and arms, and that was good and this is good. There's nothing bad about this.

When we woke in the night we were hot and caressing each other. She felt each of my scars. Looked at them. Asked me about them. I told her about each one. There are a lot, so it took a long time. Mostly I don't mind talking about them. I told her about the tattoos as well and what Wallend did to me. The scars on my wrist are ugly but they're just scars. The tattoos are a sort of reminder to me of how bad the Council is. I don't really need reminding but there's nothing I can do to get rid of them. The scars on my back are different again. They look the worst. I guess they are the worst.

She said, "That day changed everything. I had no idea what Kieran was going to do. But when he told me to run home, I did. I thought I could tell my mum and dad, that they'd stop him, not for your sake but for Kieran's, so he wouldn't get into trouble.

"But I got home and Dad wouldn't listen. He approved

of what Kieran was doing. Mum just went along with everything he said, as usual. Dad told me that I'd been warned not to see you or speak to you. They said that Kieran was protecting me and he was behaving like a good brother should. And Dad said that he must do what a good father should do too, and make me realize that you were evil. He told me you were as bad as any Black Witch, possibly worse, as you're the son of Marcus. He said that you couldn't be trusted, that I was an innocent girl, an innocent White Whet, who you were bound to prey on. He went on and on and on. How you couldn't be trusted, how you'd grow up into a Black Witch, how your nature was undoubtedly Black, how . . ." She hesitated. "How your mother was evil too and in fact worse than Marcus because she should have known better and, because of her, her husband was killed and you were born. She'd ruined her good family name and more than anything my dad didn't want me to end up like her, like your mother. And of course he loved me and he was acting out of love, and he was locking me in my bedroom because he loved me.

"I think I hate him for his stupidity more than anything," she added.

I asked, "Do you think your father really does love you? I mean . . . I know it sounds like he doesn't but . . ."

"No. He just said the words but made no effort to understand me. It was all about him. He said he was going to lock me up until I realized how wrong I was to deceive my family, to meet you. Mum came and talked to me, saying the same stuff as Dad had said." Tears filled Annalise's eyes.

"When she made no progress with me my father let Connor into my room to talk to me, hoping he would bring me round. Connor was always the only one I could talk to. He can be so gentle but Kieran and Naill push him around and he tries to be like them, tries to please Dad."

Connor was the weaker of the three brothers, the one I beat up at school, even though he was two years older than me.

Annalise carried on. "Connor persuaded me to at least say that I was sorry. He said if I didn't I'd never leave the house again. He said, 'Apologize, have your Giving, and then run away.' I knew he was right. My father would keep me locked up forever if he had to, so I pretended I was sorry. I said they were right, that I had been bad, been fooled by you. I promised to be good. I had to apologize to my dad, my mum, and each of my brothers in turn. They said I'd never be allowed anywhere without one of them being with me."

She shrugged. "It took years but that's how I escaped in the end. Connor was guarding me and he let me get away. I wanted him to come too but he wouldn't."

I said, "I should be grateful to Connor then." But I didn't feel that. I still despised the lot of them.

Annalise stroked my back gently and said, "Kieran told me what they'd done to you. He showed me a photo of you that he'd taken on his phone. You were unconscious; the blood was bubbling on your back."

I nearly interrupted her to tell her Kieran was dead. But still it didn't feel like the right time.

Annalise said, "When I saw the photo I knew then I had to get out. I knew I could never live with people who were so cruel. I realized I'd have to wait but eventually I'd have the chance to get away. I was so unhappy but every day I got through it by thinking of you. I knew you were alive. That kept me going."

And I pulled her to me and held her.

"At times I almost gave up. I never dreamed you and I would be together again, and like this: free."

I said, "When I was imprisoned I had different thoughts that kept me going. Thoughts of the good people in my life: Arran, Deborah, Gran, and you. And I had this special dream for the future. And in this fantasy future I'd live in this wonderful, beautiful valley by a stream and life would be peaceful. And I'd fish and hunt and live quietly." I hesitated but managed to go on. "I still dream of that. Of living somewhere quiet and beautiful . . . and of being with you."

"It sounds perfect." She kissed me again. "When you talk about rivers and mountains, you change. You're different then. I think that's your true self. That's how I love to think of you, at peace with nature and truly happy. Truly free."

As I lie here now with her in my arms, remembering that conversation, I know that although we seem different we're not. She was alone and a prisoner too.

The Burial

We're standing round the graves. Gabriel, Nesbitt, and I have lowered the bodies in, still wrapped up in the tapestries. Van and Annalise have joined us.

"Would you like to share any words of remembrance, Gabriel?" Van says. "Perhaps you might say something for Mercury. You knew her best."

Gabriel stands straighter and says something in French. I think it's a poem. It sounds nice and isn't too long. Then he spits on the ground and says, in English, "Mercury was a coward, cruel and slightly mad, but she loved her sister, Mercy, and she loved Rose. Mercury was a great Black Witch. The world is less for her passing." He picks up some dirt and throws it, rather than scatters it, into the grave.

"Nice, Gabby, nice," Nesbitt says, and shuffles his feet. He picks up some dirt and shakes it in his hand as if he's going to throw dice. "Mercury, you were one in a million. The world is duller but a lot safer without you." He tosses the dirt into the grave. He turns to Pers's grave. "And you were a nasty little piece of work. I wish I'd shot you the first time I saw you."

Van also picks up a handful of earth. "Perhaps, in the future, witches like Mercury will be able to live more peacefully. Pers was a young whet doing what she thought was right." Van throws the grains of soil over both graves.

I pick up some dirt and scatter it in Mercury's grave. She was amazing. Wonderful in her violent way but I killed her and there are no words I want to say. But I remember her love for Rose and I pick up more dirt and throw that down on the ground too, for Rose. And I pick up more dirt and throw it into Pers's grave for her and for Pilot. Then I pick up more for all the Blacks killed by each other and by Whites, for all who are dead and gone. I toss it in the air and watch it fall.

I say nothing. I can't find words for all that; there are none.

Nesbitt is watching with a bemused look. Annalise stands beside me. She stays quiet and still. Van goes into the bunker and Annalise touches my arm to tell me that she's going in too.

Gabriel gets the spades that are lying by the entrance. He throws one to me and we start to fill in the graves.

Mapping

After burying Mercury and Pers, I join Annalise. She's been given the task of continuing the search of the bunker and wants to make a map of it. She says, "I keep getting lost. All the corridors look the same."

I draw the map: the main corridors and the numbers of doors off each. There are three main levels of rooms, each with sublevels, and each connected by steps and slopes. The top level is smallest, the middle a bit larger, and the bottom is the most extensive; that's the one with the great hall and the entrance tunnel to the bunker. There is definitely no way in other than the one we came through.

The kitchen and food stores are on the top level. The bedrooms, hallway, library, and music rooms are on the lower level, and the intriguing rooms are in the middle. These are the storerooms. The rooms full of the stuff that Mercury has acquired over the years. These are the rooms I expect might contain some weapons—not guns but maybe magical things similar to the Fairborn.

One room is full of clothes and shoes stored in drawers and wardrobes. Annalise holds a dress out. It's pale pink, silk. "So beautiful," she says. "Do you think she ever wore them? They all look like new."

"I don't know. Mercury only ever wore gray dresses as far as I know." All the clothes appear to be for the same-sized woman. Mercury-sized. But also the size of her beloved twin sister, Mercy.

The next room contains men's clothes, but there are fewer things. Three suits, some shirts, three hats, two pairs of shoes, and two pairs of boots. I hold one of the suits up against me. I can tell it'll fit. I think these might be the clothes of Mercy's husband, my great-grandfather.

Annalise says, "Do you think it's OK for me to take something? Something different to wear and maybe something to sleep in? Some shoes as well?"

"No one else is going to use them."

I wait outside while she tries things on. She joins me, smiling nervously, looking a bit like Van in a masculine pale gray suit.

"It's nice to put clean things on. They aren't musty or stale at all. Maybe you should try one of the suits?" I know she's joking but I don't want to wear my great-grandfather's clothes.

"What's the matter?" she asks.

I shake my head and realize that I don't feel good but I try to ignore it and say, "I'm glad you're happy. You seem like you have a purpose."

"Trying clothes on?"

"No, you know what I mean. The Alliance seems to have inspired you."

"Yes, it has, and you have too. You've shown me that

you can do so much if you fight for it. For the first time in years, I can see there's hope. Hope for me and you and all witches."

Annalise slips round to stand in front of me and reaches up to kiss me but I feel dizzy and lose my balance and have to lean against the wall, taking deep breaths. The bunker is like a dungeon. The walls feel like they're coming in on me. It's the feeling of being inside at night. I say, "I need to get outside."

On the way we find Nesbitt in the great hall.

He says, "Van thinks that now Mercury's dead her spell to make it bearable inside is fading. It's back to the night-smoke."

He has already poured some into a bowl and now he lights it. We both lean close and inhale.

Not Resisting

The nightsmoke lights the bedroom with a pale green glow. I move my hand through the cool green flame and watch it move across the surface of the milky liquid. Annalise is behind me, snuggling against me; she slides her hands up my T-shirt, saying, "Let's go to bed."

I turn and kiss her but hold her arms and back away a little. "I've been thinking about that."

"So have I." She slides her hands inside my T-shirt again.

"I mean . . ." I can't say it. We've slept together but I can't talk about it.

"What do you mean? Are you trying to say we should be taking precautions?"

"I don't want . . ."

She kisses me. "And I definitely don't want . . . But . . . but I feel that I've been given an amazing second chance at life and I'm so lucky to have found you and I don't want to be sensible; I want to be with you. I don't want to sleep alone." She kisses my lips. "I want you to stay with me."

"And I want to stay with you but . . ."

"We'll be careful."

I think I know what she means.

"Or you could just resist me?" And she slides her body against mine, smiling.

"I don't see how if you do that."

"I'll wear a nightdress."

"I really don't think that's going to help."

She kisses me. "Has it occurred to you that I might be finding you irresistible?"

It hadn't.

"Well?"

"Um. No."

"Well, you are." But she folds her arms and steps back from me. "However, I'll do my best to resist."

"OK. Me too."

"So . . . what shall we do? Play cards?"

I laugh. "Haven't got a pack."

"I Spy?"

"I don't really like games."

"Me neither. And I've just discovered that I don't really like resisting."

We're lying in bed, cuddled together, going through my lists of good and bad qualities. I'm giving her my good points and she's giving me the bad.

"Thoughtful."

"Ha! Uncommunicative."

"I communicate OK when I have to." I kiss her. "See, like that. That means . . ." and I was going to say *I like you* but it means more than that and I can't say it and I know I'm stuck.

"What does it mean, Mr. Communicative?"

"It means . . ."

She kisses me back and says, "I think it means I've won that point."

"Your go then."

"Loner."

"What's wrong with being independent?"

"Silent."

"I think you mean 'thoughtful,' as I've just said."

"Grubby."

"I knew that one was coming. Tough."

"Rough."

"Am I?" I try to be gentle with her.

"I mean the skin on your hands is rough."

"As I said, tough."

"Your turn."

I say, "How about . . . sexy?"

She laughs.

Obviously I'm not sexy. I didn't think I was and I was sort of joking but I didn't think she'd laugh at me.

She says, "I love it when you blush and look confused."

"I'm not blushing."

"And you can add 'liar' to the list too."

"So I'm not sexy?"

"I really don't think that's the right word. That makes

me think of fains who spend lots of time in front of the mirror, styling their hair. Which definitely isn't you. But there's something about you that makes me want to kiss you and hold you and stay with you."

"Sweet. I remember you called me sweet once."

"I don't remember that. You're not sweet."

"Phew!"

"But you are gentle and huggable." She hugs me.

"I thought you were doing the bad points."

"Let's do mine," Annalise says.

"OK. You do good points, I'll do bad."

She says, "Right, well, obviously . . . I'm highly intelligent."

"A little big-headed."

"Accurate and precise."

"Yet unable to follow simple instructions to give one point at a time."

"Accurate and precise are the same thing."

Something suddenly occurs to me and I ask her, "Have you found your Gift yet?" It's almost a year since her Giving.

"Whoa! That's a change of subject! Or is that a weakness?"

"No, I was just thinking about you being intelligent, accurate, and precise. I mean, it does all sound like potions will be your thing."

"Oh, I see. Well, I always thought it would be potions but I'm really bad at them. It's definitely not that."

"You must have some hidden strength then, one we haven't worked out yet." And I kiss her nose. Then I kiss her cheek and ear and neck, climbing over her.

"Um, Nathan, I thought we weren't . . ."

"I've realized what your Gift is." And I'm kissing down her neck and on to her shoulder.

"What?"

"Being irresistible."

Dresden, Wolfgang, and Marcus

The next day Van wants Annalise to spend time in the library with her and Gabriel. Nesbitt and I are to continue to search the bunker for anything that will be of use to the Alliance. We head for Mercury's corridor, as we call it.

There are two rooms of "treasure": jewels and furniture and several paintings, which we assume are either valuable or magical in some way. "But it's impossible to know what they do, and I can't see them being bugger-all use to us," Nesbitt declares and walks out of the room.

The next room is the "blood room." Shelves of bottles of blood, stolen from Council stores, that Mercury used to sell for potions or to carry out the Giving ceremony for those without parents or grandparents willing or able to do it. There must be one for my mother here: the blood Mercury would have used if she'd performed my Giving. Each bottle has a glass stopper fixed with a wax seal. Through the wax is a ribbon and to that is attached a label giving the name of the blood donor. There are eleven shelves on three walls and each shelf holds thirty or more slim bottles. Except that some bottles are missing—there are gaps. Perhaps where a bottle has been used or sold. The blood will be useful for Half Bloods, such as Ellen, who helped me when

I was in London after I escaped. Ellen's father is a fain, her mother dead, and the Council will only allow her a Giving if she works for them. Her mother's blood is probably here: *we* could ensure she had a Giving.

"This stuff is more valuable than all those jewels and paintings. It'll bring in more Half Bloods to the Alliance than anything else." Nesbitt grins at me. "Power to the people, eh?"

We move on to the final room in the corridor, which is hard to move around in because it's so full of jars, packets, and sacks.

Nesbitt says, "It's like a Californian wholefood salad: packed with natural ingredients." He passes me a jar and adds, "Not for the strict vegetarians, though." It's hard to see through the frosted glass and the light is dim but I can make out two eyeballs floating in clear liquid.

"What use would they be?" I ask.

"None to Mercury now. And, like most of this crap, not much use to the Alliance either." Nesbitt puts the jar back on the shelf.

We head to the library to find the others. I'm surprised to see Gabriel and Annalise sitting at a table, talking to each other. Before I can join them Van takes me by the arm, saying, "They're getting on better without you, I think. Leave them to it." She steers me to the back of the room. "Anyway I want to show you something."

It's a tall bookcase filled with absurdly large leather-bound books, each almost a meter high and some as wide as my hand. In the wood of the bookcase is a small brass keyhole. Van takes one of Mercury's hairpins from her pocket and puts the point into the keyhole. The front of the bookcase opens out to reveal another behind it. This too is filled with leather-bound books but they are all small and flimsy, like school exercise books.

Van pulls one out at random. "They're Mercury's diaries. A daily record of all she did and whom she met. I started going through them yesterday, hoping to find details of when and where she made her cuts. I think that's the way Mercury traveled, and it's certainly quicker and easier than by car."

"You've not found anything yet?"

"Not about the cuts but Mercury describes everything, including the people she meets. She assesses them, working out who will be of use, how they can be manipulated or controlled, who's a danger, and who can be trusted—not many in the latter category."

"Does she say anything about me?" I ask.

"I'm sure she does but I've not come to that yet. However, there are other things that might interest you." She picks up a book that's lying apart from the others, and I see a page has been marked in it.

She says, "Gabriel found this. Let me read it to you."

"In Prague for three days. Saw Dresden. She had a child she wanted me to take, a girl, six years old. A nasty little thing, scrawny, sulky, and far too intelli-

gent for her age. Dresden was keen to show her off, as if I might be impressed. The girl's clever, I'll say that for her, but I wouldn't trust her for two seconds. Dresden calls the girl Diamond, as if she's a precious little star, but she needs far more than a polish. She would not be worth the effort. I wouldn't train her for all the diamonds in the world. I'd rather eat my own liver.

"Dresden is an amazingly simple soul. I can almost feel sorry for her. She's no great beauty: slight, small, brown hair and eyes; she should be forgettable but when she smiles . . . ah . . . her Gift is as simple as a smile, and the room changes, the mood changes. She is mesmerizing. When she wants to she can even lift my mood, make me smile. And Dresden's laugh is a thing of beauty even to my heart. Her Gift is joy, which is ironic, of course, given that she really brings little true happiness.

"Dresden used her Gift to work her way upward in Black circles, most interestingly with Marcus. She met him when he was going through a particularly miserable phase, and expected to bring joy to him as was her wont. But, while to start with he was captivated, her influence on him grew weaker and he eventually saw her for what she was: a simple girl with a big smile.

"I asked Dresden where she met Marcus. 'Near Prague' was her answer, and I got the feeling that could have meant as near as New York or Tokyo. When they met? Here she was a little more giving—'last summer.'"

Van breaks off and goes back a page. "This was written thirteen years ago. So Dresden met Marcus when you were four." She carries on reading.

"Dresden is bitter about Marcus. She tries to pass it off as if she broke up with him but everyone knows that he has no real interest in her—or any other woman for that matter. A day with Dresden these days is a dreary time and I couldn't wait to leave once I realized I wasn't going to get more from her.

"Pilot joined us for one evening. She's a good companion, such an intelligent contrast to Dresden. She's moving to Geneva. Told me of a remote valley that I'd like. I'll go to see it, travel with her. It sounds a suitable place for visitors.

"Pilot seemed taken with the girl. I couldn't be bothered to argue. I think Pilot is somewhat under Dresden's spell—though I don't think that will last long either."

That's all Van reads and I don't feel like discussing it.

I walk to the corner of the room, sit on the floor, and lean against the wall. I wonder about my father. I do believe he loved my mother and I'm sure she loved him. But she was married to another man, to a White Witch, one of her own, and maybe she did try to make that work. Gran told me that my mother agreed to see Marcus once a year, when it was totally safe. But there's no such thing as totally safe and their final meeting ended in disaster: her husband dead and me conceived. And because of me my mother was forced to kill herself. As for Marcus, what did he get? Not even one meeting a year but a son who's predicted to kill him.

So it's not surprising if he sought solace, sought love, elsewhere. I can't blame him. I wish he'd found it. But I think it's clear it didn't happen, and Dresden doesn't sound like a promising candidate. She definitely smacks of desperation.

He must feel very alone. Totally alone.

And I look across the room at Gabriel and Annalise and I know they love me and I love them and maybe with the Alliance we have a chance of changing the world and making things better, not just for me but for those who care about me.

Gabriel comes over to sit with me.

I say, "You're speaking to Annalise."

"Know your enemy," he replies but smiles.

I'm not sure if he's joking so I say, "She's not your enemy."

"Don't worry. I'm being polite. We're both being very polite." He holds up another of Mercury's diaries, saying, "Annalise found this; she thought I should read it to you."

"In Berlin, what was East Berlin. Rain. Damp apartment. Met Wolfgang. Haven't seen him for twenty years. He looks much the same, only a few more lines on his face. But he's different: weary, older obviously, and surprisingly a lot wiser too. He wasn't happy to see

me and he made the point that he was leaving for South America now he had.

"He'd spent a few days of the previous month with Marcus. They were never exactly close friends but then Marcus has no friends, though for some reason Wolfgang was one person Marcus could put up with, one person who didn't irritate him. It is Marcus who has irritated Wolfgang, offended Wolfgang, as he offends all people eventually, by killing someone Wolfgang loved. Wolfgang's friend Toro, it seems, irritated Marcus in the extreme and Marcus killed him. Toro was jealous of their friendship, Marcus dismissive, then angry, and then violent. Toro sounds like a fool and Wolfgang admitted as much but he says, 'Marcus knew that. He could have let him go, let him live, but he has this power thing and no patience. None. I mean, not even for a second before the whole animal thing takes over. He can control it but he chooses not to. He killed Toro. Ripped him apart. I found them. Marcus covered in blood. Covered in Toro.'

"Wolfgang went on to say, 'Marcus should have killed me. I could see he was thinking about it. He washed himself and chunks of Toro fell off him, off his shoulder; a piece was stuck on his arm. He washed in the lake and dressed and walked up to me and I'm sure he was thinking of killing me—not eating me, not that—but just killing me, cold-blooded, with a bolt of lightning or whatever he chose. But he didn't. I think that's all about his power too.

He takes life, he doesn't take it. He can do what he likes.'

"Marcus had said to him, 'I know you don't believe me, Wolfgang, but part of me is sorry about Toro: the part of me that loves you. I know you hate me for killing him. I think you should go. Don't come back.'

"Wolfgang's response was: 'I left. That was a month ago.'

"He was quiet. A tear ran down his cheek and I thought it was because of Toro but it was because of what he was about to tell me. Because he was about to betray Marcus.

"He told me where Marcus was living. He said, 'He'll have moved on but it shows you the sort of place he likes. Always places like that. That is where he feels comfortable. That is where he can make a safe place to live.'

"And I have to say I'm surprised. Marcus has no home. He lives mostly like an animal. In a den. A den made of sticks. Partly underground. A small clearing near a lake. He spends long periods as an animal. He hunts and eats as an animal. Wolfgang says, 'Sometimes it's as if he's losing his humanity.'

"Wolfgang asked him about the infamous vision that his son would kill him. Marcus said, 'Yes, Wolfie, I believe it. I've avoided Nathan all my life. Best put it off for as long as possible, don't you think? The inevitable. Or do I get it over with?'

"Wolfgang thought Marcus was so lonely, so sad, that part of him, the human part, wanted to get it over with but ironically the animal in him was the part that

wanted to live. Marcus told him, 'As an eagle I know nothing. I feel nothing but flying and living. Imagine that . . . wonderful . . . forever.'

"Wolfgang told me that Marcus meets others only rarely, to keep aware of what's happening within the different witch communities and to hear any news of his son. That is his only real interest in the human world now—Nathan. For the rest, I think he'd gladly leave it all behind. Marcus washes, pampers himself, and dresses smartly for the few occasions he meets others. There's still a lot of vanity left in him: he still likes to look in the mirror and the human side comes back. But when he's in the woods he's wild.

"Wolfgang said, 'Wild is an interesting word. We imagine wild to be untamed and out of control but, of course, nature isn't like that; nature is controlled, ordered, extremely disciplined by all its elements. Animals in herds have leaders and followers; there are disputes but still there is an organization. And animals hunt in certain ways, at certain times and for certain kinds of prey—it is terribly predictable. Marcus is like that—know his ways and you'll find him. And, if you have his son, eventually he'll come to you.'"

Gabriel looks back a few pages in the book. "This was dated just a year ago. Mercury must have thought she'd won the lottery when you came looking for her."

The Cut

•••••

The day wears on and I'm still sitting on the floor of the library, watching the others reading through the diaries. Van finds a reference to Pilot visiting Mercury at the bunker and then leaving to go to Basle.

"Basle is a historic meeting place," Van says. "It sounds like one of the cuts comes out there."

"I was thinking about Pilot," I say. "If I have access to Pilot's memories about Mercury then I must have a memory of going through the cut. But I can't find anything. Even the images of her building dams are getting fainter."

Van looks over to me. "The memories will fade if you don't access them. Alas, we didn't realize that the cuts would be important. Before, you were focusing on the outside and a place name."

That's when Nesbitt shouts, "Bingo!"

He's at the other end of the library, looking through scrolls of maps. He walks over to the central table, carrying one, a big grin on his face.

"Of course," Van says as she looks at it. "Mercury made a map of her cuts."

I get up to look. At least I can read maps.

It looks similar to the map I made of the bunker. Nesbitt

points to a small, fine blue line in one of the rooms. "Each blue line is a cut and each one is numbered. There are eleven. The key says this one goes to Germany." He points to others. "These go to Spain. New York. Algeria. This one is 'Switzerland: closed.'"

Van lights a cigarette and says, "So. We need a couple of volunteers to check out one of the cuts."

Gabriel and I look at each other and grin.

Van wants us to go through the cut to Germany, as it appears to come out near Basle where the next Alliance meeting is. That cut is in a room down one of the corridors off the great hall. We all go there. It's a small room, bare except for a thick rug.

"But where exactly is the cut?" Annalise asks.

Gabriel moves to the middle of the rug, saying, "Only one way to find it. I think she'd land on the rug when she came through so . . ." He takes a step nearer to the back wall and slides his hand into the air, feeling for the cut. He moves his hand just a centimeter or two along for each try, working his way sideways. He finds nothing. He repeats the process, this time lower, still moving along slowly. Then he repeats it again and then one more time before he snaps his hand back, saying, "It's there."

Van claps her hands. "Excellent!"

Annalise says, "I've been thinking about Mercury having visitors. She wouldn't want them coming through and wandering around her home without her knowing. Would she have a trespass spell in here like the one on the roof of the cottage in Switzerland? Would you need her to help you across the boundary when you get back?"

"She never allowed anyone she didn't trust here," Van says. "Her diaries only show Rose and Pilot gaining entry. She believed no one would find the cuts. I don't think there's a trespass spell."

"So let's test it out," Nesbitt says, eager to get on.

"Yes," Van agrees and looks at me and Gabriel. "All you have to do is go through. Find out where in Germany you come out: nearest roads, towns, transport. Check for Hunters, of course. And report back."

So that's us told.

Gabriel grabs my hand in his and interlocks our fingers, puts his sunglasses on, and says to the others, "We'll be back." He slides his left hand into the cut and we're sucked through.

I breathe out slowly as I twirl through the darkness: a tip from Nesbitt. I suspect it's a trick and will really make me feel worse. There's dim light ahead, which brightens briefly as we land on grassy ground. I'm surprised that I don't feel anywhere near as dizzy and ill as previous trips through cuts have left me.

We're in a forest by a ruined stone building. The air is still and quiet. The trees are full of summer's green richness. It's hot too. There is birdsong and I can hear distant traffic.

I say to Gabriel, "Cars. That way," and indicate to my left with a nod.

He's already feeling around for the cut. "Gotcha," he says, and smiles.

"So that was easy," I say. "Now what?"

"Let's head to the road, see if we can work out where we are."

That evening we're back round the table. Things are going well. We've been through two cuts. The one in the small, bare room leads to the place we went to in Germany, which is 150 kilometers from Basle according to the road signs. The cut in Mercury's bedroom goes to a place in Spain in the mountains. We went through that cut and walked to the nearest village and found it on an atlas when we got back. It's a couple of hours' walk from Pilot's home.

Van is meeting with the White rebels tomorrow morning and she wants me and Nesbitt to go but I want Gabriel with me and I can't leave Annalise.

"We're all in the Alliance. We all go," I say.

PART FIVE

RIVERS OF BLOOD

Die Rote Kürbisflasche

We all came through the cut last night. Nesbitt got a car and drove us to the outskirts of Basle. Now Nesbitt, Gabriel, and me are in the center of the city. We're the advance party, on the lookout for Hunters. Van and Annalise are following us in.

Basle is a city of young people, it seems, on the border of Germany, France, and Switzerland, but I hear English spoken too. There are tourists, families, and people going to work. We try to blend in with them but we don't look like tourists or a family, though I suppose we are going to work. Nesbitt knows the way to the meeting place at Die Rote Kürbisflasche—the Red Gourd—and he's taking us the long route.

Nesbitt says that the Red Gourd is a bar in the oldest part of town. We cross the wide, fast-flowing river and make a circuit of the hill on which the old town is built. We see no Hunters. We take it slow and work our way in spirals up the hill, the cobbled streets getting narrower and older as we go. There are fewer and fewer people until we reach an alley with only a cat walking down it and an old woman cleaning her windows. We don't go down the alley but walk away and wait and return half an hour later. The old woman has disappeared and so has the cat. We haven't seen any Hunters.

Halfway down the alley is a wooden door, and above that, hanging out over the street, rather than a written sign, is a metal gourd, small and more rusty orange than red. This is the place.

The door is oak and almost black with age. Nesbitt pushes it open and enters. Gabriel is ahead of me and he holds his arm up toward me as an indication to go slow and take care. We move forward, down four stone steps which curve to the left, and go through a dull red, heavy, woven curtain that hangs from a black metal rail.

We're in a low-ceilinged, narrow room with a bar running the length of the wall and a number of wooden tables with red candles on them and chairs with red padded seats. Behind the bar is a tanned, middle-aged man with spiky blond hair and intense blue eyes with black glints crackling in them. A Black Witch.

Nesbitt greets him and introduces us. The barman is called Gus. When he's introduced to me he doesn't shake my hand as he does Gabriel's. He says in a strong German accent, "Half and half, eh?"

Nesbitt laughs. "You got that right: half human, half animal."

Gabriel says, "And always pissed off—though I can't imagine why when he's in your company, Nesbitt."

"Anyone else here yet?" Nesbitt asks Gus.

"Celia and a Half Blood girl with her. Two more Whites due any minute."

So Celia has avoided being caught since we last saw her in Barcelona.

I walk to the end of the room to check it out. There's a cubicle at the far end and it's occupied. I expect to see Celia but she isn't there. A girl is. She stands when she sees me and smiles.

"Good to see you, Ivan," she says. "You're looking as scruffy as usual."

I go to her and put my arms round her. "Nikita." And it really is her, my friend from London. I keep hold of her. She feels small and I look at her face, still so young, her eyes that amazing blue-green of Half Bloods.

"It's good to see you, Ellen," I say.

She suits the name Nikita better. That's what she said her name was the first time we met, when I called myself Ivan. But, whatever she's called, I trust her totally. I hug her again.

She smiles. "You'll ruin your reputation. You're supposed to be mean and moody."

Nesbitt appears at my shoulder and says, "Don't worry, kid, he can change in an instant."

I don't, though. I really am in a great mood, seeing Ellen again.

I introduce her to Gabriel and Nesbitt and, while she explains who she is to Gabriel, I scan her face, trying to gauge if she has any news, any bad news, from the world of White Witches.

She says to me, "I know you're worried about Arran but he's fine. He's left London and is on his way to France. I'm going up to meet him after we leave here."

"He's joining the rebels?"

"Yes. Things are moving fast now. It's all gone crazy. The Hunters attacked a gathering of Black Witches outside Paris a week ago. Twenty were killed in the fighting and the rest were captured; the adults were taken prisoner but the children were executed. Jessica had them all hanged. Soul put out an announcement about it, saying it was an important victory and a step forward for all White Witches. He said the children didn't have to suffer Retribution in this case, that he was being lenient. But the adults he took aren't to suffer Retribution either. He's using them for research into witch abilities."

"What does that mean?" I ask.

"Basically Wallend is experimenting on them."

I shake my head but somehow I feel I shouldn't be surprised. "He's sick" is all I can think to say.

"The Council says that it's valid research for the protection of all White Witches. Course no one knows exactly how this will protect them, but the Council says that anyone who objects is against White Witches and is supporting Blacks. Everyone is having to declare which side they're on. And most of the White Witches are saying they support Soul and Wallend."

"And Deborah?" I ask. "Is she in France with Arran?"

"You'd better ask Celia about her. That info's above my pay grade."

"And what is your pay grade? Aren't you a little young to be a rebel fighter, Ellen?"

"I'm not a fighter; I'm a scout. But, Nathan, you have no idea how useless most White Witches are. Honestly, most of them are like fains; none of them have ever learned how to fight. They left it all up to the Hunters. The best you can say about them is that they're good at healing potions. The most useful people in the Alliance are the ex-Hunters and the Half Bloods. Except there are only two ex-Hunters and nine Half Bloods."

"What about Black Witches?" I ask.

"Some have joined but few have your skills, Nathan." I reel round to face Celia, who continues: "Which is why we're grateful that you're here."

"I don't care how grateful you are." I swear at her and my hand is on my knife. "Keep away from me, Celia. I'm serious. Don't sneak up on me."

"I wasn't sneaking up, Nathan."

"And don't fucking argue with me!"

I walk away from them to the far end of the room. Gabriel comes with me.

He says, "You're shaking."

"I'm OK." He gives me a look and I repeat, "I'm OK."

After a pause he asks, "What do you want to do?"

"Kill 'em all." I'm joking but only a bit. "Wallend is experimenting on other witches like he did on me. He strapped me down and tattooed me. That was worse than being with Celia. That was the worst thing of all. At least Celia occasionally treated me like a human being. But to Wallend I was just some kind of lab rat. No one should have to go through that."

"No," Gabriel agrees. And I think that even Gabriel is beginning to believe that the Alliance's cause is just.

I say to him, "We work with the Alliance until Wallend and Soul are dead."

He nods.

Van and Annalise have arrived and I take a deep breath and join them.

There are ten of us. Three Black Witches: Van, Gabriel, and Gus, who it seems is more than just a barman but also a key Black Witch with extensive contacts throughout Europe. On the White Witch side is Celia, another White Witch from England called Grace, a third White from Italy called Angela, plus Annalise. There are two Half Bloods, Nesbitt and Ellen. Then there's me.

Celia says, "I believe we're safe here but we'll keep the meeting short. First I take it that, as you're here, you are joining us, Nathan?"

"Until I change my mind."

She looks into my eyes; hers are a pale blue filled with white shards. Then she does something I'm not expecting. She holds out her hand. "Then we're on the same side," she says. "Welcome to the AFW."

"The what?"

"The Alliance of Free Witches."

"Ha! Well, it's no thanks to you that I'm one of those."

"But we're all very glad you are one and that you want to help ensure other witches remain free too."

Her hand is still out and I ignore it, saying, "What I want is to see Soul and Wallend dead. And quite a lot of other White Witches too. That's why I'm here."

She says, "Am I one of those you want to see dead, Nathan?"

"You'd have a bullet in your brain if you were."

"If you join the Alliance you'll have to take orders from me. Can you?" she asks.

I manage a smile. "As long as they're not stupid ones."

"Do you expect them to be?"

I make her wait before I say, "No."

"Good. I don't expect they will be either but I'm sure you'll be the first to tell me if they are."

Her hand is still outstretched. She says, "Will you shake hands?"

"I'm struggling not to spit on you at the moment."

She laughs a loud bark of a laugh and withdraws her hand. "I have missed you, Nathan. Even though I'm sure you've not missed me."

And, sitting across the table from her, I don't think she has any idea what it was like for me, or for any prisoner, being chained up and beaten. She's an intelligent woman but she hasn't got a clue sometimes. Only if you've been there can you know.

Van asks for an update since her last meeting with Celia. That was only two weeks ago but in that time there's been the massacre in Paris, and Soul has replaced all the Council members with his own people: Wallend is now on the Council. Several White Witches have been arrested for colluding with the rebels. "Including Clay," Celia says.

"What?" says Nesbitt.

"A trumped-up charge but Clay was having serious doubts about Soul. He'd lost his job, his status, his reputation, everything. Well, everything except his freedom and now he's lost that too."

Celia continues. "I heard that Isch's house in Barcelona was raided shortly after we were there. Isch took poison and died; some of the girls were captured and tortured. I knew that my name would soon pop up on their lists. Soul has named those he wants for interrogation, including the ex-Council Leader Gloria; her husband and sister, Grace; plus myself and another Hunter called Greatorex. Soul was right to have them on his list—we're all members of the AFW.

"Jessica is leading the Hunters. And I have to say she's doing a good job. The Hunters are a mostly female organization and they're delighted to have a woman in charge again. She has plenty of new recruits and has made attacks on Black Witch communities in northern France,

Holland, and Germany. The biggest has been the one in Paris but as far as I can tell she's killed over sixty Black Witches so far and has lost no Hunters in those attacks.

"But Jessica has problems too and they'll grow. Even with all her new recruits, she's going to have to spread the Hunters thinly if she wants to cover all of Europe. And many of those recruits will be less well-trained and certainly less experienced than the core Hunter army.

"Our own disadvantage is numbers. But, being small, we can move quickly to attack the Hunters. We need to move now to attack, to slow the recruitment and training of more Hunters. We must use guerrilla tactics to do that, and to win—but they happen to be what I specialize in.

"However," says Celia, "there is one final problem. Black Witches are beginning to wake up to what's going on but they don't trust me and we need to attract them to our cause. The Alliance is mainly made up of White Witches and Half Bloods from Britain. We have few influential Black Witches among us. Though we do, of course, have Van and Gus."

Gus nods. "My influence is minimal, Celia. And, as I've said before, to be a true Alliance we need to have a strong representation of all witches: Whites, Blacks, and even Half Bloods. But the Black Witches I speak to are not interested. They don't believe they should fight alongside White Witches. They say they'll fight back against the Hunters if they're attacked. I tell them about the Black Witches who've already been killed but . . ." He shrugs. "Black Witches aren't interested in causes or armies or alliances."

Celia counters, "But you and Van and now Gabriel have joined us. So some Black Witches do listen."

Gus turns to Gabriel and asks, "Why are you here, Gabriel?"

"Because I'm with Nathan."

"So if Nathan is killed or leaves?"

"If he leaves I leave. If he's killed"—he looks at me—"I don't know . . ."

Gus says, "We need someone who will attract other Black Witches to the cause. But I don't know of any other Black Witch who will join just because Nathan is here." He looks into my eyes. "He's not a Black Witch." The black in his own eyes gleams at me and I stare back at him.

Gus is just another racist snob. The witch world is full of them.

"What are you really suggesting, Gus?" asks Celia.

"To attract Black Witches, we need someone they respect, someone who is the embodiment of all that is Black."

"And who is that?" Van asks, trying to suppress a smile. "I'm rather disappointed it isn't me."

Gus laughs with her. "Sorry, Van, but you've always been seen as too willing to work with non-Blacks, even fains."

"So you're thinking of someone who represents 'old Blacks'?" Celia sighs and ruffles her spiky hair. "Mercury would be one, I suppose?"

"Yes, she—" Gus begins.

Van interrupts. "Mercury's dead."

"Killed by Hunters?"

"No. Killed by . . . us." And she waves her hand vaguely toward Nesbitt, Gabriel, and me. "In self-defense, I hasten to add, and with this as my memento." And she turns her face to the light to show her burns. "But even if she was alive, I couldn't imagine Mercury joining the Alliance. She would have seen no benefit to herself in joining, no . . . honor in it. I understand that. There are several Black Witches as powerful as Mercury: Linden, Dell, Suave . . . but they all think the same way. All the most powerful Blacks will surely be unwilling to risk everything to fight with us—except one. Fortunately he's the most powerful of them all." And she looks at me and somehow I knew it was coming to this all along.

"Marcus?" I ask.

"If he joins there's a chance others will too," Van says.

Gus smirks. "If he joins we won't need the others."

"Is this why I'm really here, why you wanted me to join the Alliance: to somehow bring in Marcus?"

"No. I want you because you're an excellent fighter," Celia says. "And I don't want Marcus. He'll cause too many problems with the Whites in the Alliance."

"Including yourself, Celia?" Van asks.

She doesn't answer but she's having to think hard.

"Nathan has put his past behind him and come to work

with you. We all must do the same if we're to move forward," Van says.

Celia still doesn't answer.

I say, "I can't see him joining anyway."

"But you'd be willing to try to persuade him?" Van asks.

"Well . . ." I'm not sure.

"No. We haven't agreed to this." Celia looks around the table. "Marcus is murderous. He's killed too many White Witches. The rebels won't stand for it."

"They won't stand for losing," Van says. "Marcus will make all the difference to the Alliance's success. Yes, he's killed many White Witches but he's killed a lot of Black Witches too. Most importantly, he's killed lots of Hunters. And everyone knows that. They may not like him but the White rebels want more than anything to be on the winning side because, if they lose, they'll find no mercy from Soul. Marcus will make it a winning side."

Celia says, "I can organize our army without him. We'll manage it. It'll take time but—"

"You said yourself a minute ago that we need to attack immediately. And I agree; if we don't stop Jessica now our fight will only get harder. Exactly how many people do you have that can fight, Celia?" Van asks.

"There are nearly a hundred in the Alliance. I'm training the able ones and—"

"How many could you send out to fight the Hunters today?"

Celia sticks out her lip and glances at me. "At this moment? Very few."

"How few?" Van persists.

"Including myself, Nathan, Gabriel . . . nine."

Gus shakes his head.

"But the training is coming on well; they're just not fighters at the moment. The younger ones, the ones with certain Gifts, will be good soldiers in a few months—"

"We won't have a few months if the Hunter army grows," Van says. "And if this is a new society we are creating, a new order, we should be willing to forgive past crimes and go forward together."

"But—"

"No, Celia. All witches must be given a chance, even Marcus. If he then breaks our rules, that's different, but past crimes should be under amnesty."

Grace says, "This is going nowhere. We need to vote on it. A representative of each part of the Alliance: White Witches, Black Witches, Half Bloods, and Half Codes. Nesbitt, you vote for half Blacks, Ellen for half Whites. Celia for White Witches, Van for Blacks, and you for the Half Codes, Nathan."

"Those in favor?" asks Van.

Hands go up round the table. Everyone apart from me and Celia votes to invite Marcus to join the Alliance.

"So three to two, the vote is carried," Grace says. She looks at me. "Why did you vote against, Nathan?"

I don't know the answer, except that I don't think my father will fit with these people: people who vote. I remember Wolfgang's story about him killing his friend and I have a bad feeling—he's too wild. But I don't mention that; I just say, "It's a waste of time. We have no way of contacting him and he won't join anyway."

Gus says, "You're wrong. I do have a way of contacting him—and it's your job to get him to join."

"You've got his phone number?" Nesbitt smirks.

"How I contact him is confidential," Gus replies.

"Fine," Celia says. "How soon, though?" She's full of urgency now. She's not happy about Marcus but she's used to working for Hunters and doing what she's told. I know she'll just get on with it.

"I'll arrange for Nathan to meet him in the next few days. I can't promise faster than that."

Celia turns to me. "If he joins us then he must understand the terms."

"What terms?" I ask.

"He follows my orders, as all the fighters do."

"That's it?"

"In battle and at camp. He has to behave . . . like a soldier."

I can't imagine Marcus doing any of this.

Celia continues. "I need to meet with him as soon as I can. I'm sure you'll tell him all about me."

"Yes, I'll make sure he knows the conditions you kept

me in. What was your phrase? 'I wouldn't want him to think you were in any state of comfort.' "

Celia straightens and I wonder if she'll say, "I was only doing my duty" or "following orders" or some crap like that but she doesn't. She was never the sort to deny responsibility.

The group disperses. I have time to catch Celia alone before she goes and I ask about Deborah. "Has she left England yet?"

Celia hesitates before replying. "She says her work is too important. Everyone on the Council knows that in the past her sympathies have been with you but she's also Jessica's sister and somehow she's managed to convince them that she's changed. She's still working in the records department. It's through her that we've learned of the Hunters' past movements and their future plans. It's vital information, but even so I've told her she should leave. She's chosen to stay, though. She's trying to get more information on Wallend and his experiments on the Black Witch prisoners. She's incredibly brave."

I don't know what to say. Deborah always was brave. If she believes something is right, that's that; there's no other way for her.

Celia moves off to talk to Van, and Ellen comes over to say good-bye.

I say, "Tell Arran I hope to see him soon. I think of him loads."

She nods. "I will. He'll be so pleased you're with the Alliance but more pleased that you're alive and well, and that you got your three gifts. Was it Mercury who performed the Giving ceremony for you?" And, by the way she asks, I'm fairly sure she knows it wasn't.

I shake my head. "Marcus did it."

Ellen smiles. "So that's why they think you'll be able to persuade him to join. They know that he wants to help his son."

Celia calls, "Ellen, we're going. Now."

And Ellen throws her arms round me and hugs me and I notice Celia watching, a look of surprise on her face. Celia still sees me as more Black than White, more violent than gentle. Ellen treats me as a person rather than a Half Code. But she's a Half Blood; she knows what it's like to be judged by a label rather than the person you are.

A minute after they go Van says that she, Annalise, and Nesbitt are returning to the bunker and that Gabriel will stay with me here while I try to make contact with Marcus. We'll all meet again at the Red Gourd in a week.

I have a short time to say good-bye to Annalise. I pull her over to the side of the room, not to talk but just to hold her and say good-bye quietly, without everyone staring at us, which they are doing anyway, except for Gabriel, who is standing at the bar with his back to us.

"Are you worried about your father joining the Alliance?" she asks.

"A bit. But I don't think he'll join anyway. I don't think he'll be interested, not in me, not in the rebels."

"You're his son. He cares about you. He found you for your Giving."

"That's different. He made it as short and as unsweet as possible. He doesn't trust me. He won't fight with me. And I can't see him following Celia's orders and acting 'like a soldier.' It just won't work."

Annalise kisses me and says, "Talking of working with Celia, I'm so proud of you, that you agreed to work with her after how she's treated you in the past, what you've been through with her." She kisses me again and leans close. "You're my hero. My prince." She kisses my ear and then whispers, "I love you."

And I'm not sure I've heard her right but I know I have and I don't know what to say.

She moves to kiss my lips and look into my eyes, and with her lips close to mine she whispers again, "I love you."

And I think I ought to say it back but it's really difficult and I'm sure everyone's listening, and then she says, "I've got to go. They're waiting."

And I kiss her.

And I've still not said it.

And she's moving away from me and I pull her back and I put my lips to her ear and I manage to say it, incredibly quietly. And she starts to giggle and I can't help but smile. And we kiss again. And then harder and

I'm not bothered about the others anymore.

There's a loud cough and clearing of the throat from Nesbitt. Annalise giggles again but I keep kissing her until she slides out of my grasp.

And they're gone.

And it was over too quick but I did say it and so did she. And we'll be together again in a week. Just one more week and I'll see her again.

Peanuts

•••••

We're still in the pub. Gus and I are sitting in the booth. Gabriel is standing at the bar, sipping a beer and eating a bag of nuts, occasionally throwing one up in the air and catching it in his mouth. Gus is bigging himself up, and his role in this "mission," and I'm trying my best to knock him down. It's childish of him and of me, and I'm not sure which of us is the bigger kid.

Gus says, "Marcus has a few contacts in the Black Witch community. Those he knows he can trust and rely on, those who will never betray him."

"Is anyone stupid enough to try?" I ask.

Gus ignores me. "Marcus likes to know what's happening in the world. But he rarely goes to gatherings these days. He relies on me for information."

"Just you? Didn't you say he has a few contacts?"

"It doesn't matter who else he uses."

"So you don't know who they are."

"What is important is that he trusts me."

"You're very honored."

"What I am is extremely discreet and equally cautious."

I yawn.

"I leave messages for him in a secret place and he picks

them up. He knows I'll be leaving him another message in the next twenty-four hours."

I stretch and look over to Gabriel. He's moved on from catching the peanuts to missing them and sending them bouncing off his nose and cheeks.

I'm telling myself this is serious; in fact, it is very serious—if not deadly serious—but Gabriel seems to think that the mood needs to be lightened and he's doing his best to make me smile. He throws a handful of nuts up in the air and turns to look at me, mouth open as the nuts shower over him, and I snigger.

Gus can't see Gabriel from where he's sitting but looks round and works it out. "You can clear that mess up now!" he shouts and Gabriel does a mock salute and throws another nut in the air, which he catches perfectly in his teeth and crunches on.

Gus says to me, "You're like children."

I shout to Gabriel, "Gus thinks we're not serious enough!"

Gabriel replies, "Gus doesn't know us very well at all."

"That's fine with me."

Gus curls his lip. "And with me too."

"OK. So we leave a message for Marcus to meet me somewhere," I say.

"No, dipshit. You wait for him where I leave the messages. You're the message."

I swear at him and ask, "When?" I expect him to say dawn or midnight or something like that.

Instead he says, "Now. The sooner you're out of my sight, the better."

"I need some lunch first, for me and Gabriel. We'll go after that."

Gus sneers. "This is more important than your stomach."

And I want to say that yes, of course it is. But, on the other hand, I haven't eaten since I don't know when, and if I go to see my father I'm not sure when I'll eat again, and I'm hungry and now I'm totally pissed off.

I get to my feet and walk out of the booth, saying to Gabriel, "Let's get something to eat."

Gus says, "You spoiled brat. This mission is more important than you—or do you think that because your father is Marcus you can swagger in here and expect everyone to run around after you?"

Gabriel is by me now and I don't turn back to Gus because if I do I might kill him. I carry on to the door, saying to Gabriel, "I'm hungry. Let's go."

"You shouldn't risk being seen," Gus snarls.

Gabriel stares at Gus. "You should make sure he doesn't leave. You should get him something to eat. You're the fool."

Gus is no fool, of course, but he is a Black Witch, and no lover of Half Codes, and he's not going to back down. So Gabriel and I walk out of the Red Gourd onto the street. When we get round the corner I suddenly remember practicalities.

"Have you got any money?"

"As a matter of fact—and I have to say I hope you're as impressed with me as I am—yes, I do."

"Buy me lunch then?"

"Anytime."

We find a small Italian restaurant and order mountains of pasta but I eat only a little.

"Yours no good?" Gabriel asks.

"It's OK. Gus ruined my appetite." I stab a piece of pasta with my fork. "He despises me for not being a 'proper' Black Witch and for being the spoiled son of the blackest Black Witch."

"Some you lose and some you lose."

"Sounds like my life. Though it doesn't look promising for the Alliance. We're hardly one happy family. If all Blacks are like Gus . . ."

"I hate to bear bad news, Nathan, but most of them are. No one's used to trusting witches who are different from them. Even here in Europe, they're just used to ignoring them. Gus would love to ignore you but he can't."

"Great."

"We can only hope that once he realizes what a wonderful, warm personality you have he'll become one of your greatest admirers."

I start to laugh.

Gabriel leans back and smiles at me. "So, as one of your current greatest admirers, can you tell me what's happening? What's the plan?"

I nod and tell him everything Gus told me.

"Gus would be very upset if he knew you'd divulged his top-secret information," Gabriel says.

"*Would* be? I hope he will be."

"You want me to let him know you told me?"

"Make him suffer."

Gabriel smiles. "It'll be good to have an objective while you're away."

Two hours later Gus has taken me out of the old town and into a smart area of closely packed houses. These aren't exactly new but they're grander and each one stands in its own walled garden. We look more than a little out of place: the people around here are well-dressed fains, smiling and looking happy with their position in the world. We turn down a side street. There are no cars here and it looks like the back entrances to the houses, high walls with gates in each.

Gus stops at one old worn gate, pulls out a large rusty key, and opens the gate.

Inside is a garden: small and surrounded by the high walls. The garden is completely overgrown with bushes. There's one old tree and a shed that's falling down.

"You wait here until he comes," Gus says. As if I'm going to do anything else, as if I'm going to do it just because he says so.

I call him an idiot or words to that effect with some swearing to enhance it.

And it seems as though that's all he's wanted and he's got me by the throat and a knife is in his hand and he's saying,

"You cocky little mong bastard. Just do as you're told. You're not worth shit. You're not a true Black; you're not even a true White. So do the thing you're here to do and—"

I push forward so that the knife is digging into my throat and Gus pulls back, surprised. I knock the knife out of his hand and punch him short and hard, then turn and elbow him in the stomach. He's big and all muscle but it's got to hurt a little.

We stand there, staring at each other, and I tell him, "Just go."

"And you just do your job." He turns to leave but before opening the gate he says, "With your father the Alliance will win. And, when we've won, I'll be settling down to a world where Whites get on with their lives and I get on with mine, like we've managed here for hundreds of years. I won't go near them and don't want them near me, and everyone should do the same so there's no more of your kind around." And he spits on the ground.

A few minutes after he's left I've calmed down enough to think over what he's said. According to Gus I'm not a true witch as I'm not pure Black or pure White. According to Gabriel I'm the ultimate witch, being the reunion of Black and White. According to White Witches I'm Black. According to Van I'm just an ordinary witch. And according to my father . . . I'm not sure what he thinks. Maybe I should find out when he comes. But I'm not going to ask any stupid questions about what he thinks of me.

Marcus

I'm lying on the ground in the walled garden. The sun has dropped behind the buildings and the shade has slid over me. The tree's leaves are gently swaying in the breeze. The sky is blue, dotted with small, thin white clouds. It's still sunny and bright up there.

I've been through the will-he-come, won't-he-come thoughts and now I'm just waiting, staring up at the tree and the leaves and the sky. The leaves are hardly moving. In fact, they aren't moving at all . . . I stare at one branch and I'm right: none of the leaves are moving, not even a slight tremor. And the little clouds: they were moving slowly left to right but the small one that is behind the branch above me is in exactly the same position as a minute ago, as a few minutes ago.

I sit up and at that moment the gate opens.

Marcus sees me and stops. For a second, I think he's going to leave straightaway but he comes into the garden and closes the gate.

I'm standing, though I don't remember getting up.

He turns to me but doesn't come forward. "I take it Gus brought you here?" he says. It's the usual enthusiastic welcome.

"Yes. I wanted to speak to you."

"We don't have long. I use the magic to stop things, to give me time to scout out an area, check for traps."

"I'm not a trap."

"No, I don't believe you are." He comes to stand in front of me and I realize how similar we are: the same height, the same face and hair, and exactly the same eyes. "But still I'd prefer to make it short."

"I know you don't want to spend any time with me, don't worry. But I need to tell you what's happening with the Council of White Witches and a group of rebels."

"And with you?"

"If you're interested."

"I'm always interested in you, Nathan. But our circumstances mean that short is usually a lot sweeter." He looks up. "I can't risk staying here any longer." He goes to the gate and opens it.

I can't believe that's it. Hello and good-bye. One look at me and he's out of here.

"Aren't you coming?" he asks.

"What?"

"Aren't you coming with me?"

"Um, yes. Course."

He walks through the gate and I trip in my rush to follow him. Once through he locks it with a similar key to the one Gus has and starts to walk away, saying over his shoulder, "Do your best to keep up."

* * *

I'm running after Marcus and it feels amazing to be with someone so fast. In the next street, we pass a car as it starts to move and, within a few strides, time is back to normal. We keep running. The houses end and we're in a wood of slender young trees and ferns, running uphill and over the brow. The countryside is gently sloping down and it gets much steeper and I'm almost out of control, taking huge strides to keep my balance, and there's no way I can stop, no way I want to stop, and the river is ahead of us and Marcus runs at it and leaps out over it and turns a somersault in the air and dives into the water.

I do my best to copy him and manage a dive. The water is cold and a shock but in a few seconds I'm used to it. My father isn't swimming so neither am I. We're floating but moving fast, carried along in the current. The banks are wood-lined, the city upstream in the distance, and we're just bobbing along in the middle of the dark river, the sky pale blue ahead of us, the sun below the hills to our left.

Then Marcus swims fast but easily to the left bank and I keep close to him. I think he's going to climb out of the river but he takes hold of my hand and puts it on his belt, saying, "Keep hold of that. Take a deep breath. Stay with me through the cut."

I sink and swim with him toward the bank of the river. The water is slower here and so clear that I can count the stones on the bottom, which Marcus seems to be navigating by grabbing one and then another to pull himself along. When we get to a large flat stone I see him reach behind it and he slips down into an impossibly tiny crack and I'm being sucked through with him from the bright, gray, cold water of the river to empty darkness that feels even colder, and I'm spinning round but remembering to breathe out too as Nesbitt told me. I'm spinning fast and the cut is so long that I run out of air and I'm desperately looking for light at the end but there's none and all I can do is concentrate on holding on to the leather of my father's belt.

I'm spewed out of the cut and suck in a new breath, and another, and another.

I try to look as if the experience wasn't that bad so I straighten up but I feel my heart pounding. I have to bend over, breathe, get air. I laugh. That was serious.

I'm on my knees in the shallows of a river. This is definitely a different one: much smaller, though powerful and fast too.

Marcus is already sitting on the bank. I get up and wobble a bit and hope he hasn't seen. I sit next to him. "You still use cuts, even though Hunters can find them?"

"What do you think? Will they find that one?"

"I don't know. But you're the one who told me that Hunters have found a way of detecting cuts and Hunters are good at hunting."

"Yes, there's at least one Hunter who can do it. It's her Gift. I think she has to be within a certain distance, though—what do you think? A mile? A few hundred meters? Ten? I'd imagine quite close but I don't know. So I expect the worst and make new cuts every month." He turns to me. "Always moving on, always staying safe." He looks at the river. "At the moment this is a good home, a decent view and fresh water. I've stayed in worse places. But, if I stay here too long, they'll be here: one day, later, sooner, who knows? I stay in one place for three months, sometimes less. Never more."

I look at the river and the trees. The sun is setting here too.

"Still, I'm not due to leave here for a few weeks, so we should have time to talk."

"That would be good."

"We'll see."

And I wonder about telling him about the Alliance but I get the feeling that this isn't the right time and I don't want to talk about that. I've spent so little time with my father, know him so little, that I want to talk about us, about him—but I don't get the feeling he wants to do that either.

I look around. Behind me is a wall of trees that seems to be the edge of a forest cloaking a hillside. The first tree isn't for a few meters, though, and the bank is covered with brambles and ferns. It feels safe and clean and open. I turn, kneeling to face the forest. Even the shade and the smell of it are seductive and the river behind is surprisingly quiet.

This is close to how I dreamed my home would be but there's no meadow, no cottage. Ahead of me the brambles are thick, fairy-story thick; they'd be impregnable without hacking through with a sword. It's a safe boundary; no one could come at us from that direction. The brambles remind me of my cage bars but they're somehow enticing too and I see that there's a gap in them, a gap barely big enough for a human. I crawl toward it and discover that once I've started along the tunnel I can't go back: my clothes get caught. I keep going. The entrance slopes down and I have to follow it lower and further.

Ahead the brambles open out into a wide, low den. It's dark inside but warm and lit by the natural light that makes its way through the myriad tiny gaps. It's like an animal den but this is definitely a human home. A low room, mostly empty. There's the remains of a fire, just off the center. A small log store is to one side and the wood is all dry. An area around the fire is bare earth, where my father must sit, feed the fire, and cook and eat. It's hard to imagine the most feared of Black Witches making soup or stew, eating with a metal spoon from a simple dish, but that's what he appears to do. And I know he spends his time here only briefly human. Mostly he's an animal. This is his life. Lonely. Alone. Human only sometimes. And I have to sit down.

He doesn't want to talk about his life. Instead he's showing it to me so that I can know him. And, if I know him, I will know myself. But this is not the life I had envisaged he'd have. I'm not sure what I expected, perhaps something impressive, grand, a place full of treasure and history and power, but I realize now that that isn't him, no more than it would be me.

And I'm crying, and I'm not sure if I'm crying with sadness or joy, for him or myself, or just a connection with him or because of all of it. I recognize this is a place I might end up living in if I'm like him. But I don't want it.

He still hasn't come and I know he's letting me get used to it. Or maybe he's just taking in the sunset.

In a corner are some wool blankets, worn and riddled with holes, and a pile of sheepskins, seven of them. They've been rolled up to keep them dry. I pull them out and lay them by the cold ashes of the fire.

He comes into the den when the light is fading to nothing. He lights the fire in seconds, getting the flames licking up some twigs he's brought in with him. He feeds the fire and we both watch it. I'm sitting, then lying, and I find I'm crying again and I can't stop and I look up at him and see no tears on his cheeks. And I close my eyes and the Alliance and all those people, even Gabriel and Annalise, feel like they belong in a different world. This is my father's world and it is another place. It's wild.

I wake. The den is light but I can tell it's early. I'm lying where I fell asleep; the fire is cold now and I'm alone.

I crawl out of the den. Marcus is sitting just by the exit, close to the riverbank. I sit by him. The sun is coming over the hill ahead of us.

"Hungry?" he asks.

"Yes."

"You want to hunt with me?"

I nod.

"Ever been an eagle?"

Me and my father are sitting together. I hunted with him. He transformed and I copied him. I wasn't sure how to choose what to become and I'm not sure I did. But the animal in me knew what to do and we did it. We copied my father the eagle and did what he did. We flew for the first time, clumsy to start with but quickly getting the hang of soaring and turning, swooping, diving. Hunting was too hard, though. My father caught a weasel and a fox. We weren't accurate enough or fast enough to catch anything. It didn't matter. We all ate together.

Now Marcus says, "Who is to judge if that me is better or worse than the human me?"

I know my father is talking about the other side of himself, the animal part.

"I'm still getting used to him, my animal. I sort of think of him as separate from me but we're trying to work together."

"It took me a while. I fought it." He shakes his head. "I thought he was trying to take over my body. He isn't. You're just discovering another side of yourself. The more natural part. The old part. The part of you that belongs to the earth more than any other. He's what you need to survive and without him it's not worth surviving anyway. Trust him and he'll trust you. Be as close to him as you can."

I sit with my father and watch the river until it gets hot

in the afternoon and then we hunt again. We soar higher and higher and hang there, waiting. A rabbit appears far below. My father lets the air take him higher. The animal me stays focused on the rabbit and we drop lower. We both want it.

That night, back as humans, my father and me watch the sun set. I ask him about his other Gifts, those he took from other witches by eating their hearts. "Can you use them?"

"Yes. It's like using my own Gift. They're mine now. But none are as strong as being an animal. Some are weak. Most I never use."

I'm itching to ask what he does use but I daren't. I feel shy sometimes with him.

He says, "The plants thing is useful."

"Making plants grow or die: Sara Adams, Council member."

"What?"

"Celia made me learn all the Gifts you took, all the people you killed."

He's quiet for a while, thinking about that. He says, "Well, it's useful. At least when you live like me."

"You grew the brambles for your den?"

He nods. "And invisibility is handy, especially when you're hiding or tracking. As is doing the spell to stop time. Being able to make cuts is another useful skill. Few can do it."

"Can you fly?"

He frowns. "No. Who was that supposed to be from?"

"Malcolm, a Black Witch from New York. That was always questionable. Can you make big leaps, though?"

"No bigger than you." He's quiet again, then says, "I can fly when I'm an eagle. I can make big leaps if I'm a leopard. Is that impressive enough for you?"

I think he knows I'm impressed enough anyway.

"Do you hear noises in your head, from mobile phones and things?"

He turns to me. "Yes. And you?"

I nod.

He goes into the den and I follow. He lights the fire and says, "I live like this most of the time now. It looks poor but it isn't."

I don't say anything. I can see the pleasure of being in the wild but the loneliness would be too much for me.

He says, "It's not what you imagined, I suppose."

"We found Mercury's bunker. I thought it would be more like that."

"And did you find Mercury?"

I tell my father about Mercury and all that has happened since I last met him, about Van, Nesbitt, Annalise, and Mercury. About Celia and Gus and the Alliance. It's dawn by the time I say bluntly, "They want you to join them."

"The Alliance?" Marcus laughs. "They must be desperate."

"Yes, I think that sums them up."

"And are you determined to join them? Do you really want to risk your life for a cause?"

"It's my cause. Bringing Black and White Witches together."

"I don't think that is the cause. I think the cause is getting rid of a lunatic White Witch leader and a bunch of power-mad Hunters. And, once that's done, winning the peace, as they say, will be much more problematic than winning the war."

"You don't need to worry about that."

Marcus smiles at me. "Possibly not. But may I still worry a little about a war I'm likely to get killed in?"

"Will you join then?" I'm surprised. "I didn't think you would."

"I'm not interested in bringing Black and White Witches together. However, I am very much excited by the thought of getting rid of Soul and the Hunters. That definitely appeals. I'm not ready for retirement just yet. I'm not really a joining kind of person. But I'll help you fight Soul and the Hunters. I'd like to meet Celia. I think I should see the woman who locked my son up every night for two years." He shakes his head. "She's offering me an amnesty but maybe she should be asking me for one."

I look at him and wonder if he's serious or joking.

"I'm not interested in amnesties or bargains, Nathan, for me or for her. I despise all that. And I hope you do too. We each do what we have to do. Maybe that applies even to

Soul, I don't know, and I don't much care about him, except I'd like to see him die."

And the cold way he says all this makes me realize that my father is as capable of killing a man as he is a rabbit, with no more regrets, possibly fewer.

"There's a meeting in Basle at the Red Gourd in five days. Celia will be there."

"I can hardly wait."

"I should go back and tell them."

"No. You should stay with me. We go back together or not at all."

I look at him, uncertain as to why he says that. I ask him, "Don't you trust me?"

He looks me in the eye and I see the same black triangles turning slowly in his as in mine. He says, "I want you to stay with me. Is a week of your life too much to ask?"

I shake my head once and feel tears fill my eyes.

He turns away. "Good."

I finally do the thing I've wanted to do for so long. I pull the Fairborn out of my jacket and hold it out to him.

He takes it from me and slowly pulls the knife out of the sheath.

"It's not a happy object, is it?" he says.

"It's yours."

"Yes, I suppose. My grandfather had it for a time."

"It recognizes us, our blood. It won't come out of the sheath for anyone else."

He slides the knife back in and places it on the ground by his side.

It feels over too quickly after all the effort to find the Fairborn and return it to my father.

“I won’t kill you,” I say.

“Perhaps not. We’ll see.” He turns and lies down. I put another log on the fire and sit watching it and watching my father, and I realize that I am happy here with him.

The Alliance

Nearly a week has gone by. It feels like a lifetime in some ways and like just a few hours in others. My father and I have done so much hunting, walking, running, and just being together, and now we're ready to go back to the Red Gourd for the meeting tomorrow.

"Are you sure you want to?" Marcus asks me.

"Yes. There's Annalise."

I've told him about her, about how I like her, and he's not commented on that. As with most things he just listens and doesn't give his opinion. I guess I'm like that too.

But now he says, "Annalise . . . the situation was like that between me and your mother. It's not a good situation, Nathan. Not in the long term. At the beginning we were so involved in each other, we lived for nothing but the next time we were to see each other. We kept meeting and it was never enough. It was a miracle we managed to keep things secret for so long. I wanted her to leave with me but she couldn't survive like this"—he waves his hand at the trees and river—"and she was wise enough to realize that. She married that man instead, which was less wise. Her marriage was a disaster." He pauses and looks into the distance. "I admit I didn't help but . . . at the time my main concern was to be with her at least a little."

He turns to me. "You should learn from us, Nathan. Look at yourself. You are like me. I've been looking for your mother in you and"—he shakes his head—"I don't see her at all. I see me. I see Black."

And I know he's right. I am like him and even more so now that I've spent time with him, but when I'm with Annalise I feel that side of me, the White side, come to the surface.

I say, "I know what you're saying but—"

"You look like me, you have the same Gift, you have the same loves and desires and possibly the same limitations."

"What limitations?"

"Living in a city. Being with people. Being in buildings."

"I admit I have a problem with buildings. But I'm OK with lots of people. Some I really like."

"I liked your mother. Look where that ended. You're a Black Witch, Nathan. You're darker than most Black Witches I know. You shouldn't have anything to do with them, with White Witches. You should leave the girl."

I shake my head. "I can't. I don't want to."

We're silent for a while then I ask him the same question he asked me. "Are you sure you want to go? Risk losing this beautiful life?"

"It's time I risked things for you. I'm getting old, Nathan. Not very old but before I get too old I want to spend some time with my son."

* * *

We go back to Basle through another cut that doesn't involve getting wet.

"How many cuts do you have?" I ask.

"Lots. I figure if they can find them then let them keep busy doing that." He glances at me. "It gives the Hunters something to do!" He laughs. "I should fill the world with them."

We're in Basle the afternoon before the meeting. Marcus insists on scouting the city and says I can't help as I'm too conspicuous, and I know that the Hunters do know what I look like. He arrives back at the walled garden when it's dark and says, "Two Hunters. One of the benefits of being able to turn invisible is that I can follow them and listen to them for hours without much danger. They're talking to informants or rather they would be if they could find any. It seems that the Half Bloods have disappeared. I guess they've fled or gone over to the Alliance, which is a good sign, though it's making the Hunters very curious."

"But they know nothing about the meeting tomorrow?"

Marcus shakes his head. "Those two definitely don't."

We sleep on the ground and I look at the stars and wonder about the future. A war is definitely coming and I have to admit that I'm curious to see my father fighting in it.

The next morning Marcus does another check of the city and the two Hunters and he returns, saying, "No change. Let's go."

We head to the Red Gourd. He becomes invisible for the journey, guiding me by my arm and keeping me moving fast. We approach the alley that the bar is in from a different side and I only recognize it at the last moment. As I push open the heavy wooden door and step inside, my father says, "I'll stay like this for the moment."

I don't nod or acknowledge what he's said but move down the first of the stone steps, and as I pull aside the heavy curtain I see the inside of the Red Gourd for the briefest moment before it's gone and we're sucked through a cut. It's black and swirling and as empty of air as ever but I feel Marcus's hand tight on my arm and, although I don't know why we've gone through a cut, I'm reassured. I feel indestructible when my father's with me.

And we're out. It's the shortest and widest cut I've been through. I don't fall to the ground like I've done every other time, possibly because the cut is so wide and possibly because my father is holding me up.

I look around for Hunters but there are none.

We're in a bar but not the Red Gourd or at least not the original one. This bar is in the open air, in a forest clearing. It is laid out the same as the Red Gourd with tables along the wall, only here there is no wall, though the booths at the far end are still booths. To my right is the long bar but there's no wall behind that either and instead of the low, timbered roof of the Red Gourd there is a canvas sail that is tied taut between trees.

Gabriel, Van, Celia, and the other White Witch, Grace,

are sitting at the furthest table and Gus is standing with them, his back to me. I take a step toward them but my father holds me still.

Gabriel sees me, and Gus turns and says, "Talk of the devil."

My father lets go of my arm.

I say, "Hi."

They all look at me expectantly and I'm not sure what to say or what my father wants me to do.

Celia says, "Are you alone?"

"My father is . . . thinking about your offer."

"So you've failed," says Gus. "You were supposed to bring Marcus with you."

And then Gus screams and grabs at the right side of his face, blood pouring between his fingers. He drops to his knees. Blood is running down his neck, his arm, and onto the floor. He's still screaming and grasping at the side of his face as Marcus appears, standing over him. The Fairborn is in his left hand and something else, something small and bloody, is in his right hand. I think it's Gus's ear.

Everyone is still and silent, except for Gus, who is wailing now.

Marcus says, "Gus. I really must thank you for working with me over the last few years, acting as such a . . ." Marcus looks at me with a mock confused expression on his face. "What was the phrase, Nathan? An 'extremely discreet and equally cautious' messenger. However, pulling a knife on my son strikes me as being neither discreet nor cautious. So I felt I had to do the same to you. You can take that as an end to our working relationship."

Gus looks like he's going to be sick.

Marcus drops the ear on the ground and wipes the Fairborn clean on Gus's shoulder. "So, Nathan, do you want to introduce me to your friends? I'd particularly like to know which one is the Hunter who kept you in a cage."

Celia moves to stand but Marcus says, "No, don't get up."

He doesn't say it out of politeness but as an instruction. I can see Celia is thinking about it but she remains sitting, cool as ever. She says, "And I have always wanted to meet the man who killed my sister."

Marcus smiles. "Really? I had no idea." He moves to stand behind Celia but speaks to Van. He says, "Thanks for the invitation to come here today, Van. I get very few, as you can imagine."

Gus is now vomiting on the floor.

Marcus looks at him with disgust and says to Celia, "We need to talk. But I'm finding Gus here a little distracting. If I stay here any longer I'm likely to cut more than his ear off."

Celia gets up. "Well, I suggest we take a walk then."

And off they go together into the forest. And I'm not sure if Celia will come out alive, with both ears or what.

Rivers of Blood

Two hours later Celia and Marcus return to the camp. Celia has both her ears. They walk back side by side, deep in conversation, not looking at each other but staying close enough to keep their voices quiet.

Soon we're all back sitting round the table, except Gus, who has wisely disappeared from Marcus's sight. Van helped him heal and reattached his ear. It looked a mess to me, though.

Van has told me we're in the Black Forest of southern Germany. Celia plans on using this place as the main camp for the Alliance.

Celia opens the meeting by stating the principal aim of the Alliance: "To remove Soul O'Brien from the leadership of the White Witches, by killing him if necessary, and to return Britain to a state of peaceful coexistence among all Witches.

"Our first objective is to drive the Hunters out of Europe. They are moving down from the north but are still concentrated in northern France and Germany. They're growing in number, recruiting as they move south. The longer we wait before attacking, the harder it will be to stop them. We must attack, both to deter new recruits and to remove the ones they already have before they're fully trained.

"However, we have few fighters and can afford to lose none of them. Each attack must succeed on three fronts: killing the enemy, demoralizing the enemy, raiding their stores—seizing their weapons, equipment and food—"

"I take it you have no weapons?" Marcus interrupts.

"Few, and nothing to match the Hunters' guns. Those are what we need to get our hands on most of all. When they realize that they're going to be killed with their own bullets—a slow, painful death—that's another small advantage we win."

I say to Celia, "I don't see how the raids will deter new recruits. The Hunters are hardly going to tell anyone about them, are they?"

"News will travel. White Witches keep much closer contact with each other than Black Witches do. But we will also spread the word about Alliance successes. We need recruits too. Van will let the Black Witches know that Marcus is working with us. Once they hear that, and see us succeeding, more will join.

"But it won't be easy," Celia adds. "Hunters pride themselves on learning from their mistakes. They analyze all their battles, victories and defeats. They'll soon work out our tactics."

"And what are our tactics?" I ask.

"We have an elite group of fighters—"

"We do?"

"Yes. Myself, Greatorex, Nesbitt, Gabriel. And now you and Marcus. Plus some good trainees."

"Not huge numbers then!"

"That's fine. We attack, raid, and run. In and out quickly. We pick the weak groups of new recruits to attack. That's what the scouts are out looking for at the moment. We choose our first target when they get back to base."

"Is this base?" I ask.

"Yes, all those who join the Alliance will come here. It will soon grow and will need organizing. Everyone will have to do their bit."

Celia explains that each person will be put in a task group. There are four groups: Scouts and Fighters; Foraging and Stores; Cooking and Camp; and Healers. Gabriel and I are fighters. Ellen, Greatorex, and Nesbitt are scouting at the moment. Annalise is in Foraging and Stores and is with one of the groups now, helping bring provisions to this base.

I look over at Marcus. He's not in any task group. Our eyes meet and I think he's thinking the same thing. He says, "When do I get to kill some Hunters?"

"The scouts are back tomorrow. The first raid will be tomorrow night."

Afterward I hang back and ask Celia about Deborah. "Has she left the Council yet?"

Celia looks relieved as she answers. "She's agreed to leave. It's become impossible for her to get more information out without it being obvious that it's coming from her. She should make it to us. I've sent someone to bring her here."

That night I don't sleep well. I don't have nightmares but I wake and can't get back to sleep. I wonder where Annalise is, hoping she's safe. I thought I'd be with her tonight but she's not due back until tomorrow. I feel sick thinking about her. She's regained much of her health since being under Mercury's spell. And she's agile and great at running but if the Hunters find her group the truth is she doesn't stand a chance. In the end I get up and start to walk through the forest. It's still dark and Gabriel falls in beside me.

"I couldn't sleep either," he says.

"I need to burn off some energy," I say. "Coming?"

"Of course." And we set off running, fast.

It feels good, so good, to be running and free. Just free. A fine, misty rain begins to fall. It's sharply cold on my cheeks as I run. It's beautiful. I call to Gabriel that I'm going ahead.

I pick up my pace and go as hard and fast as I can, over a hill and down into a glade. There's a clearing near a stream. It's getting light now and I stop. I sit on the ground cross-legged and wait, listen. It feels good sitting here, taking in the smell of earth and trees, and watching the stream run silently by. It's so calm and peaceful that it seems absurd that soon we'll be fighting and I'll have to kill again. The forest reminds me of the place where I woke after I killed the fast Hunter. I was in shock, and the Hunter was dead, but the forest was the same as ever, as beautiful and peaceful as ever. And maybe that is all we can hope for, that the forest will go on being beautiful.

I hear Gabriel's footsteps after a while, then they stop and I start to smile: I know he's trying to sneak up on me. I remain still, my hearing straining for the slightest noise. He's either stopped completely or he's improved a lot. But then I hear a rustle of leaves close behind and I turn as he rushes to me and then shouts and leaps on me. We mock fight, then roll apart but remain lying on the ground.

"You'd be dead if I was a Hunter," he says.

I laugh; he knows that isn't true. I say, "You were good. I only really heard you right at the end."

"Damned with faint praise," he says.

"What does that mean?" I ask.

"It means you'd have killed me."

"Well, yes. But I think you'd have surprised most Hunters. There are some good ones and some less good ones." I shrug. "You just have to hope you get lucky and only get the less good ones."

"I have no intention of finding out what I get, as I intend to shoot them from a great distance anyway."

"Good plan."

He shuffles closer to me and we sit looking down the gentle slope through the trees to the stream.

I say, "There'll be plenty of shooting. And soon."

"Yes, there'll be plenty of that and worse, much worse. '*I see wars, horrid wars, and the Tiber foaming with much blood.*'"

"We attack tonight," Celia says.

"Our target is a new training camp with ten recruits and two Hunters," Nesbitt explains. He arrived back early in the morning and now we're being briefed. "I've watched the camp for the last two days. The trainees are mostly young; six are German and four French. They all understand English. They're all female. They are all pretty good with guns but hand to hand they're hopeless. One of the Germans can send out a noise similar to Celia's but it's weak and won't disable you. One of the French girls can become invisible. Again it's a weak Gift and she can only hold it for a few seconds but it's enough to disorient opponents, or cause you to miss her, or give her a chance to sneak up on you. The two Hunters are old hands: English, female, early thirties, excellent shots, excellent hand-to-hand fighting."

Celia says, "The recruits will be dangerous if they get to their guns. And they usually sleep with them. We attack at first light: some will still be in bed; some will not be fully alert."

"Which brings me to the location," adds Nesbitt. "They're in an old airfield; it's open ground with a fence round it. They sleep inside, in one of the small hangars. They have two on guard at the gate on three-hour shifts, but the new recruits don't see the point of it and don't patrol the fence."

"How far is it?" Gabriel asks.

"It's in France, over five hours' drive from here, but Marcus set up a cut for us to go through. It comes out half a mile from the airfield."

Celia says, "It gets light at six a.m. Nesbitt and Nathan leave here at four a.m. to scout. The rest of us leave at five."

"I'm not a scout," I say.

"No, you're not. Nesbitt is our best scout and very valuable he is too. So your job is to protect him, with your life if necessary."

Nesbitt grins at me. "I know you'll dive in front to take the bullet for me, mate."

"I'll push you out of the way into a cowpat."

Nesbitt shrugs. "Whatever works."

"I will lead the team," says Celia. "We all go. We all learn. We work in pairs. The pairs may change in future; this is for tonight's raid. It's up to you to make sure you've got the equipment you need from the stores we have."

The little group of fighters has naturally split into two groups, Celia in the middle. Gabriel, me, Nesbitt, and a young woman, a Half Blood, are standing together and looking at three White Witches. I can spot Greatorex straightaway. She's the ex-Hunter, the deserter. She's tall, with pale, freckled skin and hazel eyes, a broken nose. I guess she's in her early twenties but she looks younger. She's wearing similar combat gear to Celia. The other two Whites are also young. They've spent the whole meeting so far trying to look tough.

Nesbitt smiles at them. "Sorry, ladies, but you've missed your chance to be partnered with me. Better luck next time."

The girls don't even look like they've heard him.

He mutters but in a voice loud enough for them to hear, "Shit. You'd think we were the enemy."

They begin to loosen up and almost smile until Nesbitt adds, "You'd better partner up quick; whoever's left over goes with Marcus."

The girls look around and laugh nervously.

Celia says, "Marcus will not be having a partner. I'll brief him separately on what's happening. Greatorex, you go with Claudia. Olivia with me. Gabriel with Sameen. And Nathan is with Nesbitt."

I grumble quietly to Gabriel, "This better just be for tonight."

Gabriel replies, "It's a sensible plan to put Sameen with me. You'd terrify her and Nesbitt would confuse her totally."

Sameen is the Half Blood: half Black, half fain. Her eyes are a strange brown and turquoise mix.

I say, "Yeah, it makes sense. But it is noticeable that we're not exactly mixing—Whites and Blacks."

"I think that's sensible too for the first mission. We've not even had time to train together. We have to trust our partners."

"Easy for you to say. You're not with Nesbitt."

The Forager

That afternoon Annalise and a group of White Witches walk into camp, carrying heavy loads. Annalise looks tired. She's supposed to help put up some tents and I ask her to leave her chores for a while but she insists on finishing all her work so I help her. One of the other girls, Laura, looks terrified of me and jumps if I look at her. The other girl, Sarah, can't stop asking me questions: "Do you have the same Gift as your father?" "Which are the other Blacks?" and "Is Marcus really in the camp?"

I'm relieved when Celia sees me and shouts, "Nathan, the others are training! You should be too!"

I find the other fighters and watch for a few minutes. Greatorex is giving instruction on basic self-defense. She's good and the trainees aren't complete beginners. I'm not sure what I'm supposed to do so I sit and watch. Sameen is practicing with Gabriel, Olivia with Nesbitt, and Claudia with Greatorex.

They take a break and Gabriel comes over with Sameen. She says, "Hi!" and smiles and keeps glancing at Gabriel. I think she's already got a crush on him.

Nesbitt is talking to Claudia and Olivia but they keep looking over and smiling at Gabriel too. Gabriel, it seems, has more chance than anyone of winning over White Witches: he just has to smile at them and they go weak at the knees.

Thankfully, Greatorex seems immune to his charms and is still business-like. After a few minutes she says, "Right, let's partner up again. But change partners. Nathan can join in on this with Claudia."

"No," Celia says, striding quickly to us. "I'll spar with Nathan."

I say to her, "You sure? You're looking a bit old and slow these days."

"I want to see how much you've forgotten."

I give her a smile. I've forgotten nothing.

Later, when it's getting dark, Annalise finds me where I've set up my own little camp on the edge of the trees away from everyone. I don't have a tent but I do have a small fire and a sheltered spot by a tree. Annalise and I sit together, a blanket wrapped round us both.

She asks me what happened at training. I say, "I trained."

"I heard you beat up Celia. They had to pull you off her."

I remember seeing Sarah standing with a group of White Witches after it was over. They'd been watching. No doubt Sarah has been gossiping.

I tell Annalise, "That's not true."

And it isn't, though Nesbitt was making jokes about who would replace Celia when I'd killed her. But mainly I blanked them all out. I was concentrating. Celia landed one good kick. I landed about twenty, not that I was counting.

"Anyway, Annalise, that's what we do. Celia can heal fine. She's done worse to me many times. We used to practice fighting every day and she beat me up every day." I reckon that's seven hundred times minimum over two years, so there are six hundred and ninety-nine more of those due to Celia.

"I'm glad I didn't see it."

Annalise has never seen me fighting, which is good, I think. I take her hand and kiss it as gently as I can. I don't want to talk about fighting when I'm with her. I say, "And how was your day?"

"Oh, OK." She tries to smile at me and says, "I know Sarah and Laura were driving you mad but I think they'll get used to you. It's difficult for everyone in different ways. They've both lost family. Sarah's parents were killed and Laura's lost her sister . . ."

And again I think maybe now is the time for me to tell Annalise about Kieran. But already she's talking about the things they did, sorting out stores and the shortage of food.

I ask her, "Are you OK with doing that? I thought you might want to be in with the healers."

"Ha! I can't even make a simple medicine. No, Celia is right to put me in Foraging and Stores. I'm good at organizing things, which is not a strength that a lot of the Witches around here have, and everything has to be made use of and accounted for. If all the rebels come here we'll need more food and sanitation and tents. Boring but essential. And I can only see that more people will flee as the fighting escalates. That means more mouths to feed. There'll be babies and children. We might need to set up schooling. It's complicated."

I'm beginning to realize that fighting is a lot simpler.

We're silent for a while and then Annalise says, "I haven't seen Marcus yet but everyone is talking about him being here."

"The camp gossip seems to be in full swing."

"Sorry, I'm beginning to sound like Sarah, aren't I?"

I kiss her and say, "Definitely not."

Marcus watched me fight but left straight afterward. I say, "He's not exactly sociable. He likes to be alone."

I look into the trees, where I met him hours ago, when I was looking for a place to make my camp. He told me he was going to stay away from everyone. "There's too much staring for my liking."

Now I say, "I think it's a good thing he keeps away from people."

"You haven't told me what happened when you went to meet him. I didn't think you'd be gone for so long. I thought you'd maybe talk for a few minutes."

"Same here."

"So what did you do for a whole week?"

"You really are beginning to sound like Sarah," I tease her. "He's my father, Annalise. I just spent time with him. It was good, for both of us, I think. He's not what I expected."

"No? But he sounds dangerous. He attacked Gus? Caroline, one of the healers, told me he cut Gus's ear off."

Before I can reply she continues, "You are so different from him. He's so much a Black Witch, so violent."

"He can be violent," I say. "Violent and impulsive. Everyone knows that, including Gus. Anyone who annoys him is stupid. But that doesn't mean people won't be stupid. Marcus won't change. But at least he's on our side."

"Tell that to Gus."

I think I'm best avoiding Gus for a while. I don't tell Annalise that Marcus attacked Gus because Gus attacked me. And I'm not sure how different my father and I are.

I say, "So I think that's enough gossip for one evening."

"Well, there is one more piece of gossip I have to tell you about." And now she's grinning. "Guess?"

I shrug.

"All the girls have crushes on Gabriel."

"Ah, nooooo!" I pull the blanket over our heads and hold her to me, saying, "Please, no more."

She laughs but carries on. "It's his hair. They were talking about it for hours; how he tucks it behind his ears, how it falls forward, how it curls. They also like his eyes and his lips and his nose, his shoulders and his legs. But mainly it's his hair."

"Do they know they're wasting their time?"

"Wasting their time because he's only interested in boys? Or only interested in one boy?" And she points her finger at my chest.

I remember kissing him, holding his hair. But I say, "He's my friend, Annalise."

"I know," she says, and kisses me gently on the lips.

And I kiss her more.

Later she falls asleep in my arms but I stay awake, just holding her and feeling her warmth against me.

I know I'll have to leave soon. And in a few hours I'll be fighting and it'll be bad and here I am now holding Annalise. All of it feels unreal.

She stirs and asks, "What's wrong?"

"Nothing. It's fine."

"You're gripping me so tightly I can hardly breathe."

"I didn't mean to wake you but I've got to go soon. I'm not supposed to talk about it but . . . I'll be back later."

Now she grips me tightly, wrapping her legs round mine. After a while she says, "When we were in the Red Gourd in Basle, you said . . . something."

I reply in a whisper, "And I remember you said something too." I pull the blanket over our heads so it's totally dark. I want to be brave and say it before she does. My lips are close to her ear, brushing it as I whisper, "Annalise, I lo–"

"Time to go, partner!" Nesbitt flings the blanket back. "Oh, sorry to interrupt, mate. Thought you were asleep."

The First Attack

Nesbitt leads me to the cut, which is a short walk into the trees, two minutes from where Annalise is in bed. Annalise and I said a quick good-bye. She looked worried about me, which was sort of nice and sort of not. I told her I'd be OK but really I haven't got a clue what'll happen. All I know is that Marcus is on our side and that has to be better than not.

I've thought about using my Gift and being in animal form for the fighting but I know that isn't right. That's for a different sort of combat. This is more tactical, human stuff, all the stuff that Celia has trained me in. I asked Marcus about it and he said the same thing. After the week with him I know I can control that part of myself, my Gift, and I can transform as quickly as Marcus can, but it's not a Gift for war.

At the cut Nesbitt says, "Seems your dad's checking up on you." And he nods over to the far trees. Marcus stands, half hidden, and he holds his hand up in a gesture of "good luck" or "see you soon" or something. I hold my hand up too.

I grab Nesbitt's wrist and he slides his hand through the cut and we're on our way. I manage to stay standing at the other side; bent over, but standing. Nesbitt is on his feet in a second and sets off at a swift jog. Well, it's swift for him.

I follow a few steps behind. It's dark and still, and even though I can't see as well as him I can sense the path, and following Nesbitt is easy. I've only just started to warm up when we get to the airfield. It's in darkness and I can make out little more than the pale shape of three hangars side by side, a hundred meters away. We follow the fence along until the hangars are aligned to our right. Nesbitt stops and produces some cutters from his jacket and sets to on the fence. My job is to hold the fence so it doesn't rattle or shake. When he's got a gap big enough to get through he indicates to me to wait while he has a scout around. I nod.

He runs to the hangars, keeping crouched low, and disappears behind them. The lookout guards are on the fence further round the other side. If they patrol the circuit it'll take them twenty minutes, I reckon, but, as Nesbitt said, they don't look like they're going to be doing that even once.

After ten or more minutes Nesbitt appears round the back of the furthest hangar and he runs to the middle hangar and then the near one and then toward me. I keep my eyes on the guards but they're so still they might well be asleep.

Nesbitt stays on his side of the fence, flattened to the ground as I am now.

"Well?" I whisper.

"Can't see in. They've covered over all the cracks in the walls. There are no lights on in there. I could hear voices in one hangar but that was empty last night."

"So there could be a load of Hunters here that weren't there before?"

"Or new recruits, or they've moved them from the other hangar. I don't know."

"Shit!"

"What do you think?"

"I think you should go back and have a proper look."

Nesbitt swears at me. "I have had a proper look."

I shake my head. "Well, you're telling Celia."

We have to wait about half an hour before Nesbitt has the pleasure of doing that. Celia runs to us, swift and silent despite her size; she always has been surprisingly agile. Behind her follow Claudia, Gabriel, Sameen, Greatorex, and Olivia. Marcus brings up the rear.

Gabriel drops to the ground by my left side and Celia to my right.

"Well?" she asks me.

"Things have changed. Nesbitt wants to tell you."

She talks through the fence to Nesbitt. They talk so quietly that I can't make out what they're saying.

I can see Celia raise her head and look around and Nesbitt runs off again to the hangars.

I whisper to Gabriel, "Something's changed. Not sure if it's for better or worse."

"You worried?"

I shake my head. But inside there's a part of me that's

anxious. Even with Marcus around there's always the chance of a stray bullet or a lucky shot or a Hunter with a special Gift or something.

Nesbitt has disappeared round the farthest hangar. A light comes on inside the nearest one, a faint glow under the door at this end. It's getting light on the horizon too. The Hunters are beginning to wake. We should be attacking any minute but we're far from ready and at this rate Nesbitt is going to get caught. So much for an easy first mission.

I keep my eyes on the hangar where I expect Nesbitt to reappear but still he doesn't. Celia turns to me and says, "You and Gabriel to the first hangar. Marcus is to take the guards and follow to the furthest hangar where I will be. Greatorex takes the middle."

Marcus goes through the fence first, then he turns invisible. The rest of us slither through and I set off with Gabriel and Sameen, fast.

I reach the door ahead of Gabriel and kick it in with so much force it almost hits me back in the face. I'm stunned by what I see, though. It's not an empty hangar—there are three rows of bunk beds extending the full length. Enough to sleep nearly a hundred people. All the beds are empty, or so it seems, but we have to check. I drop to the ground and look under them. It's so new and unused that there's nothing here. But I can't see to the far end and now I wish Nesbitt was with me.

Gabriel says, "Sameen, stay here. Guard the door. I'll

take the right. Nathan, you take the left." And he runs past me down the right-hand side to the far end of the hangar, shouting, "Empty. Empty. Empty. Empty."

I get up and go slightly slower down the left aisle. But I see no one; there are no corners to hide in. Gabriel meets me at the far end and we come back, running and double-checking. As we reach Sameen gunfire bursts out from another hangar.

Five Hunters run from the middle hangar toward the gate. And I'm chasing them, going for the fastest one first. I tackle her, my knife in my hand, and slit her throat in a single movement. She was a novice; she didn't even fight. The girl behind is now running past me and I tackle her, punch her. She's out cold. I look round and see Gabriel has shot one of them, two I think, as there's only one still upright. Sameen caught her but she's knocked Sameen back.

The Hunter starts to run but I'm in her path and I catch her, swing her round, and stab her in the stomach, ripping upward. I let her body drop to the ground and notice Marcus coming toward us from the gate. He passes the unconscious body of the Hunter. The second one I got. She's starting to groan.

Marcus goes to her and breaks her neck.

More shots coming from the hangars. Marcus heads to the far one. I run to the middle one with Gabriel and Sameen.

Olivia is at the doorway. She looks terrified. She says, "They've shot Greatorex. She can't get out."

Greatorex is inside the hangar on the floor, surrounded by dead bodies of trainee Hunters. She's alive because she's being protected by a body lying on top of her. More gunfire comes from the far end of the hangar.

I say to Gabriel and Sameen, "I'll crawl in and grab Greatorex. You two'll have to pull us both out."

Gabriel shoots at the back of the hangar while I slide in along the floor as low as possible, the bodies around Greatorex providing cover for me too. I grab Greatorex's wrists. They're thinner, more delicate than I was expecting. She's light.

"Pull!" I shout. Gabriel and Sameen drag us out. The Hunter's body comes with us. But we slide out and onto the grass and then roll to the side.

Greatorex has been shot in the leg. Olivia cuts her trouser leg away to look at the wound.

"How many in there?" I ask.

"Four, I think," Greatorex replies. She looks like she's going to pass out.

"What do you want to do?" Gabriel asks.

"Not commit suicide," I say. "Wait for Marcus." The hangar next door has gone quiet and we don't have to wait for long.

Celia, Claudia, and Marcus join us.

"Are we all clear here?" Celia asks.

"No," Gabriel replies. "There are four more inside here, at the far end. Fully armed."

Marcus says, "Don't come in for a few minutes." Then he goes invisible and we wait.

There's a blast of lightning, and the far end of the hangar is in flames and then there's a burst of gunfire, and another and another.

Finally it goes silent. We hold the door of the hangar open to see in. The only movement is of flames and smoke.

Marcus appears beside me. "Five of them," he says.

Celia looks at Gabriel and says, "Do a body count, now. And make sure it's right. If any are alive I want to keep them that way. I want to talk to them."

Gabriel and Sameen disappear and Celia moves to check on Greatorex.

Nesbitt limps over and slumps down on the ground beside me. His face is bruised and one eye is swollen shut.

"Where were you, partner?" I ask.

"One of the Hunters came out and saw me when I was scouting about. Bloody expert in kung-fu or something, she was. Took me ages to sort her out. What did I miss?"

I'm tempted to make a comment about lots of people dying but I'm too tired.

"Greatorex got shot in the leg. It's lucky none of us got killed," I say.

Gabriel and Sameen return at a run, sliding to the ground beside us. Gabriel says, "Twenty-two. Four older-looking Hunters, so I guess they're the trainers, and eighteen younger ones. All dead."

"A few more than ten recruits and two Hunters," I say. Though I can't blame Nesbitt. I'm angrier at Celia for taking the risk. If Marcus hadn't been with us it would have been harder for sure. Some of us would be dead.

Celia says, "We need to get Greatorex back to base. Start collecting whatever we can use. We go in ten minutes."

Blondine

The next raid is six days later in France again and we are up against fourteen Hunters. It goes smoothly: none of us are injured. Greatorex is healing well but misses that raid and the one after that, which is even smaller. The big difference, which I'm not happy with, is that, on the third raid, Annalise, Sarah, and another two foragers are brought along to help carry away anything we find afterward. They stay well back from the fighting and only come when one of the trainees gets them after the fighting's over. But I'm uncomfortable with Annalise seeing me. The others fight with guns, so don't get messed up, but I use a knife and end up looking like I've stepped out of a horror movie. I want to find somewhere to wash but first I decide to cover the bodies before the foragers arrive. This is something we never normally bother with.

There are ten bodies and I start to cover them with blankets from one of the tents. As I lay a blanket over one of the furthest bodies I notice that her eyes are closed and I can't see any wound on her at all. I think she may be playing dead. I'm not sure if she's got a gun in her jacket but I cover her with a blanket. I look over to the others but they aren't paying any attention to me; they're all busy with their jobs.

I get my knife out, pull the blanket back, and say, "Open your eyes."

I'm not sure she can speak English but I bet she has the basics so I say, "Open your eyes or I cut the left one out. Now!"

She opens her eyes. They're brown with silver sparks. White Witch sparks.

I shout now for the others to come. I'm still not sure what weapons she's got. Marcus arrives within seconds and Gabriel not long after that.

It turns out she hasn't got a gun but two knives. She's French. Her name is Blondine but she won't say more than that. At this stage Celia arrives and I'm about to leave her to it and go and find somewhere to wash when she says, "Nathan, she's your prisoner. Stay with her until we're ready to go back to camp."

I look for Nesbitt, who is still my partner, so he can guard Blondine while I go and wash. But, of course, Nesbitt is never around when I need him.

I've never had a prisoner before. I've been one often enough but that doesn't mean I'm sure what to do. The others leave to do their jobs and I see Annalise glancing over at me.

The only person who doesn't have another job to do is Marcus. He stays with me. He's staring at Blondine and not in a good way. I move to put myself between them.

He says, "You should kill her now. She deserves to die. They all do."

Blondine whimpers. I say, "No, she's my prisoner." I grab hold of her arm as I have a bad feeling she might run. I can feel her shaking. I tell her, "Stay with me."

It'll be safer for Blondine if we go back into the center of the Hunter camp. I say to her, "We'll go over to the others. Stay close to me. Say nothing."

She's so close to my side she's almost tripping over my legs and she's crying now and moaning quietly.

Marcus walks with us too, staring at her the whole time. It's only a hundred meters but it feels like miles. With each step I think he'll just lash out and kill her.

I head to where everyone is gathering. It looks like we'll be heading back to base camp in a few minutes. I stop. Blondine stops too. Her arm is touching mine. Marcus is leaning in on her and I know that if I don't get him away he'll kill her.

Nesbitt is pulling on a huge rucksack of swag he's collected. I say to him, "Stay with her. She's our prisoner." I point at him and tell Blondine, "Do as he says."

Then I turn to Marcus but before I can speak he says, "Hunters caught my father, your grandfather, and tortured him to death. My father. And his father. And his. And his. If they caught us what would they do?"

"That doesn't mean we do it."

I walk past him, hoping he'll come with me. I have to get him away from her. I half turn to him and say, "Don't hurt her. Please. I don't ask much from you."

I keep walking off and he says, "Why?" But I think he's heading my way. I keep walking. He's with me. He asks again, "Why?"

We're in farmland and I vault a gate and go into the next field. I get to the far end of it and stop.

He looks at me. "I can easily walk back and kill her."

"I know." I shrug. "But I don't think you will if you don't see her."

"Out of sight, out of mind?"

"Something like that."

"Why won't you kill her?"

"I don't want to be the sort of person who kills prisoners."

"When I look at her I don't see a prisoner. I see a Hunter. I see an enemy," he says. "We see things differently. This is the first time I've seen your other side."

"My White Witch side?"

"The side of you that is like your mother. Don't think of her as a White Witch. I don't. I think of her as a good person and that can't be said of many White Witches. Can't be said of many people at all."

I look at him and see him differently too. Not as a great Black Witch but just as a person. A person whose father was tortured to death; whose mother, Saba, was chased down by Hunters and killed. A man who couldn't live with the woman he loved and whose son was imprisoned in a cage.

"Don't you think you could have been good? Under different circumstances, I mean."

He laughs and says, "The point of being good is doing it when it's tough, not when it's easy. Your mother was a good person."

We all go back to base camp together, carrying as much as we can. Blondine is hooded, her hands tied behind her back. Nesbitt stays with her. I stay with Marcus. At the camp Celia takes Blondine and I wonder if she'll have a cage fixed up for her. But I really don't care. I'm just glad that Marcus hasn't killed her.

We're all starving and I go to the canteen area with the others. It's already lunchtime and there's a lot of people getting food. As I get my stew I hear the complaints. The stew is thin. There's no bread. There's no fruit. There's no this. There's no that.

Nesbitt joins me. He says, "Do they think it's a holiday camp?"

Gabriel jokes, "If they find out Blondine got the last of the bread there'll be murder."

Nesbitt says, "If that's true I'll murder her myself."

I look around and notice that as usual we, the fighters and scouts, are the only mixed group. Everyone else sits in groups of Whites, Blacks, or Half Bloods. I can hear a group of Whites near us talk about "the prisoner"; some want her tried and executed, others just want her executed.

"That girl's a problem," says Nesbitt. "And if we get more prisoners then we've got even bigger problems. Feeding them, guarding them." He finishes his stew and says, "Killing them is simpler."

"I think Celia will question Blondine and then send her back," says Gabriel.

"What?" Nesbitt and I both stare at him.

"It's a logical thing to do. As you say, keeping prisoners is a hassle. If she lets them go, the Alliance seems reasonable, and when this is over people will remember that. Forgiveness is important."

"Being sensible is too. Blondine will have a gun shoved in her hand and be sent off to fight us again," I say.

Gabriel says, "Will she? I'm not so sure, and Celia knows how the Hunters think as well as anyone. Hunters kill deserters. They hate any sort of betrayal and being captured isn't far off that: they're supposed to die fighting for one other. She won't get a hero's welcome, that's for sure. They may even execute her. I imagine Blondine might rather take her chances as a prisoner with us than back with the Hunters."

It does sound logical the way he says it but I'm not sure Marcus will see it that way.

It's not until that night that I get to see Annalise alone. She always comes to my spot by the tree when she's finished her chores and we spend the night together.

This time I want to talk. I have to tell her about Kieran; I've waited long enough and Annalise needs to know about her brother. But as usual the opening line is the difficult one. She says, "You're even more silent than usual."

"I'm thinking."

"About?"

"How to tell you something. Something serious."

She sits back.

"I should have told you weeks ago. But I didn't. I kept putting it off, waiting for the right time and crap like that. But there isn't ever going to be a right time and so I have to tell you now."

She's looking into my face and I keep my eyes on hers when I say, "It's about Kieran."

She waits. I think she must already have a good idea what I'm going to say.

"What about Kieran?"

"You remember I told you that I killed a Hunter in Switzerland? There were two of them at Mercury's cottage while I was waiting for Gabriel. They found my trail. Followed me. They attacked me and Nesbitt. Nesbitt killed one; he was Kieran's partner."

Annalise waits.

"The other one was Kieran."

Annalise looks into my eyes. Hers fill with tears. "You killed him?"

"I should have told you before. I'm sorry I didn't."

"And are you sorry about Kieran?"

I can't lie about that so I say nothing.

Annalise gets to her feet and I do as well. I think she'll

leave. I say, "I had the chance to kill him before then but I didn't. If Kieran and his partner hadn't hunted me, they'd be alive."

She says, "You should have told me before." She sits down on the ground again. "He was a bully, a Hunter. But he was my brother." She wipes her eyes and says, "I wish the world was different. I wish he'd been different." She starts crying again.

And I wrap her up in my arms and hold her and she cries and eventually she stops and is still, her breathing steady. I lie with her, looking at her, kissing her cheek as gently as I can, and I whisper to her that I love her, that I don't want to hurt her. I fall asleep holding her.

I wake. It's gone cold. Annalise is sitting up. I reach for her hand but she slides it away, saying, "Kieran was a great fighter. The best, everyone said. My father said Kieran would never get killed because of his Gift. So how did you beat him?"

I've told Annalise what my Gift is but I've never explained it. Whenever she asks I change the subject. I've never told her what it feels like or that I've killed anyone or anything when I'm an animal.

"Tell me, Nathan."

"It's hard to explain."

"Try."

"I transformed into an animal. I could hear Kieran. Sense him, even though he was invisible. We fought. He stabbed me."

"And what did you do to him?"

"Annalise, don't ask these things, please."

Annalise starts crying again. "My father once told me that Marcus transformed to kill. To steal Gifts. He took the same Gift, invisibility, from another White Witch. It's a handy Gift to have."

"I didn't take Kieran's Gift, Annalise."

She looks into my eyes and I can see she's not sure.

"Would you really tell me if you had?"

"Yes! I wouldn't lie to you."

"You've been hiding the truth from me for weeks."

"I've said I'm sorry about that, Annalise. And I'll tell you again, I'm sorry. I should have told you about Kieran before."

"Yes, you should have. And you should have told me about your Gift. It's the most important aspect of being a witch; we always agreed that it reflects what a person is really like, but you never talk about it. Even now you've hardly told me anything. You're more like your father every day." She gets up and says, "I need to be on my own for a while. Need to think." And she walks away.

I sit up and get the fire going again, watch it, and wait for Annalise to come back but she doesn't.

A Walk

The next day Gabriel and Celia aren't at morning training. When we break for lunch Celia comes over to me and asks me to walk with her and Gabriel. I think it's something to do with Annalise.

We go into the trees away from everyone and she says, "I've asked Gabriel to come with us because I thought he should tell you."

I look over at him. He's hanging back and I can tell from his face what it's about. It's nothing to do with Annalise. It's either Arran or Deborah.

I feel sick.

Gabriel comes over to me; at least he's going to tell me.

"It's Deborah."

And I know she's dead.

"They executed her two days ago. She was shot for spying. They killed her husband too, for helping her."

And it's so wrong. So wrong. She was clever and good and a great White Witch. And I know they'll have questioned her, tortured her. And it'll have been bad. And I'm so angry and I want to hit things but Gabriel is holding me. And I don't know what to do but there's nothing I can do about it, about any of it. It's too late for Deborah and I want to see her again and I can't ever and I can't even think of her being happy and I hate them for that. I hate them.

With Arran

I haven't seen my brother for over two years but I recognize him easily. He's tall and handsome and everything you'd expect of a White Witch. He walks into camp with a group of Whites and Half Bloods. They all look tired but relieved to have arrived at their destination. Arran doesn't seem relieved. It's a few days since I found out about Deborah. I was told that Arran knows.

I'm standing in the trees, watching, and now I move half a step to the left so that he'll spot me. I've so wanted to see him, to be with him again, but this is not how I wanted it. He'll be feeling Deborah's loss more than me.

It's another minute before he glances my way and then he freezes. I see he says my name and he smiles and I think I smile as he comes toward me. We embrace. He's thinner than I expected and not as tall, though still taller than me.

He says lots of things about missing me and maybe I say things, I'm not sure. He tells me Deborah was doing what she believed in and he cries a lot and I do too. And I'm thinking of when all three of us were together, tussling for room to brush our teeth in the bathroom, and her brushing her hair in the mornings on the landing and listening to me and

Arran talking, and then I remember us all having breakfast together with Gran. It was only three years ago. I feel like I'm so old and yet Deborah was so young and none of it is fair and none of it makes sense.

The next few days are different. Arran is working with Van in the medical unit but he spends all his spare time with me. It's over two years since I was taken from our house and he wants to know everything that's happened to me while we've been apart. I can only do a bit of it. I don't like to tell him the bad stuff. Ellen has told him everything she knows but that isn't much and he wants to know more. He glances at the tattoo on my neck and at my hands and he reaches out to touch the scarred skin of my wrist. I tell him to ask Gabriel if he wants any details.

Then he asks me about Gabriel and I say the same thing. "Ask Gabriel if you want any details."

"I will," he says.

"You have to promise to tell me what he says." I smile. I am actually curious at the thought of what it might be.

Arran says, "It's good to see you smile."

"And you."

Then I remember I wanted to tell him something. "Remember that time when I climbed the tree and you came up after me and I went further up and out and you wanted me to come back? And I did and we sat there for ages together, our legs dangling down either side of that branch, and you were against the trunk and I was leaning back against you?"

He nods.

"I think about that a lot. When I need something good to focus on."

And Arran's eyes fill with tears and he hugs me and I hug him back.

Laughter

Celia and I are having another talk.

"Before she was arrested Deborah sent out one last piece of information," Celia tells me. "It's probably what led to her being caught but she thought it was so important that she was willing to risk her life for it.

"Wallend has been experimenting on Black Witches, those ones that were first caught outside Paris a few weeks ago. He's developing some kind of tattoo. Tattooing them over their hearts. The experiments are on Black Witches but we think that the aim is to develop the tattoo to be used on Hunters."

"Why?" I ask. "What does it do?"

"Deborah couldn't find that out. Have you seen any Hunters with strange tattoos on their chests?"

"I haven't been looking."

"From now on we need to." She hesitates, her eyes locked on mine. "As long as you're ready for another mission."

"Why wouldn't I be ready?"

"I just want to check that you're in control. Losing your sister is difficult. I know that."

"I didn't lose her. They took me from her years ago and now she's been executed."

Celia sticks her fat lip out.

I sigh and say, "OK. Leave me off the mission. But I'd suggest you leave Marcus off too in that case. Cos he's more likely to go off on one than me."

Celia nods. "I haven't thanked you for that yet. But you did well with Blondine and controlling Marcus that day."

"What's happened to Blondine?"

"I sent her back. I saw her name on the last list of executions that we got from Deborah. Executed for desertion, it said."

"You knew they'd do that."

"I wasn't certain. But she was a deserter. She should have stood her ground and fought."

"If Marcus had killed her, everyone here would have called him an animal. You send her back and no one bats an eyelid."

Celia doesn't reply.

I say, "Blondine would have suffered less if I'd let Marcus kill her."

The next raid is a small one. Among the final material Deborah provided is a list of locations of Hunter bases in northern France, along with details of how many Hunters are at each point. Without this the raids could never take place and never work. We all owe her so much. Celia is busy in meetings with new arrivals. She's spending more time in administration now, hasn't been to a training session for days.

So Greatorex is to lead the attack, which is fine: she's a good leader. She's serious and professional, like Celia, like all the Hunters, but she seems to have a more human side and to understand her fighters as individuals, each with a different personality, and to each of us she speaks a little differently. With me she jokes a lot, laughs at me. With Nesbitt she's tough but never critical. With Gabriel she's business-like. With Sameen she's encouraging. I respect her and the others do too.

Nesbitt has a constant battle with her about her name. Greatorex is her surname; no one knows her first name. I guess she's embarrassed by it. She won't say and she certainly won't tell Nesbitt. I ask him, "Anyway, Nesbitt, what's your first name? You ashamed of yours too?" He swears at me. And I start trying different names for him. "Gerald? Arthur? Not . . . Gabrielle?" He doesn't mention Greatorex's name too often after that.

Greatorex goes over the plan for the attack. There'll be eight Hunters. We go in at dawn. We work in pairs, except for Marcus, who uses his invisibility and does most of the initial dangerous work. I'm fast so I go after runners. If any of the Hunters try to make a break for it my job is to chase them down. Nesbitt is good at tracking so he's my reserve but so far no one has got away from me. Runners are my specialty.

The attack sounds like it's going to be routine.

Only it's never really routine. There's always something worse or bad or shit about killing people. I hate Hunters. I have no sympathy for them. I'm not sure what I feel about Blondine but it's not sympathy. I'm angry, I guess. Like Gabriel says, I'm angry at just about everything. I'm angry at Blondine for being stupid enough to join the Hunters. At Wallend for experimenting on people. At Soul for killing my sister. At the world for being shit. Oh yes, and Annalise for not getting it, cos she's hardly talking to me and since I told her about Kieran we've slept together once but it wasn't the same and I somehow felt she was doing it because of Deborah, and I can't believe that I told her I loved her again. Again. And this time she didn't say it back.

The raid goes to plan. There are eight Hunters. Marcus goes in and kills most of them. There's one runner. A boy, not even that fast. I chase after him. Catch him easily. I slit his throat. I always make sure I kill them. I don't want another prisoner. I go back to the Hunter camp, my hands dripping in blood.

When I reach the others they're all standing slightly back from Gabriel, who is kneeling by a Hunter. She's wounded, shot in the stomach. She's dying and there's nothing anyone can do to save her. She won't be a prisoner but it'll probably be an hour before she loses all her strength.

My hands are wet with blood and I wipe them and my knife's on the clothes of a Hunter whose body is at my feet.

Gabriel is talking to the dying Hunter, asking her if she

has a tattoo. The Hunter swears at Gabriel. Gabriel says he's going to see if she has a tattoo. I'm surprised that Gabriel does check; he cuts into her jacket and T-shirt but there is no tattoo.

I look at the body at my feet and cut her jacket open. Her T-shirt. Exposing her chest. There's nothing. I can't believe I'm having to do this.

Gabriel asks again, "What are the tattoos for? Do the tattoos help you heal? Make you stronger? Give you a new Gift?"

Nesbitt says, "Make bullets bounce off you. Make your farts smell like rose blossom."

I realize I've forgotten to look if the boy I killed, the runner, had a tattoo. I turn to go back to check him. Annalise is right behind me. She's been watching us, listening to us. I don't know how much she's heard but somehow I know it's a lot. Her face is pale.

She says, "Can we get a healer to help her?" She's not talking to me, or to anyone really, just thinking aloud.

I say, "She's been shot in the gut. There's nothing anyone can do."

She looks at me and says, "Except laugh, maybe."

I hadn't realized I'd laughed at Nesbitt's joke but maybe I had. The whole thing is a sick joke.

At that moment Greatorex steps up and tells everyone to get on with their jobs. "Including you, Gabriel. Leave her."

The Hunter curses and says we're all going to die and

we deserve it and we're all scum. Her voice is surprisingly loud. And Marcus walks up to her, kneels beside her, and slides the blade of the Fairborn into her throat. The blood oozes and bubbles out and she shakes once, quickly, and dies quietly. Marcus cleans the knife on the Hunter's clothes and walks away, saying, "Someone should have done that ten minutes ago."

I look round to Annalise. Her eyes are wide, staring at the Hunter. Sarah is beside her now. I know I'm not wanted.

I go back to camp with Marcus and wash in the stream that runs through the forest. I stay there with Marcus for the rest of the day.

I see Annalise at breakfast the next morning. She's sitting with Sarah as she does all the time now. I ask if I can sit with them. Annalise nods. I sit opposite her rather than next to her.

"Do you blame me for what happened to the Hunter yesterday?" I ask.

"No," she replies. But then she looks me in the eye and says, "But you laughed, Nathan. She was dying and you and Nesbitt were joking."

"Do you know how many people I've killed, Annalise? Twenty-three as of yesterday. Do you know how funny it is?"

"Not very."

"Exactly. It's shit. It's all shit. Most of the Hunters we're up against are like that lot yesterday. Trainees. Kids.

Useless. But they could still kill us all. So we kill them first. But maybe tomorrow they'll get lucky. I don't know. Next time one of us may not come back. So don't judge me or any of us. We get through it. That's what we do."

I get up and leave. As I walk away I hope she'll run after me and we'll make up. When I reach the trees I turn back and look and Sarah is with her again, her arm round her, walking into one of the many tents that crowd the clearing round the bar.

The next day I tell Arran what's happened between me and Annalise. I tell him about my Gift and about Kieran.

He says, "You're not evil, Nathan. You're not wild either. And you're not your father. Talk to Annalise; be honest with her. That's all you can do."

"Do you approve of me being with Annalise now?"

"I didn't disapprove before because it was too dangerous. Now, though . . . well, at least that isn't the problem."

I go to find Annalise, determined to talk to her without getting angry, though I'm not sure what I'm going to say. I go in the store tent looking for her, but no one's there. Sarah walks in. I half expect Annalise to be with her as they seem to be joined at the hip most of the time.

"She's not here," Sarah says.

I walk to the door and Sarah moves out of the way. As I pass her she says, "She doesn't want to see you."

I stop.

I know I shouldn't get angry. I take a breath and say, "Well, I'd like to see her, so—"

"You shouldn't see her. She doesn't need you."

"So who does she need? You?"

"She needs nice people."

"You mean nice White Witch people, I suppose?"

"You said it, not me."

"Well, I'm not interested in what you think. And anyway you're wrong." I move closer to Sarah and spit out, "Let me tell you something. All the nice White Witches were quite happy to lock Annalise in a room and would have been quite happy to let her die a prisoner of Mercury. Not one of the nice White Witches was willing to risk their life to help her. So the less-nice, non–White Witches had to do it."

"She told me what you did. All very brave I'm sure. But let's face it—you enjoy it."

"What?"

"You can't fool me with all that pretense that the killing is awful. No one's taken in by that; everyone knows you love it."

"And how would 'everyone' know what I love?"

"It's well known that in the raids you don't use a gun. You cut the Hunters up, slit their throats, and slice their stomachs open. Everyone says it's only a matter of time before you start eating them."

I shake my head in amazement.

"That's what your father does—turns animal and eats people. That's what you'll do, if you've not done it already."

I lean closer to her. "I would spit on you but you're not even worth that."

She steps back, looking scared, but says, "I'm right, aren't I?"

I turn from her and walk away.

She calls after me, "You shouldn't be with her. If you cared about her you'd leave her alone."

The Meeting

Four days later we're summoned to a meeting in Celia's tent, which isn't that unusual as that is where we meet to plan raids and debrief after them. On my way I see Annalise and Sarah. I haven't had a chance to get Annalise alone since my run-in with Sarah, though I've wanted to. I've seen Annalise in the canteen twice but when I went to talk to her she got up and left.

I hang back now, expecting Annalise and Sarah to go to the stores, but they go into Celia's tent. I hesitate and wonder if I've got the wrong instructions. A couple who work in the canteen turn up next and also go in. Gabriel arrives, sees me, and walks over. I ask him, "Do you know what's going on?"

He says, "Rumor is Van's back."

Inside, rows of chairs have been set out and Celia and Van are sitting at the front facing them. I haven't seen Van for a few days; Arran told me she'd been away, trying to get more Black Witches to join the rebels. Nesbitt is standing near the front, almost jumping around with excitement. He's just got back from a reconnaissance trip. Gabriel and I stand at the back. The tent fills up with all the fighters and scouts but there are more from the other groups: Healers,

Cooking and Camp, and several from Foraging and Stores, including Annalise.

Last to arrive is Marcus, who comes to stand next to me. Virtually everyone in the room takes the opportunity to turn round and look at him. I say quietly to Gabriel, "I know most of them don't see Marcus around but they behave like he's some sort of sideshow."

Gabriel turns to me and even he seems to stare too. He says, "It's more than that, Nathan. When you're standing next to your father it's more obvious how alike you are." That's when I notice that Annalise is watching us but when our eyes meet she turns back to face the front.

Marcus says to me, "Don't you sometimes wish the whole lot of them could be swept away in a giant tidal wave?"

And I have to say, as I look around the room, that some of them I wouldn't miss, but some I would. I don't want Annalise to be swept away. I want her to come and stand with me.

It's not Celia but Van who starts the meeting. She says that the camp is having problems. There are nearly two hundred people here now but few can fight and they all need to eat. Basically there are lots of people and not enough of anything else. Certainly food and water is a problem that everyone is aware of, and sanitation too. There aren't enough tents or blankets. Torches and even cups are in short supply.

Celia explains, "The foragers will be obtaining all the items we are short of in the next few days. They will go to buy them from fain shops as before, but we've had an extra twenty people arrive and we must always be careful when we leave camp."

That seems to keep people happy but someone complains about the food: no fruit, no variety, not enough meat, not enough veg, and on and on. And then the other complaints start to escalate. Why is nothing happening? Why is Soul still in power? Why is it taking so long? Why aren't we helping the White Witches who've been imprisoned by Soul? And I realize that another problem is that most of these people have nothing to do all day but whinge and complain and gossip.

Van refuses to answer. She says, "That isn't the purpose of this meeting."

Then it's Greatorex's turn to explain that the fighters are short of weapons, and particularly Hunter bullets. She says, "But we get by." And I'm grateful that she doesn't look at Marcus as she says that. What she means is that if it wasn't for Marcus none of our raids would have succeeded, at least not without casualties.

Now Celia takes over. She tells us that we have learned the location of a significant Hunter cache containing weapons, other equipment, and food. It's an opportunity for us to improve our situation significantly and deal a blow to the Hunters.

"There are just sixteen Hunters guarding the cache. Six of them look experienced, the rest are trainees. Greatorex will lead the fighters in at dawn. All foragers and anyone else who can walk and carry must be ready to go and clear everything they can as soon as the fighting is over. Everyone from the camp must help."

Annalise will be one of the foragers and in the past I hoped she wouldn't see any of the battle but now part of me thinks, *Let her see the horror of it all because that's what it is.* It's all very well Celia saying the rebels have the moral high ground but really there is none in war. It's all shit.

Connor

Greatorex leads us into the cut. It's a relief to be away from all those people and all the complaining and into the quiet of the forest. We're running through trees at the other end in no time. It's a two-hour jog to the Hunter camp. All the foragers and everyone else are coming close behind but they'll walk and will arrive well after the fighting is over.

We slow near the camp. It's at the end of an unpaved track through the forest. There are two trucks parked and a number of small tents that look like they are where the Hunters sleep. There is also one large gray tent, more like a marquee. In front of that are a couple of wooden crates stacked up.

It's just getting light. There are two Hunters on guard but already another is appearing out of one of the small tents.

Greatorex takes it all in quickly and gives instructions. There are sixteen Hunters and sixteen of us. We're a good fighting unit. We have a few more trainees but they're serious and good. Sameen, Claudia, and Olivia are all excellent. We fan out; we know what to do. I'm still partnered with Nesbitt. But we know each other's ways now. It works.

Marcus goes invisible and attacks first.

I look out for runners. There are two. I go for the fastest

first and by the time I've caught the second runner the fighting's over. I check both the runners for tattoos but find none and I'm about to head back to the others when I realize there's a hissing noise in my head. I'm not usually thinking about this when I'm fighting because all the Hunters have mobile phones. But this noise is strong, like many phones hissing at once.

I head back to the Hunter camp, expecting the hissing to get stronger. I think it must be something there. Perhaps one of the crates has phones in it.

As I get back, though, the hissing hasn't really changed. I can't work it out. There are phones here but if each Hunter has just one that's only sixteen. The hissing in my head is louder than that. I want to ask Marcus but I can't see him. I ask Nesbitt where he is.

"Dunno, mate. But look at this lovely loot." He's almost dancing round two wooden cases open on the ground, full of guns. "And there's more in here," he says, going inside the large gray tent.

Greatorex shouts to Sophie, a new trainee fighter, "Go get the foragers and the others! Tell them to hurry."

I can't see Marcus anywhere. I want to concentrate on the hissing noise but there are bodies of Hunters here, all with mobiles. I'm standing in the middle of it, trying to work that out, when Nesbitt comes out of the tent with a different problem. He's pushing a prisoner in front of him. "Look what I found hiding in the back."

The Hunter has his head down and his straight blond hair has fallen forward.

Nesbitt shoves the prisoner to his knees and the young man looks up.

I haven't seen him since I was thirteen but I'd know him anywhere. And he recognizes me too.

"Nathan."

My first thoughts aren't about him but of Annalise. I know she cares for Connor more than her other brothers. I know he helped her escape. I try to think positively about him.

But then he says, "Nathan, they made me do it. My uncle made me join the Hunters. I don't want any of this."

And that makes me mad. I'm knee-deep in dead bodies and he's complaining about being made to join them. He's still as cowardly and pathetic as I remembered. I walk over and spit at him.

Nesbitt puts on a mock reasonable voice, saying, "Hold on, Nathan. He's telling the truth, you know. That's why he was hiding in the back. He doesn't want any of this."

I back off, trying to control myself, but then Gabriel comes over, asking what's going on, and I tell him, "Oh, Gabriel. Let me introduce you to an old friend of mine. This piece of shit is Connor. Connor O'Brien. Annalise's youngest brother. I used to be at school with him. He's a Hunter, but don't worry about him, Gabriel. He doesn't want to be one. He doesn't want to hurt anybody. At least not until they make him. And, when he does, he's really,

really sorry about it. So that's all right." I turn away from him to control myself but I can't and I turn back and kick at Connor's stomach, shouting, "Isn't it, Connor?"

He doubles over and is on his knees with his face in the ground, groaning.

"Oh! I'm sorry, Connor, I didn't mean to hurt you. It's just part of my job. I don't want to do it really."

Gabriel stands between me and Connor, though he doesn't need to. I don't want to kick Connor again, even though I'm still mad. I say to Gabriel, "I'm OK. I just lost it for a second." But I lean round to Connor and say, "Connor is the one that put the powder on that burned the cuts into my back. Not the *B*, just the *W*."

"Then I'll carve *my* name on *his* back," Marcus says. He's striding toward us now. He pulls Connor up by the hair, the Fairborn at his throat. Connor stares at me, his eyes wide.

"Or do I just cut his head off?" Marcus asks me. "Yes or no?"

"Connor!"

It's Annalise. She's at the head of a stream of people coming through the trees, running the last few steps closer. She shouts, "Let him go!" She picks up a Hunter gun that's been dropped in the fight and points it at Marcus.

I step between them, holding my arms out. "Annalise. Put the gun down."

"Keep away from me, Nathan. Tell Marcus to let Connor go."

I've stopped. I've still got my arms out. I'm trying to keep my voice low and calm. "Annalise. We won't hurt Connor. Please put the gun down. This isn't helping. Put the gun down. Please."

I can see she is shaking now but she says, "Not until you let my brother go."

I turn to Marcus and say with as much authority as I can, "He's a prisoner. We give him to Celia to deal with. She'll want to question him. He's her problem."

I turn back to Annalise. "Please put the gun down."

"Promise me," she says. "Promise you won't hurt him."

"Yes. I promise. He's a prisoner."

She lowers the gun.

I turn back to my father and say, "We give him to Celia."

Marcus says, "I'll carve my name in his back when she's finished with him." But he lets go of Connor's hair and Connor collapses forward.

And at that moment there's a gunshot from my left and one of the foragers near me falls to the ground. There's another shot, a scream, and another forager drops.

"Hunters! Hunters!" someone shouts, and the shout is taken up by others. Already the foragers are running away, back the way they came, but I see the black shapes of Hunters beyond them. That was the hissing noise. They were hidden in the trees all the time. Invisible. But now we can see them and we're surrounded. The whole thing is a trap.

Gabriel shoots at the Hunters but more are appearing.

Greatorex shouts, "Everyone, get down! Stay low!" But

we can hardly hear her for shouting and gunfire.

Annalise is still standing, protected by the tree to her right. I'm low. There are bullets hitting the ground near me. I shout, "Annalise, you have to get down." She doesn't hear or she isn't listening, and she stays standing. I'm about to shout again when she raises her gun, and I turn, expecting to see a Hunter running to attack her. But it's worse.

Connor is scrabbling over to the crate of guns. I shout at him, "No, Connor. No!" But it's too late. Marcus is too angry. He grabs Connor by the hair and drags him round to face me and looks at me as he stabs Connor in the throat.

Annalise's gun fires and fires again.

Marcus staggers.

The second bullet hits him a few centimeters above the first, both in his chest. Small red marks are spreading on his shirt and he drops to his knees. And I'm frozen in place, staring at him.

My father, shot.

I turn to Annalise, her gun still held straight, pointing at Marcus.

I step between them to protect him. I'm standing upright. She screams at me, "You promised! You promised!"

And there's more shooting around us and Gabriel leaps on me and pulls me to the ground, lying on top of me to protect me. When I look up Annalise has gone.

Slowing Time

I scramble back to Marcus, keeping low to the ground. I have to pull him behind the crates. His wounds are bad but they're not fatal. And this is Marcus: his healing powers are huge. He'll be all right.

"You can keep yourself alive until we get back to Van," I tell him.

Marcus coughs. "I'm not sure how you're going to get me back there. Back anywhere."

It's true: most of the Alliance members have fled now but if some of them go back to the cut, and the Hunters find it, all will be lost. There are four or five bodies of rebels on the ground and I see a straggler fall in the distance. And it hits me that this has all been well planned. The Hunters will have watched to see where the cut is; our camp may already be in their hands.

Nesbitt crawls over to join us. He says, "Most of the Hunters have followed the foragers but we're surrounded still."

Gabriel helps Nesbitt drag some wooden crates over to form a makeshift barrier to one side of us. The cases of guns are by our feet. Gabriel goes through them and tries to fire them. None of them work. They're all broken in some way.

We're trapped.

Greatorex, Claudia, and Sameen are nearby, hunkered down behind some other cases. I can see Olivia's body close to them. Everyone else has run.

Nesbitt offers his flask to Marcus. "It's just water," he says.

Marcus takes it but his hand is shaking.

"Any bright ideas, anyone?" asks Nesbitt.

Gabriel says, "We need to get away as soon as we can. I make out sixteen Hunters around us. But the others will be back."

"There might be more," I say. "I think these are the ones with Wallend's tattoo. I think they can all go invisible."

"Shit!" Nesbitt says.

"Yes," Marcus agrees. "Shit!"

"Can you run, Marcus?" Gabriel asks.

"I don't think—" Blood bubbles out of the corner of his mouth and he coughs. I can see he's healing, and his healing is strong but it won't last. "I don't think I can even stand at the moment. These bullets are bastards, aren't they?"

"Can we cut them out? Like you cut mine out?"

"One is in my lung; if you cut that out I'll die anyway."

There's more shooting and I know Marcus certainly won't be able to outrun Hunters. I look around. I'm not sure *I* can outrun them.

Nesbitt and Gabriel have crawled farther away and are shooting at a group of four Hunters who have crept up on us.

Marcus says, "I haven't much strength but I think I can help you to get away. I can slow time enough. It probably won't last more than a minute, maybe not even that. But it should allow you to get past the Hunters around us."

"And what about you?"

"I stay here."

I shake my head. "I'll carry you. We'll get you out."

"No. That's not what happens. I'll be too slow. You have to get away."

"No."

"I can't heal these wounds. I'm dying, Nathan. You have to fulfill the prophecy. You know that, don't you? This is what I saw in the vision."

I shake my head. "No. I can't."

"You can. The Fairborn will help you. It'll want to cut me. Pull open my ribs. Eat my heart. Do it as a human. That is how it is in my vision. Take my Gifts. Take them all and use them."

I have a feeling that everything in my life has led to this point but I don't want any of it.

"It's the only way, Nathan."

"I can't do it." But I can see Marcus is determined for himself and for me.

Gabriel crawls back to us and Marcus says to him, "I'm going to tell you the plan. I want you to make sure Nathan does it and escapes safely. I think I'm still strong enough to stop time for about thirty seconds, maybe a little more. It'll be enough for you to run. Kill as many Hunters as you can in that time and meet up at the far side over there." He nods in the direction away from the cut. "Nathan will stay with me. When he's ready to go you must cover him. If there are any Hunters left alive draw them away from Nathan."

I shake my head but Gabriel says, "Yes. I'll make sure he's safe. I'll tell the others." And he crawls off to where Greatorex and Nesbitt are.

Marcus reaches up and puts his hand on my shoulder. "Nathan, I'm glad I got to know you briefly. Maybe too little and too late. I wish it had been more." His hand drops and he pulls the Fairborn out of his jacket. "I'm dying, Nathan. But I don't want to die for nothing. I want you to have my Gifts."

I shake my head. There's no way I can kill him, never mind eat his heart.

"You're strong. You can do it. Kill me and then kill Soul and the rest of them. Kill all of them."

He pushes the Fairborn into my hand. "Will you do this for me, Nathan?"

I look into his eyes and see black triangles moving slowly, too slowly. I know there is nothing I can do to save him. I have to do as he asks.

I take the Fairborn out of its sheath, feel its desire, and tell my father, "I'll kill them all."

"Always remember that I wanted you to do this. I'm proud of you." He coughs again. "Doing the spell is tiring. As soon as time speeds up again I will be weak, unable to heal any more. That is when you have to use the Fairborn."

He rubs the palms of his hands together, making circular movements that go faster and smaller. He stops. Takes a breath and starts again. Then stops and starts again. This time he stops and raises his palms to the side of his head. He looks at me then and I can see the spell must be working and he's concentrating but it's hard for him. It's taking his energy. His hands are shaking. He says, "Tell them to run."

I look over to Gabriel. I can tell from the stillness that time has stopped. I shout to him, "Run!" though I'm not really aware of anything now.

Gabriel, Nesbitt, and the others charge off. There are some shots. I see a Hunter fall. And another. And then all too quickly the world speeds up.

The next thing I do is the worst thing.

If it wasn't for the prophecy I couldn't do it and not without him telling me to and with his eyes on mine the whole time. He says, "I love you, Nathan. I always have." His eyes are black, the empty triangles tumbling and turning slowly to a stop.

I do it while I stare into my father's eyes. The Fairborn is keen to go in and sever everything. It helps me. I pull my father's chest apart and eat him and watch the triangles in his eyes fade to nothing as I taste him and swallow his heart.

Seeing Jessica

I'm not sure exactly what happens after I kill my father. I'm aware that there are Hunters around still but Greatorex and the others are attacking them now. The change in their position has confused the Hunters, at least enough for me to get away. I leave my father's body. It's hard to do but once I get up and start to move my legs just carry me.

I see Gabriel ahead and run to him. But really all I see is my father looking at me and his eyes staring and the triangles fading to nothing. The taste of him is strong in my mouth. I'm on the verge of gagging but I'm determined not to.

"Nathan, look at me," Gabriel says. I realize he's grabbed my arms. "Look at me!"

I do as he says. But I'm not sure what I see. I can't focus on him.

He says things to me. I'm not sure what. I'm remembering my father saying he loved me. I've hardly known him. And now I've killed him. There was so much blood. So much blood. My knees feel like they'll give way and Gabriel pulls me up and shouts at me. "Nathan!"

Nesbitt runs up to us, sees me, and stops, exclaiming, "Shit!" He didn't know what I was going to do.

Greatorex and the others arrive and stare. I know I've got blood all over me: my face, my chest, my hands.

Greatorex says, "We need to go. More Hunters are coming."

Gabriel is pulling me along now. Pulling me by the arm.

Greatorex and Sameen are ahead of me, Claudia to the right, Gabriel close to my left.

Running helps. I'm feeling more like myself. But we're not fast enough. The Hunters are after us. We keep going, and the more I run the better I feel, the stronger I feel. I'm in the lead now. There's another shot and a scream and I turn to see Sameen fall. She's not dead. Gabriel slows and stops and I go back to him. Sameen is twenty paces behind us.

I tell him, "Keep going. Stay with Nesbitt and I'll catch you up."

He shakes his head. "No, she's my partner. I told your father—"

"No! I'm faster than you. I can get away. Go. If I don't catch up with you in a few minutes I'll be at the meeting place, as we agreed. But the longer you take the more danger I'm in now."

He points at me; he knows I need to be alone. "The meeting place, as we agreed."

"Yes. Go."

He runs off.

I go back to Sameen. I've still got the Fairborn in my hand.

I kneel by her. She's been shot in the back but blood is coming out of her mouth and nose. I say, "Sorry, Sameen."

She doesn't say anything, just looks at me. I slit her throat.

More blood. Blood everywhere. My hands are dripping.

I stand and look back at the Hunters, making sure they see me. There's one of them whom I notice not far from the front. I just get a glimpse of her. But I know it's her. My sister, Jessica. It was her trap.

I know I can outrun them. I'm in shock but my body's strong, stronger than ever. I don't need to think when I run. I don't want to think. Just run. I break to the left. Going hard and fast away from Nesbitt, Gabriel, and Greatorex, drawing the Hunters after me.

Red

You can't let yourself think too much about numbers; how many are dead. There's a lot. There always seems to be another one. You can't let yourself think about much really. You need to just keep walking. But every time you think there won't be any more bodies you come across another. A woman, a man, all members of the Alliance, all dead, usually shot in the back.

You've ended up in a gentle valley and a few rebels must have run down here. There are bodies lying in clumps, as if they surrendered but were then shot, some shot in the head—executed. You count them. It's the only thing you can do. Nine of them.

If Marcus had been alive, if Annalise hadn't shot him, most of these people would be alive too. Marcus would have been able to slow the Hunters enough. Kill enough of them. These deaths are on Annalise's head.

Still, you need to get out of the valley or you'll be dead too. The Hunters will come back this way to check they haven't missed anyone.

It starts to rain as you climb up the side of the valley and into the next one, down its steep side and through the old trees. Between the trees are rounded, moss-covered stones and the floor is deep with ferns: it's a lush, green, and beautiful place. You sit, too tired to go on. The ferns arch over your head and the rain patters down. You rub your face. And inside you feel on fire. Marcus's heart has already given its Gifts but it has exhausted you and it's doing something else to you too.

You bow your head and the rain runs off you, rivulets of red, to join the mud and the blood around you.

You want to sleep but when you close your eyes you see it all again: Annalise pointing the gun at Marcus, the Fairborn going into Marcus, cutting into his skin, you pulling his ribs apart and all the blood and everything that you had to do.

You would never have had to kill Marcus, would never have had to do all that, if it hadn't been for Annalise.

You lie in the rain. Going over it again and again. There's nothing else you can do today. But tomorrow will be different. Tomorrow you go after her.

Acknowledgments

Half Wild is my second published book, and writing (and rewriting and rewriting) it was a completely different experience from that of *Half Bad*. I really must plan my next story a lot more before I jump in. I'm extremely grateful to everyone in the great teams at Puffin and Viking for their help in getting this story out of my head and on the bookshelves—and not just bookshelves in the UK and US but around the world (even in places I have to Google to find out where they are). As always my agent Claire Wilson has been a star.

In case you're interested, the quote "I see wars, horrid wars, and the Tiber foaming with much blood" is a translation of Virgil's *Aeneid*, "bella, horrida bella, et Thybrim multo spumantem sanguine cerno" (6.86–87), which I found as a result of reading through Enoch Powell's "Rivers of Blood" speech, and then looking up (with the help of Google) the original "river of blood" quote. I think it is more appropriate in *Half Wild* than as mistakenly used by Powell (http://edithorial.blogspot.co.uk/2013/04/how-enoch-powell-got-vergil-wrong.html).

European travel is a great thing and I did hope to do at least some in my research for *Half Wild*. Sadly time was not on my side so I had to rely on my memory of places (Spain,

Basle, that lake with the iceberg in Norway), Google, and the AA's online Route Planner for all my fictional journey routes and times.

Thanks, too, to all the lovely, friendly *Half Bad* fans and my followers on Twitter, and especially those who helped with the names for my White Witches. I received ideas from the following: Lisa Gelinas @InkdMomof3; Jan P. @janhpa; Caitlin @caitlingss; Charli @Charli_TAW; Artifact #1 @themefrompinata; Daniel Rowland @danialii; Fiction Fascination @F_Fascination; Oswaldo Reyes @readers WRITER; Emily Ringborg @RingEmily; Colleen Conway @colleenaconway; Damien Glynn @damog7; Finlay and Ivor @tmbriggs; Jo Porter @joanneporter_1; Caroline Pomfret @CazPom.

But I eventually chose the names:

– Sameen, suggested by MSA @MsaMsa85;

– Olivia, suggested by Renee Dechert @sreneed;

– Claudia, suggested by Jayd Amber @dragonslibrary.

I hope I've included everyone. Apologies if I've missed you off that list.